PRIMORDIA

IN SEARCH OF THE LOST WORLD

GREIG BECK

SEVERED PRESS
HOBART TASMANIA

PRIMORDIA

Copyright © 2017 GREIG BECK

WWW.SEVEREDPRESS.COM

ISBN: 978-1-925711-47-9

What if it were true?
What if it were all true?
What if it was never make believe at all – that the Lost World was real?
Sir Arthur Conan Doyle didn't make it all up. I believe he was reading
about a lost expedition that really happened. We need to find the
notebook. And then we need to go there.

Benjamin 'Ben' Cartwright, 2018

A comet impact on the Earth would be devastating depending on its mass and composition. However, even if it didn't make landfall, the full astral effects of a comet simply passing close to our planet are not yet known or fully understood.

October 2014 – Approaching comet, C/2013-A1 (designate name: Siding Spring), has plunged the magnetic field around Mars into chaos.
NASA's Goddard Space Flight Centre, Greenbelt, Maryland

PROLOGUE

1908 – South America, somewhere in South Eastern Venezuela – the Wettest Season

Benjamin Cartwright ran like never before in his life. Damp green fronds slapped at his face, thorns ripped his skin, and elastic vines tried to lasso every part of his body. But he barged, burrowed, and sprinted as if the devil was after him.

Because it was.

The thing that followed him pushed trees from its path, and its carnivore breath was like a steam train huffing and hissing as it bore down on him. He whimpered, pivoting at a boulder and changing direction. The roar came then, making leathery-winged avian creatures take flight from the canopy overhead, and causing his testicles to shrink in his sweat-soaked trousers.

Cartwright accelerated, and immediately an explosive breeze hit his face as the jungle opened out. He skidded to a stop, squinting against it. He was at the cliff edge that dropped away to a green carpet over a thousand feet below.

He stared for a split moment; the strange low cloud swirled all around him, and he knew he only had hours before he'd be trapped forever. He grimaced and turned. Already the trees were being pushed aside as his pursuer caught up to him. He'd seen what it did to Baxter, and the thought of it happening to him liquefied his bowels.

Arm-thick creeper vines ran across the clearing and hung down over the edge of the cliff face but didn't reach anywhere near safety. In the few seconds he had left, Benjamin Cartwright realised his choices were to be eaten, or suicide – death either way.

The foliage burst open behind him, and the hissing-roar made him cringe back with fear. He couldn't help but turn – the creature rose up, towering over him, all coiled muscle, glistening scales, and teeth as long as his arm. The remains of Baxter still hung ragged between those tusk-like fangs.

Cartwright fired his last bullet from the gun he had almost forgotten in his hand – it had no effect, and he threw the Colt revolver to the ground. He turned back to the cliff edge, grabbed up one of the vines, said a silent prayer, and leapt.

PART 1 – WHAT IF IT WERE TRUE?

There's many a man who never tells his adventures, for he can't hope to be believed —

Arthur Conan Doyle, The Lost World.

CHAPTER 01

2018 – Greenberry Cemetery, Ohio – Today

Benjamin Cartwright stood with his arm around his mother's shoulders. *It shoulda been raining*, he thought. Instead, belying the somber mood, the sun shone gaily, and the verdant green lawn gave off a pleasant odor of cut grass and fresh soil. The leaves on the large trees ringing the cemetery quivered slightly as a soft breeze moved through their shimmering leaves.

Perhaps it was fitting, as his father, Barry, was an outdoorsman ever since he was a kid. Being here, surrounded by this forest-like setting seemed, *perfect*.

His mother sobbed again, and Ben squeezed her slim shoulders and felt her continuing to shudder as her tiny frame was wracked by sorrow. His own eyes blurred with tears momentarily, and he blinked several times to clear them.

It was the surprise and suddenness of it all, he guessed. His dad was only 63, and he had seemed strong as an ox…right up until chopping wood had turned into a clutched chest, and then it was lights out big guy, forever.

Cynthia, his mother, had called him first, telling him that Barry had a bad fall, *very bad* – that was it. Ben could tell by her voice that it was no simple fall. Both his parents were the type that brushed off trauma as a mere annoyance – even a broken wrist was described as just *having a bit of a scrape*. So Dad having a *very bad fall* set off alarms in Ben's head.

Her voice became tiny then. "I don't know what to do," she had said.

Ben felt sick from fear then, but he swallowed it down. Trying to impart calm, he had told her to phone the police or an ambulance, or a neighbor, and he was on his way. He lived in Boulder, Colorado, and even though the flight was just a little over 2 hours, it would still take many hours on top of that to go point-to-point.

"Keep him warm. And Mom, just stay calm, okay? I'll be there soon." He checked his watch, blew air through pressed lips, and ran to his room to grab a few things and stuff them into a bag. He snatched up his wallet and phone, and then ran to the door, praying there'd be a flight he could jump on.

He'd phoned anyone and everyone he could think of; sending emergency services, plus Hank the neighbor. His mom sounded disorientated, having only said that Barry was still asleep and that she had placed his jacket over his shoulders to keep him warm.

After the longest 5 hours of his life, he was there.

When he arrived, he thankfully found that an ambulance had come and gone, but Hank from next door had grabbed his shoulders. "Sorry, Ben," was all he'd said.

He had steeled himself, knowing what to expect, but it still hit him like a kick to the guts.

He trudged up to the house, where a local police chief he remembered from when he was a kid waited on the porch. He saluted Ben and shook his hand.

"Sorry for your loss, Ben. Your father was a personal friend of mine. He was a good man." His jaw worked for a moment. "Massive heart attack. Probably never felt a thing."

Ben nodded. "Mom? Cynthia?"

"Inside. She's okay…wanted to wait for you."

Ben went past him and into the house. He found her in the family room, sitting on the sofa, just staring at the fireplace. He had sat down next to her and put an arm around her shoulder.

"Stupid old man; chopping wood like that," she scolded, and then collapsed into tears.

Ben felt his own eyes fill. Barry had been the perfect father – happy, strong, always there, and had taught him everything from how to do his shoelaces, to being able to drink from a soda bottle without the backwash sliding back into the bottle.

Guilt nagged at him for not coming back sooner, to have one more laugh, one more beer, or maybe one more chance to tell him he loved him. All gone now.

That all had been just two days ago. Now, family and friends were gathered at his funeral, staring at the polished coffin that gleamed in the sunlight. No one talked, and few even met his eyes after the initial handshake greeting – all bar one – Emma Wilson, a high school sweetheart. She nodded to him, and he gave her a flat smile of acknowledgment in return.

He also turned slightly, hiding the scar on his cheek – a parting gift from a grenade-throwing ISIS asshole in Syria. The line down his face from temple to chin was a reminder of his time in the military. The grenade had been a lucky throw, and landed in the center of five of them – he dived for it, but his buddy, Mad Max Hertzog, had beat him to it, shouldering him aside and covering the frag device with his body.

Then came the madness: the explosion, the smell of burning flesh, the warm wetness that rained sticky blood and flesh onto his face, his hands, and into his eyes and mouth. There was the siren sound of perforated eardrums and the faint shouts of men hauling him up.

There wasn't much left of Max, blown in half, and another of their team lay on his back with smoke rising from charred and ripped flesh. They were being overrun, and he was dragged away, but not before he thought he saw the dead man's fingers twitch. He tried to pull away, tried to scream that the man needed help, but his mouth wouldn't work.

He was later told the man, Henderson, was dead. His head told him that was the truth, but his subconscious whispered that he had left a man behind and those bloody fingers twitching, beckoning to him, still haunted his dreams even today.

The shrapnel had opened his face, but he knew he was one of the lucky ones; he served, and survived, with everything intact. Many others didn't, or they came home missing pieces.

Ben let his eyes drift again to Emma and didn't realize his hand had reached up to touch the scar; his mother said it made him look handsome in a brutal sort of way. Others said it just made him look meaner, and that was fine by him.

Ben continued to stare with dark brown eyes that had a hawk's intensity. Years ago, he and Emma had dated. She was a cute girl then, but now had grown into a beautiful woman, and he wondered whether she had kept in contact with his family, or she was here just to catch a glimpse of him. *You conceited ass*, he thought, but then, *I hope so.*

Afterwards, there was a wake planned at the family home, which was agonizing to endure, and then his mother asked could he stay for a few more days to help tidy things up, and to just be there.

He knew what she had meant – tidy things up, meant to pack away objects she couldn't bear to look at anymore. Of course he would. Besides, Ben was diplomatically termed *between engagements* right now.

After the grenade, and then the two hundred and fifty plus internal micro-stitches to his face, he had left his Special Forces unit and the Army for good. He had felt like he was running away, and the guilt still hung over him like a shadow. But he knew then that he had seen enough, endured enough, and delivered enough violence to last a dozen lifetimes.

Now, he just wanted peace and quiet, and may even resume his studies to become a vet – animals he loved; it was human beings that were capable of atrocities and that he had walked away from. He was like his dad, and his grandfather, and he guessed all the other Cartwrights who yearned to live life simply and in the sunshine. Even his namesake,

Benjamin Cartwright, who died somewhere down in Venezuela in 1908 after trekking into the jungle, was just a dreamer with an adventurous soul.

His mother came back into the living room and picked up an old photograph, stared for a moment, and then sobbed again.

Ben sighed; yep, *should be raining*.

CHAPTER 02

Ben woke with a start. The house was quiet, and he turned his head slowly, wondering what woke him.

He read somewhere once that if a person dies suddenly it could take days for their spirit to actually realize it. They'd carry on like nothing had happened, wandering along hallways, opening and shutting doors, and even trying to speak to their loved ones.

"Goodbye, Dad. I love you," he whispered to the still air.

Ben sighed and sat there for a few more minutes; it was late, or rather way too early, and he silently got to his feet. He stepped carefully, trying to avoid squeaking floorboards that might wake his mother who had finally got off to sleep.

He decided to continue with his tidying up and carried a box of his dad's clothing under one arm and a beer in the other as he made his way up to the attic.

His grandfather, Errol, had made his fortune in mining and left his father a sizeable inheritance and home on a gentle hilltop with 20 acres of surrounding land. The family home itself was impressive with plenty of sandstone and wood, filled with antiques, memories, and things the family had picked up over several generations.

The third floor was all attic space and was filled with boxes, chests, and dustsheet-covered excess furniture. He flicked on the lights, placed his beer on a covered table, and hiked the box of clothing over to the existing pile of chronologically layered personal items.

He still had much to bring up, but the man's pictures would remain downstairs. He noticed his mother had turned them face down, as if even looking at him would cause her to crumble all over again. Ben figured his dad's ghost would be in the house for a long time to come.

He pulled a sheet off an armchair and sat down, breathing in the smell of dust, old wood, and aging papers. He put his feet up on a chest and just let his eyes move along the piled towers of their family history – like geological layers, Barry would now have his things added to the piles, joining those that belonged to grandfather Errol, great grandfather Julius, and his namesake, his great, great grandfather Benjamin.

In a moment of feeling his mortality, he wondered whether one day someone would be sitting right here with their feet on his lifetime's collection of papers, pictures, and old track and field trophies.

Ben shifted his feet on the chest. When he was a kid, his dad had told him that they were all full of treasure. But upon opening a few of them, he had been disappointed to find that there was nothing but papers, old letters, antiquities, and faded photographs. Nothing a kid valued at all.

His dad had just smiled at the downcast look on his face and told him that knowledge and information was the greatest treasure that a person could ever be given. Back then, he wasn't impressed; but time has a way of changing perceptions.

He lifted his feet from the ornate box and unlatched it so he could lift the lid. The hinges squealed in protest like tortured banshees, and he *shushed* them.

He clasped large hands together and ran his eyes over the contents. This one belonged to his grandfather Errol and contained thick folders of papers and old books on geology and mining. He dug down; there were even sealed packages in a waxed paper and bound with string. He lifted several free and read the notes scribbled on the front in pencil. Some were addressed to Errol's father, Benjamin, some to Errol, and some just to the Cartwright Estate, with a few dated as far back as 1912, well before Errol was even born. Another was inscribed 1930 and both felt like books, and both seemed to be from a similar source.

He ran a hand up through his thick, dark hair and left the fingers there, massaging his scalp as he read the notations – they were from the Estate of Sir Arthur Conan Doyle. Being an avid adventure fiction reader, he recognized the name and his interest was immediately piqued. He unwrapped the first package dated 1912.

"*Whoa.*" As he suspected, it was a book – *but what a book* – an immaculate first edition of The Lost World. The gilt and blue cloth-bound book was heavy in his hands.

Ben didn't even know Doyle had written the book. He always thought he was well known for his Sherlock Holmes adventures, but thought The Lost World was actually a Steven Spielberg movie.

He lifted it to his nose and sniffed; he detected a slight mustiness, but overall, the dry attic coupled with the book's wax paper covering had preserved it over the entire century.

But why wouldn't Errol have opened it? he wondered. Maybe because it came before he was born and wasn't addressed to him? Or perhaps it had been put away and he hadn't even known it existed?

Ben opened the book and read the inscription. It was from the great man himself:

To my good friend, Benjamin Cartwright,

Your experiences ignited my imagination, and this is the result. Hope we can correspond again soon.

Your friend, Arthur Conan Doyle

Ben smiled wistfully; *we Cartwrights had friends in high places,* he thought and then sighed. The letter told him that Doyle obviously didn't know that Benjamin died down in Venezuela some four years before the book was printed.

He carefully began to read pages here and there, picking up the gist of the story – a newspaper reporter, Edward Malone, is sent to interview a professor by the name of Challenger, who claims he knew of a hidden plateau in the South American Amazon that was inhabited by living dinosaurs.

Ben smiled as he read. In no time, Challenger had convinced a small band of supporters to embark on a perilous adventure to find this plateau, where they certainly *did* discover creatures from the dawn of time.

Well, of course they did, Ben thought dryly. He turned the book over in his hands, admiring the fine binding; he couldn't imagine what the book was worth, but he'd certainly not let it linger in the old trunk any longer. He partially rewrapped it and placed it on the table beside his beer.

The next package he drew forth was a bundle of letters tied together with age-stained string. He undid the knot and spread them out. He could see they represented earlier correspondence back and forth between Benjamin and Doyle.

Ben snorted softly. *So it was true then,* he thought. He remembered his father regaling him with tales of Benjamin, the adventurer's adventurer who went on many expeditions to remote corners of the globe, with the 1908 one being the fatal last. His wife had to organize recovery of his body from some remote village down in South America at the edge of the Amazon jungle.

He opened the first letter dated 1906, prior to his ill-fated trip. It discussed his preparations for the expedition he was organizing. He even invited Arthur Conan Doyle to come along and document it.

He read quickly; there were also meandering discussions about finances, who and what he should take with him, and then the rest settled on more mundane political matters of the time.

Doyle's response was to express a keen interest in the expedition, but he politely declined to join Benjamin. However, he did offer to finance part of the trip if Benjamin ran into difficulty raising funds.

Ben looked at the dates of each letter and grinned – they were dated many weeks, and sometimes months apart, and the time lapse would have represented communication times between continents at the beginning of last century. Today, talking to someone anywhere in the world was near instantaneous and would have been something so astounding that Sir Arthur Conan Doyle might have only entertained the concept in one of his fiction novels.

Ben sipped his beer again and opened another letter, enjoying immersing himself into the minds of great men from over a century past. In this one, Benjamin described what he hoped to find – he had heard tales of a place of great beasts appearing once every decade during the wettest of seasons. And also of a hidden plateau in an unexplored Amazonian jungle that, in Benjamin Cartwright's own words, would rewrite everything the world knew about biology and evolution.

"Get outta here." Ben's forehead creased – *the hidden plateau, South American jungle, rewriting what we know about biology and evolution* – he recognized all the basic elements from Doyle's fantastic tale. He swung to where he left the copy of The Lost World and carefully unwrapped it again. He reread the dedication:

To my good friend, Benjamin Cartwright – your experiences ignited my imagination, and this is the result, Arthur Conan Doyle had written over a century before.

Is that what Doyle really meant? That over 100 years ago, Benjamin Cartwright had actually done what he had only described in his work of fiction? He chuckled as he closed the book, placing it back on the tabletop.

Impossible, he thought, but his interest sparked up more than ever. He reached for the next item in the pile – a single letter on top, once again in the famous author's handwriting. Ben eased it open and read.

Dear Benjamin,

My dearest friend, I write this to your spirit, or perhaps to your heirs. Your passing has wounded me and serves to remind one of their mortality. But you, sir, will now remain the brave and youthful adventurer, forever.
Your notebook was, and is, invaluable, and so it will be kept with my favorite things in the secret place only we know – under the earth in Windlesham Manor.

Your friend, forever,

Arthur Conan Doyle

Under the earth? *He freaking buried it?* Ben snorted softly. "Way to go, Arthur." Ben placed the old letter aside and lifted the next. This one was a larger envelope, dated 1931, and much more formal looking. It was still unopened and sent to the Benjamin Cartwright estate, just like with Doyle's last letter, confirming they knew that Benjamin was no more. He carefully slid a finger along the gum-line and the ancient glue easily gave way.

The paper inside was of high-quality fiber. He immediately saw this one was written in a different hand and was from a legal firm representing the estate of Sir Arthur Conan Doyle. He read down:

To whom it may concern,

You may now be aware that Sir Arthur Ignatius Conan Doyle has now passed away, and we have been charged with tidying up his affairs. Many items of Sir Arthur's collection will be kept for posterity, some will be provided to museums, and some he had wished returned to their owners on his demise.

One such item was to be the leather-bound notebook of the late Benjamin Bartholomew Cartwright of Ohio, United States of America. This notebook was something Sir Arthur valued immensely and always wished to hand-deliver back to its owner, Mr. Cartwright. Obviously, events overtook both parties before this outcome could be satisfactorily achieved.

Unfortunately, our searches to date have not located the item referred to in previous correspondence. Should knowledge of its whereabouts come to light then this letter will serve as proof of ownership for a Cartwright heir to take possession of the notebook in person.

Yours sincerely,

Horatio William Bartholomew, Solicitor of Law
Windlesham Manor, Crowborough, East Sussex

The corner of Ben's mouth turned up as he looked at the dozens and dozens of large chests in the attic. He held up his hands.

"And did you ever go and get it, Great Granddad or Granddad?" He sighed and lowered his hands, looking down again at the letter. His brows knitted as he remembered something that now seemed to answer his question – the letter had been unopened.

"Or perhaps it was never even claimed."

He exhaled slowly through his nose and let his mind wander. The thrill of adventure coursed through his Cartwright veins and he let his eyes rise to the stacks of trunks, crates, and chests. But there were so many, it wearied him.

Ben yawned. "*Nah*, more likely there was another attempt at communication and probably somewhere in this museum warehouse is old Benjamin's notebook."

He sat in silence for a few more moments, staring into space and watching as the rays of early morning light streaming in through the attic's dormer windows illuminated dust motes gently floating for an eternity, waiting patiently for the next large body to move through them and whip them into swirling agitation once again. As he watched them dance in the sunbeam, his eyelids began to lower, and lower.

Ben was back in the jungle and running hard. He tried to remember if it was the mission in Thailand, the Congo, or even Colombia, but his mind refused to identify it. The only thing he knew for sure was something was after him – not some one, but some *thing*.

He barged on as vines tried to snag him, huge palm fronds slapped at his face and body, and he was coated in perspiration, rain, and fear.

Behind him, trees were being flattened and he tried to accelerate but hit a wall of weird tree trunks that barred his way. He spun and reached for his gun – it wasn't there.

Before him, the trees were prized apart and he finally saw his pursuer – he screamed.

"*Jesus Christ!*" The sound of the front door bell was like an electric shock and jolted him awake to jump in his chair, beer sloshing in his bottle and onto his groin.

"Ah, crap." Ben grimaced and quickly got to his feet, put the bottle down plus the pile of letters, and headed for the steps. He checked his watch – full morning already – and he moved quickly, taking the steps two at a time. He didn't want his mother woken.

On the first floor, the doorbell rang again.

"*Argh!* Keep your hat on!" He sprinted now, the last dozen stairs to ground floor taken in three giant bounds.

Out of breath, he reached for the door handle and wrenched it open. "Can you please keep it...?"

"Well, someone looks out of condition." Emma Wilson smiled up at him, holding a cloth-draped box in her arms.

Ben cut off his demand and instead sucked in one last big breath right to the bottom of his chest, flooding his lungs with oxygen. He held it for a second and then let it out in a whoosh. He shrugged. "Yep, and that's what living the high life will do to you."

He stood there staring at her, knowing that the grin he wore was a dumb one.

He'd seen her at his dad's funeral, but up close, she looked even better – luminous green eyes, and her brown hair shone with red highlights in the sunlight. Freckles still smattered across an upturned nose and cheeks, and she wore a T-shirt showing off an athletic figure – very athletic; there were corded muscles in her neck and arms. Whatever she was doing was obviously working for her.

He and Emma had dated for a while and got really close. But he enlisted, their roads forked when he went away, and that was that. Seeing her again, made him feel…good. He suddenly remembered his scar and angled his face slightly.

She held the box in one hand and reached up to his chin. "Did it hurt?"

Her fingertips were butterfly-light on his skin, but he still felt their warmth. He shook his head. "Really, I don't remember a thing. Could have been worse." He shrugged.

"Yes." She dropped her hand. "You kept your looks." She tilted her head. "I kinda like it. So…" She held up the box. "I made these for your mom; just an orange sponge cake with marmalade jam. It's her favorite."

"Her favorite?" His brows rose slightly.

She beamed up at him. "Um-hmm. And she also likes pecan cookies and brownies done crispy on the outside and gooey on the inside." She tilted her head, her eyes narrowing. "If you got back here more often, then you might…" her smile vanished as she seemed to remember. "I'm sorry, your dad… I didn't mean…"

"No, you're right; I should have been here." Ben waved it away. "Forget it; you wanna come in?"

"Yes, please. But only if it's a good time." Emma shuffled in, now looking a little less sunny than when she arrived. "I can come back."

"Don't be silly." He gently closed the door and then led her into the living room. "So, how do you know my mom likes orange sponge cake?" He cocked his head.

"We-eeell, you do know that she does cycle classes down at World Gym, right?"

He shrugged. "I knew she was exercising, but…"

"It's the same gym that I go to." She lifted her chin. "We kinda ended up hanging out from time to time."

"Good for you, the pair of you, and thank you." He looked her over. "And that accounts for the body of iron I detect."

She raised an arm, making a muscle with her bicep. "Dude, this is rock-climbing beef. Ohio is home to some of the best climbing faces in the country. I'm rated 5.11, expert level."

He reached out to squeeze her arm. "I'm impressed." He grinned. "But I'm afraid mom's asleep right now. Hate to wake her as she hasn't been sleeping well of late."

"No, no, it's okay." She held up a hand, while still cradling the box. "I thought I'd drop this off, see how she is. Maybe say hello to the prodigal son while I'm at it." She looked up into his face as she held the box out to him. "So, how are *you* holding up?"

He bobbed his head as he accepted the box from her. "I'm good; feeling a bit guilty for not being here, but, good."

"Don't feel guilty." Emma's eyes glistened. "No one could have expected…this."

"Yeah." He scoffed as he stared at the box she had given him. "Like, who knew the guy was even sick? I'm betting he didn't either." He pulled in a cheek. "Mortality; one minute you're here, and then next, you're not."

"Big Barry was a great guy. And he and your mom proved that love could stay strong forev…" She looked up. "She'll miss him."

"We all will," Ben said and motioned to a sofa. "Get you a coffee?"

"Sure, cream, no sugar," Emma said as she eased down on the broad couch.

Ben headed to the kitchen where he opened the box. He was blissfully assailed with the smell of fresh baking.

"*Mmm*, maybe a slice each as well."

The coffee had already been made so he poured a couple of mugs and placed two slices of cake on a plate – two small and the other doorstop size.

Emma beamed when she saw him bring the cake. "Good boy. Maybe it'll become your favorite too." She took the cup and broke off a small piece of cake and popped it in her mouth.

"So, how long do you think you'll hang around this time? Ohio, I mean."

"Hadn't really thought about it. A few days, I guess. I'll make a call on it after I see how mom is getting on at the end of the week." He shrugged. "Maybe longer if she needs me. Not much going on at home right now."

Emma's eyebrows turned down, but there was a slight gleam in her eye. "Um, no one at home for you to miss?"

He half smiled. "No Miss Right, and not even Miss Right-Now." He sipped his coffee. "Since I got out of the military, I've been doing some freelance security and advisory work, but I thought maybe next year I might go back and finish my studies."

"Oh yeah, I remember. The animal lover." She nodded. "That's great."

"And what about you?" he asked as he bit off half the cake wedge and pushed it into the side of his mouth.

"I have a small business running rock climbing classes, adventure tours; that kinda stuff," she answered.

"You were always the maths whiz. And weren't you studying economics?" he asked quickly.

"Yeah, but how many economists get to spend their day outside, every day?" She lifted her chin. "Have you ever sat amongst a field of wild flowers in spring? Just the bees and birds talking to you, with the warm sun on your back and the mountain peaks lined up before you?"

He shook his head. "No, but you make it sound like a dream. Seems like its captured your heart. And speaking of that…what about you? Any Mr. Rock Climber in your life?"

"Not really. I mean, no." She laughed. "Hey, maybe I've been waiting for you to come back." She laughed again, but this time her cheeks reddened.

Their eyes locked for a moment, and Ben almost fell into them.

"Ben, is that you?"

He turned at the sound of his mother's voice.

"Down here, Mom." He stood up. "I better…" He thumbed over his shoulder.

Emma also got to her feet. "Yeah, you better." She brushed crumbs from her jeans and headed for the door. She jammed both hands into her back pockets.

Ben opened the door for her and she turned back to him.

"A few of the old gang are getting together tonight to throw back a couple of beers, have some ribs and a few laughs. Why don't you come along?"

"Um." His first instinct was to decline. But looking down into those eyes made it impossible. "Sure, where and when?"

She grinned. "*When*, is 7pm. *Where,* is across town; I'll pick you up at quarter to seven, deal?"

"Deal." He reached out a hand and she took it. This time, he felt the calluses on her hand and he turned it over. "Oh yeah, these really are rock-jock hands."

She pulled her hand away. "They can be soft when I want them to be, soldier boy. See you tonight." She turned and skipped down the steps, a lightness in every bounce.

*****

A car horn honked at 6:45 on the dot.

Cynthia looked up from her book. "Your date's here, darling." She smiled.

Ben rolled his eyes. "It's not a date. Just gonna catch up with some of the old crowd."

"Emma's nice; I like her." Cynthia watched him as he pulled on his jacket. It was tight across shoulders that were more at home on a linebacker.

He nodded. "She sure is. And she makes a great cake."

"And she'd make a great wife. Not that I'd match-make, you know." She raised an eyebrow.

He chuckled. "What? I'm back a few days and you're trying to marry me off already?"

"Well, you're not getting any younger, handsome. Barry missed out on seeing any grandkids, and I sure don't want to."

"Aw, Mom." He scowled but couldn't help the corners of his mouth turning up.

There was a knock on the door.

"And impatient to see you – good sign." Cynthia lowered her voice. "She often asked after you, you know."

Ben waved her to quietness and was about to turn to the door when he paused. "Do you need anything?"

She shook her head. "Just for you two to have a nice time."

"It's not just us two," he whispered back. "I won't be late. Call me if there's anything you need." Ben quickly crossed back to kiss her on the cheek.

He then headed back to the front door and pulled it open, immediately smelling wonderful perfume. Emma stood there in a clinging cotton dress, and her smooth, tanned skin, perfect figure, luminous green eyes, and shimmering hair made his heart leap in his chest.

"Wow, you brush up real fine." He meant it.

"You make me sound like a pair of shoes." But she grinned appreciatively. "And you look pretty damn good yourself. Even if you could do with some new clothes."

He opened his arms. "Shabby chic; it's all the rage in Colorado."

She nodded. "I believe you; thousands wouldn't." She leaned around his large frame. "Hiya, Mrs. Cartwright; need anything?"

His mother waved. "No, and thank you for the magnificent cake. Even though Ben ate most of it before I even got to take a peek."

Ben raised his hands. "Guilty."

"I'll make some more," Emma replied, beaming.

"You two have a nice night." Cynthia settled back in her chair. "And no need to bring him back early; he needs a break from looking after an old woman."

"Aw…" Ben grimaced at her.

"Go." Cynthia shooed him out and Emma grabbed his arm.

"See ya, Mrs. Cartwright." She waved and dragged him down the steps, barely pausing long enough for him to drag the door shut.

Her car was an old Land Rover that was covered with dust up to the door handles.

"Whoa, the best of British muscle, huh?" He smiled appreciatively.

"It's open." She jumped in and he followed. "Yup; 1998 Land Rover Discovery. Tough as all get out and damned cheap; it also has a V8 engine, four-wheel drive as well as great angling for off-road activities – there aren't many tracks that I can't get to in this bad boy."

"Nice." He strapped in. "So, where to, driver?'

"You remember that hokey bar and rib joint that all the cool kids used to hang out in?" She started the Rover.

"Ricky's?" His brows went up.

"Yep, that's the one. Well, the cool kids still go there; they're just a little older and less cool now." She chuckled.

"And some of us don't need fake IDs to sneak into bars anymore." He gave her a wry smile.

She chuckled. "Yep, that's me; Emma the law breaker." She half turned to briefly flash him a dazzling smile before facing the road again.

Ben enjoyed her company, and they talked like they had never been apart. He was almost disappointed when they arrived at Ricky's Bar and Rib Joint as it meant he'd now have to share her.

She parked the Rover with a jerk and jumped out. He followed.

"Hasn't changed a bit." Ben looked up at the neon sign, still glowing cherry red with an image of sauce-laden ribs on a plate. Through the windows, he saw a few family diners and a group of younger people gathered at one end of the bar.

The door squeaked as he held it open, and she led him over to the group.

"Get outta town, *it's true*." A slim, stubbled young Asian man stepped out, grinning widely. He wore casual, but expensive clothing.

Ben returned the smile. "Mr. Daniel Murakami; you still here?" They embraced and then others swarmed around.

"Nah, I come back from time to time; you should too, buddy. Long time no see," Murakami chided.

"He's slumming it." Another hand slapped his shoulder and Ben turned. The blond man was lantern-jawed, as broad as Ben, and had an easy smile. "Welcome back, big guy." He stuck out a large hand.

"Steve," Ben scoffed with a grin. Steven Chamber's hand felt like wood and leather. He turned seeing another member of his old crew.

There was Andrea Ashley, still as intensely beautiful as she was at school. He distantly remembered that she headed off to Hollywood to find her future. He doubted she was now back in Greenberry just to see him.

"Andrea." He smiled, and she looked back at him with an appraising eye before stepping in to hug him, and then continue hugging him.

"Jesus, someone throw a bucket of water over them." Steve jammed a bottle of beer between them and another into Emma's hand as she also wedged herself in front of Andrea.

Steve then held his own beer aloft. "To the return of all prodigal sons and daughters – *saludo!*"

"*Saludo!*" Bottles and glasses were raised and then clinked together.

They spent the next few hours catching up, talking crap, laughing too loud, followed it with ribs and more beer, before finally settling at a corner table to finish with coffee and whisky.

"Bummer about your dad, Ben. He was a good guy." Steve gave him a glum smile.

"Yeah, thanks. Mom's still a little messed up." Ben continued to stare at his coffee.

"And will be for a while; but she'll be okay," Emma said. "Those guys come from tougher stock than us."

Andrea reached forward to lay a hand over his. "It's good that you came back to support her. Are you staying?"

Ben saw Emma's lips compress. For some reason, he felt flattered. He patted her hand and then slid his out. "Only for a while. Thought I might try and finish my veterinary studies. Then settle down somewhere...for good."

"You? A vet?" Dan comically widened his eyes and then grinned. "Suppose it'll be good to use your brains rather than just brawn for a change."

"Aw, thanks, buddy." Ben grinned back. "I'll make a fortune off rich guys like you; I hear they have houses full of fluffy little dogs."

Dan nodded and raised his brandy. "And peacocks; don't forget the peacocks."

"Hey, Greenberry needs vets too, you know?' Emma raised her coffee.

"Do they now?" Ben smiled at her.

"So I guess right now you're helping your mom; anything we can do, just let us know," Steve Chambers said.

"Thanks, buddy." Ben looked into his coffee for a moment. "Right now, I'm just getting all Dad's things squared away. I've been picking over the Cartwright ancestor history in the attic." He snorted. "Hey, want to know something cool? Did you know my great, great grandfather was a friend of Sir Arthur Conan Doyle? I even found a first edition copy of a book, 1912, still wrapped in paper – was never even opened."

"Very cool; which one?" Emma asked.

"The Lost World," Ben replied.

"No way! That's one of my favorites; I read it as a kid." She turned to the group. "It's where these explorers find a hidden mountain covered in dinosaurs."

"Something like that." Ben leaned forward. "But you want to know something *really* weird?"

"Always," said Dan, leaning closer.

"What if it was true?" Ben looked up.

"Say what?" Steve's forehead creased.

"Oh, Ben." Emma started to giggle.

"No more whisky here." Dan grinned as he shouted to the bar.

"Hear me out." Ben cleared his throat. "What if it was true? Seriously, what if it was *all* true? What if it was never make-believe at all, and that the Lost World was real? Sir Arthur Conan Doyle didn't make it all up. I believe he was reading about a lost expedition that really happened."

The group just stared. Emma's cheeks reddened slightly.

"I found out that my great, great grandfather, Benjamin, actually went to South America and found something amazing." He opened his hands on the table. "And Arthur Conan Doyle used it as the basis for his story."

"I believe you, or want to," Steve said, with a hint of a smile. "But, ah, how do you know that? Know that it's true, I mean?"

"Benjamin wrote it all down in a notebook; in 1908." Ben sat back.

The looks went from disbelievingly to quizzical.

"Wait a minute here. You have a notebook that proves all this?" Dan blew air between his lips. "Now, I'm *really* interested."

"Can we see it?" Andrea asked.

"Well…" Ben grimaced.

"Here it comes." Steve grinned again.

"I don't have it." Ben sighed. "Apparently, Benjamin sent it to Arthur Conan Doyle, and then according to some old correspondence, when Doyle learned that Ben the 1st had passed away, he kept it, and then hid it somewhere on his estate so it wouldn't be lost."

"You mean like it is now," Dan said. "Good plan."

Ben then spent the next few minutes giving them a thumbnail

overview of what he'd found out. The group was spellbound, especially Dan, who seemed to fully suspend his disbelief and had moved to the very edge of his seat.

When he was finished, Ben sat back. "All I have is a letter from a lawyer verifying that the notebook exists and belongs to me, or at least to one of Benjamin's heirs."

Ben sprang forward. "Oh, one more thing; apparently this place in the Amazon can only be found during some sort of weird seasonal thing that only happens once every ten years. And the next year it can be located is…" he held up a finger for a moment, before jabbing it down on the table. "…*now*, in 2018. In fact, we probably missed it; the window for locating it is in just a few weeks."

Dan clapped. "Oh man, that is awesome."

"That notebook's got to be worth a fortune…if you could ever find it," Steve said.

"As long as the notebook hasn't been destroyed, then anything lost can be found." Dan waved over his shoulder, calling the waitress for more drinks. He then pulled his chair so close his chest bumped the table. "And forget selling it; the value is in its secrets. And by the way, Ben, we haven't missed *anything* yet. I say, we need to find the notebook, find this place, and then go there."

"Nah, gone now," Ben said. "Wouldn't even know where to look."

"Is it? Gone, I mean." Andrea tilted her head. "I've never heard of this notebook or whatever it is coming to light. Have any of you?" She then looked at each of them for a moment before turning back to Ben. "So it might still be hidden. Maybe it's still hidden there. I bet he left clues. So the million dollar question is, where is *there*?"

Ben bobbed his head. "In some sort of secret place that only both of them knew." He sighed.

"That's it?" Andrea frowned.

"Well, he mentioned it being *under the earth* in Windlesham Manor." He hiked his shoulders. "So, buried somewhere there, I guess. If it exists, and if it hasn't already been found or inadvertently destroyed by the elements."

Dan put his hands to his head. "Bullshit." He slapped a hand on the table. "Think positive, man. I say it's still there somewhere. We can find it. We use science and technology. Like I said, we find it, and then we go there."

Ben chuckled and lifted his glass. "Not the whisky talking at all."

"Why not?" Dan implored, his almond eyes now wide. "This is the most exciting and interesting thing I've heard of in years." He turned. "Guys, what do you think?"

"In England, right?" Steve raised an eyebrow. "We'll just all pop over to England, each of us with a shovel on our shoulders, and start digging. I hear they like Yanks doing stuff like that."

Dan laughed out loud. "No, smartass, with a little more investigative finesse than that. I can't believe you don't see this as the biggest and most exciting opportunity, like *ever*." Dan rubbed his hands together, looking like he was warming to his own idea. "I'll even pay…for everyone."

"Well, I'd go." Emma straightened.

"Me too," Andrea added.

"Now wait a minute." Ben couldn't believe how fast this was getting out of hand. "To the United Kingdom? Jesus Christ."

"Yeah, to start. I mean, the whole shebang – we go and look for this hidden jungle as well." Dan rubbed his chin. "Windlesham Manor, you say? Tell you what, by morning, I'll know everything there is to know about it. I'll have some of my guys do a full search." He grinned. "I smell a plan coming together."

"Good grief." Ben shook his head, but couldn't help being swept along by Dan's excitement. "Guys, maybe Dan is keen to waste his money and time, but we should think about this. It could all be a wild goose chase…and a deadly one at that. As I mentioned, the book might be nothing of interest, or it might already be found."

"You're right." Dan eased back in his chair. "And I can find that out as well. I'll have two-dozen tech guys on it in 20 minutes; we'll put a search out on the networks, and even the dark web. The traders, collectors, and even the black marketeers would know if something like that has ever come to light." He grinned. "Let's rustle a few bushes and see what we scare up."

"And tell everyone we're looking for it." Emma frowned. "Is that a good thing?"

"So what?" Dan said. "Like Ben mentioned; most people don't know, don't care, or have long forgotten." He held a finger aloft. "We'll also need an *in* for Windlesham Manor."

"I know someone who lives over there." Steve opened his arms. "An English girl, zoologist; she might help us."

"Done and done." Dan slapped the table.

Emma and Steve high-fived and Andrea leaned across to hug him.

"Meet back here for breakfast at 9am, and I'll tell you what I've learned." Dan stood, pushing his chair back and pulling his phone at the same time. He jammed it to his ear, talking rapidly as he headed for the door.

Ben sat with an open mouth grin. "What just happened here?"

Emma sniggered. "I think we just got Murakami'd."

*****

Later, pulling up out front of his house, Emma switched off the engine and turned in her seat.

"So, do you think any of it is true? I mean, *really*?"

"Yes, no…maybe." He grinned. "Could the notebook have existed? Yeah, I think it probably did at one time. But seriously, a hidden plateau where monsters lived? Come on."

Emma rested her chin on the seat watching him. Ben smiled at her as he went on.

"Remember, Sir Arthur Conan Doyle was a fiction writer. Maybe there was something Benjamin found that was fantastic. But back in 1908, a lot of things were being discovered and probably seemed fantastic. I'm pretty sure that all the rest came straight from Doyle's imagination."

"Well, you know what I think?" She smiled, her eyes almost glowing. "There's only one way to truly find out…find that mysterious notebook." She rested her chin on her hand. "Besides, the only thing we've got to lose is time. If there's no notebook, then at a minimum we'll all get a nice holiday out of it. Be good for the old gang to hang out again."

"And if there *is* a notebook?" He looked deep into her beautiful eyes.

"Then it could solve one of your family's greatest mysteries. And just think; it might even lead to an adventure none of us will ever forget. You'll be famous."

"I don't want to be famous." Ben put a hand on the door handle and began to turn away but paused. "But I do like the sound of hanging out with the old gang again. Didn't realize how much I missed you all."

Ben felt her hand on his arm and he turned back. She leaned forward to kiss his cheek, but managed to catch the side of his mouth. He felt a tingle run all the way through him.

"Did I say *you all*? I meant, just you." He lifted a hand to her chin and kissed her on the lips.

They sat back, staring at each other for a moment. "Um, would you like to come in, for a…coffee?"

Emma smiled at him from under lowered brows. "Not tonight." She put a hand over his. "I like being with you, *just you*, too. Please say yes to the trip."

He groaned theatrically. "Oh, maybe."

He went to turn away again, but she grabbed his shoulder. "Ben-*nnn*."

He groaned louder. "Oh, okay." And pushed the door fully open with a scream of rusting hinges.

"Yay! See you tomorrow; 9am – *sharp*."

CHAPTER 03

1948 – South Eastern Venezuela – the Wettest Season Returns

The hurricane-like winds had died down and an armor-plated *Ankylosaurus* raised a dull expression skyward for a moment, seeing the clouds part to let rays of brilliant sunshine in through the hole that was widening above its jungle.

The creature was 18 feet in length, weighed in at around 4,000 pounds, and was heavily armored with a horned beak-like mouth. As well as its plated hide, its armory also included a tail that ended in a club of solid, dense bone that it used to great effect on any overly interested predators. It wasn't invulnerable to attack, but rarely did the carnivores of the land bother it.

The lumbering beast pulled at the hard grasses, chewing down great clumps, grinding them up with its fist-sized molars, and then moving on to the next. Its path led it towards two tree trunks only six feet apart, and rather than go around, it wedged its huge bulk between them and relied on its powerful stump-like legs to pull it through.

The tree trunks and canopies shook, and from above rained down hundreds, possibly thousands, of spindly red ants in defense of their nest. The inch-long insects had spikes on their heads that resembled horned helmets, and upon alighting on the body of the perceived threat to their colony, they immediately commenced their attack.

Formic acid was injected, magnifying the pain from the countless bites, and then the insects began to swarm towards the head where they had learned that the massive, thick-hided beasts were vulnerable. They quickly found the tiny eyes, ears, nostrils, and also the soft inner tissue in the mouth.

The *Ankylosaurus* screamed with fear and pain and charged forward. Its bulk smashed trees from its path, and its cries reverberated through the jungle, silencing the other chattering, skittering, and squealing inhabitants. Winged creatures took flight above it as it found a watercourse and charged along it.

It was nearly blind when it entered the stream, washing away many of the insects, but the damage was already done. Fear and pain maddened, it blundered on.

Nothing seemed able to stop it, until the impact from above drove it to its knees as something grabbed its neck and shoulders. The grip was large, and the *Ankylosaurus* felt the scrape of sharp teeth across its armor-plated back.

The teeth couldn't hope to penetrate its hide, but the grip of the jaws was strong enough to hold it in place. The dinosaur got back to its feet and began to lumber on. But then more of the thing that held it piled down on top of it and started to loop around and under, eventually completely enfolding it.

Once done, the constricting began. Titanic muscles compressed, and then unbelievably, the armor-plated hide began to buckle and crack. The plant eater bleated its fear, but when it did, precious air escaped from squeezed lungs that it could never hope to recover.

A rib broke, and then another, and then its entire chest collapsed as its body was slowly pulverized. Only then did the mouth's grip on its back shift towards the *Ankylosaurus'* head. The long, fanged mouth opened, stretched, and then inched forward, beginning the swallowing process.

As the dinosaur's head and shoulders were fed into the maw, the coils gave one more mighty squeeze and the great beast's heart finally exploded.

CHAPTER 04

Edward Barlow's phone buzzed on the top of his Brobdingnagian-sized, antique oak desk. The cavernous hunting room he was working in had been tomb silent save for the deep ticking of a seven-foot-tall grandfather clock in the corner.

Along each of the room's walls, mounted heads watched with wild-eyed but eternal glassine stares, and a monstrous polar bear reared up, jaws gaping and paws aloft as if to tear any unwary passerby limb from limb.

Barlow was a hunter. Or rather a collector, and one of the idle rich whose family had left him billions from a mining business he had no interest in. But what he *was* interested in was sport shooting, and the more elusive, dangerous, or rare the specimen, the more he would seek them out.

Barlow's great, great uncle had been Douglas Baxter, and he had heard the family stories of his ill-fated expedition with Benjamin Cartwright, and the rumors of them setting off to find a secret place inhabited by fantastical creatures never before seen by modern man.

No matter how much he invested or how much time he spent, he could never find any clue as to where to look or even where to *begin* to look. He had scoured the Amazon and had even paid a small fortune for satellite images. But in the land of the *Boraro*, the South American demons, his searches had come to a dead end.

Barlow had always suspected that there was something he was missing or misreading – the clues, the place, or maybe even the timing. He remembered that Douglas Baxter related a sense of urgency about dates and needing to be down in the Amazon during a certain time – rainy season, eclipse, breeding cycles – he never found out exactly what.

His final throw of the dice was a technological one; years ago, he had engaged a software company to lay sophisticated *bear traps* on the Internet and also the dark web. They used trigger words, and a combination of each would spring the trap: *Benjamin Cartwright – expedition notebook – 1908 – Amazon Jungle, and – dinosaur.*

Nothing had come of it; nothing ever got triggered.

Until now.

Every online trap they had burst into life as multiple word combinations were being searched for: *Benjamin Cartwright, expedition notebook, 1908, Amazon Jungle.* It was obvious that someone was looking for a missing manuscript related to the mission to the Venezuelan Amazon in 1908. *His damned mission.*

Barlow had felt the hair rise on the back of his neck when he had read the report. The technical document also traced the search back to its source. He sat back for a moment, clasping clubby fingers across his belly.

Why now? Why did someone suddenly begin to look? he wondered, but immediately had an answer: *Because more clues had come to light, or whatever cyclical event needed to occur was about to reoccur.*

Barlow sprang forward, beginning to type on his computer. Whoever this person or people were, they were in the lead. But he had an advantage – he knew about them, but they didn't know about him.

If they had something that could lead them to the manuscript, he wanted it. And he would have it at any and all costs. He had searched for years, his life, and if anyone were going to find that hidden world, it'd be him.

He paused, thinking. He needed to assemble a team and include people who were prepared to break the law if necessary.

He began to type again; he knew just the man. Someone he had worked with before, someone who was as ruthlessly efficient as they were unscrupulous.

Barlow smiled. As Sir Arthur Conan Doyle once wrote: *the game's afoot.*

CHAPTER 05

Ben took a taxicab to meet the gang rather than letting Emma pick him up again; he wanted to think on the way. After getting back home last night, he had spent a little more time rummaging through much of the attic looking for more clues, and maybe the missing notebook. Perhaps rendering this adventure over before it started.

He yawned and rubbed tired eyes; he ended up with only a few hours sleep and no evidence that the notebook belonging to his great, great grandfather was ever found. Wherever Doyle put it, that's probably where it stayed.

Ben smiled as he remembered Emma's enthusiasm. Her eyes had lit up just like the kid he remembered from all those years ago.

It was weird how close they had all been, and now being back, if he squinted real hard, he could see them all as they were then.

Twenty-five years ago, he, Dan, Steve, Emma, and Andrea had their own pushbike gang, hanging out at the local park and racing each other on the jogging track. They were normal kids with freckles, braces, and knobby knees. And little Emma Wilson, with her huge front teeth and just the hint of tiny breasts beginning to poke at the front of her loose T-shirt.

He remembered her stacking her bike and grazing a knee. His mom always made him keep some band-aids in his pocket, which he thought dumb at the time, but it meant he could pull one out and slap it on her wound. She pressed on it and then looked up at him. Those large green eyes crinkled at the corners and stared, and he felt his kid heart bump up a notch. No one had even looked at him like that. Well, no other girl anyway.

Then came the hanging out at the mall as young teenagers, and then high school and following that, they all ended up at Ohio State, where he and Steve were picked to try out for the Buckeyes football team; a big honor. Andrea even got to be a cheerleader.

It was an away game and afterwards, he and Steve were to meet Dan and Emma in the car park. But before Ben even got there, he saw the four, big raw-boned young men around Emma and Dan. Perhaps they were Wolverine supporters and had taken exception to the grey and scarlet that his friends wore. Regardless, Dan faced them down, the small Japanese man barely coming up to their shoulders. But he was all heart and refused to step back or take whatever shit they were dishing out.

Dan got punched then. Emma screamed and lunged and was immediately grabbed by the upper arm, jerked hard and thrown to the ground. Ben saw red and dropped his bag and sprinted at them.

Ben's father had taught him to box when he was young, and he shoved one guy out of the way and then spun the leader around to face him. The guy went to double-hand push Ben in the chest.

Ben's father also told him that in a street fight to always make the first one count – he did. While the guy lunged forward, Ben used his momentum to throw a straight right into his face, a bulls-eye to the nose.

Blood and snot sprayed, and the cartilage flattened. The guy went down, and Ben spun to the next. He hoped they wanted more; he wanted to punish them all. Steve was now at his shoulder and a few seconds of glaring resulted in the three guys yelling a few *fuck yous*, and then picking up their buddy and limping away.

Steve went to help Dan, Ben crouched down beside Emma, and she held out a hand. He gave her a crooked smile.

"I've got another band-aid if you need it."

She beamed back at him. "My white knight rides in to save the day again." Emma squeezed his hand, and he fell into those beautiful eyes.

"Whenever you need me, I'll be there." He smiled sappily and hauled her up.

"I need you now." She still held his hand.

They went steady after that, loving, laughing, and making plans for some perfect future they'd make together.

But life's roads have bends and turns, and after a while, their worlds tilted and they slid in different directions. And before he knew it, she was gone and then someone else's girl. And he was left wondering what to do with himself. Maybe that's why, and when, he decided to leave town.

But now being back made him realize how much he'd missed them all. And maybe how much he needed them all.

The fact was, his mom was more settled now, and he'd be lying to himself if he said he wasn't more than a little intrigued by the whole idea of the adventure. Besides, if Dan wanted to pay, then the only thing he stood to lose was a few days time. And for that, he got to hang out with his old friends, Emma, and probably do it all first class – no downside.

"Here you go, buddy." The driver pulled up at the rib joint. "Enjoy your breakfast."

"Will do." Ben paid and stepped out.

In the harsh light of day, it looked shabbier than when it had its neon makeup in place. He grinned; it was the first rib joint he knew that reinvented itself as a diner throughout the day. Good – he didn't actually feel like ribs for breakfast.

He saw through the window that the gang was there and he was the last to arrive. Emma spotted him first through the window, and he suddenly hoped she had been looking out for him. On entering, she bumped her hip up against Dan, forcing him to move along in the booth. Steve Chambers lifted his chin in acknowledgement and Andrea's eyes were on him all the way to the table.

Ben snatched up a menu as he sat down. "What did I miss?"

"The eggs, over easy. Plus bacon good enough to make an angel weep," Steve said.

"Sounds good." Ben dropped the menu.

"*Erk*, grease." Andrea stuck her tongue out.

"A-*aaand* that's where the flavor is." Steve saluted her with his coffee.

"Sad but true." Ben looked up as the waitress appeared like magic, wrote down his order that included a toasted bagel, and also poured him a coffee. He waited until she was gone, then leaned forward to interlock his fingers on the table.

"I spent a bit of time hunting through more of the attic but didn't find anything any more illuminating. That's the bad news, so I guess the good news is, that I found nothing that indicated the notebook was ever returned, or ever found. Wherever Doyle hid it, then that's where it could still be today."

"Ditto," Dan added. "I had my tech teams send out searches far and wide looking for anything that might indicate the Cartwright expedition notebook of 1908 ever came to light – we got *nada, zero, zilch.*" Dan's brows waggled. "And that's good; means we are still good to go."

"We'll need anti-malarial shots," Steve said

Dan nodded. "Good thinking."

"Wait, what? I thought you guys meant that we were just going to find the notebook." Ben frowned.

"We sure are…to begin with." Dan reached forward to grip his forearm, his dark almond eyes intense. "Let me ask you a question: if you went to the hardware store to buy a shovel, are you doing it because you want a shovel, or are you doing it because you want a hole?"

Ben nodded slowly. "A hole, obviously."

"Exactly," Dan went on. "So the objective of finding the notebook is not just to *find the notebook*, though interesting and valuable, but to find out the secrets contained within it."

"Yeah, I see that. But this is leaping a few paces, or rather miles, from what I was thinking," Ben replied. "We should take it one step at a time."

"And we will." Dan looked earnest. "But come on, man, you gotta admit, this is the most intriguing thing, like *ever*. Imagine if that hidden place in the jungle actually exists."

"And every speck of logic says it probably doesn't," Emma said with a smile in her eyes. "But then again, just imagine for a tiny second that it does...and you were given a way to find it." Her eyes gleamed. "And I think your ancestor, Benjamin, would want his namesake heir to be the one to do it."

Dan opened his arms, sharing his best entrepreneurial smile. "Look around you, buddy. Each of us has an abundance of a few very important things – enthusiasm, youth, curiosity, and time." He grinned. "What say we use it – strike while the iron's hot?" He shrugged. "All on my ticket, for all of us, and gold class all the way."

"Whoa; hey, what do you get out of it?" Steve asked, one eyebrow up.

Dan snorted. "Listen; I sold my tech company five years ago for $180 million bucks. Since then, I've been bored, bored, bored. I've spent my time parasailing, rock-climbing, deep sea diving and jungle trekking, and I always come back feeling unfulfilled. But this... *this*, is a real adventure. Something with intrigue, danger, hidden clues, and a purpose; I gotta tell you, I feel alive again." Dan raised his hands and looked skyward, evangelically for a moment before lowering them flat to the tabletop.

"Me too," Emma added her hand on top of his.

"Me three." Steve laid his on the pile.

Andrea raised her hand, smiled, and then slowly laid it on top of Steve's.

Ben saw the fire in his friends' eyes. And truth be known, he felt exactly the same. The thought of retracing an ancestor's steps, and perhaps finding something unique and wondrous, was compelling to the point of being irresistible.

Andrea then placed one thin arm on the table and then rested her chin on the palm. "So, why don't we just go and knock on the door of this place in England, and get their permission to start looking? After all, you said you have proof it belongs to you."

Emma shrugged. "She's got a point, Ben. You've got a lawyer's letter telling you it's your property. Let's just knock on the door of Arthur Conan Doyle's estate."

Dan held up a finger and waggled it. "Umm, yeah, about that; we did some investigation on the Doyle estate; in a nutshell, it doesn't exist anymore. His final home, this Windlesham Manor, is a freaking retirement home now."

"Are you thinking what I'm thinking?" Steve started to chuckle. "With all that gray hair, there'll be no resistance to a little onsite digging."

Dan sighed. "If only it were that easy. Windlesham Manor sits on 20 acres; more than 870,000 square feet. That's a lot of places to hide something *under the earth.*"

"Good God, that'll be impossible." Emma's mouth hung open.

Dan nodded, his lips compressed. "We either need more clues to pinpoint it, or we need to have the Manor's approval to go looking around – and that might take some time."

Steve bobbed his head. "I've got a friend over there, a zoologist, who could get us in. But like you said, the bottom line is we need more clues to narrow our search."

Ben ran a hand up through his hair. "Yeah, I can have another look through the Cartwright history, but I'm just not sure there's anything else significant to find."

"Well, let's think this through logically." Dan interlaced his fingers on the table. "You told us that Doyle valued it so greatly he didn't want it lost. That's why he kept it rather than simply sending it back to your ancestor's estate if there was a chance there was no one to either receive it or appreciate its importance. Right?"

"I guess so," Ben replied.

"So, if he valued it so greatly, he would have wanted it safe, and close. My gut feeling is it'll be in the manor or real close by on the grounds. I don't think our search area will be all that big."

"That sounds a little more promising." Emma beamed.

"Kinda makes sense," Ben added.

"Well, doesn't matter anyway." Dan grinned sheepishly. "I've already booked our flights."

"Jesus." Ben straightened. "For when? I still haven't told my mom."

Steve chuckled. "What, are you still 12?"

"Two days time, Friday morning." Dan held his arms out. "Now or never, buddy." He turned and pointed. "Steve, you contact your friend in England and let them know we're coming. See if he –"

"*She,*" Steve added.

"Of course." Dan gave him a wry smile. "See if *she* can get us an invite into the Manor. The rest of you, pack, get your shots, and grab your passports."

Emma snorted. "I suddenly feel like Dorothy being lifted up by the tornado and swept away."

Ben laughed. "Well, we've got a few days, and I think Mom is going to need another cake when I tell her."

Emma grinned back. "Sure, but she'll be fine when she knows I'll be looking after you."

CHAPTER 06

Heathrow Airport, London, United Kingdom

Out front, Ben inhaled, taking in the mixed odors of car and airplane exhaust, cold mist and an ever-present dampness. He looked up at the leaden sky.

"There is a sun up there, right?"

"No wonder they're all so pale." Steve put both hands on the small of his back and straightened it, causing a popping and cracking sound that made Andrea wince.

"Ouch," she said.

"Yeah, I know, right? Fourteen hours on a plane is murder," he said to her and then turned to Dan. "And all crammed into business class. Why no first class, you tightwad."

"Oh really?" Dan's brows went up. "You ever been in first class before?"

"Let me think." Steve grabbed his chin for a moment. "Um, nope."

"It's overrated. Besides, Chambers, I've never seen anyone eat so many little pastries and mooch at the stewardesses so much."

"Just getting my money's worth. Oh wait, I mean, *your* money's worth. Thank you, Uncle Daniel." Steve saluted.

"I'm cold." Andrea pulled her thin coat tighter.

Ben saw that she had dressed for fashion rather than practicality; even though Dan had warned her it'd be cooler, a silk scarf just wasn't going to cut it.

Dan began to rummage. "I might have a spare pullover you can..."

"I've got one here." Emma pulled a top from her bag and tossed it to the woman. She hoisted her carryall to her shoulder and groaned. "Hey Steve, this friend of yours was meeting us here and now, right?"

"Yep, Jennifer Brock, zoologist who works at the London Zoo." Steve turned about looking up and down the street.

"The zoo, huh?" Ben grinned. "No wonder she likes you."

Steve turned back momentarily. "She said I'm a fine specimen." He pointed. "There."

Ben turned – a slim, athletic-looking woman with a dark bob haircut waved back. She wore a khaki shirt with a monogram on one of the pockets. She marched straight up to Steve, hugged him hard, kissed his cheek, and then pulled back to stare up into his grinning face.

"All this way just to see me?"

"Of course, Jenn." Steve turned side-on. "My friends." He counted each off. "Ben, Emma, Andrea, and Dan our mobile bank account."

"Thank you, Steve." Dan held out his hand. "Nice to meet you, Jennifer."

"And you." Jenny took his hand first. "And you, and you…" She then shook all of their hands. "Please call me Jenny, and come on, we can formally introduce ourselves in the van." She turned on her heel. "Let's get to the car-park before it sends me broke."

*****

Jenny had loaded them all into a Ford Transit Kombi van with the same London Zoo logo stenciled on the side as she had on her breast pocket. There were six seats, three in the front cab, three in rear, with plenty of storage for their bags.

Ben immediately smelled hay, with a hint of damp fur, and suspected people weren't the only things that had been transported in Jenny's van.

Steve slid in next to the zoologist, and Emma jammed in on the opposite window seat. In the back, Ben slid across to one window, Andrea quickly jumped in next to him, and Dan took the last seat.

As they sped out of Heathrow, Ben hung an arm out the window, watching with a mix of alarm and amusement – New York rush hour had nothing on some of the turnpikes out of the airport ring.

The real difference was that where American drivers would jam a hand down hard on their horns, or lean out of their windows to give you a piece of their mind, English drivers tended to glare or quietly fume in their vehicles.

Jenny half turned. "Tomorrow, I've arranged an interview for you at Windlesham Manor. As a background story, I told them you were planning on placing your dear old mother there. I can take you, but it should be only two of you – you guys choose which ones."

Jenny turned back to the road. "Oh, and dress well; this place is expensive."

Steve grinned. "Well, I'm out."

Emma turned in her seat. "Got to be Ben. Only he really knows what to look for." She smiled at him. "And I can accompany him as I just bought some new clothes. We can pretend to be a couple."

"Or brother and sister," Andrea added with a smirk.

"What do *we* do?" Dan asked.

"Enjoy our hospitality." Jenny shot back. "I've put you all up at Fairstowe House; it's a bed and breakfast down at Crowborough, so close to the Manor. It's nice; there's a traditional English pub down the road, and the place has a lot of history. So while Ben and Emma visit the estate, the rest of you can go for nature walks, exploring, or just sleep off your jet lag."

"Well, that works just fine for me." Steve sighed and eased back in his seat.

"Well done, and thank you, Jenny," Ben said. "How far exactly to the Manor?"

"From Fairstowe House, just a few miles. From here, 50 miles, so sit back, take in the scenery, and get comfortable, as it'll still take us about 3 hours, with most of that just getting out of this damned city."

"Well then." Ben also eased back in his seat. "I'll be working off my jet lag right now." He closed his eyes.

*****

The squeal of breaks and a sharp elbow in the ribs told him they'd arrived, and Ben opened his eyes to a scene that reminded him of a cross between Harry Potter's Hogwarts and the cover of one of his mother's prized House and Gardens magazines.

"Wow," Steve said from the front seat.

Fairstowe House had to be 200 years old if it was a day. Its sandstone and dark brick façade was covered in climbing roses, and leadlight windows held glimpses of golden lamps burning within.

"Looks inviting," Ben observed, pulling back the door on the van. The group piled out and stood in the courtyard, smelling rose, lavender, and a hint of wood-smoke.

"Oh yeah, I could get used to this." Emma turned slowly, hands on hips.

The front door opened and a woman holding a tea towel wiped her hands on it, and then flicked it up over her shoulder. She smiled, making her cheeks glow even more.

"Jennifer?"

"Yes, hello, Mrs. Davenport." Jenny strode forward to shake the woman's hand. She turned. "And my American friends." She pointed at each, giving names. Ben and the group grinned and waved as their names were called.

Jenny looked pleased. "And let me know if you need help translating. Their accents can be a little difficult."

Steve laughed. "Wait until she gets a load of our manners then." He gave the older woman a wry smile. "Don't believe a word of it, Mrs. Davenport, we're a well-behaved bunch."

The older woman smiled warmly. "Well, of course you are. And call me Margaret, please." She stood to the side. "This way, this way, do come in."

"Beautiful house, Margaret," Andrea said, following first. "Looks old, um, I mean, *grand and historically* old."

Margaret stopped in the living room. "Not that old; the Fairstowe country house, stables, and even rose beds are all approaching two centuries, but inside, you'll find all the mod cons."

The fireplace popped behind her, and Ben smelled burning cedar. Except for the slightest waft of mustiness, Ben loved it – it was warm, comfortable, and they seemed to have it all to themselves.

Margaret beamed. "I have a room for each of you." She raised her chin. "I was told that you each wanted a single room; was that suitable?"

Dan nodded. "Sure, still all single for now, but we're working on it." He let his eyes slide to Ben. Emma glared in return.

"It's absolutely perfect, Margaret, and thank you." Jenny then checked her watch. "It's 4pm now, and we'll be going out for dinner, so I think we'll get settled and clean up." She raised her eyebrows. "What say we then meet down here at 7pm? I know a perfect place for dinner."

CHAPTER 07

48 Hours to Apparition

Comet P/2018-YG874 wasn't a big one by any astral mapping standards. Its designate name was Primordia, and it probably originated in the Oort cloud a hundred million years ago.

To date, there are nearly 6,000 known comets in the inner solar system and many billions more in the outer system. Only about one comet per year can be seen with the naked eye, and most are unremarkable.

Primordia had been travelling in an elliptical orbit in a periodic recurrence of every 10 years. It would approach the Earth, pass by it, and then head back to the inner star where it was grabbed again and then flung back out into the solar system for yet another cycle around the 3rd planet from the sun.

Due to the effects of solar radiation, the small body emitted the usual coma and icy tail, giving it the distinctive comet streak. When a comet finally appears to the naked eye, it is called an apparition.

The Primordia apparition was unremarkable, except for one thing – its comet nuclei, or central core, had a significant concentration of iron and other rare minerals that created a significant magnetic distortion on the surrounding solar geography.

The Primordia Earthly cycle had it passing closest to South America, directly over a vast tabletop mountain in Venezuela. It was only observable for a few days, but in that time, strange distortions occurred on the mountaintop – things became rearranged, reordered, pathways created and doorways opened.

In 48 hours, Primordia's first magnetic wave effects would be felt. And in Eastern Venezuela, the season was once again at its wettest.

CHAPTER 08

Venezuelan National Institute of Meteorological Services

Mateo bobbed his head from side to side as he read the data on the bank of screens before him. "Storm gathering, but centered." He switched to the satellite images. "Very strange; just over the deep eastern jungle."

Mateo was fresh from university and armed with a degree in meteorological and climate sciences, and he'd never seen anything like what he was looking at; he didn't even know of a precedent for it in any textbook. There looked to be a small developing hurricane, but coming out of nowhere. It was tiny and centralized. But strangely, *staying* centralized.

He cursed under his breath as his computer systems refused to give him the data he wanted. The cloudbank swirled and was so dense that it wasn't allowing any thermal or even geographic readings over the site. Worse, as he watched, the satellite image started to blur over the affected area as if there was a smudge on his screen.

"Hey, boss, this can't be right. Look." He rolled his chair backwards and pointed.

Santiago sighed and also rolled his chair backwards. The slightly portly man was Mateo's superior and had been in the role for over 30 years. He rolled himself closer, took one look, and grunted.

"Yeah; wet season, and this year, the wettest. It's rare, but it happens." He rolled back to his own workspace.

"Huh?" Mateo's frown deepened. "This is unprecedented. It looks like a hurricane, small, but so dense it's now almost impenetrable."

Santiago snorted. "Not everything that occurs within the boundaries of what we collectively group under the term *weather* is in textbooks. Um… " He reached up to pull a battered old paper folder from a shelf and thumbed through it for a moment before handing it to the young man.

"Here, see, every 10 years, like clockwork, there is a unique phenomenon that happens in these parts. Only during the wettest of wet seasons." He shrugged. "The conditions manifest over a single area, only remain for a few days, and then just as abruptly, dissipate and then vanish." He shrugged. "Theories are that it is caused by an upwelling of thermal activity in the area that alters ground heat, and then the associated humidity and air density."

"Wow." Mateo grinned. "And we can't see anything through that cloud?"

"Mmm, yes and no." Santiago pointed to the folder. "Turn the pages, there, that's it. We flew a high-altitude plane over the site twenty years back, and used LIDAR to bounce some laser off the area. Those images are what came back."

Mateo frowned. He knew of LIDAR; they were the Light, Imaging, Detection and Ranging devices that were used to map areas by illuminating them with a laser light, and then reading the reflected pulses with a sensor – they were extremely accurate.

Mateo frowned. "It can see everything, except for this one large tepui in the inaccessible eastern zone – the top, it's...*not there*." He looked up, open-mouthed. "I don't understand."

Santiago winked. "A mystery wrapped in a conundrum, hmm?"

Mateo grinned back. "This is why I love this job."

Santiago chuckled. "And that's why they call us the bureau of climate guessology – we only know what's happening *some* of the time."

CHAPTER 09

Next morning, 8am sharp, Ben and Emma met Jenny downstairs. Ben still felt like he was going to burst; Margaret had made them toasted muffins, little sausages as long as his thumb, eggs and bacon, plus hot tea. Ben ate most of it, but stopped short on the bacon – it was floppy and undercooked and not crispy like he preferred it. He found out later that this was the way it was usually eaten here – *yech*.

Jenny led them back into the drawing room, and Steve, Dan, and Andrea soon joined them. They all flopped down into oversized armchairs and couches.

"What's your plan, Jenn?" Steve asked his friend.

Jenny had a teacup to her lips and seemed to gulp the remaining contents. Ben was amazed at the quantity of tea that these guys put away; it put American coffee drinkers to shame.

Jenny replaced the cup in its matching fine china saucer and smacked her lips. "Our meeting is set to occur in another hour, and one of the reasons I chose Fairstowe was that it's only 10 minutes from the Manor. Our cover story is that Emma and Ben are considering moving to the area for work, and will be bringing their elderly mother with them. You'll be wanting help with her, of the highest standard." She looked at Ben. "She's 86, has no real health or dietary issues, but is slightly foggy of thinking, okay?"

Ben nodded. "Got it."

"You drive the conversation. Don't get bogged down in your details. You ask the questions and get them to show the pair of you around. Even better if once they've given you a quick tour, you're allowed to do a bit of wandering around by yourselves." She sat back and sighed. "And the million pound question is, *looking around for what?*"

Ben exhaled slowly through his nose. It was a question he had raked over his memory many times trying to tease out some clue, but came up empty every time.

"All we know is that the author, Arthur Conan Doyle, hid my great, great grandfather's notebook at Windlesham Manor somewhere on the estate." He gave her a wry smile. "And he didn't exactly say where."

"Good lord." Jenny's brows went up. "Do you know how big…?"

"Yes, yes." Ben looked skyward for a moment. "I know, *huge*. This might be damn mission impossible."

Emma sucked in one of her cheeks. "All we know is it's somewhere *under the earth*, in a place that only Doyle and his ancestor knew about."

"Hmm. This is just like Doyle, a man who liked mystery and intrigue." Jenny's eyes narrowed. "But this does mean that your ancestor had been here before. We could have used that, but unfortunately, all connection between the Manor and Doyle has now been severed. So we can't expect them to give you any good graces in relation to the search." She grimaced and shook her head. "I don't like your chances."

"Me either," Ben said. "Just hoping that something jumps out at us." He sighed.

"Might it have already been found?" Jenny asked.

"Maybe, but we think it's unlikely," Dan said. "There's been no mention of it, and this notebook would have rated a mention, somewhere."

"Unless it was purchased on the black market and went straight into someone's private collection," Ben added.

"I still think, no," Dan said. "There isn't even a mention of the notebook existing other than in the correspondence between Benjamin the 1st and Doyle. I think wherever it was put, it stayed there."

Jenny checked her wristwatch. "Well, we got a date, so we better just keep our fingers crossed. Otherwise, at least it will have been a nice holiday for you."

In 20 more minutes, Jenny herded Ben and Emma back into the van. Dan, Andrea, and Steve had come out onto the front steps to wave them off, and Steve gave them a thumbs-up as they pulled out.

Ben waved back in return, and then began to chuckle.

"What?" Emma nudged him.

"Well." Ben still grinned. "One minute I'm at a funeral, then you turn up, and suddenly I'm on the other side of the world about to try and trick my way into an old folk's home." He looked across at her.

She smiled. "Yeah, and one minute, I'm running an everyday adventure tour business, you turn up, and suddenly I'm swept away by Hurricane Cartwright. See, I could say the same about you." Her smile widened. "But at least no one can accuse us of having a dull life together, huh?"

He lowered his brow. "You do know I was thinking about moving back home *just* to enjoy the dull life."

"And yet, here you are." Emma jiggled her eyebrows.

"Windlesham Manor coming up," Jenny said.

The van turned off the main road onto a heavy tree- and bush-lined avenue. The magnificent oak and chestnut trees created a green tunnel for them to pass through before they arrived at an impressive sandstone entrance gate with a single silver pole by the side with intercom. Jenny slowed and lowered her window. She reached out to press the button.

"Jennifer Brock with the Cartwrights; we're expected." She turned to wink at them.

They only had to wait a few moments before the gates buzzed, clicked, and then slowly began to swing ponderously inwards. Ben noticed that there were discrete cameras mounted on each of the sandstone pillars.

"Good security," he observed.

"Hm-hmm." Jenny eased the van forward. "But I'll wager it's more to keep the elderly from wandering away rather than keep intruders out."

They drove up a winding gravel driveway and pulled up in front of the magnificent house. It was only two floors, but enormous. Climbing fig adorned one wall, and roses bloomed all around its perimeter. Everything seemed so green and lush, and Ben saw under a few leafy canopies there were huge garden umbrellas with wheelchairs pulled up beneath them. Tiny heads of fluffy white hair turned to watch them approach.

In another moment, a woman appeared on the top steps and gave them a friendly wave. She had a powder-blue cashmere cardigan over a silk blouse, and pearls the size of marbles adorned her neck.

She first crossed the lawn to the wheelchairs and chatted to a few of her residents. She patted shoulders, poured tea, and laughed at something one of them said. Then she began to head towards them.

Ben smiled at the perfect pastoral scene. The sunshine was warm on his face, the gardens fragrant, and guests looked happy. Ben turned to Emma.

"Make a note; this is where I want to retire."

She scoffed. "I thought you were retired now."

"Ms. Brock?" The woman's smile was open and honest.

"Mrs. Hurley," Jennifer responded and stepped forward, hand outstretched. They clasped hands, and Jennifer motioned to her friends.

"The Cartwrights: Benjamin and Emma."

"Of course." She held out one firm and dry hand. "Pleased to meet you."

The older woman's eyes ran up and down Ben from his hair to his shoes for a fraction of a second, missing nothing.

Ben noticed that the woman's attire could be described as understated elegance. She was dressed simply, but expensively. And though he and Emma were dressed nicely, it probably told Mrs. Hurley they might just not be in the Manor's league. Ben only hoped that being from out of town, she might give their casual attire some leeway.

"You're making inquiries on behalf of your mother, Mr. Cartwright?" Her perfect eyebrows rose.

Ben nodded. "Yes, she's getting on, and always wanted to move somewhere with a nice climate, and plenty of class. Windlesham Manor was recommended to us."

Mrs. Hurley nodded as though this would be expected. She turned and started to walk towards the garden beds, talking as she went. Ben briefly looked to Emma, shrugged, and they followed.

She took them in a circuit around the house, pointing out the plantings, a separate building she called *the aqua room* that contained a swimming pool, aqua-aerobics center and sauna, plus a full gymnasium. Ben wondered what Arthur Conan Doyle would have made of his grand old house turning out like this. Being a visionary, maybe he would have approved.

She stopped underneath a large oak tree. Its wizened trunk was gnarled, heavily aged, but yet they could make out the initials, *A.C.D.*, carved into it.

"Arthur Conan Doyle was here." Ben smiled.

She tilted her head. "I assume you did some research prior to arriving and would know this was his home and where he wrote many of his wonderful stories." She waved an arm around gently. "This impressive Edwardian country house was where Sir Arthur Conan Doyle spent the final 23 years of his life living happily with his wife and family."

"Yes, we did," said Emma. "We also found that in 1955, the last of the Crowborough estate grounds were sold out of the Doyle family. The remains of Sir Arthur and his wife Lady Jean Conan Doyle were removed and reburied at All Saints Church, Minstead in the New Forest, Hampshire. I guess all that remains now is his spirit."

Mrs. Hurley gave Emma a cool look. "And perhaps also his memories." She waved an arm around. "I like to think we've done the Doyle legacy proud. The Manor needed significant restoration work, and the grounds were in a terrible state. This tree is the only thing that remains of the gardens as they once were."

Ben had a sinking feeling. "Even the gardens have been replaced?"

"My word, yes; *everything* out here has been replaced. Even the soil has been rejuvenated." She smiled benignly. "It's why the roses do so well."

Mrs. Hurley marched back towards the front of the house, and Emma turned to him with her mouth slightly twisted down. "So much for *under the earth*," she whispered.

Ben just grunted and followed.

Mrs. Hurley led them up the sandstone steps and in through a waiting open doorway. Ben saw the large men immediately – all dressed in white jackets and dark pants. They looked like a cross between butlers and doormen. Each of them looked formidable and fit. They were obviously male nurses who doubled as security – no wonder the front gates seemed so lightly guarded; the Manor had its own private army.

Ben watched for a moment as the men pushed wheelchairs, polished furniture and mahogany rails, and carried trays up stairs. Every one of them glanced at the newcomers with their eyes lingering on the large frame of Ben and perhaps recognizing another body trained for confrontations.

The next 30 minutes comprised of them touring rooms, the library, dining facilities, and then talking budgets. The annual costs made Ben's eyes water, and that was for the basic package. When dear old mom or dad needed additional medical care and supervision, the costs went skyward and kept going until you sailed past the moon.

Ben and Emma smiled and nodded, trying to keep straight faces.

"Very reasonable," Ben said, while Emma turned to him and made her eyes go crossed.

Eventually, Mrs. Hurley began to lead them back down the staircase. The mahogany banister now gleamed, and Ben felt the silken surface still had a touch of orange oil that made it feel like silk and also gave off a faint but pleasant citrus odor.

Jenny was still downstairs waiting for them and he nodded to her. His plan was to ask Mrs. Hurley to be able to wander around unescorted, but didn't like his chances. Even if the hawk-eyed woman left him, he doubted they'd be out of sight of one or more of the large nurse-butlers.

They came to the last few steps; Ben still trailed his hand on the banister, preparing to lift it over the carved newel post, when he saw it.

On top of the stair post was a carved globe – the planet Earth. Ben nudged Emma and leaned closer to her.

"Are you seeing what I'm seeing?"

She turned to him, and then followed his gaze. Her brows knitted for a moment before her jaw dropped into an open-mouth grin. "Could it be?"

"Under the *Earth*. Not, *under the earth*," he whispered. "Got to be."

CHAPTER 10

1988 – South Eastern Venezuela – Once again, the Wettest Season

The torrential rain abruptly stopped as if it had been turned off at the tap. For many minutes on the plateau top, water ran from treetops, palm fronds, and also ran in rivulets along the jungle animal trails.

Above the treetops, the boiling purple clouds opened in a circular hole, letting in a widening column of light and making the massive lake shine like a blue jewel.

Leathery winged creatures glided from the trees to skim a surface that was lined with motion ripples, popping bubbles, and upsurges as unseen things below got on with the business of eat or be eaten.

Along the far shoreline, a herd of plant eaters grazed on rich mosses or lichens at the water line, their duck-like bills grazing on the protein-rich soft, green growth right down to the water.

A hundred feet out from them in the lake, an enormous dark lump appeared. Bulbous eyes popped open to watch them. After another moment, the lump glided closer, and then slowly eased back down below the surface. Huge muscles coiled.

For one unlucky plant eater, the price of a good meal was death.

CHAPTER 11

"What is it?" Jenny asked, after seeing Ben and Emma's animation on the staircase.

"A clue, we think," Ben whispered back. "Keep Nurse Ratchet busy for a minute."

Jenny nodded and then strode towards Mrs. Hurley who was signing some forms on a computer tablet for one of the hulking male nurses. She looked up and smiled as Jenny approached.

"Can you please tell me about visiting hours and guests staying, if you don't mind?" She stood where it made Mrs. Hurley face away from the staircase.

Ben grabbed Emma's arm and quickly guided her closer to the post. He placed a hand casually on the globe and tried to tilt it, turn it, and even press down on it. He rapped on it with his knuckles. Nothing; seemed solid.

Too obvious, he thought.

"Cover me," he whispered and positioned Emma between one of the nurses and the post and knelt down to untie and slowly retie his shoelace.

He looked at the wooden post; it was unblemished on its carved and buffed sides. He reached around Emma and quickly felt the bottom step – tight, no give in it, no flaps or hidden doors on the riser or step top.

Ben then checked where it met the floor; thankfully, the lower ground had rugs and not carpet, and the floorboards were polished to a mirrored sheen. They also fit flush. There were several screw holes at the base – 3 of them, with the furthest post side being flush against the steps. He put his fingers over the screw holes and pressed – left side, nothing, front, nothing. Then pressed the last, the one at the back – a small panel at the base of the steps popped open.

"*Bingo*," Emma said softly.

Ben looked up and grinned, and then quickly looked around for any spectators. He was in the clear, so he reached in, and immediately felt something covered in cloth. He grabbed at it, just as from behind he heard a growing electronic whine. He looked over his shoulder.

Ah crap, Ben thought as he saw the old lady in a motorized chair was wheeling towards him, her pale, rheumy eyes moving from him to the open panel.

Ben grabbed the package and drew it free. It was bigger, thicker, and heavier than he expected. He'd never be able to sneak it out.

Emma kicked back at him, and he looked up to see Jenny and Mrs. Hurley approaching.

Shit. He looked around and grinned as the old lady was now only feet away. She raised one drawn-on eyebrow at him.

"Hi there." He shut the panel. "Mind this." He reached out to place the book on her lap, and then quickly turned and stood in front of her.

"Well, this has been most informative." He forced his smile.

"Did you get everything you needed?" Mrs. Hurley smiled back tightly.

"I think we did." The corners of Emma's eyes crinkled.

"Emma and I will talk to mom tonight." From behind Ben, he heard the whine of the wheelchair and he glanced over his shoulder to see the old lady motoring down the length of the room towards a set of the open doors.

"Well, we'll be in touch." He looked around, and at the same time grabbed Emma by the arm. "Thank you for everything; your facilities are wonderful."

Jenny went to head to the front doors, but Ben held Emma back. "Um, do you mind if we have one last look at your magnificent gardens?"

"Be my guest." Mrs. Hurley offered him her slim and manicured hand.

Ben shook it and turned on his heel, dragging Emma with him. Jenny was left behind with knitted brows, and he could feel Mrs. Hurley's eyes on him every step of the way.

Ben headed to the open door, moving quickly.

"What is it?" Emma asked.

"The notebook; the old woman's got it." He stopped.

"Which one?" Emma's eyes widened as they stepped out into the sunshine.

"The one in the wheel…" Ben groaned; there were around a dozen men and women in wheelchairs, all nearly identical, save for the odd book or teacup in their hands. All had nicely coiffed hairdos of cotton-white and maybe a hint of purple here and there.

"What was she wearing?' Emma said.

"Old lady stuff," Ben replied, chuckling.

"Great, that at least rules out most of the old men." Emma exhaled.

"Come on; meet and greet time." Ben led her forward.

Ben pasted on his most endearing smile, and Emma hooked her arm over his. Together, they walked along in front of the row of men and woman, smiling, nodding, and stopping to chat to a few here and there.

Ben wished he had paid more attention when he threw the book at the woman.

He felt a knot of impatience growing in his stomach. They were fast running out of time, and also out of white hair, when Emma nudged him. "*Hello*, look, over there."

In the shade of a huge camellia japonica tree, an ancient woman sat staring back at them, a tiny smile on her lips.

Ben craned his neck. "Maybe."

They approached, and Ben started to feel more confident.

"An adventure is afoot," she said and her smile widened. She then threw back the shawl that was over her shoulders and lap to reveal the hide-covered package.

Ben crouched before her. "Thank you, and thank you for not telling them."

"Dare I ask what it is?" she asked.

"A notebook that belongs to my family, to my great, great grandfather, Benjamin Cartwright. It had been held and then hidden away by the late Sir Arthur Conan Doyle. It was to be retrieved by one of Benjamin's heirs, but it got lost and forgotten." Ben smiled up into her lively eyes. "I came to claim it; but needed to find it first."

"And you are?" She tilted her head.

"Ben Cartwright." He smiled back. "The new one."

She nodded. "And now the heirloom has been found." She ran a hand over the oilcloth surface of the package. "Rose Pennington." She looked into his eyes. "And I'll tell you right now, when the chance presents, I'm going to look in that secret place myself, and see if there are any other treasures."

She reached out to grasp Ben's hand. He felt the small bird-like bones wrapped in the papery soft skin. "Ever since I was a little girl, I loved adventures. But age makes them more difficult to pursue." She squeezed his hand. "Give me your number. If I find anything else, I'll call."

Ben nodded and did so. He held out the scrap of paper and she gripped his wrist.

"And you tell me what you find; I smell adventure, mystery, and danger." She hiked her shoulder and smiled. "If I was 50 years younger, I'd make you take me with you."

She handed the ancient notebook to him. "Good luck, and good hunting, Benjamin the 2nd."

CHAPTER 12

The package lay open on the table before them. For several moments, everyone just stared.

Dan looked up. "I say we go for it…*now*." His eyes blazed.

"We're not ready," Steve said.

"And how exactly do you get ready for something like this?" Dan tilted his head. "We're all here, all fit, I have the funds for the expedition." He pointed at Emma, and then to each. "We have climbing skills, military skills, trade skills…" He looked at Andrea, smiled, and then skipped her to Jenny. "We even have a zoologist."

"Dan, you don't trek into the Amazon jungle as if you're planning a picnic in Central Park. That's how dumb guys like us vanish." Ben sighed. "I've been there briefly, and it's one big damn green hell."

"Well, I've been there, several times actually," Jenny said. "And we even work with the local tribes for animal procurement, habitat advice, that sort of stuff."

"*Yes*." Dan fist pumped. "All objections neutralized." He sat back.

"Something else to think about; didn't you say that whatever window of opportunity was going to present itself was only going to be open for a week? And that was coming up soon." Steve shrugged. "Maybe this once in a generation wet season causes a river to flood that leads the way, or something to drain, or even a certain flower to bloom that points the way. I kinda get excited just thinking about it. And if it's not going to happen again for another 10 years, well…" He hiked his shoulders even higher.

"Now or never," Emma said dreamily.

Ben had also placed on the table before them the rare copy of The Lost World, now unwrapped. He clasped his hands together as his gaze went from one book to the other.

Even from where he sat, he could smell the ancient pages of both. The package they'd recovered from Windlesham Manor was now revealed – beneath the oilcloth there had been a layer of wax paper. Once he'd carefully opened it out, the century-old, leather-bound notebook was revealed – it was roughly 12 inches by eight, and a spine-bursting three inches thick. The thing was battered and worn and had been well used in its day. There were even brown streaks marking the leather that he recognized from his military days as undoubtedly being blood.

There were other odors as well; the smell coming from the notebook was of oil, paper, and perhaps the sweetness of some sort of plant resin. There were initials pressed into the cover – *BBC* – Benjamin Bartholomew Cartwright, his great, great grandfather.

He opened it – the inside had loose pages stuck there, some dried leaves, and even a large butterfly's wing, still iridescent blue, and looking as fragile as the most silken gossamer.

Jenny had leaned forward, smiling and nodding. "*Morpho peleides* – the Blue Morpho Butterfly, and sometimes called the sapphire of the Amazon."

"It's beautiful," Andrea said in a hushed tone.

"And so big," Steve added.

Ben's mouth curved into a smile. "Long before the days of any sort of quarantine procedures, huh?"

Jenny nodded. "And I didn't see a thing. In reality, I'm supposed to report or destroy that specimen. I'm just going to hope any potential hitchhikers on that wing are long dead."

Ben continued his examination. The date and notations told him it was Benjamin's missing field notes for the ill-fated Venezuelan expedition of 1908. Ben had always been impressed with the writing style of the earlier generations, and how they managed to make their script look both precise and beautifully calligraphic at the same time. While his shabby jottings would look right at home on a doctor's prescription.

Ben sipped his tea, winced at the bitter taste, and then went back to carefully turning the notebook's pages. Emma dragged her chair to crowd in beside him on one side and Andrea on the other. Steve, Dan, and Jenny were also craning necks to read alongside him once again.

"These guys," Emma began, "were all artists. So many skills."

"Yep," he replied, looking at an artistic drawing of a steamer boat and a detailed description of the ride he and the trip's sponsor, Douglas Baxter, took to Caracas on the South American continent. Then they endured weeks on horseback to the small town of Zuata in the interior where they picked up a team of bearers – Pemon Indians, Benjamin had called them. He had added in a drawing of a group of a dozen fierce-looking young men with smooth faces, hair in dark bowl cuts, and daubs of paint on their cheeks.

Ben turned the page, seeing some of the ink had been blurred, perhaps by a sort of sap. "I can't imagine what the Amazon had been like then, in 1908." He picked up the words and read, relating the story to his friends.

"From there, they had set off into an area of unexplored jungle in search of a hidden plateau that, in Benjamin's own words, would rewrite everything they knew about biology and evolution."

"Hidden plateau," Dan read over his shoulder. "Oh boy."

Ben nodded. "In a land, hidden under a permanent cloud – hmm, the rainy season thing, perhaps." He tilted the notebook towards Emma. "Great artwork." He had stopped at a pencil picture of Benjamin Cartwright's hunter friend, Baxter, crossing a river, rifle held above his head to keep it dry. Even in the quick etching, Benjamin had captured a face that was determined, eyes gun-barrel steady and a jutting mustache.

He placed the leather-bound notebook open on the table. "The later editions of Doyle's story had fewer and fewer drawings. But the first editions contained a lot of hand-drawn ink sketches, copied from the notebook."

He then carefully opened the 1912 edition of The Lost World and flicked through several pages until he found what he searched for. He laid it open next to the notebook.

It was the drawing, this one of the story character, Lord Roxton, not Douglas Baxter, but exactly the same features, same rifle held aloft. This one was far more stylized for the printing, but there was no doubt the similarities were breathtaking.

Ben turned back inside the book's cover board to the inscription by Arthur Conan Doyle.

"*To my good friend, Benjamin Cartwright – your experiences ignited my imagination, and this is the result.*" He rubbed his chin. "Is that what Doyle really meant; that over a 100 years ago, Benjamin had actually done what he had described in his work of fiction?"

"Yes, yes, of course he did," Dan urged. "And there's your proof, right in front of you."

"I don't know." Ben noticed a folded piece of paper in the notebook and flattened it out. He looked at it momentarily, before snorting softly. "And what would a modern zoologist make of this?" He slid it towards Jenny.

She peered down at the drawing, her lips curving up at the corners. It was a magnificent rendition of a jungle in the rain, the penciled shading managing to impart dripping fern fronds and vines. But they were just to frame the main subject – through a tunnel-like portal of jungle could be observed a dead creature lying in the mud.

Jenny read the ancient notations. "Unknown dinosaurian." She looked up slowly. "*Un-bloody-known dinosaurian.*" She grinned at Dan. "If you guys do go, you damn well count me in."

"I'm in too," said Steve.

"Me too," Andrea said. "This adventure will make me famous."

Emma raised her hand and grinned sheepishly at Ben. "Don't know about being famous, but I'd die curious if I was dumb enough to say no."

"Ah Jesus Christ." Ben sighed and leaned back. "This could get us all killed. I don't want to be responsible for –"

"I speak for myself, and am responsible for myself," Jenny said. "Ben, if there's even a one in a million chance of this being real, you need to check it out. And if, as you said, there is only a small window every half a generation, then what do we do? Wait until we're all in our forties before finally making up our minds?"

She folded her arms. "One more thing, the Pemon still exist, are still used as guides, and I can arrange for them to be with us."

"It's all lining up, buddy." Dan's smile widened.

Emma pushed her dark hair back off her forehead. "The wide-eyed kid in me says, go, go, go! But the adult, the one who's supposed to be sensible, is asking, do we really think we can find this plateau with just a few notes?"

Ben leaned forward to carefully flip pages again, first of the old edition of the Lost World. He came to a hand-drawn map. Then he did the same to the notebook. "A few notes, and this."

There was a map, hand-drawn, but surprisingly detailed. There were even longitude and latitude coordinates. He turned a few more pages. "And this, and this, and this." There were more maps, just as detailed as the first.

"Oh my God," Jenny breathed. "This can work. It can *really* work."

Ben nodded. "The ones in the novel and my ancestor's notebook aren't the same. Maybe Doyle decided to keep some things secret, huh?"

"*Ho-ooo-ley* shit," Steve said with a broad grin. "He *knew* it was real."

Ben sat forward and clasped his fingers together. "If we go, we run this like a military operation. Agreed?"

Everyone enthusiastically agreed.

"I've been on jungle missions before; it's damn hard work. We're gonna need a plan, and some serious kit."

"The kit I can take care of," Dan said. "You just give me a shopping list."

"I'll help," Steve said.

"Me too," said Emma.

"I'll make contact with my friends in Venezuela and let them know we'll need local guides and transportation."

Andrea smiled. "And I better call my agent. This is gonna be fun."

Ben sighed and put his hand on the book. "And I need to study this and draw out anything and everything we need to know."

The group broke up quickly, each excited and eager to get their allotted tasks in motion.

Ben climbed to his room, sat on the bed, and kicked off his shoes. He punched both pillows into a single mound and stuffed them behind his head and shoulders, and then opened the notebook to read.

As he read, the drawings, the words, and descriptions all began to transport him back over a hundred years to that fateful expedition of 1908.

CHAPTER 13

1908 – South America – somewhere in South Eastern Venezuela

The torrential rain had finally eased back to a greasy drizzle. Benjamin Cartwright raised a hand to his small party. The smell of death was growing stronger. Last night's storm had passed over, but the ever-present cloud cover remained.

The stories had been true; the once in a half-generation wet season was here, and that meant in this area apparently the sun never shone much above a twilight, rendering everything damp, humid, and like a bottled greenhouse covered in shade-cloth.

They had been following a game trail for days, and still were, even though he knew it was a dangerous ploy in that the smell of carrion usually attracted large predators. But they had no choice. The jungle here was near impenetrable, and it was either hack, hour by hour, through the green morass, moving ahead at only a few feet every hour, or burrow along readymade caves.

In amongst the constant drip of water on large broad leaves, Cartwright overheard the Pemon guides muttering their discontent – coming this far had meant entering lands that were taboo to them. He was now leading them closer to a sacred plateau that rose over a thousand feet from the floor of the jungle and up into the clouds.

It was his destination, and home he had been told of a civilization older than the Egyptian pyramids, and a place of flora and fauna not seen since the dawn of time. As a rising archeologist, he'd be famous overnight. But it wasn't fame or riches that drove him forward, but a curiosity that had burned within him since he was just a small boy.

Cartwright looked up at the cloud cover. He had wanted to bring a hot air balloon to traverse the jungle and also raise them to the plateau. But the cloud would make navigation impossible, plus the fact that for some strange reason his compass had gone haywire.

He sighed. If they ever found a way up to this secret land, they'd have to climb hand over hand. He'd never done that before but would meet that challenge when it came.

Cartwright rested beneath the huge trunks of trees that defied any known classification – their massive trunks were covered in hair, or the bark that coated them was like wooden scales. They were close; he knew it.

He pulled out his notebook to look briefly at the maps he had made – all crude and sketched from conversations he had with the Pemon village elders. What he sought was something that was at the foot of a sacred tabletop mountain, or tepui – they were called various names from sky lands, houses of the gods, and cloud kingdoms, and all of them were taboo. The unique geological formations were massive flat-topped mountains and were composed of sheer blocks of Precambrian quartz arenite sandstone that rose abruptly from the jungle, and for some that was a half a mile into the air.

But the one he searched for was supposedly so tall it was hidden in a thick cloud cover that constantly masked its roof. The massive vertical walls sealed off whatever was up there from life on the ground, and also vice versa.

Climbing them was said to be impossible, but paradoxically, it was strictly forbidden to even try. According to the Pemon, legend had it that generations ago, a young, foolish man had climbed up, and within a day, his remains were flung back down, missing limbs and head. So, as far as the Pemon were concerned, whatever was up there, having it cut off from them was a good thing.

Cartwright jumped as a hand alighted on his shoulder.

"Goddamit, Baxter, creeping up on me." He shrugged it off and turned an indignant glare on his friend.

Douglas Baxter chuckled. "So, you step over giant spiders, alligators, poisonous vines, and sucking bogs, but it's my hand that makes you jumpy?"

Cartwright grinned and pushed his notebook back into the pouch. "Yeah, well, if it wasn't raining, after eight weeks without a bath, I should have smelled you creeping up on me."

"Who needs a bath?" Baxter snorted. "And the only reason we can't smell each other is because of that stink."

Cartwright's face became serious as he looked back out to the jungle. "Some sort of big animal, I guess. Dead leopard, maybe? You tell me, you're the hunter."

Baxter straightened and also scanned the dripping jungle. He was the archetypical outdoor's man and adventurer. He was also a renowned game hunter on several continents, and from a wealthy family – it was his family's money that was financing their expedition – a grand adventure not to be missed, he had called it.

Baxter sniffed deeply. "Can't place it, but doesn't smell like game." He inhaled again. "More like dead fish."

Cartwright turned back to the jungle. "Yeah, maybe." It did smell a little like the ammonia corruption of something washed up on a beach at low tide. He looked over his shoulder. "Pemon won't be with us much longer."

Baxter crossed his arms, cradling his Springfield rifle, and glanced over his shoulder to the huddled group of natives. "Yeah, I think you're right; surprised they hung on this long. My friend, if they turn back, we're gonna have to make a call on it." He turned about. "Without our supplies, it's going to be a long trek back…with little food. There's no damn game." He nosed towards the jungle. "Other than whatever that stink is from."

Cartwright sighed. "According to the maps, we should have found something by now." He turned about. "We'll try for another few miles, and see how much longer they stay with us."

"Works for me." He shouldered his rifle. "Lead on, sir."

In another 30 minutes of burrowing through the wet, green caves, the smell had become so strong that the very air around them felt like it was coating them in rank oil. Cartwright started to think it might have been some sort of mass death area, like an elephant's graveyard or the like. It only made him more interested and determined.

He pushed through the curtain of vines and froze. His second guess was that the thing was of such a great size that it produced the massive amounts of rotten gas. And this turned out to be the correct one, as framed in the green tunnel, the thing was revealed.

The creature was, or had been, enormous. It was a small mountain of decaying, mottled flesh. There were clouds of furious black flies crawling over and swarming around the beast, and Cartwright had to shut his lips tight to keep them out. For several more seconds, all he could do was stare.

"Well, holy hell," Baxter scoffed.

"Hell is right," Cartwright replied softly.

Curved ribs as thick as tree trunks poked through torn flesh, a long tail trailed away into the ferns, but there were spikes showing from the grasses where it finished. The legs ended in stumps, with three horn-like nails on each and every one of them bigger than his fist.

"Some type of dinosaurian," Cartwright breathed. He followed the long neck to where it ended in a head that at first seemed equine, but was five times its size, and lined with ridged, flat teeth.

Eager to see more, he pulled the vine curtain back a little further. He now saw there were gouges in the great beast's side and how the ribs that poked through hadn't just burst through the skin but looked raked out, as if by huge talons. The thing was a monster, but it had been attacked by something even more ferocious and formidable.

"Attacked and killed," Cartwright said. "But what would attack that? *What could?*"

"By the look of those gouges in its flanks, I'd say something bigger and meaner – a carnivore, a hunter. And not sure about that being what killed it; look at the impact crater it's lying in, and also the neck." Baxter now held his gun ready in his hands. "It's broken."

Cartwright looked heavenwards, but there was nothing but thick cloud above them. "Perhaps it was running away, running for its life, and then fell…from where?"

"You did say we should have found something by now, right?" Baxter grinned. "Then we must be close."

Huge flies picked at Cartwright's lips and he held a hand over his mouth and nose. "The stink – can barely breathe."

He and Baxter turned at the sound of a commotion behind him and expected to see the Pemon preparing to leave. But instead, their leader, a wiry young warrior by the name of Inxthca, was busy issuing rapid orders. His men scurried away, digging out dry tinder and wood.

"Hey, don't do that." Cartwright held out an arm.

They ignored him and began to cover the great beast over. Inxthca then called for the firestones to be struck – shards of chert and pyrite that gave a spark and then a flame.

The small warrior drew closer to the pair and spoke rapidly. Cartwright could only speak a little of their language, but he got the gist of it.

"He's telling us, *no*; warning us not to go on. This was the place of bad gods, something called the Boraro."

Baxter snorted. "Then we're very much at the right place."

They spun as a horrifying noise from within the flames turned their heads. From the swollen belly of the beast, something burst free, screeching its pain from within the fire. It was a vision straight from hell. Coiling and hissing, the enormous diamond-shaped head split open to reveal fang-lined jaws.

Baxter raised his gun, sighting at the thing. From high above them, as if in answer, came a roaring hiss that shook the very trees around them. The Pemon jabbered and began to drop their packages.

Cartwright spun to them. "Wait!" He knew what would happen.

It was too late. They fled.

Baxter watched them vanish for a moment and then turned back to the flames, thankfully, seeing the hideous thing also consumed.

"What manner of place is this?"

"One of gods and monsters." Cartwright stared at the fire and grimaced. "Was that thing one of its young?"

"Didn't look like the dead animal. Might have been scavenging on it...or in it." Baxter shrugged. "We should get moving."

"Yes." Cartwright hurriedly pulled out his notebook and started to scribble in it. "Just...want to...make some notes. Describe the thing."

"Well, hurry it up." He looked down at the leather-bound book, with the hand-drawn maps and notes tucked into it. "What are you going to do with all that stuff anyway?"

Cartwright half smiled but kept writing. "I have a friend I correspond with. A famous author actually, a Brit named Arthur Conan Doyle."

Baxter's mouth turned down. "Never heard of him."

Cartwright looked up. "He wrote Sherlock Holmes."

"Nope." Baxter just shrugged. "Don't read that much these days. Action is what I'm interested in."

Cartwright nodded. "Yeah, well, that reading thing is not for everyone, I guess." He finished with his notes and shut the soft leather cover, sliding a string over it to keep it closed. He then pushed it into a leather satchel at his side.

He waved Baxter on. "Come on. Like you said, we've got to be close now."

*****

The rain had started to fall again. Heavy drops that drummed down on the broad leaves, their hats, and their shoulders. Underfoot, the ground squelched and sucked at their feet, every step becoming a battle against the mud and their fatigue.

Cartwright, leading, snagged an ankle and fell forward, crashing through elephant ear palm fronds to sprawl onto the slimy, composting jungle floor.

"Dammit."

Baxter followed and was beside him in an instant, but didn't bend to help. Instead, he froze and just stared.

"Hoo boy."

Cartwright wiped mud from his face and eyes and looked up. He saw what had grabbed Baxter's attention and his mouth immediately split into a grin.

"Oh my good God." He got to his feet. "*Oh my God!*"

There was a structure; temple-like, set into the side of a sheer rock face that vanished up into the clouds high above them. Holding it in a muscular embrace were gnarled tree roots as thick as his waist, and the heavy-cut stonework was moss-green with age. Everything about it exuded artistry, antiquity, and spiritual reverence.

"Looks like a church, old man." Baxter crossed his arms, cradling his rifle.

"It does, doesn't it? But there's no religious icons, or at least none I recognize."

"Could it be Spanish?" Baxter asked.

Cartwright wiped water and more mud from his eyes and took a few steps into the small clearing before the building.

"Well, the Spanish have been here since the early 1500s. But this looks more like thousands of years old, rather than hundreds." He pointed. "See that dead tree trunk that had thrown roots over the foundation stones? That's an *Acomat boucan* tree; they can live to be over a thousand years old, and that huge guy looks to have died of old age."

Baxter whistled.

Cartwright craned his neck, trying to take more of it in. "It's not really my field, but looks a little like Mayan, but different."

"Check out the gargoyles." Baxter flicked water from his hat and then jammed it back on sodden hair. "Or are they more of your dinosaurian beasts – with two heads?"

Cartwright cast his eyes over the stone statues standing rampant on each side of a huge doorway. They were strange, wrong; they rose up on two muscular legs, but seemed to be wrestling with something – a long muscular body wrapped around them, fangs bared and with unblinking eyes.

"No, not two heads, but two creatures, their gods maybe, or perhaps creatures from a superstitious culture." Cartwright had done his paleontology subjects at university, and there was nothing like these described in the fossil record. "Usually designed to warn strangers away."

"Well, no wonder the Pemon said this land was taboo." Baxter spat rainwater onto the ground.

"Jesus." Cartwright cringed as a roar blasted out from the clouds above them. Baxter's arms unfolded in an instant, holding his gun ready. After another few seconds, the hunter relaxed.

"What the hell is up there?" he asked.

"Gods and monsters, remember?" Cartwright straightened.

Baxter looked back and forth along the sheer wall. "No way up."

"And no way down...unless you fall." Cartwright turned about. "Undoubtedly a good thing."

"Well, as a betting man, I'd lay money on someone having been up there," Baxter observed.

"What makes you think that?" Cartwright tilted his chin at the bigger man.

"Those statues, for one. And I bet this temple, or whatever it is, has clues to find a way up there. We should check it out."

Cartwright licked lips wet from the rain and felt a knot of tension, or maybe excitement, coil in his belly. "Yeah, we should."

"Well, let's go; I didn't come all this way just to look at stuff." Baxter gave him a lopsided grin. "There might be a secret passage, or treasure, or adventure."

"Well then; here's to adventure." Cartwright hefted his pack and sucked in a deep breath. "Let's take a look, shall we?"

*****

There were several blank pages, and then when the notes resumed, Ben's brows drew together as he noticed that the handwriting, word choice, and even grammar changed.

Someone else was now writing – he quickly flicked to the end to find the signature notations. And then, there it was:

Alonzo Borges, Capitán de Policía – El Callao, Eastern Venezuela.

And a date indicating three months had passed. But what had happened? Ben quickly turned the pages back and began again. His heart sank as he read on.

*****

Alonzo Borges watched as the man was stretchered from the jungle. His emaciated frame made it easy for the bearers to carry him. He had a matted beard, rags for clothing, and a face marked by abrasions, rashes, and deep grime. There were also deep gashes along his ribs that had festered. But his eyes still blazed from his feverish face.

Being the police captain, Borges had all manner of problems brought to him, from the town or jungle. But it was the first time a strange westerner had been found wandering alone in the jungle. The stretcher-bearers laid the man at his feet, and the captain crouched beside him.

Borges laid a hand on the poor soul's forehead, immediately feeling the fierce heat of fever. He guessed he was not long for this world. He clicked his fingers to a small boy watching. "Get the nurse." He pointed at another boy. "You, water, *rápido.*"

He turned back to the figure. The man's pale blue eyes remained wide, and his fever-red face made them stand out like blue lights. In his hands, he tightly clutched a leather-bound notebook. It seemed all he had left.

Borges was handed a cup of water, and he wiped greasy hair from the man's brow, feeling once again the heat emanating from his skin. Borges spoke Spanish and a little English, but if the man spoke any other European language, then he would remain a mystery.

"Drink."

He lifted the man's head and allowed him to sip from the cup, but most of the water ran down his bearded cheeks. Borges gently laid him back down.

"Who are you?"

The man's rolling eyes fixed on him. "*Ca, Cart*, Cartwright." His voice was a croak and he licked flaking lips, already out of breath.

"Señor Cartwright, was there anyone else with you?"

Cartwright nodded his head. "Baxter. He was."

"And where is Señor Baxter now?" Borges leaned closer.

Cartwright sprung forward, making the captain lurch backwards. The man's eyes were so wide they looked about to pop free of his face.

"Eaten...*alive*."

Cartwright grimaced in agony and hunkered over his mutilated side. Dark blood pulsed out onto the stretcher.

Borges turned. "*Doctor!*"

The luminous eyes fixed on Borges again and the man held out a shaking hand, holding the leather book. "Get this...to...Doyle," he wheezed and gritted his teeth in agony. "Arthur Conan Doyle; *important*."

Borges took the book and only then did Cartwright lay back. "He'll know...what to do."

The pale eyes closed, and a long breath came from his mouth and his body seemed to collapse in on itself. Borges made the sign of the cross over him and imagined that his last breath was his spirit leaving the torn and battered body.

The captain stood slowly as the nurse finally came running. He turned to her and shook his head. "No hurry now." He lifted the book, opening the string and flicked through several pages, looking over the drawings. After a moment, he shook his head.

"Scribbling of a madman."

He sighed and closed the book, and turned to head back to his station. Señor Cartwright was off to meet his maker. Now he needed to see if someone wanted to claim the body, and as a dying man's last wish must always be honored, he would also see that the book found its way home.

CHAPTER 14

Later that evening, Ben sat in his room with the map sketches laid out in front of him. In the military, all soldiers had to learn basic cartography, map reading, and landmark plotting. Bottom line, if you got separated, you needed to be able to find your way home or to a rendezvous point with a map, sun/star positions, or just your memory.

Following his reading of the notebook, he now believed that there *was* something unimaginable down there; and something dangerous and unique. Benjamin the 1st had a skilled eye for landmarks and mapping, and today, Ben could use modern maps, satellite images, and even photographic libraries to pick up the trail.

He knew that the fateful expedition of 1908 had been somewhere deep in the eastern jungles of Venezuela – that was good and bad.

The good being that it was still largely thick and unmapped jungle, meaning that if there were any secrets, they still might be hidden there.

And the bad being that it was still a thick and unmapped jungle, meaning that if there were secrets there, it'd be damned hard to get there, find them, and also survive.

Ben knew jungles; he'd been to the Amazon, the Congo, and to the jungles of New Guinea. Frankly, the Amazon was the best and the worst of them, as the humidity was at a constant 90%, the ground cover was as thick as the overhead tree canopy cover, and everything that could possibly slither, creep, bite, nip, and infect you lived down there.

They'd all arranged to get shots for malaria, diphtheria, tetanus, typhoid, hepatitis, rabies, yellow fever, fungal infections, and a half-dozen other shots for blood-borne parasites. He even knew of certain flies, like the chigara, that burrowed into skin, releasing maggots just under the surface to feed on the living flesh.

"We're all mad," he mused. Taking a team of novices was lunacy. Most people when they imagined jungles conjured images of lush green plants, rainbow-colored birds, and maybe clear streams with sharp-toothed fish. But he knew they were really hot and wet miasmas that sapped strength, health, and sanity. "*I'm* mad," he added.

He went back to the online map of Venezuela. The first major clue he was given was the large river that wended its way into the northeast of the jungle. He groaned as the number of candidates were listed – dozens and dozens, and way too many to explore in their window of opportunity. And as he only had drawings and descriptions of some aspects of the waterway he was looking for, he'd need more clues. But at least he had a start and a good piece of the puzzle.

The notebook described a place of permanent cloud cover, but it also indicated that this cover was an unusual event that only occurred during the wettest of wet seasons. Still, he knew there were several drainage basins in the Amazon where cloud cover could remain collected for months or even permanently, only ever rising slightly and then sinking back depending on the humidity, temperature, and prevailing winds.

There was a small notation on one of the pages. *"Must hurry, only days until Primordia returns."*

A ship for their transport? Ben wondered.

He exhaled through pressed lips. He needed to take it back a few steps. There were clues, but he'd need to tease them out. In the notebook, the original Benjamin and Baxter arrived at the edge of the jungle and then travelled east, overland for several days on horseback, before boarding a riverboat. Given that a fully laden packhorse would only travel about 5 miles per hour, travel for about 10 daylight hours and only break for an hour in that entire time, then that should be between 40 and 50 miles per day, before arriving at their river.

Ben went back to his map, using the scale and plotting to where he believed they ended up. He found a promising candidate – the *Rio Caura*. It emptied into the *Orinoco* Basin and was termed a *black-water river* – that meant the water was the color of dark coffee from being stained by all the tannins leaching out of the rotting vegetation. The problem was it split into dozens of tributaries.

Ben sighed as he tried to find names for them – most didn't have one – at least not to the mapmakers. He checked the renditions in his ancestor's book again and read the notes.

He smiled. "Benjamin, I'm afraid the sound of drumbeats or an indication of where Professor Challenger lost some specimens is just not going to cut it."

But there were other indicators more promising – rocky slopes, large plains of tree ferns, low hills, and spongy morass of swamps – they would be something a local should recognize. And then there was the area that was headed, *concealed river*. Ben knew that places like this existed, where a narrow and remote tributary had large trees on either side growing up over it to meet in the middle. From line of sight, it was invisible, and if you didn't know it was there or weren't travelling along it, it didn't exist.

He stared hard at the map, concentrating on an area of river and surrounding geography that might just suit the profile for Benjamin's expedition, making notes as he went.

The knock on the door was almost welcome and he sat back and rubbed tired eyes. Ben checked his wristwatch – 9pm – *whoa*; he'd been staring at maps, old notes, and pencil drawings for hours. Ben got to his feet and crossed to the door pulling it open.

Andrea stood there in jeans and casual cotton shirt, collar up, and unbuttoned down to just show the top of a pair of full breasts. In her hand, she held two bottles of a local dark beer and a pair of glasses. She held them up.

"Nightcap?" She smiled, showing a neat line of expensive white teeth.

"*Um.*" He wasn't sure this was a good idea and wracked his brain for a polite excuse without hurting her feelings. "Well…"

"Well, thank you." She ducked past him.

"Huh?" He watched her shapely figure walk lightly to the small table and two chairs, and then use a napkin to twist the top off one of the bottles, while the tip of her small pink tongue just touched her top lip.

She poured two glasses of the beer that was the color of dark honey. She sat and slid one of the glasses over in front of the opposite chair. "Come on, sit down and tell me what you've found."

Ben checked his watch again and shrugged. A few minutes wouldn't hurt. Besides, he kinda liked English beer.

He sat and lifted the bottle – *Earl of Brixom* dark ale. He sipped and immediately got hints of roasted malt, chocolate, and caramel, and after he swallowed, it turned to a slight, black-coffee bitterness. He liked it, but would have preferred it chilled.

He saluted her with his glass. "Good choice."

She leaned forward to clink his glass with hers. "All they had, but I still accept your compliment." She sipped, her eyes on his for a second. "Well…" She nodded to the maps. "Anything interesting?"

Ben bobbed his head from side to side. "Yes and no, I guess. I think I know where we start, but at about 500,000 square miles, if I'm wrong, we'll never find what we're looking for."

"The hidden plateau?" She raised her brows.

"Eventually. We're just trying to pick up the thread to begin with. Like I said, I think I might know where to start, but the bottom line is we'll need to rely on Jenny's contacts on the ground. Local knowledge is going to be crucial once we're there."

"Once we're there," she repeated softly while looking at her glass. "I can't believe we're actually doing this."

"You and me both; we must be insane." He gave her a half smile. "*Extremely* insane." His smile dropped the more he let himself think about it.

Ben looked up at her. "So why do you want to go? The Amazon is no place for novices. In fact, it'll be weeks without shelter, and it'll be hot, humid and uncomfortable, and not to mention deadly." He leaned forward. "You, me, we could all die there."

She sipped again. "You'll protect me." Her eyes were direct, but after a few seconds, her face broke into a smile. "But honestly, Ben, I'm 32 years old, and haven't exactly been getting that many casting calls lately."

"Seriously? You're still a very beautiful woman, Andrea." He hiked his shoulders.

"Thank you, but in a land of beautiful women, you need more. I'm tipping towards invisibility in my agent's office. The thing is, I'm boring." She put her glass down with a clunk. "The very thought of this fills me with excitement, curiosity, and hope. I'm going to write down everything we do and see, get a writer to turn it into a script, and then I'm going to take it to a producer." She leaned forward with a cat-like smile on her lips. "And I'm going to play the lead."

"Good plan. But let's not count our chickens just yet, Andrea. We might not even make it there." He sipped again consciously, struggling not to look down at her open shirt.

She also sipped her ale, her eyes on his. The tiny curve of her lips gave Ben the impression she was reading his mind. She slowly put the glass down.

"Well, I for one wouldn't want to be the guy who was on his deathbed and didn't bother to see where this adventure might lead."

Ben grunted, knowing this to be true for himself. "I never said never, Andrea. I'm not trying to be a handbrake, more a…reality check."

"A shock absorber will do." She got to her feet.

Ben walked her to the door and pulled it open. She turned in the doorframe and leant forward quickly to kiss him on the lips.

She eased back, but only a few inches. "*Never say never*; I like it." She kissed him again, harder.

Ben's eyes were open, and he couldn't help his hand finding its way to her waist. She was soft and firm at the same time, and he felt himself become rock hard between them. Over her shoulder, he saw movement and looked up to see a horrified Emma.

Shit, he thought, and immediately pulled back from Andrea who saw the look on his face and turned. She giggled and turned back to him.

"First come first served." She looked down at his waist. "Ouch, that looks painful." She then sashayed down the hallway, nodding to a fuming Emma as she went past.

He turned to Emma, but her eyes blazed and her fists were balled. She turned on her heel and also vanished.

Ben groaned as he shut the door and leaned against it. *Good grief,* he thought. He seemed to stumble from one thing to the next without being in control of any of them.

He sat on his bed and contemplated calling Emma on the in-room phone, but bet she'd never take his call. Ben turned to look at the table with the two beers, one only sipped at and the other, his, empty. The maps, notebook, and old novel stood open. He couldn't be bothered resuming his research again right now.

"Tomorrow's another day." He stripped down to his boxers and T-shirt and flopped back down on the bed, pulling the duvet up over himself.

In another moment he was asleep.

*****

Ben Cartwright ran, fast and hard, from what he had no idea. He just knew he must not let *it* catch him.

He put his head down to push harder and suddenly needed to skid to a stop – the jungle ended and he was at the edge of a cliff that dropped away to a ground that was lost in the clouds below. A breeze blew into his face that seemed to come from everywhere at once. He squinted, staring down.

Beneath his feet, the ground shook as something of enormous weight came through the jungle like a truck. The thing that pursued him filled him with a terror he couldn't even measure.

Ben turned back to the cliff edge as his panic was causing his mind to short-circuit with indecision. Behind him, the foliage burst open and the roar made him cringe with a panic he hadn't known even when he was under siege by terrorists.

He didn't want to look back, didn't want to see, but slowly his head edged around anyway. His teeth clamped together hard and pure horror made the gorge rise in his throat. The thing poured towards him, and he threw his hands up in front of his face.

Ben's eyes flicked wide open. He was back in the dark of his room, and safe.

But then knew he wasn't alone.

There was the faintest creak of a floorboard and an impression of movement in the room's still air. He lay still in the near pitch darkness, listening some more. Ben was sure of it now; there were moving bodies in his room. At first, he was hopeful that somehow Emma had managed to get in and was going to forgive him.

But then he knew different. There was more than one person, being silent as wraiths, and he lay there just using senses other than his eyes. He could smell them then, the tangy sweat of men, musty clothing, and worryingly, gun oil.

Another floorboard complained with only the faintest of sounds, but it told Ben that the men were big and heavy. Anyone else might have wondered if some guests had blundered into the wrong room, but Ben's covert military experience told him that whoever they were, they knew what they were doing and were determined to be as stealthy as possible.

He heard the soft ruffle of papers – they're going for the notebook – *like hell*, he thought, and flew from the bed.

He immediately encountered a large boot to the chest. The room was near total darkness, and it told him his intruders must have been wearing night-vision. This was no casual break-in.

Ben had trained for this and went fast, using memory of the room's layout to avoid obstacles. If they had night-vision, then light was his ally. He came low, lifted quickly and flicked on a bedside lamp. The glow was low wattage, but after the blackness of the room, it illuminated the scene like a flashbulb.

Ben knew when waiting for eyes to adjust from night-blindness, the key wasn't to wait for everything to take shape, but to just take in enough and react, and let the brain fill in the gaps.

There were two big men, dressed all in black and with Cyclops night-scopes down over the faces. The light would have near blinded them, but instead of recoiling or fleeing, the pair of men turned…to fight.

Ben came low, intending to take the first intruder down, and then use an elbow to his throat or even bridge of the nose to incapacitate him. It didn't go to plan.

The guy lowered his chest and took Ben head-on. Ben was big, but this guy outweighed him by a good 20 pounds. Ben was skilled in hand-to-hand combat and had the advantage of reacting first. He dived under the barrel chest, grabbed a pair of trunk-like legs, and upended him, flinging him backwards. He heard the satisfying dull thud of skull against wood and the guy stayed down, flat out.

Within the same heartbeat, Ben spun at the second man, who had now ripped off his goggles. The eyes behind the balaclava weren't wide with shock or fear, but focused and intense – he knew it – *professionals*.

The straight-hand punch was aimed at his chin and Ben blocked it easily, catching the wrist and twisting it. There was no yell of pain or even a grunt; instead, the man planted his legs and flicked out a flat-hand strike at Ben's nose.

The blow was meant to bust his beak and cause the eyes to immediately water. Ben turned his head in time to catch the blow to the side of the face. And then it was on; the pair of big men stood toe to toe, trading and blocking blows that would have felled a normal human in an instant.

Ben ducked under a looping right cross, jabbing up with a flat hand into his attacker's diaphragm, and heard the breath whoosh out of him.

Got ya, he thought, and came up on his toes, expecting to bring a hammer blow down on the guy's neck. Unfortunately, the second intruder was now back up and a boot came down against the back of Ben's knee, forcing the leg to bend forward, and Ben with it...and straight into a short sharp left. Ben saw stars and went down.

Then the chair came down across his neck and shoulders. The thing about being hit with furniture was it's never like you see in Hollywood – they don't splinter over your head into matchwood; instead, they usually put a fucking big dent in your skull.

His training took over, and he acted on pure instinct and adrenaline now. He rolled away, still expecting the serious work of a beating to be administered to him, but when he came up, the pair was out the door. He staggered a few steps after them, rubbing the back of his head, but thankfully they were gone.

Ben stood in the doorway, breathing hard, and wiping his face. *Shit-damn.* He grimaced and flexed his knee a few times – a foot race was out of the question. People started to appear in the hallway – Steve, Dan, then Andrea and finally Emma, who folded her arms, looking at him from under her brows as though he had been having a party.

"They stole..." He briefly turned back to his room. Thankfully, the notebook and novel was still there. But all the maps he had been creating were gone, and with them the copious notes he had been making on landmarks.

His groan turned into a long sigh. "They took all the maps."

"Ah, *shit*...those freaking assholes." Steve quickly pulled on a jacket and went to head down the steps.

"*No.*" Ben held up a hand. "Don't."

Ben knew that Steve was a big and fit guy, but the two people who had been in his room were professional hitters. If they had taken *him* down so easily, Steve could get seriously hurt.

"But..." Steve turned, brows knitted.

Mrs. Davenport appeared at the top of the steps, tying a cord on her thick, powder-blue dressing gown.

"What's happening here?" Her face was creased with worry, and the frown deepened when she spotted the blood around Ben's nose. "Is everyone okay?" She looked from one of the group to the other. "It's a bit late for all that noise."

Steve chuckled, and Ben waved a hand to her. "It's okay, Mrs. Davenport, the party's over. Good night."

She clicked her tongue and headed back down the steps. Ben bet that her preconceptions about rambunctious Americans were all coming true. He headed back into his room and was followed by the group.

"Holy shit." Steve surveyed the damage to the small room. "Jesus, man, who were those guys?"

Ben shook his head and bent to lift a chair back into place. "I'm wondering the same thing." He leant on it. "I woke up to find them in here."

"That would have freaked me out," Dan said.

"Yeah, wasn't fun." Ben dabbed at his nose again.

Emma knelt and started to collect up papers. She lifted the notebook. "I wonder if they came for this?" She then picked up the antique novel. "Or this?"

"Well, if they did, they failed. The big guy scared them off," Dan observed. "Good."

"Unlikely," Ben said, wearily.

"If that's what they came for, how did they even know about them?" Andrea said. "We're not locals, and I doubt Mrs. Davenport has been chatting to anyone."

"Oh God, of course." Steve's eyes widened comically. "She's a spy."

Andrea grinned and jabbed him in the ribs.

"I think they got something more important – the maps I had been making and all the notes," Ben said.

Everyone's head turned to the floor, stepping back, searching. After a few fruitless moments, Ben exhaled long and loud. "I guess now we know what they came for." He put his hands on his hips. "Perhaps they *did* come for everything, but I disturbed them before they could clean me out."

Dan's brow furrowed and he pursed his lips for a moment. "Hey, you know what? This is the best news I've heard in...hours."

"What?" Emma scowled. "Ben could have been hurt, and he just lost all his maps. How is that in any way good?"

Dan turned and grinned. "Because, they came for the map, or map and notebook. Someone *actually* took the time, effort, and risk to do this." He kept grinning. "It proves how important it is...and not just to us."

"Jesus." Steve put a hand to his forehead. "But you know what else? We just got confirmation this is all real."

The room was in silence for a few seconds, before Dan's whooping broke it. "*Yes!*"

Ben nodded. He hated to admit, but he was right.

"But the map's gone," Andrea said. "Can we get it back?"

"We don't need it; Ben made it *and* the notes. We have something far more valuable; that wonderful brain of his." Dan threw an arm around Ben's wide shoulders and turned to the group. "Plus, we still have the notebook, which is more important as far as the landmarks are concerned. Right, Bennie?"

"Maybe." Ben's mind had already turned to the *who* and *how*. "Your search, Dan." He turned to his friend.

"What?" Dan's eyebrows went up. "My search?"

"Yeah, when you searched for the notebook online, I think someone saw it. Maybe someone has been bird-dogging us ever since," Ben said.

"Poss-*iiiibly*." Dan's lips turned down. "I mean, you can set alerts, traps, nets, and even alarms on the Internet." His vision seemed to turn inward. "My searches might have been picked up on a sweep. Unfortunately, there's no way to avoid that."

"What do we do now?" Emma asked. "Ben could have been really hurt. These guys were thugs."

"What do we do?" Dan asked. "I'll tell you what we do; we still go, but move faster. It seems someone is looking for the same thing we are. This is not just a search, but a race now…and we need to get on the front foot; right, everyone?"

"I hate to admit it, but he might be right, Ben. If you want to find out what really happened to your ancestor, then you need to do it before someone else shuts it all down." Steve shrugged. "Or else beats you to the punch."

"We're not ready," Ben said.

"We're as ready as we'll ever be," Steve replied. He raised a hand. "I vote we leave in the morning."

"Aye." Dan immediately raised his hand.

Ben saw Emma raise hers, followed by Andrea. He turned to Jenny, who also gave him a half smile coupled with a nod. "Just say the word, and I'll have guides waiting for us," she said.

Dan folded his arms. "And I can get us on a connecting flight to South America by midday," he said. "Go hard or go home, people."

Ben looked from their faces to the mess of his room. What happened to his great, great grandfather had been a family mystery for a hundred years, and he was dying to get to the bottom of it. But there was something else; now he also wanted to find out who attacked him, and who else knew about that mystery.

He knew he couldn't do that from here or from home. He decided.

"Let's do this."

CHAPTER 15

24 Hours to full Apparition

Comet P/2018-YG874, designate name Primordia, was on its approach to the third planet from the sun. The magnetic bow wave that preceded it caused collisions between electrically charged particles in the Earth's upper atmosphere, creating an Aurora Borealis effect over the jungles of South America.

In one of the most inaccessible parts of the eastern Venezuelan jungle, clouds began to darken, and in another minute or two, they started to swirl and boil like in a devil's cauldron, throwing down a torrent of warm rain.

Beneath the clouds, a gigantic tabletop mountain became cloaked in the dense fog, and brutal winds began to smash at its sides and surface. Thunder roared and lightning seemed to come from the sky, air, and even up from the ground.

The first of the bestial roars that began to ring out even drowned out the crash of thunder, and before long, the hissing, roars, and screams rose to be like those from the pits of hell.

It had been ten years since the primordial sounds had been heard in this part of the Amazon, and even the creatures on the jungle floor over a thousand feet below the plateau scurried away in fear.

It was the wettest season and Primordia was returning.

CHAPTER 16

2018 – South Eastern Venezuela – The Wettest Season

The plane ride from London across the Atlantic to Venezuela took nearly 10 hours. Caracas was Venezuela's capital and largest city, located in a mountain valley on the northeastern side of the country.

Ben rolled the stiffness from his shoulders and looked down. The city had two million inhabitants and was a modern metropolis nestled in amongst mountains and lush green forests. They were close to the Caribbean Sea, but still separated from the coast by a 7,200-foot range of mountains.

He'd been on longer flights before, and even though Dan had booked them all business-class seats with extra legroom, constant snacks, and movies, it still felt like it was never going to end. Perhaps it was the anticipation, impatience, or maybe even the feeling they were now in a race and speed mattered.

True to her word, Jenny had organised people to meet them at the airport. Following a brief delay at immigration control, they were quickly shepherded to a small and cramped Cessna airplane – destination Canaima.

It meant another three hours flying time, but the only other option was 14 hours by bus, which would have been murder on the narrowing tracks through the thickening jungle.

Canaima was an area that encompassed three million hectares on the border of Brazil and Guyana. It was jungle, thick jungle, and remarkable for its numerous tepuis, massive flat-topped mountains, that rise from the jungle floor and are usually covered in mist.

Once again, Ben looked down as they soared above the canopy that was now so dense there wasn't a trace of the ground visible below them. From time to time, a reflected shine from a ribbon of snaking river glinted back at him, and flocks of birds soared across the green rooftop that could have been ten feet or a hundred up from the ground. This was the Amazon jungle he remembered – dense, unforgiving, and sometimes damn deadly.

In the seat in front, Emma dozed and made a small squeaking noise that Ben found cute and a little child-like. Everyone else was also pretty wiped out by the amount of travelling they'd just gone through in the past 24 hours. They'd soon land in Canaima airport, and then it'd be a short hop to their accommodation.

Dan had organised an overnight stay at a hotel, and the following morning, they were to meet the contacts Jenny had organised. According to the plan, which he had reviewed, they would travel overland, first by truck, then by riverboat, and finally via canoes where they'd enter areas of the jungle that just fell off the map.

Ben sighed and let his eyes slide to Andrea. She had earphones over her head and read a glossy magazine. He wondered what would happen if she decided she wanted to go home – would they be able to send her back if they were hundreds of miles from nowhere? Would she be safe even attempting that, even if they split the guides?

He doubted it. Once they decided to travel to the Amazonian interior, like it or not, they were all committed. He'd need to impress this on her, and everyone else, before they left – last chance to pull out and all that.

The plane started to drop, and Ben leant forward to peer through the porthole window. He smiled as he beheld the sight of the Angel Falls – the cliff-top river looked like it fell off the Earth. It was the world's highest uninterrupted waterfall and dropped 3,200 feet from the top of the Auyántepui Mountain. In the air, the powerful watercourse spread and finally turned to a shimmering spray before it made it to the river below.

He narrowed his eyes as he looked back at the massive tepui – this is what he expected they were looking for. The Canaima jungles were in thousands of square miles of national park, but beyond that were largely unexplored wilderness. In addition, the park was renowned for the strange and prehistoric-looking tabletop mountains. These geological wonders weren't just millions, but billions of years old, with vertical walls rising thousands of feet to almost perfectly flat tops. Most, if not all, had been found, mapped, and climbed. But out in the deep jungle, there could be others. And that's what they were banking on.

Ben reached forward to grab Emma's shoulder and squeezed. "Hey, wake up, sleeping beauty, or you'll miss the show."

"Huh." She looked around groggily, turning first to him. Ben pointed to the window.

"Angel Falls."

She sprang forward to the window, and her mouth dropped into an open grin. "Oh, wow."

Jenny leant forward onto their seat backs, also looking out. "Those tepuis are amazing."

"I did some research on them," Ben said. "They date back to when South America and Africa were part of a super-continent. Some are nearly 3 billion years old."

Jenny grinned as she looked from the window. "Well done…and *they* told me you were just the muscle."

He shrugged and smiled back at her, but then put on a mock frown. "Hey, who's *they*?"

She nudged his head. "Something else. The Pemon have an intimate relationship with the tepuis, and believe they are the home of gods and monsters. And also demons."

"My ancestor, Ben the 1st, made mention of them, and also the Pemon. Same people?" Ben asked.

"Sure, they've been here for thousands of years. They have no formal writing, but they have a fantastic inherited knowledge system via stories and songs. If there's any hidden tepuis out there, they'll probably know about them."

"The trick will be getting them to show us." Emma turned around in her seat and rested her chin on the back of it. "We're outsiders."

Jenny nodded. "Yep, true. We're going to need to win their trust. I've worked with them before, so hopefully that's going to help." She headed back to her seat.

Emma turned to look at him…and kept looking.

"What?" he asked with a grin.

"I can't believe I'm here." Her grin widened. "I've never been to a real jungle before. I've been to forests, deserts, seashores, and mountains, but never a real, real jungle. But you have."

He nodded. "And this is about as real a jungle as you can get." He smiled back. "Emm, they're no picnic. Quick mud, spiders the size of your hand, bugs that drink blood, or try and lay eggs under your skin. Big cats, caiman alligators, and even the plants can sting you. You really have to respect it, and then maybe it'll let you walk out in one piece."

She nodded for a moment. "Thank you for bringing me."

He laughed out loud. "That's it?"

She inhaled and let it out through her smile. "I feel so…*alive*; so yeah. Besides, your experience and expertise will make a difference."

"Hopefully." Ben gave her a lopsided grin. "The most important thing we can bring with us is common sense. You'd be surprised how many novices strike their camps on soldier ant nests, or on the banks of rivers where a big caiman lives, or even under trees that a band of monkeys live in." He grinned. "A few hours of having dung rained down on you clears the sinuses."

She chuckled. "Well, I'm still glad I'm here…we're *both* here."

He bobbed his head. "I'm glad you're here, but seriously, I'd prefer you weren't."

"Big brother syndrome? Or..." She blushed a little. "Just be free with the advice, okay? I'll be paying attention."

"Will do." He meant it; Ben planned to keep them all safe, but especially Emma.

The plane bumped down on the short runway, veered hard to the right, to the left, and then straightened. The small craft slowed quickly and turned before switching off its engines. There were a few golf-cart-style cars waiting to take them to Waku Lodge – somehow, Dan had managed to find the only five-star accommodation at the edge of an Amazonian rainforest.

Ben would have preferred them all to begin to acclimatize to the new geography, hours, and climate, but he knew that they were all tired, and there was no harm in a last night of luxury before a few weeks of doing it tough.

The plane door was swung open and they clambered out. The first thing that hit them was the wet-heat that immediately made their shirts and underwear cling to their bodies. The second thing was the smells; though they were in a domesticated area of the jungle, there were the suspended odors of plant sap, fragrant blooms, and a hint of rich, composting earth.

Ben caught a whiff of something else – his body odor – a damn shower would be his first priority. He didn't know what it was about plane travel, but it managed to squeeze a lot of weird scents from the body. He jammed his hat on his head and headed for the vehicles.

In the first buggy, Dan was up front, he and Emma were in the back; Steve, Andrea, and Jenny were in the other. Dan turned in his seat.

"Got someone coming over this evening." He looked both self-satisfied and conspiratorial as he leaned even closer. "Arranged for some *stock* for us." He winked and then made a gun from his hand, jacking the thumb up and down.

Normally, Ben would have called him an idiot and told him to cancel it immediately. But he knew the dangers within a rainforest, and there was also the unknown danger factor of those assholes that attacked him and could well be moving in parallel to them right now. He *knew* they were armed.

And then the notebook had told them there might, *just might*, be something at their destination that gave him a strong desire to have more than a sharp knife for protection.

"Good." He nodded. "Jenny comes too. Her local knowledge will be useful."

"Okay." Dan nodded, looking pleased with himself, and turned back around.

"*Whoa*." Emma leaned out of the side of their buggy as they approached their hotel. She turned and grinned. "You're unbelievable, Mr. Murakami."

"We Japanese have class." Dan winked at her.

Waku Lodge was done in a tropical grass hut style, but the large buildings in the center of verdant green grass were far from holiday hokey.

They eased to a stop on a glass-smooth asphalt driveway, and the drivers immediately leapt out to shepherd them inside, promising to bring their bags in after them.

"I like it." Ben nodded his approval. "Grass hut outside, first class inside."

"Mr. Murakami?" The young woman behind the reception counter flashed them a stunning smile.

"*Yo*." Dan raised an arm and almost jogged to the desk. He looked around. "Beautiful place."

"Thank you." She beamed.

"Hi." Ben came and leant on the countertop. "Any other guests?"

"No sir, we –"

"Any booked, or been here in the last few days?" he pressed.

Her smile dropped a fraction at his abruptness. "No, sir, and none for a few weeks; until the tourist season really starts. You have it all to yourself until then."

"Thank you." Ben felt relieved. Though he would have loved to administer a little payback justice to his intruders, he didn't want them using this as their launchpad as well.

Dan had booked them in for the night, and then again for a few more nights later. But it was left as a standing order and line of credit – whenever they got back, everything was prepaid.

They were each shown to their rooms, and when Ben pushed his door open, he just stopped and took it all in. The rooms were each a jungle fantasy – lamp shades designed to look like birds of paradise, bamboo wall paneling, with ceiling fans slowly rotating to move the warm flower-scented air. New porcelain gleamed in the bathrooms, and thankfully, the mini-bar was well stocked.

"Oh yeah, this'll do just fine."

His bags were already on the small blanket table beside the bed, and on a side table, a pitcher of fresh pineapple juice. He sat down, poured himself a glass and drank half, before letting himself fall backwards and then threw an arm over his eyes. It was only three in the afternoon, but he could have drifted off then and there. In the past week, he had travelled more in a few days than he had in years. Though he was only

35, right then, he felt about a hundred.

"Anyone home…or at least awake?" Emma grinned in his doorway.

He turned his head. "How can you look so fresh?" Ben groaned as he tried to sit up. "Whatever you're taking, Ms. Wilson, give me some right now."

She laughed softly and came and grabbed his arm to haul him up to a sitting position. "What sort of people is our military turning out these days?" She crossed to the side table and sipped at his juice.

"*Ex*-military." Ben rubbed his face. "A quick shower, something to eat, and about a weeks sleep, and you watch, I'll be good as new."

"*Pfft*." She knelt up beside him on the bed. "Come here." She grabbed his shoulders and started to knead his aching muscles. Then put the point of her elbow in at the base of his neck and ran it down his spine a few inches.

He moaned, feeling like he'd been sent to heaven. "Okay, yep, that's it, right there."

She changed hands. "Feels like a stack of knotted wood in there."

"Thank you, you're not too bad yourself." He chuckled and tilted his head back, mouth open.

Emma moved her hands up to his head, and her fingers began to gently make circles at his temples.

"O-*oooh* boy." Ben felt like he was floating. He opened one eye. "Knotted wood, huh?"

"Hmm, maybe something a lot more dense." She sniggered.

Ben felt himself relax, and he breathed deeply. He felt the small movement of the air from the overhead fan as it stirred the balmy, tropical heat. But he also caught the delicate scent of Emma's perfume, mixed with a slight hint of perspiration. He found it intoxicating.

After another moment she gently slapped his shoulder. "There you go, big guy."

Ben rolled his neck muscles. "Thanks." He turned, and she still knelt on the bed. Emma's eyes locked with his, and they both just stared for several moments. Her eyes seemed to darken as her pupils dilated.

She reached a hand out, and the tips of her fingers gently ran down along the scar on his face. Her hand stayed on his chin, the thumb stroking there for a second.

Ben's lust rose and he reached out a hand, first to her shoulder, and then to her chin, cupping it. Her eyes never left his as he drew her face to his.

"Yes," she whispered. "I've waited so long for you."

Their lips just touched.

"*Knock, knock*." The door handle turned and Dan poked his head around the door. "Sorry, hope I wasn't disturbing anything." His eyes widened theatrically. "Oh, *was I?*"

"Wassup?" Ben asked, easing back from Emma.

"Dinner at six, and then we have a date with, *ahem*, some gentlemen who'd like to sell us some portable self-protection." Dan waggled his eyebrows.

"I'll be there," Ben replied.

"Great; see you at six." Dan went to shut the door, but paused. "Carry on." He sniggered as he shut the door.

Ben sighed and looked back at Emma. "Where were we?"

Emma slid from the bed. "Getting interrupted." She headed for the door.

"But…" Ben groaned, feeling annoyed – primarily with Dan.

She got to the door, but instead of leaving, she locked it and turned, smiling wickedly back at him. "And *that* fixes that." She pulled her T-shirt up over her head. She didn't wear a bra, and two small but perfect breasts jiggled slightly.

"Beautiful." Ben got to his feet and she crossed to him. He grabbed at her small figure, pulled her close, and kissed her deeply, tasting pineapple as her tongue danced in his mouth.

Emma stepped back and began to unbutton his shirt. She looked up into his eyes with a dusky expression. "I've dreamed about this." She finished his buttons and pulled his shirt open. "Oh wow." She stood back, admiring his physique. "And now my dreams come true."

Following leaving the military, Ben worked to stay in shape, and his body was still ripped and powerful looking. The downside was the multiple scars – the burns, stab marks, and surgery scars.

Emma traced one with a finger. "I'm glad you're not doing that anymore."

"No." He enfolded her in his arms. "These days, I'm playing it safe by coming to a deadly jungle to search for a lost world that may be inhabited by monsters. *Oh*, and with some bad guys willing to bash my head in along the way."

She smiled and shrugged. "Keeps the boredom gremlins away, huh?"

He kissed her again, and she pushed him back onto the bed and climbed on top of him. Her legs came up on either side of his hips. Ben had never wanted a woman so much as he wanted Emma then. And it seemed she was the same with him.

She moved herself back and forth, grinding down at him; making him so hard it became painful. Emma leant forward to kiss and then nibbled at his ear. "Mmm, I can feel more knotted wood – better take care of that too." She reached for his belt.

*****

After a dinner of roasted meats, local fruits, and vegetables cooked with way too much precision for a hotel on the edge of an Amazonian jungle, Steve, Andrea, and Emma retired to the bar for a nightcap, and Ben, Dan, and Jenny prepared for their rendezvous.

Having Jenny there was bad enough, but she *had* to be there. However, it had taken all his persuasive skills to keep Emma out of it. He liked that she was concerned and wanted to be with him, but meeting gun smugglers in the night for a cash transaction has the potential to go wrong in so many ways that he knew he'd need eyes in the back of his head, as well as all the military intuition he could bring to bear.

Ben drove the buggy out into the darkness. Both Dan and Jenny sat in silence, and he could sense the nervousness coming off them in waves. Ben hoped the transaction was going to be fast and uncomplicated. As it wasn't his money, and Dan had plenty of it anyway, haggling over price was not going to be an issue.

Ben had seen the results of dumb people trying to deal with black market weapon militias before and trying to play hardball – sometimes the militias just decided to keep both the money and the guns, and if they left behind a few bodies, well, then that was just bad luck and the cost of doing business for the patsies.

Dan checked his GPS and then held up a hand.

"Pull in here."

"Here?" Ben scoffed. "You're kidding, right?" It was dark jungle on three sides, plus the sound of the falls in the distance masked any potential sound of approach.

"I don't like it."

"Neither do I." Dan grimaced, his teeth showing white. "What do you suggest?"

Ben looked one way then the next. "How long until our meet?"

Dan checked his watch. "I said oh eight hundred. So, in ten more minutes."

"Got it; stay in the car. I'll do a quick recon." Ben went to leap out, but paused. "You guys speak Spanish?"

"Yes," Jenny replied.

"A little," Dan added.

"*Suficiente para tener una conversación?*" Ben said, and raised his eyebrows.

"Okay, well then, no, not really." Dan grinned back sheepishly.

"Let Jenny do the talking. But first prize is to get them to speak English." Ben reached into the cart. "And I'll take this." He grabbed the moneybag. "See you soon. And remember, be cool."

"*Wait, what?*" Dan hissed, but Ben had already slid into the brush.

Ben moved back along the edge of the track, and then did a big loop back towards the vehicle, staying low and quiet.

The sound of the Angel Falls was a constant background roar, so he didn't need to creep. He pushed bracken out of his way and was thankful the moon was near full; the silver light gave him more than enough vision even though the jungle was raw and thick in this area.

He had worn a hooded pullover and drew it over his head; though his tanned and stubbled face wasn't that pale and reflective, he had refused to wear insect repellent, as the odor was distinctive in a jungle, and so the only protection he had against biting insects was his clothing.

He heard movement above the background noise in the jungle – it was *them*. He eased down to watch.

*****

Dan fidgeted in the front seat. "Jesus, I don't like this." He looked over his shoulder. "Where's Ben? I wanted him here, to goddamn be *here*, not be out *there* somewhere."

"Heads up. Company." Jenny reached forward from the back seat to grip his shoulder.

"Fuck." Dan felt his heart rate kick up threefold.

"*Hola?*" The three men ambled from the jungle, each carrying large bags. All had sidearms.

"*Hola*," Dan replied, hating that his voice had a tremor in it.

"*Buenas noches para los negocios, ¿sí?*" The lead man held up a hand.

"Jesus, I have no idea what he just said." Dan licked his lips.

Jenny leaned forward, whispering. "He said it was a nice night for business."

"Okay, got it," he whispered over his shoulder before turning to the men. "Yes, it is. You speak English?" he asked.

He went to step out and Jenny grabbed him. "Stay in here…"

"I got this." He got out anyway.

"*Damn it.*" She got out as well.

"A little." The man's grin was luminous in the dark. His two colleagues spread out to the left and right, hands hanging loosely over the holsters on their belts.

"You are Mr. Dan, yes?" the man asked.

"Yes, that's me," Dan replied. He tried to project a cool confidence, but felt his legs shaking.

"Jose." The man tapped his chest.

"Nice to meet you, Jose." Dan swallowed.

"Yes, yes, good to know you too." He looked about. "Just, *ah*, you two?" he asked.

"Don't answer that." Jenny whispered. "Let's get this over with."

"Did you bring the guns?" Dan asked.

"Sure, lots of guns. Not easy to get. Did you bring the money?" Jose had stopped but his two friends walked forward a few paces to stand at each end of the buggy.

"You stay right there," Dan said.

One of the huge men kept coming in, and then stuck one huge hand out. "Money."

"Sorry, it doesn't work that way," Jenny said evenly.

"I think we will tell you the way it works." Jose laughed corrosively, and then spoke rapid Spanish to his man.

"Oh shit," Jenny said as the guy lunged in and put a hand on Dan's shoulder, grabbed a handful of shirt, and started to drag him closer.

"I haven't got the money," Dan said.

There was a thump and a grunt, and the guy who held Dan looked over his shoulder. Dan also peered around him.

Ben was holding the other of Jose's henchmen from where he had knocked him to the ground. He lifted him and turned the still groggy man around, holding him by the collar.

"I've got the money." Ben's voice was full of controlled menace. Immediately, the dynamic changed. The guy who held Dan let him go and swung around to focus on the bigger threat.

Dan felt relief wash over him. "My security. Protection against wild animals and all that."

Jose stood side on and waved his remaining man to be at ease, who now had his hand on his gun. "You are armed, señor? Why don't you let my friend go and come out where we can see you? All friends here."

"You think I'd come to this transaction unarmed?" Ben stepped further in, and shook the men he held. He kept his other hand in his pocket.

Jose cursed under his breath. Ben was a big man and obviously immediately had an impression on the smaller Venezuelan.

"Ex-military," Dan said. "And I'm afraid, very short-tempered."

"I hope we can conduct a pleasant transaction, and then all go home happy," Ben said continuing to maintain an edge to his voice. He pushed the man he held forward where he sprawled for a moment, and then got up to crawl forward and rub his jaw.

There was silence for a few moments, and Jose's colleague looked to him and then back to Ben. After a moment, Jose chortled and waved his hand.

"Sure, sure." He turned to his men and snapped his fingers. *"Poner las armas, rápidamente."*

The two men set to laying a sheet on the ground on which they placed row after row of handguns, rifles, and ammunition.

Dan exhaled with relief as Ben came in closer, and Dan and Jenny came to his sides.

"Flashlights," he said and kept his eyes on the men, as Jenny and Dan turned on their lights and shone them down on the weapon's cache. Ben glanced down briefly, his experienced eye running over the cache.

"We'll take six of the Sig Saur, 9mm semi-automatic handguns."

"Six?" Dan straightened. "One for Andrea as well? I don't think she can even shoot?"

"She'll learn." Ben eased Dan out of his line of sight. "Also two spare magazines a piece." He edged closer, looking at the larger weapons. "Nice. I'll take that M4A1 carbine, and two spare mags."

"Very good, señor." Jose grinned. "But not elephants down here." He chuckled. "Maybe in a zoo."

Ben grunted. "The zoo, huh? In that case, I better take that Mossberg shotgun as well. Plus two boxes of shells."

Jose rubbed his hands together. *"Excelente."* He waited.

"That'll do." Ben stepped back. "Best price."

Jose blew air through his lips. "These weapons, top of the line, very hard to acquire." He began to shake his head. "And premium for discretion." He shrugged. "Fifty thousand, American dollars."

Ben snorted. "Make it –"

"We'll take em," Dan shot back. And turned to Ben, nodding vigorously. "No haggling remember?" he whispered.

Ben hiked his shoulders. "It's your money." He turned back to Jose. "Collect them all up into one of those bags, ammunition included for me to do a spot check; then we're done here."

Jose had his men separate out their chosen weapons and lay them in the bag. Ben put his hand in, took one of the handguns, snapped a magazine in, and quickly turned, firing two test rounds into a tree trunk.

"Now, I'm armed." He tucked the gun into his belt. "Pleasure doing business."

Jose snorted, and Dan handed over several wads of cash. Jose quickly counted it off. He then saluted with two fingers. "Good luck, señors and señorita, with whatever war you intend making in our beautiful country." He chuckled and then the three men vanished into the darkness.

They watched them go for a moment and over the sound of the waterfall, they could just hear the faint rev of an engine for a moment before that too vanished.

"They're gone." Dan exhaled and then slapped his thighs as he bent over. "*Je-zuz*, was that a rush or what?"

Ben grinned. "Expensive day's work, Mr. Murakami."

Jenny smiled. "Oh well, we got the guns, and no one has any holes in them, so, there's that."

"Yep. I'm happy with that," Ben said.

"Now what?" Dan asked.

"We get these home. We leave tomorrow morning, and when we're in the jungle, we do some limited practice shooting."

Dan looked in the bag and hefted the Mossberg shotgun. He looked up at Ben. "So, looks like you're starting to believe there really might be something out in that jungle, huh?"

Ben closed the bag. "Well, as the saying goes, it's better to have a gun and not need it than need a gun and not have it." He hefted the bag. "And yeah, this jungle, the Amazon, is a land of mystery and myth. If there's anywhere in the world where something can remain hidden, this is the place."

He headed to the buggy. "Let's go."

CHAPTER 17

Edward Barlow held onto his broad-brimmed hat as the helicopter took to the air. The riverbank grasses flattened, and he squinted momentarily as he waited for the whirlwind to abate while the craft lifted away.

He opened his eyes and grabbed his hat to swipe it down his side to dislodge grass, seeds, and dirt. He quickly jammed it back on his sweating head as the sun stung his pate, yet it was still only just past nine in the morning.

Janus Bellakov checked their gear, and already had a rifle thrown over one shoulder with his sidearm strapped to his waist. Bellakov's two men worked tirelessly; Walt Koenig and Arthur Bourke were experienced hunters and trackers, and both had brawny arms hanging from sweat-soaked shirts. Although, truth be known, Bellakov was more mercenary than hunter.

They had been dropped fifty miles southeast of the Canaima National Park, and well into the uncharted areas of the Amazon. The river here was still free-flowing, but only a few dozen feet in from the bank, the walls of the jungle were like a green cliff face.

Barlow had invested in the best mapping technology money could buy and had used the 1908 notes made by Benjamin Cartwright, as well as his hand-drawn maps, to check the geography at the turn of last century to find his launch position. He also made use of the observations the young Ben Cartwright had made in his own notes, and these too had proved invaluable.

The software had pinpointed this area, and the small clearing was as close as he could get. Further inland, the visibility vanished in thick tree canopy cover and low clouds that obscured everything below it. Somewhere in there were rocky slopes, large plains of towering tree ferns, low hills, and also spongy swamps.

Barlow smiled. Nature hid her secrets well. But he was determined, and unfortunately for nature, now he was here.

Bellakov and his two men hefted the packs onto the shoulders. Barlow just hefted his own considerable bulk. He guessed by now Cartwright would be on the ground.

Barlow knew his job was simple: get there first and claim whatever discovery as his own. His guns for hire would ensure there was no protracted negotiations or disagreements. Of that he was sure. The boys weren't afraid to dish out a bit of violence when it was necessary. He turned to them.

"Mr. Bellakov, please lead us out."

"You got it, boss." Bellakov drew a long machete and headed in.

CHAPTER 18

The boat was about fifty feet long, belched diesel, and probably hadn't had a coat of paint in too many years to think about. The captain was a round-faced man who smoked like a chimney, causing the teeth on one side of his mouth to be an interesting shade of chocolate brown. He also had a squint that'd make Popeye envious from holding his unrecognizable brand of cigarette clamped between pressed lips.

Also onboard was their Venezuelan guide, Nino Santiago. The wiry young man was someone recommended to Jenny by the local zoo, and who was reputed to know most parts of the jungle on or off the map. He'd been responsible for assisting the zoo in locating many of the harder to find species they needed to stock exhibits, and the expectation was that he could find what others couldn't.

The boat ride down the Rio Caroni was faster than Ben expected as they moved with the flow. Still, the antique engine chugged hard, and he, Emma, and Steve were up on the front deck, while Dan, Andrea, and Jenny were either below or out at the rear. Nino chatted with the captain.

Hours back, the last of the small fishing boats had vanished, and now only occasionally they saw a canoe or fishing platform, which was little more than a raft of lashed logs. One of the reasons for the growing isolation on the waterway was that as they entered more remote parts of the Amazon, the crocodiles got bigger and fishing became more a high-risk game.

They also noticed the water also got darker, to the color of coffee, and smelled of decomposition and earth, as it was stained by the tannins from all the rotting vegetation that fell into it.

In another hour, the boat slowed and turned towards the left bank. Ben marveled at the captain's navigation skills as to him the river had been nothing but identical green walls for many miles, but sure enough, there was a side river with three long canoes already waiting and just tied off on the bank.

"Did you call an Amazonian taxi cab?" Emma grinned.

He chuckled. "Hats off to Jenny for her organizational skills – everything's going to plan so far."

The big boat turned off its engine and a deckhand scrambled up on deck, lifting a long, slim barge pole to slow them to a stop and then jamming it into the river bottom to anchor them close enough to the shore so they could all jump free.

Once again, Dan paid the man in dollars, and Jenny also handed him a few mini bottles of scotch she bought from the hotel.

"What's with the firewater?" Steve asked.

Jenny shrugged. "Universal sign of gratitude down here."

"Remember, señor, we wish the captain to be here when we come back." Nino agreed. "Or it will be an extra five-day trek back to base."

Ben leapt to the shore and turned to help Emma down, but she had already landed beside him.

She grinned. "I do this for a living, buster."

He grinned back. "Then you should have helped me down."

Dan jumped down and stumbled a little. He righted himself and brushed mud from one of his gaiters.

"Like armor plating." He grimaced.

"Yep, exactly," Ben responded.

The snake gaiters were a snake shield worn on the lower leg, from knee to foot, and the ones Ben had chosen for them were constructed from a weave of high-strength ballistic fibers and polyester. They even had a top-of-foot guard.

Dan grinned. "I'm getting used to them. *Slowly.*"

"You'll be glad of 'em when we push in." Ben scanned the dense wall of jungle. "Down here, they've got more venomous pit vipers than anywhere else in the world. Plus a big mother called a Bushmaster – 10 feet, long-fanged, and venomous as all hell, and will actually chase you down to bite you." He turned back to Dan. "Thank me for that armor plating if you ever walk into one of those."

"Not complaining." Dan grinned back.

Ben sighed. *Really, they had no idea what they were in for*, he thought. As well as the gaiters, he'd also had Dan order them bush knives, rain ponchos, head nets that fit over their hats and hung down to their necks, plus full nets for sleeping, as well as hammocks so if they needed to stay up off damp or insect-infested ground, they could.

Last and most importantly they all got Coyote Tactical Gloves. In a jungle, hands were something you used a lot but were extremely vulnerable. The gloves he ordered were rubber backed, canvas front with leather patches over the meaty areas of the palm. They were tough, durable, and light; you could climb, shoot, scale a fish, and then rinse 'em out afterwards to be good as new.

Everything they had was impregnated with Permethrin to keep creepy crawlies from sneaking into their packs, or just plain eating them down to nothing.

He saw Andrea wave at an insect that refused to leave her alone. He sighed. "Andrea, have you put on your repellent?"

"Um, just on my shirt." She walked stiff-legged up the bank in her snake gaiters.

"Put it on, all over you, please, or at least put the netting over your head." Ben's mouth set in a line.

"But I read it's got DEET in it." She sniffed. "And that's poison."

"Sure, but more poisonous to the bugs. It's military-grade insect repellent, and yeah, it's loaded with DEET. It's not something you'd want to wear all the time, but even the CDC uses it." Ben placed his hands on his hips. "Just don't spray it in your eyes or get it in your mouth, and you'll be fine."

He saw she didn't look convinced.

"C'mon, Andy, this isn't Florida in June, this is the jungle," Steve implored. "If you get bitten down here, you won't end up with just a tiny red spot; you're liable to end up pretty damn sick."

"How about *Leishmania* parasite?" Ben said evenly. "Spread by sandfly bites. Causes large rotting ulcers on the flesh, and especially likes the nose and mouth."

Andrea stopped and turned to stare for a moment. "Okay, okay." Her eyes rolled and she exhaled in a big sigh. "Steve, can you *please* help me put some on then?"

"Sure." He trotted over to her.

Ben smiled, watching her work her charm on him. For now, he'd hold back on telling them about everything that could bite, sting, or infest them. But he'd be providing some rapid education as they went.

The packs were still being unloaded and Ben walked a few hundred feet further along the bank. Both the jungle and the water became darker the further in he went. The smell of the water was like a warm heady brew of compositing, loamy earth, bracken, mosses, and then as a scent layer above it there was the ever-present sweet nectar from exotic-looking flowers, with the chemical tang of plant sap.

Clouds of insects swarmed around him but kept their distance thanks to a lathering of repellent he wore. Dan appeared beside him.

"So we turn off the main highway, and head down this side-road, huh?"

Ben nodded. "In Benjamin's notebook, he mentioned finding a concealed river; I'm not sure this is it, but it gives us a good idea of what we're looking for." He pointed overhead. The branches were interlocking, and only filtered light streamed through from above. It actually looked like a green tunnel with water at the bottom and even close by the smaller river would have been near invisible. But then again, most of them were.

"This can't be it," Dan said. "Hardly a secret, hidden river if even the captain there knows about it."

"You're probably right," Ben replied. "Their expedition followed a side river for half a day, and then found a smaller tributary they called a *river of paradise*, in a secret opening. That took them many more miles into the interior, well, as far as they could go anyway. Apparently, they had to take to wading when it shallowed out."

"Wading…" Dan grinned. "… in an Amazon river? Oh yeah, good plan."

"Think of it as a dip in a tropical pool." Ben nudged him with an elbow. "Might be no choice if we're to find the landmarks he depicted – a large rock on the shoreline that looked to have been carved. And at the very edge, there was the huge trunk of some sort of tree. He called it an Assai palm and it should be hanging out over the water."

Jenny had joined them, overhearing. "He probably meant Acai palm, but close enough. Problem is, after over a century, don't expect anything much to be left of a tree trunk. Things vanish in this humidity after a few years."

Ben sighed. "Then we better keep our eyes peeled." He pointed. "Looks like our rides are ready to go."

"Oh boy," Dan said, chuckling softly.

The canoes were long, narrow, and looked hewn from a single tree. Crossbeams had been added, and there were several inches of muddy-looking water in each of them.

Ben and Emma took the lead canoe, Dan, Nino, and Jenny next, followed by a grumpy-looking Andrea and Steve at the rear. Their boatmen, local Pemon, were all no more than five feet tall, but well-muscled. Their nut-brown limbs were matched by even darker hair that was cut in a bowl-cut and shaved up at the neck.

In the canoe behind, Ben heard Jenny and Nino chatting to their boatman, but he had no idea how to converse. After a moment, he leaned around Emma and nodded, smiled, and his rower returned the gesture.

"English, *Español?*' Ben raised his eyebrows.

The man just stared. He had a vivid red stripe running from under his fringe, down his forehead and to the tip of his nose. After a moment, he curled his lip and shook his head. Ben refused to at least find out his name. He touched his chest. "*Ben.*" Then reached forward to touch Emma's shoulder. "*Emma.*"

The small man continued to stare as he paddled but then nodded. He took one hand off his oar to touch the center of his own chest. "*Ataca.*" He nodded and tapped again. "*Ataca.*"

Ben and Emma repeated the name, nodding theatrically and

repeating the name. Ataca then pointed to the two other paddlers in the canoes behind them. The first paddler had what looked like long sticks poked right through his earlobes.

Ataca pointed. "*Ipetu.*" He turned, making sure that Emma and Ben understood.

"Ipetu," they repeated.

Ataca grunted, and then pointed to the last canoe paddler, who seemed the oldest of the three, and by the way his jaw sat, possibly had few teeth remaining. "*Mukmet.*"

"Mukmet," Ben and Emma repeated again.

And then that was it for conversation. From time to time, Ataca would lift his arm to point at something or other off in the brush, but after a while, the canopy closed in even tighter overhead, and the jungle got gloomy with only occasional bars of light penetrating through to the steaming, coffee-colored water.

Though the sunlight was heavily filtered, the humidity was not, and there seemed to be a mist threading its way along the jungle floor that was strangely devoid of vegetation. Large tree trunks acted as columns to a canopy a hundred feet above their heads, and giant fingered epiphyte plants clung to forks in trees and knots in the bark to give the appearance of broken, green umbrellas hung up after a heavy storm.

Above them, things moved about, shaking limbs, occasionally screaming their fear or anger at the intrusion. Discarded berries, leaves, and possibly dung rained down, but whether it was a band of monkeys, birds, or some other climbing species, they remained invisible to them.

Emma trailed a hand in the water for a moment and lifted it out to rub her thumb and fingers together. "Like a warm, gritty bath," she said and went to dip her hand back in.

"Uh-uh." Ataca waved a hand at her, one finger up. He shook his head. Emma had already pulled her hand back and watched as the native put his hand towards his mouth and made a show of his teeth biting at it.

Ben nodded. "I'm guessing there's more than just a few goldfish beneath the surface of that soup."

"Got it." Emma gave him a thumbs-up and kept her hands in the canoe from then on.

Ataca slowed his paddling, his eyes shining white and round as the darkness closed in even tighter around them. Ben could see he was becoming fearful and remembered what Jenny had told him about the superstitious nature of the locals. But he also knew that the jungle was home to plenty of physical horrors that could take a life in an instant.

At a narrowing bend in the river, they needed to come in closer to the shoreline. The jungle was at its darkest here and below them the water was the shade of ink. Ben looked over the side, and in some of the shallower places, he saw submerged logs trailing slimy, green beards. Tiny things zigzagged below the surface, and he wasn't sure if they were small fish or some sort of water insect.

Ben squinted into the darkening jungle – some of the tree trunks here were huge, massive columns reaching up to merge with the roof canopy. Others were covered in strangler figs that grew their own lattice up and around the living tree trunks and used their bodies to climb to the sunlight. They eventually choked their host of nutrients and light, and the result was a hollow shell of fig-lattice where the fig survived, but the host tree died and rotted away.

Ben pulled his flashlight from his pack and the others did the same. Shining it over the jungle floor, he saw something the size of a football lump the soil as it burrowed along, never breaking the surface as it searched for food, or hid from the light.

There were also insects and spiders living, hunting, and feeding amongst the matted carpet of debris. Bugs as big as his hand were preyed upon by spiders of even greater size, and he shuddered at the thought of having to break camp at a place like this.

Ben had slept rough in jungles before, and the key thing was to be aware of your environment, check trees overhead and even their trunks, and make damn well sure you were up off the ground. It was surprising how many creatures could burrow up beneath a warm, sleeping body and tap into it for a quick feed.

They paddled for more hours, slowly now, Ataca and the other oarsmen carefully dipping their paddles in, pulling back, and lifting without a sound. Several times, they spotted creatures prospecting on the jungle floor – an anteater, easily seven feet long from pointed snout to the end of its wire-brush stiff tail, probed the leaf detritus. And once, they caused a family of wild boar to pause and stare back with eyes that were way too human.

Ben was tempted to bring one or more down, as he knew that they didn't have the supplies to last the entire journey and living off the land would soon be a priority. But something made him stay his hand, as the thought of letting loose a rifle shot might alert man or beast to their presence – and it wasn't the beasts he was worried about.

More hours passed as they sought out the entrance to the smaller tributary his ancestor had called a *river of paradise*. But the secret opening remained invisible to them.

While they searched, Ben continued to refuse requests to take a break on the bank, hoping that they'd soon come to a more open area or at least a rocky outcrop they could perch upon. Only Jenny agreed with him, as she also knew that the Amazon was a haven for parasites that loved to hitch a ride on their food source.

Burrowing up from out of the soil, from the water, and zooming in from the air, revolting things like the botfly injected the skin with their eggs that hatch into carnivorous grubs that feed on the flesh until they burst free as a fully grown fly, ready to mate, bite, and implant their young into a host, beginning the cycle all over again. But there were worse things that caused permanent damage, such as elephantiasis, where the filarial parasites are transmitted to humans through mosquito bites, causing the limbs or features to swell hideously to gigantic proportions.

There were also flesh-hungry nematodes in the soil that infested internal organs, eyes, and even the brain. All sought out the human body and its flesh and blood as food, as an incubator for their young, or simply as a mobile house.

The canoes bunched up, forming a raft and allowing them all to talk quietly to each other. Nino grimaced. "I have never been this far, and I have never heard of any hidden rivers."

"What about the Pemon?" Ben asked.

"If they know, they're not saying," Jenny said.

"Yeah, we kinda expected that," Emma added.

"It's got to be here," Dan said. "I just feel it."

"That's good enough for me." Steve grinned.

"We push on," Ben said, nodding to Ataca.

They travelled on all day, and Ben's GPS told him that they were somewhere about 52 miles from where they had departed. The jungle had closed in again, and the rods of light that filtered down to them were turning to a muted twilight, indicating they were coming to the end of the day.

The last thing Ben wanted was to be travelling in the darkness, or worse, be forced up onto some damp riverbank.

They glided on in silence for another 30 minutes before Emma straightened and pointed her flashlight.

"*There!*" she shouted.

A huge boulder sat half submerged at the water line, and by the edge of the first rocky outcrop they'd seen for dozens of miles.

"That's it, gotta be." Ben grinned.

Beside the huge rock, the rotted stump of tree poked out half a dozen feet. It was a good four feet round and would have been enormously distinctive when it was alive, perhaps a hundred years ago. *It could well be the tree trunk his great, great grandfather had remarked upon in his notebook*, Ben thought.

"We'll camp for the night on the rocks." Ben turned. "Ataca." He pointed to the shoreline where there were rounded slabs leading into the water.

"Where's the secret river?" Emma asked.

"Good question." Ben craned forward but saw nothing, just a line of rushes between some of the thicker tree trunks, ferns, and bushes. He held up a hand and Ataca dug his paddle in to slow the boat. Ben then saw that the rushes actually bobbed and bent gently towards them. He smiled – there was a water flow coming from behind them.

He pointed again and waved them on. Ataca nodded and paddled deeper on one side of the canoe, steering them to where Ben indicated.

As they passed the huge boulder, Ben looked up at its surface – the carving was there, a huge leering face, faint and though heavily time eroded, still unmistakable.

Behind him, he heard Ataca mumbling and holding onto the amulet that hung around his neck as the boat glided up onto the shore and ground up on the rocks for a moment.

Ben stepped out. He held onto the edge of the canoe and pulled it further up on shore a few feet as he looked from the Pemon to the rock face and back again.

Ataca refused to look at it, but he knew Jenny had been right; superstition ran strong in the Pemon, and this meant something to them. Ben looked back at the carved face. Now that he was up closer, it wasn't human at all, but something with fangs, a scaled face, and slit-pupil eyes.

"Rope," Ben said, holding out his hand.

Emma handed him a length of rope which he tied to the front of the canoe, and then while he was on the bank, dragged the canoe along the rocky edge until he came to the reed barrier, where he tugged it through – he was right – just behind it there was a small hidden river.

Ben straightened. "We'll camp here tonight."

*****

The night was uneventful, and another lathering of repellent plus a healthy fire kept insects, predators, and anything else interested in making a home or meal of them at bay.

Just before they'd turned in, Ben did a quick wide circuit of their camp, looking for anything that might have been a threat to the group. He was as satisfied as he could be, but knew he'd be sleeping light tonight.

Emma had joined him and above them in an opening of the tree canopy, they saw the clouds open momentarily, displaying a dark sky speckled with stars…and something else.

"What is *that*?" Emma asked, frowning.

Ben quickly pulled out his binoculars and pointed them up at the streak. "Weird; looks sorta like a streak of light."

"Meteor?" she asked.

"Maybe, but it's just hanging there." He lowered the glasses. "It's right over us. Well, more sort of to the right hemisphere."

As they watched, the clouds closed over them and the streak of light vanished. Emma put her arm around his waist and they continued to watch for it for a few more minutes before Ben hugged her.

"This whole place is another world," Emma said softly.

"You got that right." He kissed the top of her head. "Come on, let's turn in; going to be a big day tomorrow."

Dawn found them quickly preparing to embark on the next stage of their journey.

"Ben." Steve waved him closer to a place near a tree trunk.

"I was taking a leak and saw this." He pointed at the ground. There was the usual mat of leaf litter, but in an area where the leaves and debris had been kicked aside was the toe print from a large boot.

Ben grunted. "The Pemon don't wear shoes…or have feet that damn big. I'm thinking the guys who took our map are ahead of us." He squatted and touched the soft soil. "Maybe less than half a day."

"Do you think they came by water?" Steve turned back and then craned to try and see further out into the jungle. "And went the same way?"

"Maybe, maybe not. But we better make sure everyone keeps their eyes peeled."

Steve nodded and went to turn away, but Ben reached out to grab his arm.

"And tell 'em to keep all noise to a minimum from now on."

"You got it." Steve headed back to the group.

Ben turned slowly, peering off into the jungle. The smaller river they were going to now enter was already catching some rays of morning light, and it meant that the tree canopy was opening slightly. It was still largely hidden from above, but the type of trees here were of a different variety with thinner canopies. *Thank God*, he thought.

By the time they'd packed up and were ready to go, the sun was a little higher, and they could all now see what was before them.

"Oh my God." Emma put a hand on his shoulder.

Andrea walked forward, her arms out, and turned in a circle. The river here was shallow, of no more than a few feet, as well as being crystal clear. Where the river they had come from was dark coffee, this looked mountain-stream pure.

Unlike the previous river, each bank of the clear stream was covered with mossy rocks, orchids of all kinds and many of a hue that reminded Ben of tiny tropical birds that had come to land on the green, strappy leaves. Palm fronds dripped with dew, green-and-red striped frogs croaked, and dragonflies hummed low over the water's surface.

"It's beautiful," Emma observed and turned to grin up at him. Her eyes were luminous with excitement. "A *river of paradise,* just like your ancestor said it would be."

"He was right," Ben agreed, but then smiled. "At least about this."

As the sun rose, they took to the canoes again. The sunlight began to stream down in earnest, finding a million holes in the canopy overhead. It made the river and surrounding jungle look like some sort of giant garden pergola and leafy archway wending away for miles.

"It *is* a paradise; seems there are still a few Gardens of Eden still to be found in the world just yet," Emma added.

In the canoes behind, he saw Steve holding up a camera and filming Andrea who pouted, posed, and waved for his lens. Ben grinned; seemed the actress was true to her word and was going after maximum exposure from the trip.

The lightening of the jungle made Ben feel more at ease than he had in days. It was easy to forget they were still in the dark heart of the Amazon as they moved up a shallow sandy-bottomed stream that seemed about as dangerous as a manicured Boston garden in springtime.

He let his eyes wander from bank to bank, conscious of the fact that there was another party, and a violent one, out there somewhere. But the visibility was good for hundreds of feet, and even if the stream ended, there were huge areas of meadow-like grass that would have made travelling on foot a pleasure.

Underneath the roof-like canopy, tiny birds shot past them that were like feathered rainbows, and Ben looked at Emma, whose face was lit with wonder. She turned to him and her expression clouded.

"It's so beautiful, but why aren't there any people here?"

"Yeah, good question," he replied. "Hardly an inhospitable place, is it?" He looked briefly at Ataca, but decided the question was way too hard to try and act out with his hands so he leaned out the side of the canoe.

"Jenny, question for our guides."

She raised her chin. "Ask away."

"This area – why isn't there any Pemon, or anyone, here?" He waited as Jenny translated the question to their paddler, Ipetu.

Ipetu spoke softly but urgently in return. While he spoke, he noticed that Ataca's hand had snuck back to the amulet around his neck. In another moment, Jenny leaned back out to him.

"Taboo; this is a place of bad spirits. Some have come here in the past. But then they never come back home." She grimaced. "And bad news; sounds like our drivers are starting to get cold feet."

Ben nodded. "Thank him, and thank all of them for their courage. And Jenny, try and hang onto them for as long as we can. Though walking looks easy here, we're making good time on the stream."

They paddled for another few hours, stopped for some lunch, and then rejoined the stream again. Ben looked over the side and after the journey on the dark and foul-smelling main river, he was delighted to see that the clear water here was filled with fish.

Silver torpedo shapes darted close to the surface as they tried to pick off overly adventurous dragonflies. Other fish just hung in the crystal clear water without fear of humans at all.

It didn't make sense. *Taboo*, they'd told Jenny. Ben guessed it must have been pretty powerful magic to keep the local population out of a bountiful place like this.

The scenery was exactly like how Benjamin had described it in his notebook, and Ben only wished he could go back in time. He wanted to be standing on the bank and watch the face of his ancestor as he came along this very stream. Would he be open-mouthed in wonder, or so exhausted by now that it was only a respite from all the hard travelling he had accomplished? Back then, there would have been no air travel or luxury hotels at the edge of the jungle. But instead, a hacking, chopping and strength-draining slog every inch of the way.

After another hour or two, the sunlight began to vanish, and checking his wristwatch, Ben was confused to see it was still only four in the afternoon and many hours until sundown. Looking overhead, he didn't discern any great thickening of the canopy, and also the jungle had gone from its bright gaiety to a more somber silence – even the once ever-present rainbow birds were now missing.

They glided on for a few more moments before he noticed that Ataca had stopped paddling. He clutched at the amulet pouch around his neck and turned about, scanning the bank for a moment before then turning back to meet Ben's eyes.

He spoke rapidly in his local tongue and then both waved a hand and shook his head for emphasis.

Ben groaned, and looking over the Pemon's shoulder, he saw that Ipetu in the next canoe seemed to be having the same conversation with Jenny and Nino, both animated as they probably pleaded with him.

After another moment, the man made a rapid horizontal slicing motion in the air with his hand and said with significant force probably one of the only words in English he knew, and one he knew they would understand:

"*No!*"

Nino turned to Jenny and shrugged, and the zoologist eased back and nodded. She smiled and spoke softly to him, and the Pemon man's face softened, even though his eyes were still resolute. He nodded and paddled the canoe closer. At the rear of their canoe, Mukmet also brought in Steve and Andrea until all three boats were together.

Jenny reached out for the side of Ben's canoe and smiled with resignation, or perhaps surrender. "This is as far as they'll go. This now…" she waved an arm, "… is the land of the *boraro, cherruves,* and *churipuri,* you name it; *all* demons."

"Oh fucking great," Dan said softly.

"Yeah, I know, but what looks like a tropical paradise to us, is the start of the wettest season, they call *Xincceheka.*" Jenny looked up as she worked on a suitable translation for the Pemon word. "Dark Lands."

"*The season of the Dark Lands?*" Dan's frown deepened. "What does that even mean?"

Jenny spoke softly to Ipetu again, who leaned closer to her and whispered in return as if afraid of being overheard. Jenny nodded her understanding. "The elders have told them that this is the time of the demons. In this year, the wettest year, it is foretold that the jungle in this area is not safe." She half smiled but there was little humor in it. "They have quite accurate calendars."

Ipetu spoke again, even more urgently, and Jenny frowned as she concentrated. She nodded and turned to the group. "Once every half lifetime, the land here belongs to the gods. It becomes their kingdom."

"That's it," Emma said. "It's got to be all tied in with what your ancestor wrote about the window of opportunity when the hidden place was able to be found."

"And when the hidden place can be found, that's when the demons are about." Steve raised his eyebrows. "Anyone else thinking of Benjamin's pencil drawings of the dinosaurian?"

"The kingdom of the gods." Ben sucked in a breath.

"Sounds ominous," Steve said. "But at least it tells us we're heading in the right direction."

"Yeah, there's that," Ben said. "Jenny, will the Pemon be here when we return?"

"Good question." She immediately began to speak to Ipetu, who looked from Mukmet and Ataca, back to her. He shook his head and Jenny turned to him.

"It's okay, I got it," Ben said. "Then ask, no, *tell him* to leave two of the canoes."

Jenny nodded and then straightened. She spoke forcefully.

The bickering went on for several moments, with Ataca leaning closer to her and raising a single figure in the air. Jenny shook her head, pleading, cajoling, and then demanding. Finally, she tilted her head and spoke softly. Ipetu looked from Ataca then to Mukmet; both men nodded.

Ben grinned. "You got both canoes?"

"Yes, not easy, and I had to trade." She shrugged. "Two bush knives, a machete, and…one of the spare revolvers."

Ben didn't even have to think about it. "Done; trekking back would take us weeks… if we made it at all." He looked around. "Let's pull into the bank and unload."

In another moment, they were all on the bank, gear beside them. The three Pemon were now in a single canoe and paddled back down the clear river. The other two canoes had been pulled up, safe and dry.

Ben had a strange sinking feeling as he watched them depart – the natives knew something they didn't, and he hoped it was only superstition. He turned to the group.

"Okay, we've gone far enough for today, so let's camp here, rest, and make an early start."

*****

Palm fronds lashed his face and sticky vines tried to rope his arms, legs and torso. In firefights in the deserts of the Middle East, Congolese jungles, or urban labyrinths, Ben had feared nothing and no one.

But now, big Ben Cartwright whimpered as he ran – the thing was gaining on him, flattening undergrowth and knocking down trees as if they were kindling.

Where was everyone else? he wondered, trying to remember. Then he did – *all dead, massacred, eaten alive*, a small voice jeered back at him.

The jungle suddenly opened out onto a cloud-filled vista, and he braked hard, his feet skidding on loose gravel right to the cliff edge. Below, the jungle looked like the tops of broccoli, over a thousand feet below him.

Behind him, a blood-freezing noise made the hair rise on his head and neck, and he turned, eyes wide and teeth showing in a grimace of fear.

Instinctively, Ben's hand slapped down on his holster – it was empty. The thing burst from the jungle.

"*Jesus!*"

Ben jerked upright from his bed roll.

"Hey? You okay?" Emma sat up, rubbing her face, and then turned to stare into his. "It sounded like you were, *crying.*"

"Nah." He snorted the thought away. "I'm okay, just..." He also rubbed his face and felt his eyes were wet. "Nah, it's nothing."

"Nino," he called.

"Si?" Their Venezuelan guide was already up and fastening away his bedroll.

"Gather some firewood; I'll try and catch us some of those fish for breakfast." Ben got to his feet, and then also rolled up his mat. He reached into his pack, took out his mosquito netting, and tucked it under his arm.

"Want some help?" Emma asked.

Ben smiled. "An outdoor woman like you can help kick-start that fire. That'll help. Also, get everyone up and ready – going to be a long day."

She scoffed but agreed.

Ben walked up along the bank for a few hundred feet, noticing that the sandy bottom was starting to discolor the further up he went. Also, it began to shallow out even more, and would have made traversing it by canoe impossible anyway. In amongst the shallows, there were still a few pools where brightly colored fish, tiger-striped in red and blue, darted about, all the size of a medium trout.

He laid the netting on the downstream side of one of the pools, allowing a belly to be created in the mesh. He then moved upstream and used a long stick to chase some of the fish towards his trap. In just a few minutes, he had a good haul and dragged them out. He grinned at his luck; *if only it was this easy back home*, he thought.

Ben started to head back, but then paused, his brows knitting – on the riverbank, there were strange tracks. Almost like from a weird truck tire that had rolled over the sand. They were nearly a foot wide and continued on for a while before disappearing into the water. He crouched, looking at the impressions – they weren't old, maybe only days.

Rain started to patter heavily about him, filling the tracks. He put two fingers into one, feeling their depth. *What the hell made them?* he wondered.

Ben looked over his shoulder into the jungle, wary now. When he turned back, he saw Jenny wandering about and raised an arm to call her over. He looked back down at the tracks; the Pemon had said that in the past some foolish natives had come here, but they never come back. He lifted his fingers to his nose and rubbed them together, but there was no scent on them.

"What have you got?" Jenny asked and crouched beside him.

"Tracks, I think."

She smiled down at the markings in the dirt. "Big fella." She turned to him. "Probably *Eunectes murinus* – green anaconda."

"Jesus, these tracks are from a snake?" Ben blew air through his lips.

"Yeah, they can grow to 18 feet and weigh in at 250 pounds." She looked around, and then into the tree canopy overhead. "And they lo-*ooove* water."

"Dangerous?" Ben got to his feet.

Jenny followed him up. "Not to us, here and now. But if you were weak or sick, and they came across you when you were sleeping, they might try and swallow you...after pulverizing you down to mush."

"Nice; so not a total paradise here after all." He gave her a lopsided grin.

"Don't you read your Bible? There's a snake in every Garden of Eden, remember?" She winked.

Ben chuckled. "Let's hope there's only one then. Let's go."

By the time they returned, everyone was gathered around the morning fire. Coffee was being brewed, so he used his knife to clean the fish and thread them onto poles. He handed one to each.

"No silver service, I'm afraid."

The cooked meat was delicious, if not a little blackened on the outside. They still had some rations left, but this was the first live game they'd caught and eaten. From now on, Ben would try and have them live off the land and preserve what they had left.

In another 30 minutes, they were on their way again following the stream, the bank being a natural pathway. For hours, they watched the stream first shallow, with some grasses threading their way to the surface, and then islands of sand rising in its center. In only a little more time, the stream bottom broke the surface and turned from sand to mud, and then to sludge.

There were no more fish, no more darting rainbow birds, or even iridescent winged dragonflies. The abundant life forms now only seemed to be swarming gnats. Underfoot, the sandy ground had also changed – the bank had vanished and their feet squelched in mud and slid on oily mosses. The air began to steam up with the smell of methane and corruption.

It seemed paradise had come to an end, Ben thought. But it was when the mud became bog that Ben began to worry.

Gas bubbles popped to the surface with an eggy-sulphurous smell, and the humidity made the perspiration run from them in dripping streams that never dried. Added to that, the mud got deeper, and the snake gaiters became traps for pounds of sticky mud that made every step an energy-draining experience.

Dan stumbled and reached out a hand to some vines but immediately yelled his agony. "Jesus." He went to pull his hand back, but the vine came with him. "Fucking thorns."

He pulled out his knife and hacked away at it, then had to carefully pick the woody stem from his gloves. Jenny squelched her way towards him and took it from him. She held it up.

"Cat's claw vine." She turned to him. "Pierce your gloves?"

Dan grimaced and had his glove peeled down. "Bastards went straight through."

"Yeah." She held it out, showing him the half-inch hooks at the base of each leaf stem. "Evolved to stop them from being eaten. But they're big and sharp enough to pierce boot leather."

"Okay, spray it, slap a bandage on it, and let's keep moving." Ben waved them on.

Dan held up his bleeding hand. "Little sympathy here."

Jenny quickly leaned in and kissed his cheek. "There, all better now?" She tossed the vine out and away from them.

By late morning, the drizzle continued, and in the spaces between the overhead branches, there was only a thick cloud cover showing. Steve was now taking his turn leading them out. He was also the first one into the heavy bog.

"Crap." He tried to pull on his legs, but they were mired to the knees. He grunted and managed to lift one leg up, but it forced the other deeper.

Ben was only about twenty feet behind him and came as fast as he could but stopped before the oily-looking area Steve had wallowed into.

"Lay flat," Ben said. "Might be quick mud."

"Ah, Jesus." Steve turned about, obviously not wanting to get coated in the oily sludge. Close by was a tree with one limb hanging out fairly close to him. So instead, he strained to reach it.

"*Stop there!*" Ben yelled, freezing the man.

By now, the group had hauled themselves closer but also froze. Ben pointed to the man. "Lower your hand, and lay flat, *now*." He followed the tree branch up the limb and then higher.

Steve did as he was asked, lying out on his belly. "What? What is it?"

Jenny narrowed her eyes. "Bullet ants…in the tree. Very bad."

Ben had spotted the machine-like insects on the tree limb – he'd met them before, and Jenny's summation of *very bad* didn't even begin to describe the little monsters. The inch-long ants had enormous jaws and a sting that felt like an electric shock. Their nests were usually on the ground, but they spent their time in tree canopies. Any perceived threat to the ants, the nest, or the trees, elicited an overwhelming and sometimes deadly attack.

Steve was just a head and neck showing now, and he tried to turn to look up at the branch. "Do they –?"

"Yes, and damn painfully." Ben dropped his pack in the sludge and pulled it open, dragging out some rope. "You grab that branch, they'd swarm down onto you."

He threw one end to Steve and handed the rest to the team. "Stay flat and swim towards us." He half turned. "On three, two, one…*heave.*" They tugged, sliding Steve out of the bog.

The young carpenter got to his feet, coated in the thick, oily mess. "Thanks." He scowled as he wiped himself down. "Nothing a shower and a couple of margaritas won't fix." He held something up that was dripping with mud.

Andrea giggled, and Steve immediately brightened. "What did you find?" she asked.

Ben shook his head. *Great idea; take a team of novices into the Amazon – what could possibly go wrong?* he thought.

"There was something in there," Steve said, showing them what looked like a broken bowl.

"Let me see that," Jenny said, pushing forward.

Steve scraped more mud from the shard and handed it to her. Jenny got her water bottle and splashed some on it.

"Hey," Ben said sharply.

"Just a bit," Jenny said, rubbing at the pottery, and then holding it in front of her face. "Old, very old."

Dan grinned. "You just found yourself a souvenir, buddy."

Steve wiped more greasy mud down from his shirt. "Yeah, definitely worth it."

"So, there *were* people here once," Emma said.

"A long time ago maybe," Jenny replied distractedly. "This looks Mayan, but not as stylized. It's more primitive."

"*More* primitive?" Dan scoffed. "I thought those guys were first here about 4,000 years ago. How could it be more primitive than that?"

"Maybe it's not. Maybe they were here after the Mayans – a separate race." Jenny rubbed more of the mud from the images carved into the bowl.

Ben came in closer and saw there were small figures, many tied together by ropes around their necks. They were being herded towards some sort of large slit-eyed gargoyle thing.

"Reminds me a little of the carving on the rock face in the stream. Might be the same people."

"Long gone now, I'd say." Emma looked around. "Might have been washed down from somewhere."

Jenny handed the pottery back to Steve. "Well, someone had to be here originally to start all the myth-making."

Steve took the bowl and went to take his pack off his shoulders, but Ben shook his head.

"Leave it, Steve. You don't need the extra weight right now."

"*Aww.*" He looked at it again. "Might be valuable."

"And if it is, then our antiquities department will never let you take it from our country." Nino shrugged. "Sorry."

"I'll pay any duties on it," Dan said. "He swam in quick mud to rescue that; he deserves it."

"Yep." Steve searched for a moment and then selected a large tree where he placed the bowl at its base. "I'll see you on the way back."

"Finished?" Ben sighed and then waved them on. "Come on, and everyone keep their wits about them, and touch…"

"*Nothing,*" they said back in unison.

In another hour, Ben broke from the swamp and out into a landscape of tree ferns that reached onward and gradually upward into the distance. He shook off his backpack and gloves, and wiped his brow. Even with his large and battle-hardened frame, he felt a little dizzy with fatigue.

"See here." Nino crouched just at the edge of the forest. There was a ring of stones, and at its center burned remains of a fire as well as some fish bones. He dipped fingers into the ash and rubbed them together for a moment before standing.

"Less than half a day." He walked slowly around the stones, contemplating the ground. "Three, four people, all big men."

Ben pulled out some field glasses and surveyed the distance. There was nothing showing, but even though they were leaving the canopy cover of the jungle, the plain of tree ferns still grew to a height of about 10 feet, throwing out broad umbrella-like fronds.

"This was their camp before they headed off up the slope. We're not far behind." He put his glasses back in their pouch. "But means they're in front of us."

"Question?" Dan held up a finger. "What happens when we actually catch up to them…or them to us?"

Ben grinned. "That all depends on whether they're the ones who have my map."

"Oh yeah." Dan saluted with a grin. "Then you're in charge of negotiations."

The slope became steeper, and the climb more energy sapping. After another few hours, it leveled back out and they took a quick break. Looking back down from where they had just climbed, they could see the near endless jungle from which they had just trekked. As Ben expected, though they had traversed a river and stream for many miles, both were invisible below, and the jungle looked dense and unbroken.

"Hey." Steve had out his GPS and turned one way, then the other. "Same with my compass."

"What's up?" Emma asked.

"Look." He held out the device. "It says signal interruption. And the compass is just going haywire."

They crowded around, all offering advice, suggestions, and possible solutions.

"Oh shit." Ben quickly tried his phone and found that there was no reception, even though he should've been able to pick up any communication satellite anywhere with the new phone he specially obtained. "No signal on the phones as well. What the hell's going on?"

Dan put his hands on his hips and turned about. "I can make a few educated guesses based on spot signal black outs in remote areas." He turned to face them. "Signal jamming, shielding, or my favorite guess, a meteorite."

"Huh?" Steve's brows came together. "Did you say *meteorite*?"

"Yep." Dan shrugged. "There's a phenomenon that occurs sometimes where a large iron-based meteorite or meteorite fragments are scattered about – it can partially, or totally, disrupt signals. All I'm saying is, that maybe millions of years ago, it fell to earth and the entire mass is buried here, creating a slightly magnetic field and disrupting our signals."

Dan looked up. "You know, if it's this strong, it'd also cause a grey zone on satellite imagery." He chuckled. "And that is real cool."

The rain started to fall again, heavier. Andrea looked miserable. "Why?" she asked. "Why is it cool?"

He turned to her. "Because it means that with satellite blackout, and the remoteness, and the superstition keeping the locals away, and also that permanent cloud cover, means this place simply doesn't exist on any map. We're invisible."

"But it does," Jenny said. "This place has been mapped before. There *are* satellite images."

"It only happens every 10 years," Emma added. "So not something permanent."

There was silence for a few moments before Ben grunted. "Maybe not in the wettest months...every 10 years or so." He turned his head slightly. "In the notebook, Benjamin remarked that there was a window of opportunity when the hidden place was able to be found. Could this weird magnetic thing have any bearing on that?"

"No." Dan's mouth was turned down.

"Yes," Emma shot back. "I think Dan might be partially right."

Dan's brows went up. "Oh yeah?"

Emma folded her arms. "What if it's not a meteorite, but a comet? What if the effects are being felt, but it never actually crashed here, but was just passing by." She grinned. "Like once every 10 years."

"Fucking brilliant." Dan clapped. "That could do it. Especially if this is the absolute closest point on the Earth where it makes its pass, or apparition as they call it. This is the focal disruption point. Maybe it creates some sort of humungous magnetic storm."

"Passes once every 10 years and generates a *humongous* magnetic storm, giving this place the wettest of months." Ben thought it through as something nagged at him.

"Sure, I mean there are hundreds of comets shooting through our solar system. They are swung from the sun, they return, and then head back out after a few days." Dan's eyes were bright now.

"*Must hurry, only days until Primordia returns,*" Ben said softly. He looked up. "That was a notation in Benjamin's notebook."

"*Yes.*" Dan pointed at Ben's chest. "They give comets two names; a scientific name, and a nickname. I bet Primordia is the name of the comet that returns once every 10 years – he only had days until it was returning."

"Like it did for Benjamin in 1908." Ben turned to Emma. "We saw it; the streak in the sky."

"Oh shit; you're right. It must have been the comet's tail." Her mouth hung open.

"It's called a coma," Dan said. "So, it *is* a comet."

"And now it's back again for us in 2018." Steve held his arms wide. "We're here at the right time." He held his hand out, letting raindrops fall onto it. "The wettest season."

"This is *so* cool." Andrea clapped her small hands.

Ben pulled out his long bush knife and slashed it into the trunk of a large tree several times, marking an arrowhead formation. "From now on, we'll need to blaze a trail. With no compass, GPS, stars or sun to follow, we've only got line of sight." He looked back out at the jungle.

"Getting lost in here will be a fast trip to hell."

After another few hours, the ground leveled out a little more and once again, the jungle started closing in. Andrea continually complained now, of being tired, having sore feet, of her thirst and headache. She also seemed to be turning Steve into her personal servant. Ben smiled. Perhaps Steve didn't mind at all.

The tree trunks started to get closer together, and once again, the ever-present vines started to slow their progress. Ben turned to see Jenny had stopped to examine a peculiar-looking tree trunk. She squinted at it, and Ben raised a hand to call a halt.

"Jenny?"

She stepped back, craning her neck up the length of the trunk, and then simply pointed at it. "Impossible."

Ben sucked in a breath and crossed to her. "What is?"

"This." Her eyes gleamed.

Ben looked at the trunk; it had curious bark that was growing in segments like overlapping shingles. It was about 3 feet around the trunk, and it rose a good fifty feet into the air, where it sported only sparse branches and leaves that were flat and more like grass.

"Never seen it before." He shrugged. "But then, I don't think I've seen 90% of the plants down here before. Nino?"

The Venezuelan glanced at it and hiked his shoulders. "No, Señor Ben, never seen it before."

"You're right, you haven't, and neither have I, or for that matter, neither has anyone in modern times." Jenny took a picture. "I think it's a *Lepidodendron*; also known as the scale tree." She turned to him. "And the reason you haven't seen them before is the same reason no one has seen one before – they're Carboniferous Period remnants and been extinct for over 100 million years."

"So, old, huh?" Steve joined them and put a hand against the bark, and then rapped on it with his knuckles. "Feels soft. Not like wood at all."

"That's right," Jenny said. "Because they weren't like true trees, and probably more closely related to club mosses or quillworts." She smiled. "You only ever see these guys now as coal."

Emma turned about. "There's quite a few of them here; maybe this is where they survived."

"Unlikely." Jenny pulled out her field glasses, but there was nothing to see through the dense foliage and cloud cover. "Modern competition wiped them out. They must survive somewhere else. They reproduce by spores and so probably would have blown in from somewhere else."

"Or floated down. From where they've survived untouched for

millions of years," Dan added with a grin. "We *must* be *so* close."

The rain eased, then stopped as if a tap had been turned.

"Let's take five while we have a break in the weather. Grab something to eat," Ben said and found a rock to sit down on. He opened the notebook and leafed through the pages. Emma came and sat beside him.

"What does Benjamin the 1st have to say?"

"He also says we're close... I think." He looked up and over her head. "We can't see much with all this low cloud. But somewhere around here is the foot of the plateau, and also some sort of temple he mentions."

Emma sighed. "You do know that even if we do find this plateau, it's going to be difficult to climb. These things are usually sheer faces, and at least a thousand feet straight up. I, you, maybe Steve, could get up there, but I'm not so sure about the others."

"I thought about that. We also don't have that much rope, and I doubt Steve and I could do a free climb of that distance." Ben gave her a half smile. "Best laid plans and all that."

"Let's just hope there's a place that's not too high and easy to climb." She smiled. "After all, I doubt your ancestor was an experienced climber."

"Hope you're right. But remember, if there were an easy way up or down, then there wouldn't be any isolation of the things that supposedly live up there – according to Benjamin, it was supposed to have formed a perfect barrier against anything climbing up, or scaling down." Ben got to his feet and held out a hand.

Emma grabbed it and hauled herself up. "I guess if we find the plateau, that's something. But if we don't get to the top, we'll never know if it's the right one."

"We'll get to the top," Ben said confidently. "One way or the other, we're getting up there."

"Or at least a few of us will," Emma added.

Ben squeezed her hand. "And no, you're not going up by yourself."

"Yes, Dad." She grinned back.

The group marched on in silence. The rain set in again, and the jungle was thickening with all manner of strange plants that eluded all of Jenny's attempts at identification. Pushing aside some fronds, Dan yelled in triumph and ran a few feet forward.

"*Ha*." He turned and pointed. "The cliffs."

Like the rest, Ben couldn't help running through the ferns and vines to break through and see the orange-pink walls just peeking through the jungle. Their tops were lost in the ever-present low cloud, but he couldn't stop the grin from splitting his face.

"*Oh yeah!*" He walked forward, looking one way then the next along the impressive sight. To their left, a waterfall tipped water from somewhere high above them to change to sparkling diamonds in the diffuse light. Both ways, the cliffs continued on until they vanished in the distance without any sign of them curving.

"It's freaking huge," Jenny said.

"I cannot climb this," Nino said, looking pale. "Maybe those who do not climb should wait here."

Ben nodded. "No one has to climb if they don't want to."

"That's right, buddy. Feel free to miss out on all the fame, glory, and whatever amazing things we find up there." Dan jiggled his eyebrows

Nino frowned. "There will be treasure?"

"No, unlikely," Emma said. "Don't listen to him."

"But we don't know exactly what's up there now do we, hmm?" Dan replied. "So, *could be* treasure."

Ben turned to Nino. "You don't have to go up." He looked skywards. "And frankly, unless we find an easier way up there, no one's going anywhere." Ben pointed along the leftward cliff edge. "I think this way."

"Where to?" Steve asked.

"To an easier way up, I hope," Ben responded.

*****

Edward Barlow and his men were invisible in amongst the dense foliage. A small smile played on his lips as he eased his head around to watch as Janus Bellakov held small field glasses to his eyes even though they were only a few dozen feet from the Cartwright party as they approached – it didn't matter as the blunderers made so much noise they masked any and all approach.

Barlow didn't want any of them hurt; in fact, he needed them. The maps they had been following had now come to an end, and he cursed the bumpkins he had paid to retrieve the information. He had specified *the notebook*, and they had only brought him the notes.

He sighed; it was so hard to get good help, even in amongst the so-called *specialty pool*.

He watched as the group moved past, and his eyes narrowed. They needed to take care with the ex-soldier leading them on. Cartwright was a formidable man and only he presented any real problem – even Mr. Bellakov recognized it.

So Cartwright needed to be neutralised first.

CHAPTER 19

"We found it!" Emma yelled and plunged forward.

Ben chased after her, but then stopped dead and just stood with open mouth. There was a structure; temple-like, set into the side of a sheer rock face that vanished up into the clouds high above them. Holding it in a muscular embrace were gnarled tree roots as thick as his waist.

"Shit," he breathed out. "It's real." The heavy cut stonework was moss-green with age, and everything about it exuded artistry, antiquity, and reverence.

"And so, here it is," Dan whispered, but then threw his head back and whooped.

Ben dragged out his great, great grandfather's notebook and looked from the sketch his ancestor had made to the prehistoric structure – it was exactly like in the pencil image – everything was there; the massive tree trunk that had thrown gnarled roots over moss-covered foundation stones, the tumbled blocks, as well as the stone guards, acting as a pair of monstrous sentinels.

"Holy crap," Steve said, walking towards the colossal structure.

"Careful," Jenny said.

"Huh?" Steve turned briefly to her. "Sure." He turned back to the statues. They reared up, fanged mouths open. "Hey, no wonder our guides took to the hills; this is some scary shit."

The ten-foot-high stone statues seemed to be two creatures, sort of intertwined. One was something that resembled a two-legged beast, huge mouth open as if in defiance or pain, as another monstrous creature with a long muscular body wrapped around it. Its fangs were long broken off, but they must have jutted down like twin daggers. It was finished with a pair of large unblinking eyes with slit pupils.

"Some scary shit is right." Jenny looked skyward; high above them the clouds seemed to be lifting, and hints of green could just be made out flowing over the cliff edge. She smiled. "I'll bet a month's salary that up there is where those ancient tree spores came from…and everything else that's unidentifiable down here."

Ben had his hands on his hips, following her gaze. "Well then, we better find a way up."

PART 2 – THE LOST WORLD

So tomorrow we disappear into the unknown — Arthur Conan Doyle, The Lost World

Ben finally pulled his rifle from over his shoulder and carried it cradled in his arms. On seeing him do this, Dan also drew his gun. But Ben waved it away.

"For now, keep it holstered. We're all going to be a little jumpy, so let's not inadvertently put holes in each other." He slightly lifted the M4A1 carbine in his arms; the assault rifle was short but lethal looking. "I got this."

Dan nodded and reholstered his weapon, and then Ben led them in. He had his flashlight gripped in the same hand as the barrel hand-guard, and the other on the pistol grip.

Ben swept the light beam back and forth; his eyes were hawk-like in their intensity. The doors to the ancient structure had long since rotted away, or perhaps they never existed. Inside, it was about the size of a large barn, empty save for a single altar at its centre. Around the walls, there were more carvings, depicting scenes of large unidentifiable animals that could have been prehistoric creatures, or perhaps beasts from the former occupants' mythology.

"Hello!" Steve shouted, but there was no echo.

"Keep it down, smartass," Dan shot back.

"No return echo means the bounce back was swallowed – there's more openings somewhere," Ben said. "Spread out."

Multiple flashlights cut the dark atmosphere as the small group searched the structure. The temple had obviously been dug back into the cliff wall, or maybe there had been some sort of cave that they had modified in the past. There were no side rooms apparent, and the ancient stone blocks in the wall were occasionally forced apart as huge muscular roots poured through to then continue their journey on into the floor.

"Jesus," Emma scoffed. "Check this out." The sides of the stone altar were carved with images of bound men and women having their heads removed, hearts cut out, and limbs severed.

"Yeah," Jenny said, trailing her hands along troughs in the top. "Human sacrifice," she whispered. "Jesus, what the hell where they doing to them?" She pointed at the next carved scene that looked like men carting baskets of body parts.

"Feeding time." Andrea's voice was small. She pointed to another image on the altar base. It was a scene of the natives throwing the human meat to some gigantic beast that seemed all teeth. "Looks like the things outside." Her voice was little more than a squeak now.

"The folly of feeding the crocodile and hoping it'll eat you last," Emma said. "And maybe in the end it came for them anyway."

"Got something," Steve yelled.

Heads turned, but it was only when he leaned back out from behind a broad piece of stone that looked like the rear wall could they locate him. He ducked back in.

"A passage." Steve's voice sounded even further away.

The way the stones had been hewn made it look like an unbroken wall from the front, but the closer you got, you saw that it was just cleverly hidden by perspective.

"Stay there," Ben shouted as the group crowded towards the rear.

Ben saw that the stonework became rougher and his suspicions that it was at some time some sort of natural opening in the rock were confirmed; Steve stood aside to let Ben ease in beside him.

Steve moved his light beam around. "There's a lot of roots, and it might have collapsed further in, but I can feel a breeze."

Ben nodded. "But I can feel air rising, being sucked upwards."

Steve grinned. "Do you think it goes all the way to the top then?"

Ben returned the smile. "I'm betting on it." He also shined his light up into the inky black tunnel. It was narrow, no more than three feet wide, and thick roots crisscrossed much of the passage.

Dan wedged his head in next to them, craning his neck to look up. "What are we waiting for?"

"Let me have a look." Jenny also tried to jam herself in underneath the big men, and Ben could also hear Emma and Andrea jostling as well. He grunted as he extracted himself and jostling bodies immediately filled his space.

Standing back, he checked his wristwatch – it was 4 o'clock, and though they still had a few hours of light left, he didn't know how long it would take to get to the top, and if they did, arriving at night was an unnecessary risk.

"Good and bad news." Ben placed his hands on his hips, as a few faces turned to him. "It looks narrow, and potentially passable for us, but not for anything larger than us. That's the good news. The bad news is, we'd need to clear it to see how far we can get, and hope there's no choke points further up. Gonna take time."

Ben snorted as he saw more of the group burrow back in, shining their lights around. "Given we think it's over a thousand feet to the top of the plateau, it'll be a hellova climb and will take too long to undertake today."

Emma pulled back, frowning at him.

Ben shrugged. "Bottom line, I want us there with plenty of daylight left."

"Ahh." Dan raised an eyebrow. "The impatient side of my brain says you're a party pooper. The smart, sensible side, which is the much smaller side, says that makes sense." He grinned.

"Make camp here?" Emma said unenthusiastically.

"Yeah, sheltered, dry, and secure," Ben said, calling them back in. "Here's the plan; Steve, I want you to climb up a few hundred feet, take Emma with you, and see what we're up against."

Emma immediately brightened, and he lowered his brow at the man. "Just a few hundred, got it?"

Steve nodded. "Yeah, got it."

Ben turned to Emma. "And that goes for you too; promise me."

"O-*ookay*." She smiled.

"C'mon, promise," Ben pressed.

She grinned. "I promise." She crossed her chest.

Ben nodded. "Dan and Andrea gather wood, make a fire. Jenny and I will see if we can scare up some game. Nino, check this place out to make sure there's nothing that's going to surprise us at night."

The Venezuelan saluted. Ben waited for any further questions and when there was none, he waved to Jenny. "Let's go hunting."

*****

Ben's eyes snapped open; sleep immediately banished – the fire had died down and inside the temple the embers cast a muted, hellish glow that didn't quite reach into the nooks and crannies of the crumbling edifice.

He lay there for several minutes, breathing evenly and just letting his eyes move slowly of the interior. He had positioned himself at the rear of the room, facing the open doorway. Everyone else seemed to be sleeping peacefully, and there were no unusual sights, sounds, or even odors. But still, a soldier's intuition put him on edge.

Another sound, this time from outside – twigs snapping. The depth of it told him the twig had been of a fair size so needed a degree of weight to break it.

Ben eased to a sitting position and withdrew his handgun. He retained the old mission habit of sleeping in his boots, so he simply got to his feet and edged along the wall to the door, peering around it.

There was nothing, even though he watched and waited for a full five minutes. But just as he began to relax, there came more sounds, further out. Something or someone was definitely out there.

He crouched and went out fast, moving quickly to the nearest bank of ferns to pause, staying low and once again just using his peripheral vision to try and pick out any movement or out of place shapes or coloring. He exhaled, frustrated and wishing he had night-vision goggles – the thick cloud cover meant no moon and no stars, so it was near pitch darkness.

Ben had fought in these conditions before and was trained to rely on sound, smell, and intuition, but it became a game of luck as well as one of skill and reflexes.

A sound again, and this time the flick of a tiny light – people then – was it a cigarette lighter? He stayed low, burrowing and treading softly as he moved another fifty feet further into the jungle. He smelled the smoke in amongst the humidity and mist of the jungle – cheap, harsh, foreign tobacco. There came a pinprick of orange light – the flare of a cigarette tip as someone drew on the smoke. Ben looped around and came up from behind it.

Sure enough there he was, a big man, broad, and standing close to a tree fern trunk that looked like it was covered in hair. He faced towards the temple as though keeping watch on it. Ben gripped his gun and came to his full height. He eased closer, but the guy was so focused he never heard Ben come up behind him.

"Nice night for bird watching?"

"*Вибачте*?" The man froze, holding his cigarette in a raised hand.

Ben didn't recognize the language, and thought it might have been Russian – he tried it. "*Русский*?" In the darkness, Ben just made out the curl of the lip and shake of head. He tried English.

"You alone?"

The man just shook his head, but more from lack of understanding. He knew Dan spoke a few languages.

"Let's get you back and see if anyone else can sort you out."

He saw that the man had a sidearm, and Ben pointed with his free hand, while keeping his own gun pointed at the man's chest.

"I'll take that." He held out his hand.

The man kept his eyes on Ben's and not his gun. Ben recognized the confidence and professionalism; the muzzle of Ben's gun would transfix an amateur, but it wasn't the gun that dictated what happened next, but the thoughts of the potential shooter – and it was the eyes that usually betrayed those.

The man pulled the gun from its holster and carefully handed it over. Ben took it and jammed it into his belt.

"This way." He waved the guy on and together they headed back to the ruins – he had a hundred questions and hoped he could get someone to ask them.

The guy shuffled, walked into vines, and kept his arms out in front of himself as though he was blind. Ben knew he was a lot more professional than he was letting on, and his patience finally ran out. He grabbed the big guy by the shoulder and started to push him through the foliage towards the red glow of the temple doors.

At the entrance, he shoved him inside, keeping the gun pointed at the ground but ready, and also his free hand up to ward off a potential backhanded blow if need be. But what met his eyes made his heart sink.

*****

"At last. Good evening, or is it good morning, Mr. Cartwright?"

Ben lunged forward at the guy he had just led in and grabbed him by the shoulder to then pull him back as a shield.

The stranger who had addressed him was portly, mid-50s, and looked supremely confident. With him were two other big men, grizzled, hard-edged, and now standing over his team. All their weapons had been collected and piled to one side of the temple.

"Who the fuck are you assholes?" Ben growled.

"Language, please. After all, there are ladies present." The man honestly looked dismayed. "My name is Barlow, Edward Barlow. With you is my friend, Mr. Janus Bellakov, who was asked to escort you back here – which he has done."

Steve launched himself at one of the men, who faster than anyone anticipated, whipped out an arm holding the gun and cracked the young man across the jaw. Steve went down, holding a split lip.

Barlow's man then stood over him, gun pointed at his head. He trailed the gun over the other's heads, daring another attack.

Nino cringed, holding his hands up higher. "I just guide."

"That's enough now, Mr. Koenig," Barlow said, and his man begrudgingly stepped back.

"You sons of bitches." Ben pulled Bellakov backwards and grabbed his collar, jamming the muzzle of the gun up under his ribs. "Your friend, huh? Why don't you let all of *my* friends go and then we can talk."

"We're talking now." Barlow continued to smile. "And if you want to shoot him, then go ahead. But then we'll need to shoot one of your people, or maybe two."

Barlow spoke without turning. "Mr. Koenig, choose one of the women."

The big guy to Barlow's left pointed a gun at Emma's head. She screwed her eyes shut, but there remained a defiant set to her jaw.

Shit, Ben thought. He knew that he was quick enough, and certainly a good enough shot, to whip the gun around and take out Barlow or Koenig. But that left two others who may start shooting, and with so many civilians, the odds of someone getting killed were off the scale.

"What do you want?" Ben glared at Barlow.

"To talk. That's all." He held up a hand flat. "I promise."

"I'm betting I've met a few of your boys before, at the hotel in Windlesham Manor. That your idea of talking?" Ben's jaws clenched.

"Stupid, I know." Barlow sighed. "But if I said to you I wanted to see what you had, or even tag along, your answer might not have been what I wanted. I was wrong to attempt to steal your notebook, and I apologize, profusely."

"Who was it?" Ben growled.

Barlow grinned. "Why, your friend right there of course." He winked at Bellakov.

"Good." Ben jerked Bellakov back to club him over the head with the butt of the gun. The big man went down. "That's for the kick in the guts, you sonofabitch." He lowered his gun, but continued to hold it loosely at his side. "Lower your guns and we'll talk then."

Barlow turned left and right, nodding. His men lowered their guns and stood at ease. At his feet, Bellakov groaned and then got to his feet. He came up with the blazing, blood in his eye look of someone who wanted to charge in. Ben lowered his head, looking at the man from under his brows.

"Anytime, big fella."

"Enough." Barlow's voice was sharp in the enclosed space, and Bellakov begrudgingly backed away, still rubbing the back of his neck.

Barlow smiled. "I knew you'd find it, this place. That's why we tagged along."

Emma came and stood beside Ben. "You were in front of us."

"Only for a while," Barlow said. "Then we looped around and waited for you. We already knew you were on your way, and we had come to the end of your map and had no idea which way to go from there. And then the GPS, compass, and comms all went to hell, and with only a few thousand square miles of uncharted Amazon jungle to bumble around in, I mean, what could possibly have gone wrong?" He chortled for a moment or two before pulling a handkerchief and wiping his brow and then lips.

"No, so much better to follow the guy with the notebook." He glowered at Bellakov. "That we failed to retrieve in England."

"Thanks, but we don't need any more people on our expedition." Steve got to his feet and went to pick up his gun, but one of Barlow's men pointed the gun again.

Ben returned the favor, and Barlow raised his hand. "Not just yet, young man." He said, smiling benignly at Steve. "Soon, perhaps." He turned to Emma. "You can't overpower us, or hide from us, and you're way too nice to do anything violent or...final." He lifted one eyebrow. "Really, what choice do you have? We'll simply follow you. Best if we join forces, I'd say. After all, I don't think it's going to be a picnic up top, do you?

"So..." Barlow found a suitable piece of tumbled stone. "Everyone, please sit down." He lowered himself to the stone and then placed two meaty forearms on his thighs and took a few moments to look at each of them.

"Friends, from when I was a child, I'd heard rumors that Sir Arthur Conan Doyle's fantastical Lost World adventure was based on fact. Then in school, I read about them finding more and more of these tepuis structures, some absolutely enormous, and being so high that they really did support some life forms on top of them – whole colonies of creatures that remained in perfect isolation and indifference to the life on the ground for many, many millions of years."

He sighed. "But these things, these isolated remnants, were only insects, ground shrews, and a few nematodes. But it made me think that if there was a large enough land mass, then it goes to reason that the creatures could, *must*, also be exponentially larger." He raised his chin. "And then with some good financial fortune, my search was able to begin."

"How did you find us?" Dan asked.

"Daniel Murakami, *Dan*, really, *you* ask that? A specialist in information technology and communications, asking how we could find someone or anything these days? I simply set the trap, and you sprung it yourself when you began your search for the notebook. I already had a plan in place, I just needed something to focus it on...and you delivered."

Dan groaned, already suspecting that he had sent up the flare that Barlow had spotted.

"What do you want from this...from us?" Jenny asked.

"Nothing more than to know, to see, to experience what may be up there. The secret will remain with us, but I do reserve the right to come back here with small parties for further...study."

"Hunting parties more like," Jenny said, bristling.

"Study, hunting…" Barlow shrugged and smirked.

"Won't make any difference," Ben said. "Apparently, this place can only be found every 10 years. Come back next week, and there'll be nothing."

Barlow sniggered. "Oh really, like what happens, the entire tabletop mountain vanishes?"

Ben now knew that Barlow obviously hadn't heard that part of the legend.

"Well?" Barlow looked at their faces. There was silence for a moment or two, and then he held a hand up. "You have my word on it. And given my men are experienced hunters, trackers, and bushmen, we will be of value to you."

Ben looked from Barlow to Bellakov, and then to the stony-faced Koenig and Bourke. Both looked about as mean and hard-bitten as you could get. Bottom line, Ben didn't trust the four men for a New York second. They held the guns, and had already shown him they were prepared to use violence. If he said no, what was to stop them killing all his friends, right here, right now? *Time to play along*, he thought, *for now*.

"Agreed," Ben said quickly.

"What?" Emma's face screwed in anger.

"Hey, Ben, that's not your call." Dan and Steve also looked surprised.

"We need them," Ben said matter-of-factly. "If what's at the top of the tunnel is anything like what my great ancestor put in his notebook, then the more security we have the better."

"Good man," Barlow said and slapped his thighs. He then looked at his wristwatch. "3am – in a few hours the sun will be coming up. Might be worthwhile arriving as early in the day as we can manage. What say you, Mr. Cartwright?"

"Sure, and no hard feelings." Ben held out a hand to Bellakov who ignored it. He laughed and then turned to Barlow. "We'll pack up, grab a quick bite, and then start up." He turned to the shaft.

"Steve, Emma, for our new guests, remind us again of what you saw in there?"

Steve's eyes still burned with anger, and he mumbled through a swelling jaw. Emma put a hand on his arm and spoke up. "A shaft, not quite vertical, but steep. Root-bound and possibly a few choke points, but I'm betting it's passable – for someone of normal body weight." Her lip curled slightly as she glanced at Barlow.

The man grinned in return. "Then I better remember to suck it in, hmm, darling?"

Emma continued. "I estimate the climb to be easily over a thousand feet, maybe more, much more. And I doubt there's going to be too many places to rest. We need to decide if everyone goes or not." She let her eyes slide to Andrea, whose brows immediately snapped together.

"Hey." She scowled. "You really think I just sailed, rode, and then trekked through the Amazon to wait down here and mind your coats?" She gave Emma a tight smile. "Not fucking likely."

"That height is not bad at all," Jenny cut in. "Some of these tepuis can climb to 3,000 feet."

"That's good. Steve, you okay?" Ben asked.

The young man worked his jaw for a moment and then nodded. "Nothing a little payback couldn't fix." He glared at Koenig who just smirked in return. "I'll save it for now."

"Nino, how about you?" Ben saw that the young guide had finally gotten to his feet, but still shifted from foot to foot.

He shook his head. "I think I go back home now."

"No, I don't think you will," Barlow said. "You can stay here at the foot of the plateau, and one of my men can stay with you. But no one is leaving to broadcast our find until we say so, well, until *I* say so. Is that clear?" Barlow tilted his head, his smile benign.

Ben shrugged. "Can you climb?"

Nino bobbed his head.

"Nino, I'll give you a big bonus for your troubles, promise," Dan said and flashed him a salesman's smile.

"I can climb." He scowled at Barlow. "And I can be trusted."

"Okay, we buddy up," Ben said. "Emma, Nino, and myself will lead us up. Steve and Andrea, Dan and Jenny, and Mr. Barlow, you three can make your own arrangements. Also, we climb light; anything unnecessary we leave down here."

"Agreed," he said. "Except for one change; Mr. Bellakov and myself will climb directly behind you and your first team, Mr. Cartwright. And then Mister's Koenig and Bourke will bring up the rear. All good?"

Barlow raised his eyebrows, but Ben knew it wasn't really a question.

"Fine," Ben said.

The final rations were then eaten in silence and then done more for taking in fuel, as everyone became lost in their own thoughts. Ben turned to see Barlow's man, Bourke, fiddling with something and Ben groaned when he recognized the shape.

"What the hell do you think you're going to do with that?"

Bourke ignored him and kept at his work. Ben got to his feet and so did Bellakov.

Ben pointed. "Am I going mad, or am I seeing some asshole counting out fragmentation grenades?"

Bourke looked up and grinned as he took them out of plastic and laid the squat green canisters on the ground in a row. "F1 anti-personnel fragmentation device, five-second internal fuse and lethal detonation spread of 30 feet." He winked. "These bad boys will do some real damage."

"Damn right they will; to us if not handled correctly," Ben said, seething.

Barlow sighed. "Calm down Mr. Cartwright. We don't know exactly what deterrents we're going to need yet. And if we need them, and in a hurry, I'd prefer the good Mr. Bourke here doesn't need to spend valuable seconds fumbling in his preparations."

Ben fumed. He objected to seeing the military-grade explosives because he didn't have any. Plus, he had no idea whether Bourke had handled them before.

"You only use them when I say." He glared.

Bourke looked up and chuckled. "Yeah, sure."

Ben went and sat back down, finishing his final meal. He started to think this bad idea was looking worse by the second.

It was still dark outside when they attached their headlamps to foreheads and lined up at the bottom of the shaft.

CHAPTER 20

Full Comet Apparition

Comet P/2018-YG874, designate name Primordia, was now at its perihelion or maximum observable focus as it had now reached its closest point to Earth.

The magnetic distortion had also reached its peak, but now the field generated a form of stability. The hurricane-like winds that had been roaring above them on the top of the plateau ceased, and the boiling clouds dropped to become a mist that moved through a primordial forest.

Warm rain fell on a lost world. The wettest season was here.

CHAPTER 21

Warm air rushed past them as Emma stood on a small ledge and looked up into the natural cave tunnel. Her trained eye picked out tiny ledges, toeholds, and crevices for toe and fingertips.

The upside was it was so narrow they could go up chute-style where they braced a leg against each side of the tunnel and basically hopped their way upwards.She led the way and used her hunting knife to cut and hack away at many of the roots barring their way – so far, she found no real impediment. Added to that, the rushing wind told her that the chimney went all the way to the top. Or she hoped. There was always the chance that the chimney was going to take a turn and exit out on the cliff-face.

She looked back at Ben – he wasn't an expert climber, but he was fit and sturdy, keeping pace with her. His strong jaw and stubbled chin held a smile.

"Hey, if my dear old great, great grandfather could do it…"

She laughed. "Yeah, but he was younger than you back then." She had a small flashlight attached to her wrist, and she reached up, adjusted her forehead lamp, and began to scale again.

Way behind her, she heard Nino breathing hard, a man's voice curse, and someone else complaining. But she was in her element. This was what she trained for and what she excelled at, the hand over hand, toe hold to the next, always scaling upwards while trying not to outpace those behind.

Emma paused again to scan around a slight bend in the shaft. The rocks were good, old, but dense and looked like they were ancient igneous rock, more than likely granite, which was hard as iron, and less likely to drop stones back down on lower climbers.

She looked back down; Nino already struggled, and she saw that Ben had let him slip past so he could push up on the man's foot, basically lifting him as he climbed. She grinned as she watched him; she couldn't help it. She liked him. She'd liked him at school, and she now liked what he'd grown into even more.

Truth be told, she wasn't just here to find some lost plateau; she was here for Ben. He was her ideal man – tall, handsome, rugged, and from a good family. Any one of those attributes would have put him close to the top, but all of them together…well, let's just say, she'd already decided that big guy wasn't going to get away so easily this time.

She chuckled in the darkness.

"All right up there?" she heard him call to her.

"All good, so far." She directed the powerful beam of the mag-light lashed to her wrist up into the chimney – there was no end in sight, and by her estimates, they had come about 400 hundred feet, but had maybe three times that distance to go.

She called down: "How's everyone doing back down there? Everyone still with us?"

Ben stopped, getting her drift. "Sound off, people," he called.

One after the other, with the voices getting fainter, the group let them know they were all safe. Even the loathsome Barlow and his band of apes joined in. She didn't trust any of them for a second, and she still couldn't work out why Ben had agreed to let them come. *No choice*, she guessed.

She turned back to the chute, quickly rubbed her hands on her pants, and then continued up. For her, the climb was easy, and there were no areas that required ropes or pitons, and just as well, as she only had about 100 feet of rope in her kit and no other climbing aides. She had originally assumed she would have to scale the sheer wall of the plateau by herself, but the pipe was an unexpected gift.

About 800 feet up, she paused to suck in some air. A slight breeze still rushed past her, bringing with it all the sounds of the lower climbers – the grunts, groans, and heavy breathing.

Emma took off her forehead light and used an arm to wipe her brow – even though the cave was cooler than outside, the humidity was stifling, and she wedged herself in the chute for a moment to tug out her canteen and take a sip.

The air stopped moving.

Emma sipped again, waiting. But the air remained stagnant. She frowned, looking up, and saw it was impenetrable darkness above her. She remembered she'd removed her forehead light and quickly slipped it on, looking up again. She'd felt this sort of event type before – it occurred when something blocked a chute, and it usually meant bad news – a rock fall or something was laid over their access path.

Ben caught up to her and tapped her shoe, making her *yip* with fright.

"Jesus, Ben." She looked down at his dust-streaked face.

"What's up?" he asked.

"I think..." She looked back up just as the air suddenly began to rush past her again – whatever the blockage was, it was now gone. She licked flaking lips. "Nothing." She continued to stare upwards.

Ben squeezed her foot. "Let's go, beautiful."

"Yeah, yeah." She smiled and nodded. "Just...just tell that fat-ass Barlow to stop blocking the pipe." *That had to be it*, she thought.

She continued on, still feeling good, light, strong, and then what she thought was dust began to grow thicker. Emma held a hand up in front of her face and let her light beam play over it – she expected to see floating dust motes, but instead, there was nothing except a distinctive cloudiness.

"Ha. Mist," she said and felt an odd tingling in her belly.

Oddly, it seemed to defy the breeze blowing past them to remain suspended in the chute.

She shone her flashlight upwards. The chimney continued on until it exhausted the strength of her beam, but now there was a definite haze. She laid a hand against the stone – cool. She knew that mist and fog could form when cool air passed over warmer water or land. But the stone was cooler here.

Ben caught up again.

"Look. We've entered a mist layer."

He added his light to hers. "Humidity's pretty high. Cave wall's still dry though; that's a good thing."

"Yep," she said. She placed a hand on her belly. "You feel okay? Any tingling?"

He scoffed quietly. "Yeah, a little. Just thought it was fatigue or vertigo, or something."

"No, not that." She wiped her nose. "Weird; maybe that magnetic effect Dan mentioned."

"Maybe," Ben said half-heartedly.

"Are we there yet?" Nino had caught up and gasped up at them with a red, sweat-slicked face.

She smiled back. "No, but *nearly*."

She started up again. Higher and higher, even her trained muscles were starting to feel the ache and strain of dragging your own bodyweight upwards. Her fingertips were abraded and nails ground down, and it was only after another hour that she thought her eyes were playing tricks as it seemed that the fog was thickening. There was also a change in air density that she recognized.

She increased her speed, moving like a spider as excitement gave her muscles new energy. She quickly left Ben and Nino, as the smaller Venezuelan man unfortunately beginning to act as a plug to the other climbers. He was just lucky he had Ben with him who continued to push him skyward, as he would surely have been left far behind.

Emma's grin widened as she detected something else, and she

reached up to flick off her headlamp.

Yes, she whispered, and turned once again. "We got light, people." She started to scamper higher, leaping now.

"Slow down," she heard Ben yell, but his voice was already far behind now. The chimney narrowed a little but caused her no problem. However, she knew that someone the size of Barlow would struggle. *Good*, she thought, *hope he loses skin*.

In another hundred feet, she smelled damp earth, exotic odors, and many sweet scents that could have been pollens or flowers in bloom. Her wristwatch told her it was 7am, and sun up, but the light was still muted. She sniffed again; there was also something odd, faintly acidic, almost like cat-piss ammonia.

Emma put her hand up onto a ledge with a roof above it. The chimney had ended in a horizontal cave, flat at about two feet high, but broad and disappearing off into the darkness for both ways.

She eased off her backpack, scrambled on her belly over some sort of gravel to the end, and stopped.

"Oh my God."

Her mouth stayed open

*****

It felt, as well as heard, the animals in the cave. The vibrations in the stone that had been transported to her body told of blundering creatures, several of them, and all inside the cave. *Her cave*.

It tasted the air but didn't pick up any scent; they were still far away. It eased itself from its hiding place, prepared to defend its territory. But something else flared inside it, *hunger*, always the ache of hunger.

It also hadn't eaten in days, and nothing would be wasted.

*****

Like the rest of them, Ben had to dump his pack to crawl forward. He put a hand on Emma's shoulder. She had her chin resting on the back of her hands, and she turned to smile.

'It's real," she said dreamily.

Ben turned back to the vista. *"And there we were, upon the dreamland, the Lost World."*

"From the story?" she asked.

He nodded, letting his eyes take it all in. There was a heavy fog or low cloud, but even the plant life that he could make out was so alien to what he had seen in many other jungles before that it was near unrecognizable. And the size of everything was breathtaking – massive trunks soared high into the clouds without showing their canopies. Jagged outcrops berthed ferns and strange flowers with raw red heads, and there were the prehistoric scaly looking trees that Jenny had identified below.

But there were also strange palms with fruiting bulbs of brilliant orange, yellow, and purples, and massive columns of hairy wooded stumps that had green strips like reeds rather than leaves at their tip.

"Everything is so...*big*," Emma whispered.

Nino crawled up beside them, the gravel crunching underneath him, and scanned one way then the other. "I don't like it."

"Well, I *love it*," Emma responded.

The others came and lay beside them, with the long flat cave allowing the entire group to lie side by side.

"Well done, sir," Barlow said between puffing breaths.

Ben turned to the wheezing man; his face was so flushed and red it looked like some sort of overripe fruit about to burst. Sweat dripped from his chin and the end of his nose. He wiped it with a dusty handkerchief.

"Well done to my great, great grandfather, I'd say," he replied.

Barlow nodded. "Quite so."

Further down the cave, Dan gave him the thumbs up and took pictures, and Andrea divided her time between glancing out at the jungle and examining broken fingernails.

"What's that smell?" Emma asked.

"Sour; smells a little like cat's piss." Ben wrinkled his nose. "Something died in here?"

"Great, and we're lying in it." Emma stuck her tongue out.

Ben looked past her to see Jenny fiddling with something that looked like a lot of large chalky rocks. She was breaking them open, sniffing them, and her brow was creased. She looked up. "We should probably get out of here... *now.*"

He was about to ask what she was doing when Emma nudged him. "Let's go; I want to see...everything."

"Wait..." He grabbed her.

"Why? That's why we're here, isn't it?"

Ben shook his head. "You know, I never really thought about a plan for when we were here. I guess my goal was to see if it existed, and now that we know it does, I'm not sure what to damn well do."

"Well, I do," Barlow answered over their heads. "Now, we go forth on an adventure like no other." He rested on large beefy forearms. "I want to see the specimens, the animals, plants. Think of the opportunities, the wonders, and think of the advances in medicine, paleontology, and biology. People will pay a fortune to come here."

Emma's jaws clenched. "All about the money, huh?"

"Isn't everything?" Barlow turned back to the vista. "Ladies and gentlemen, it's like we have just been transported back in time for about 100 million years. I suggest we use our time well."

"We need to think about this," Jenny said quickly. "We also need to think about interacting with plants, animals, bacteria, and parasites that do not exist in the modern world, and haven't for millions of years. Dangerous doesn't begin to describe it." She grimaced. "But..." She looked over her shoulder briefly. "... we can do that outside, okay?"

"Agreed. And please remember, we're not the first here," Barlow responded.

"That's true," Dan said. "And not just Ben's ancestor; the Pemon or some other race, were obviously coming up here as well."

Steve snorted. "Oh yeah, the natives; wonder what happened to them and those baskets of body parts. And no offence, Ben, but your namesake ancestor didn't exactly die of old age either."

"Jesus, Steve." Emma scowled

Janus Bellakov sneered. "I think you'll find we're a little better prepared than primitive natives or a long-dead Cartwright."

"Asshole," Emma whispered.

Steve crawled forward, and looked out and upwards. "The clouds are rising."

"Thermal effect," Dan said. "The sun will heat up the surface, drawing the clouds away from the land. Doubt it will allow the sun through, but it'll at least improve visibility."

Steve hiked his shoulders. "Now or never."

"Now." Barlow turned. "Mr. Bourke, crawl back and retrieve our packs. There's a good chap."

Bourke's lip curled down and he grumbled as he turned on his belly and crawled to the rear of the cave.

Ben chuckled, but then pointed. "Okay, there's a tumble of boulders about a hundred feet forward and just to the left. I'll take a quick look and if it's safe, then we head there and stretch our legs before...deciding to do anything else. We can spend a few hours looking around and then come back here, long before either sundown or the clouds drop again."

"That is agreeable," Barlow said with a smirk.

Ben sucked in a deep breath, felt Emma give his bicep a quick squeeze for luck, and then he slid out of the flattened cave. He had his M4A1 assault rifle over his back and kept it there. But he unclipped his sidearm holster.

He stood tall and inhaled – it smelled earthy, alive, and damned *primordial*. There was bare ground for about a hundred feet around the front of the cave, and then there was the great wall of jungle. He looked along it, trying to detect the slightest hint of movement, unusual color, or even odd shape. But there was nothing.

He walked forward a dozen feet and stopped to examine some tracks in the gravel – they were bird-like, three-toed, but large like they were made by something the size of a large ostrich. He lifted his gaze again to the jungle where there were towering stump-like trees, tangled vines, and broad ferns, palms, and cycad plants. He scoffed silently – he knew it could have held a hundred creatures that had developed extraordinary camouflage abilities, and he might not even see one of them.

He turned back to the cave and saw the heads of his group as they watched from a letterbox-type crack in the wall of rock. He had expected that they would be at the cliff edge, but he remembered that the chimney was at a slight angle, so over the thousand plus feet of climbing, they had been moved a little inland on the plateau's surface.

"Looks okay," he said softly, but knowing his voice would carry. "Grab your stuff and come on out."

*****

Jenny and Nino were the last to clamber back to the rear of the cave to retrieve their packs. She saw one of Barlow's men, Bourke she thought he was called, pulling his and his master's bags towards himself and then removing weapons and sliding them into his pockets. He looked up to see her watching and blew her a kiss.

Ugh, she thought.

This far back in the cave, she could smell again the sharp tang of ammonia. It gave her an uneasy feeling after finding the large white chalk-like bundles that reminded her of the times she had to clean out the snake tanks in the zoo's reptile house. It damn well looked like snake droppings. The problem was the size made that impossible.

She had broken one open and seen the remains of crushed bones and teeth – exactly the contents she would expect to find in a large jungle constrictor-type snake. But she'd only ever seen that size as coprolite – fossilized dung.

She placed a hand down on the gravel and then looked down – it wasn't gravel at all, but thousands of teeth, mostly human. And they were ages old, possibly thousands of years. She knew that tooth enamel was mostly hydroxyapatite, a mineral form of calcium phosphate that was one of the hardest biological materials and, in fact, harder than steel.

Jenny narrowed her eyes, looking around in the darkness; was this what happened to the race who had once been coming up here? She inhaled, smelling the ammonia again – *was it getting stronger?* she wondered. She pulled her pack a little closer as she suddenly had the eerie sensation of the hairs on her neck rising.

She tried to see into the darker depths of the cave, but there were too many areas of inky blackness, and looking left and right again, what she *could* see of it travelled a long way. There was one thing she learned about caves in the jungle; they were never unoccupied. She felt decidedly uncomfortable.

"Nino, we better go," she said softly.

"Si, si." Nino started to drag his bag to the entrance, and Jenny reluctantly turned to Bourke.

"Hey, hurry it up. I don't think it's safe."

Bourke snorted, continuing with his tasks. He looked up, grinning in the dark. "Don't worry, darling, this party hasn't even started yet."

"Fine, take your time." She started to crawl back towards the light and away from the chute. She quickly caught up with Nino, and the small man looked at her and his nose wrinkled.

"He is asshole."

She chuckled. "You got that right."

Behind her, she heard Bourke grunt. Then grunt again. She turned.

It felt like her eyes actually bulged from her head – almost half of the man's body was inside the mouth of a snake so big that it had to flatten itself down to fit inside the cave.

Inward-curving, dagger-like teeth had dug deep into his body. But the tough mercenary pumped with his free hand against a head that had scales bigger than dinner plates and doubtless wasn't troubled by the defensive display of the small warm and soft animal.

"*Jesus Christ*," she shrieked and jerked up, smashing her head on the roof of the cave. Nino screamed something about a demon and started to scramble away.

The snake began to tug Bourke deeper into the cave, and she heard the muffled screams of the man still coming from inside its mouth. But then to her horror, she saw that curled in his hand was one of his grenades. Then in a practiced motion, he flicked the pin out.

"*Bomb!*" she yelled, crawling faster than she'd ever crawled in her life.

*****

"What?" Ben heard Jenny's yell and turned back to the cave. He saw her head appear just as the percussive blast shot across them, blowing him and the group flat.

Ben rolled on top of Emma who lay beside him as the rubble and dust rained down around them. Rocks, some as big as bowling balls, thumped onto the ground, but thankfully, it was mostly pellet-sized.

He sat up quickly. *That fucking asshole.* People were sprawled and struggling to get to their feet. He turned to Barlow who sat up groggily. "Your asshole just blew himself up." He turned, remembering who was still in the cave.

"*Jenny!*"

Ben sprinted back to the cave mouth that was now just obliterated rubble. He found her forty feet away, moaning with her clothes still smoking. Her hair was singed and clots of blood patterned her shirt and matted the hair on the back of her head.

"Jenny... Jenny." Ben carefully wiped a shred of flesh from her face. Thankfully, there was no gaping wound beneath it – it had belonged to someone else. Her eyelids fluttered, and he cradled her into a sitting position. She moaned. "Stay still; we've got you." He eased hair back off her face and wiped away more blood.

Her eyes opened as slits. "Can't...hear."

Ben nodded. Staring down into her face, he knew she definitely would have damaged her eardrums; he just hoped it wasn't permanent.

Forty feet away, Nino rolled on the ground, his clothing tattered. He sat up and wailed, holding his head. Ben pointed to him.

"Someone see to him," he yelled. Dan was first there.

Jenny groaned, reached up to grab his shirt, and dragged herself to a sitting position. Emma rushed over, then Steve, and they gave her water to sip while Ben checked the back of her head and neck, looking for damage. Luckily, it looked like her hair had cushioned much of the blast, and maybe she was far enough away that the percussive force spat them out before it chewed her up.

"I'm okay, I'm okay." She pushed the water away. "Nino, did he...?"

"He's alive." Ben sat in front of her. "What happened? Did Bourke use a grenade?"

She winced. "Snake, giant snake."

"Say what?" Steve leaned closer.

"Maybe Titanoboa." She started to gulp air. "So big; attacked him."

"Easy; you're fine now." Ben's lips compressed. *This happens,* he thought, *and they'd only been here a few minutes.*

"Jesus, Ben. A snake big enough to eat a man?" Steve's brows knitted.

Jenny sat forward by herself and rubbed her face. "We should have expected it – the smell, and the dung I found." She winced again. "In fact, it was only just a few years back in a coal mine in Colombia that they found fossils of an enormous snake estimated to be around 70 feet, and as thick around as a draft horse."

Jenny held out a hand and Steve pulled her up and also threw an arm around her waist, while she looped one over his shoulder. She carefully rubbed one of her ears. "*Titanoboa cerrejonensis*, lived right around here about 50–70 million years ago during the Paleocene epoch; probably ate dinosaurs. In fact, it outlived the dinosaurs, and no one knows why they went extinct."

"Obviously they didn't." Ben turned back to the cave. "Looks like we're not going home that way." He walked a little closer to the collapsed cave mouth. On the ground, there were a few huge chunks of meat that had scales like Chevy hubcaps.

We should have expected it, Jenny had said. *Sure, but we just couldn't ever imagine it*, he thought.

Ben sucked in a deep breath and turned, seeing the damage to his friends, their supplies, and their way home. Andrea wailed and Dan rushed to her as she got up hopping on one foot. There was a rip in her pants and underneath, a matching gash in her leg.

"I'm cut...*and bleeding*," she wailed.

"Oh shit," Ben seethed.

"I've got it." Steve rushed to her and eased her down to sit, kneeling before her. He ripped her pants a little to get at the wound and dab it with a cloth. He smiled up at her. "Just a small wound, but a lot of blood – actually looks worse than what it is."

"It hurts," she said, frowning.

"I'll bet it does. I'll patch it and stem the bleeding, okay?" He continued to dab at it.

She nodded but her lips were turned down. "It's going to look terrible."

Steve grinned. "But think of the publicity?'

Her frown lightened a few degrees, as she obviously thought it through.

Ben went and sat with Nino, putting a hand on the man's shoulder. He nodded, but his eyes watered from the dust and probably the pain.

Dan put a hand on the Venezuelan's shoulder. "Best I can do." He had bandaged his head, but already the cloth was damply red.

"Good job." Ben helped him up and then turned back to the group. "Okay, gather up everything we can use; anything else, leave behind.

Let's get the hell out of here."

Barlow recovered his hat and swiped debris from it with one chubby hand before jamming it back on his head. "I really think we should rest a little longer and gather our senses. Maybe make another plan, hmm? Don't you think?"

"No, I don't." Ben turned. "Did you not hear what just happened to Bourke? Up here, we're not top of the food chain – and your idiot just rang the biggest dinner bell he could find."

Everyone turned to the wall of green. It was strangely silent, and had been since the blast. It was if a thousand eyes were watching them. Almost as one, people started to recover bags, weapons, stray food, and anything else they could find. In another few minutes, they were ready.

Ben turned back to the collapsed cave and then faced Barlow. "You want to say any words for Bourke?"

Barlow nodded and faced the cave. "Goodbye, fool."

Ben snorted. "Touching; let's go."

*****

Emma was first to be at his side. "Creepy."

He nodded. "Jungles always are. But this isn't just another jungle, so we better stay on edge. Priority now is staying alive until we can find another way down." He sighed. "In 1908, Benjamin mentioned in his notes they found an inland lake that had caves at its edge. The lake has got to be what was fueling that waterfall we saw back on the ground."

She nodded. "Caves mean passages, and passages might mean more chutes."

"And a way down," he added.

"We'll need to find a suitable campsite," Barlow said. "With protection from the elements *and* the beasts: failing that, we can always stay close by here, maybe try and dig open the entrance again."

Ben grimaced. "We'd need earthmoving equipment to shift that. And then we won't know if the shaft has been compromised until we've spent several days digging – that'd be a damn poor investment in energy and time."

"Then assuming we're going to be here a little longer than expected, shelter is the priority. And a cave would be ideal as sleeping out in the open might be a little risky." Barlow's brows went up.

"Hey, I'll tell you what might be *a little risky*; sleeping in a cave," Steve bristled and jabbed a finger at the man. "Just ask your buddy Bourke."

Janus Bellakov came and stood between Steve and Barlow. The

bigger man glared at Steve.

"It was my fault," Jenny said. "I suspected that cave was inhabited; I should have said something."

"Very good; I'll send your after-the-fact admission of guilt to my dear friend Mr. Bourke's family." Barlow touched the brim of his hat. "They'll be comforted, I'm sure."

Bellakov smirked.

"It's no one's fault, Jenny," Dan shot back. "Don't talk like that. Besides, you tried to warn us."

"Much as I hate to admit it," Ben said, "a cave is the best and most defendable form of shelter. If we need to clear one out, we will."

"Ben and I were just talking; these Tepuis are riddled with caves," Emma said. "They're eroded by water. So, our best bet is to find the water."

"My ancestor referred to caves by the lake." Ben pointed. "We've got no GPS or even compass. But I estimate the waterfall was tipping over the edge about a half-mile back that way. If we head towards it, we should find the stream and then track that back to the lake. The watercourse should also make it easier to get through that tangle."

"Sounds like a plan," Steve said.

Ben pointed at one of Barlow's men. "Koenig, was it?"

The big, bearded man nodded.

"Good, your hunting skills will come in handy, so I'll want you at the back for rear security. Okay?"

Koenig turned to his boss who gave him a small nod. Barlow then turned back to Ben. "He agrees...and I'll just fit myself in somewhere towards the middle."

"Of course you will." Ben turned away. "Jenny, I'd like you close by me if you feel up to it. Your expertise will come in handy."

"Yeah sure; ringing ears, but I'm fine," she replied and felt the back of her head. Spots of blood smeared her fingertips. She grimaced either from pain or from recognizing that the blood and gore was not her own.

"Everyone stay vigilant." Ben nodded to the wall of tangled green. "Let's find that stream."

The team formed into a basic line of two by two, so it wasn't too strung out. Leading them out was Ben, Jenny, and Emma, followed by Barlow with the fearsome-looking Janus Bellakov at his shoulder. Then came Andrea, Nino, Steve, Dan, and bringing up the rear was the now morose-looking Walt Koenig.

Just as Dan suggested, the cloud began to rise, but there was still the ever-present cover overhead. It trapped the moisture, and though it seemed to be only around 90 degrees, it was easily that in humidity so their perspiration never dried, and they were all quickly drenched in sweat.

Surrounding them, the jungle had slowly come alive with sound. But oddly, not the bright sounds of parrots squawking or chattering monkeys. Instead, it was filled with hidden creatures that hissed, hooted, and roared, and even with Jenny's zoological expertise, they refused to be identified.

From time to time, just above them and out of sight in the cloud cover, large leathery-sounding wings beat overhead. From the heavy sounds, the things must have been of considerable size.

Jenny sped up to walk beside him, and her expression was still troubled.

"What's up?" he asked.

"We're making too much noise."

Ben looked down at her, seeing the real fear in her eyes. She alone had already been subjected to the horrors of this place, and he knew her fears weren't misplaced.

"Agreed." He stopped and turned, allowing everyone to bunch up before him. "Listen up; we're basically in a place that potentially has predators like we've never encountered. In fact, like *no* human has ever encountered since 1908...and they didn't survive. We need to be silent as ghosts if *we're* going to stay alive."

"These predators will hunt by sight, sound, and scent," Jenny added. "From the fossil record, we know that many dinosaurs had poor eyesight."

"Good," said Dan.

"Not really," Jenny responded. "They still had the telescopic binocular vision of a hunter. But that *weakest* of senses is bolstered by hearing that will be far superior to ours. And I can only guess what their sense of smell is like, but assume its hundreds of times better than ours." She felt the back of her head and looked at her fingers. "We stink of fear, sweat, and most of all blood, and that scent will be carried on the breeze and attract predators." She held up her bloody fingers. "We need to find shelter, soon." She briefly crouched, grabbing a hand full of dirt, and came up to smear it over the blood in her hair. "And we need to mask our scent as much as we can."

Ben let his eyes shift to Andrea who had the bloodstained bandage on her leg. It looked like the bleeding had finally stopped. He pointed. "We should change that, quickly."

"I'll do it," Steve said and dropped his pack to pull out the small med kit they all had.

"Bury the old bandage," Jenny said. "Deep, or something will track it back to its source. And that…"

Andrea looked up sharply and Jenny's lips clamped shut, biting off her thought. "Just bury it deep." She turned away to tend to her own head wound again.

Ben could also see that Nino had a streak of blood from each ear – the blast must have perforated them, and he bet the guy's hearing was well below normal. He occasionally moaned his discomfort.

After another few minutes, they were ready. Ben had his rifle cradled in his arms now, Steve also held the shotgun, and also Koenig and Bellakov had their weapons ready. Dan and Emma drew their handgun, but Ben held up a hand.

"For now, no handguns. Everyone else, no stray firing unless there is a clear and immediate danger. Okay?"

Dan immediately reholstered his gun, and Emma also reluctantly did the same but didn't clip it down.

*****

They continued on in silence. Ben had even convinced the walking wounded into stifling their smallest moans of pain and distress – he'd told them as politely as he could that it didn't help and might attract something a lot worse than the snake. He didn't know what, but he didn't want to find out.

As the heat increased with the late morning, so came the insects. Huge things that flew at them, or hung down from the tips of ferns to try and cling to them as they brushed past. All were voraciously hungry and found the humans full of fluid, and soft – perfect for them.

He regretted now having everyone leave behind their netting, but there was no use lamenting what ifs. He had allowed only a small covering of repellent for each of them, as he was keen for them to preserve it; he knew night would be the worst time for bugs. Also, the way they were sweating, anything they added would be washed off in a matter of minutes. The final concern was that the spray was an alien odor, and up here might be very attractive to scent hunters.

As if to damn his decision, something alighted on his neck and stuck there – he slapped at it. He was horrified to find it the size of his thumb, and a combination of shell-like carapace, spikes, and bulbous abdomen that both stuck in his hand but also squashed in a burst of green goo before it could bite him.

"*Yech.*" He flicked the remains from his glove, and Jenny glared at him for making so much noise.

She reached out to put a hand on his arm. "We might have a

problem." She kept her voice low.

He half grinned. "No shit – only one?"

She bobbed her head. "We need more repellant, or something like it."

"We'll need it more tonight. I've been in jungles after dark – the real bloodsuckers come out then." He remembered what it was like. "Even with repellent, I'm still not looking forward to it."

She nodded. "Me neither. But it's not just the blood drinkers that worry me. There are also parasites, ones that actually preyed off the dinosaurs; even the *T-rex* was vulnerable to infestation. To these things, we're just walking bags of blood."

He nodded. "What do you suggest?"

"If, *when*, we find the water, we cover ourselves with mud." She exhaled through her nose, looking miserable.

Ben snorted and looked down at her. "Can I tell Andrea, or do you want to?" He laughed softly, but knew Jenny was right; on jungle missions, he'd done it himself.

CHAPTER 22

Nino's head still throbbed with a dull pain, and his ears rang. His hair was singed and he knew there were wounds all along his neck, scalp, and down one side of his face. He also knew he was near deaf and had to watch the lips of the group to see if they were talking; being in near silence scared him. Added to that, his bandages itched, and the insects tormented him every step of the way.

He shook his head and then swiped at something big that landed on his scalp, nipped, and felt like it was trying to dig in before he brushed it away. He cursed under his breath, wishing he had never responded to the opportunity to work as a guide for the westerners. They had promised him a bonus; he'd damn well make sure the bonus was so big that he'd never have to work again.

He continued to grumble – if not, then he'd either sell the location to this secret place, or report them for buying illegal weapons – something the government would take great interest in when foreign nationals were involved.

In another hour, Nino became aware of the strange noise, but maddeningly, it seemed like it was coming from *inside* his head. It reminded him of someone eating an apple – *crunch, crunch, crunch* – it never seemed to end. Just like his torment.

*****

The fly larvae had hatched almost immediately where it was laid just beneath the skin. The prehistoric ancestor of the botfly wasn't used to finding flesh so soft and accommodating, and the grub immediately set to borrowing deeper for both protection and nutrition.

For larger animals with hides covered in scales, armor plates, or leathery skin, it usually meant burrowing down several inches to find the nutritious muscle mass. But in Nino's head, the first thing it encountered was the bone of his skull, and its powerful, chitinous mandibles immediately set to work, grinding it away.

In an hour, it was through and then it continued on into the protein-rich cranial matter.

CHAPTER 23

Ben held up a hand and the group stopped. He waved them down. Walt Koenig eased up beside him and crouched.

"I hear it too," the hunter whispered.

Ben nodded. "Just up ahead. Let's take a look." He turned to his friends and put a finger to his lips, and then mouthed: *wait*. He crept forward with Koenig right behind, and he slowly parted a curtain of hanging vines.

Koenig exhaled in a soft laugh. "Well, holy hell."

There were half a dozen small animals roughly the size of hogs, and just as barrel-shaped. But that's as close as the similarity got as their necks added three feet to their bodies that were striped in orange, brown, and red. The creature's eyes were large and liquid looking, like those of a cow, and their short faces ended in a horned beak. The most amazing thing was along their necks and tails there seemed to be a line of quills that might have been tiny feathers.

Ben turned and pointed to Jenny, waving her forward. The woman scurried fast and laid her hands on Ben's shoulders to use them as a perch. Ben heard her sharp intake of breath.

"Oh my God...they're..." she pointed, "...they're dinosaurs. *Real* dinosaurs."

From behind his other shoulder, he heard the whine and click of Dan's camera as he edged forward, aiming and shooting over and over.

"I told you; we'll be famous," he said. "I *knew* it was real."

"What are they?" Emma whispered as she wedged herself between him and Walt Koenig. The hunter cursed and then made room for her.

Ben shook his head and looked up at the zoologist.

Jenny shrugged. "The shape, size, hard beak; could be a *Psittacosaurus*, a parrot-beaked plant eater. But who really knows? These guys were quite prevalent 80 million years ago, but even artist's impressions of reconstructions can't even come close to how they really looked. I mean, on the tail and neck – they look like primitive feathers!"

"So, they really did turn into birds then?" Emma grinned. "This is so cool."

"I could die happy right now." Dan lowered his camera. "I have no more bucket list."

Ben looked at Koenig. "Well, good to know these guys are here – if it comes down to it, we'll be eating one of them."

"Are you serious?" Andrea looked horrified. "They could be poisonous."

Koenig scoffed. "You get hungry enough, miss, and you'll eat it raw, believe me."

"*Pfft.*" Her lips curled.

Behind them, some branches broke and the animals bleated once and vanished. Ben spun to see Nino blundering towards them.

"What the hell?" Ben frowned and watched him for a few more moments; the man was mumbling to himself again. He also seemed to stumble as if intoxicated and blood was once again leaking from under the bandage around his head.

Ben took a quick look one way then the other and then went after the man. He grabbed Nino's arm and led him back to the group. He bent forward to look into the man's face.

"Hey, how you doin' there, buddy?"

Nino looked up at him, but only one eye focused. The other seemed to slide to the side, and half his face sagged as if he'd had a stroke.

"Just gonna check this out. Hold steady."

Ben peeled back the bandage, seeing the blisters, congealed abrasions, and other damage from the blast. Those wounds had coagulated and were on their way to healing, but there was a small, round hole just below his temple that wept clear fluid. He wiped at it with the bandage, but the fluid pulsed out again. Ben started to feel a knot in his stomach.

"Stay still." Ben kept his eyes on Nino's face, but half turned. "Jenny, over here."

The woman quickly crossed to him and the others began to crowd closer.

"What do you make of this?" Ben asked.

Jenny squinted and then shook her head. "Don't know; shrapnel wound maybe? Rounded; looks like a bullet wound."

Dan eased in closer. "I bandaged him, but I don't remember that. Might have missed it."

Ben squinted and gently turned the man's head. "That discharge looks a little like cranial fluid."

"Jesus," Dan said with a grimace.

"How do you feel?" Ben looked into Nino's eyes again.

The man looked vacant for a few seconds as though listening to something, before his lips began to move. "The devil...he is inside me now." He looked up at Ben, his face slowly creasing in anguish. "*Inside me!*"

He pushed Ben's hands away and sprinted off into the jungle.

140

"*Shit.*" Ben went after him, followed by most of the group.

The small man was able to burrow and dodge around the mad tangle of the jungle, and quickly outpaced his larger pursuers. In just a few minutes, he was already fifty feet ahead of them.

Ben barged after him, following the sound of his mad dash, but in another moment, it fell silent. Ben then found the man; he was standing in the centre of a small clearing, looking bewildered.

Ben would have called out, but he remembered Jenny telling him to be silent. He pushed fern fronds aside, about to enter when he was tackled from behind, and a hand went over his mouth.

He spun, ready to fight, but was immediately released. Walt Koenig had his fingers to his lips. "We're being stalked."

The others caught up, and Koenig waved them down. Ben looked from the hunter back to Nino. "Where?"

Koenig pointed. "There and there – just past the first line of brush."

Ben followed where the man indicated but saw nothing. But then he noticed something odd; the sounds of the jungle had vanished, and it was like they had all fallen into a vacuum.

Mist curled in amongst the hairy or scaled trunks of trees and threaded its way through tangles of vines and huge flesh palms. But he couldn't see what the hunter could.

Nino started to wail and hold his head.

"We need to help him," Ben whispered as the man became even more agitated.

"Too late for that." Koenig's mouth turned down.

"The hell it is." Ben started to get to his feet, but the hunter grabbed his shirt.

"Wait, watch," Koenig said more forcefully. "Don't get all your friends killed."

Emma and Jenny crawled forward. "What is it? Where's Nino?"

Ben pointed.

The jungle came alive as the attack began – the first creature sprang from the leafy tangle behind the man, coming at him so fast it was nearly a blur. The thing was around seven feet tall, brown and green tiger-striped for perfect camouflage, and had beaded red eyes like those of some sort of bird of prey.

From 10 feet out, it leapt, landing directly on Nino and pinning him down, huge claws on its toes sprung down and dug in. Nino's scream of surprise and pain was like a signal to the rest, who came from two sides, smaller, but obviously part of the same pack.

"Theropods," Jenny whispered. "Pack hunters."

Ben couldn't tear his eyes away. He'd seen soldiers, friends, burned, blasted and shot full of holes, but this made him feel physically ill.

The creatures wasted no time tearing at Nino's flesh. Ben swallowed down some bile as he watched in horror. In only seconds, the Venezuelan's arms held up for protection were ripped away, and his screams continued even as they pulled more and more flesh from him. He was then raked and disemboweled, and then finally the pack leader reached for the man's face, and the sound of tooth on bone made Ben look away for a moment.

Even as he did, he could hear them eat, gulping their meat. He turned back. The three theropods continually lifted their heads, looking over their shoulders to scan the foliage. Their darting movements reminded Ben of some sort of horrifying birds from Hell pecking at their meals. But there were no beaks, just cruel mouths that were just rows of needle-sharp teeth.

"Sons of bitches," Koenig hissed through clamped teeth.

Ben eased his rifle off his shoulder, but the hunter shook his head, whispering, "Like a lion or wolf pack, there could be more that are just waiting their turn. We need to get the fuck out of here."

With a wet, tearing crunch, one of Nino's legs was torn from his torso. Emma made a gagging noise in her throat, and then couldn't help herself: "*Oh, Jesus…*"

Jenny threw a hand over her mouth, but the words carried. The three creatures pulled their bloody box-like heads from the mess of torn clothing, splintered bones, and rags of meat that was once Nino, and faced in the group's direction.

Ben knew they were hidden behind a stand of fern fronds, but it wasn't the thing's eyesight that would pick them out. As if on cue, the largest reared back and lifted its head, sniffing deeply.

"We'll never outrun 'em," Koenig whispered. "No choice now." This time, it was the hunter who drew his rifle.

Ben silently did the same, and used a hand to force the group back. When Ben turned back, he saw that two of the creatures were now easing towards them, and were now only 50 feet away. Their heads were pointed on long necks and their tails were out arrow straight behind them. Any second, he expected the charge to come.

One of the creatures, the smallest, remained behind, one clawed foot on the last of Nino's remains, but it also watched intently. Ben was of two minds: should they stand and fight, or run for it?

The decision was taken from him, as the first creature, the largest, hissed like a steam kettle and prepared its run.

"Brace." Ben was up on one knee, the assault rifle to his shoulder. Koenig was just behind him, his own rifle pointed and rock steady.

"Don't aim for the head," Jenny whispered. "Too hard."

The hissing of the three creatures was loud in the clearing now, and the pack leader's clawed feet began to pound towards them. But as it did so, from behind them something else burst from the brush, obviously attracted by the noise and smell of a fresh kill.

"Oh-*hhh* fuck," Steve quaked.

The thing stood about 15 feet tall on two titanic legs, small arms that had three hooked claw-like fingers on the ends of human-sized arms. Its pebbled flesh was brick-red.

Trees were shattered from its path, and it roared so loud the theropod that had been on top of Nino froze, just for a split second, but enough for the massive creature to leap and land.

Ben felt the ground shake beneath them as the thing came down on the smaller biped theropod, pinning it to the ground. The other members of the pack, outweighed, out-muscled, and out-toothed, fled in terror.

The massive beast roared again, and Ben felt the power of the sound as he too froze in fear. The huge, boxy head lowered then, and the mouth opened displaying rows of eight-inch, backward-curving teeth. The small theropod screamed and even from where Ben watched, he could feel the primal fear of the animal, as it knew it was about to be eaten alive.

In a single crunch and tear, the sound of fear was ripped away as a third of the smaller theropod was torn from the rest of the body.

"Go, go, go." Koenig dragged Ben backwards, and he and the group began to barrel through the jungle.

They ran hard, ducking and dodging tree trunks and fern fronds, and it was only after a few minutes that he realised that the group wasn't slowing, didn't know where it was going, and was basically just blundering through the jungle in a blind panic.

Ben hated to do it, but he had no choice – he yelled: "*Stop!*"

Emma turned briefly, and then slowed and stopped. Just in front of her, Koenig did the same, and then he saw Jenny come back, red-faced and eyes round. Her head constantly turned, looking from one side of the jungle to the other.

Ben sucked in huge lungfuls of air. "Where the hell is everyone else?"

Jenny shook her head. "In front, running fast. I lost sight of them."

Ben cupped his mouth with his hands, but Jenny put a hand up to his face.

"Don't." She pulled his hands down. "Please, Ben, don't. Theropods track primarily by sound and scent. I think that big one was an *Allosaurus* – there could be even bigger predators about." She sucked in a few breaths, looking like she was about to throw up. "Plus, the smaller ones are still out there somewhere. We just need to, just need to…" She gulped air again. "We just need to find shelter, and then work on finding a way down."

"We need to find them; it's Steve, Dan, and Andrea," Emma said. "That's our priority."

"Yes, but we're vulnerable now. Night time might actually be better for us," Jenny pleaded.

"I can track them better during the day," Koenig said. "Gotta find the boss, or no pay. And he's damn gonna be up for plenty from this dumb ass mission."

"Can't lose touch with them," Ben said, feeling his nerves stretch with impatience.

Jenny hung onto him again. "Look, it's all educated guessing when dealing with these massive creatures that have been extinct for over 65 million years, but we know that these things had great senses of smell and hearing. But many predatory bipeds also have something called optokinetic reflexes. Basically, it means that they are tuned in to have reflexive responses to moving visual stimuli – the eyes automatically track contrast-based movement. But it works best in the light – like now." Her features were screwed with anxiety. "Wait until it's dark."

Ben exhaled through pressed lips. "Fuck it." He looked out into the jungle. It had already swallowed the others – Steve, Andrea, Dan, Barlow, and Bellakov, all out there somewhere. Barlow and Bellakov he couldn't give a crap about, but his friends being lost worried the hell out of him.

Ben checked his watch – midday – they had time. "I don't care; we find them."

CHAPTER 24

Barlow wheezed like an old kettle and reached out to hang onto Janus Bellakov's arm. "We need, we need, to...*rest*," he panted.

Bellakov didn't look at him, but instead kept scanning the jungle. He gripped his rifle hard with muzzle up.

"We need to go back," Andrea cried. Her face was beet-red and tear-streaked.

"She's right," Steve said. "We've become separated and need to find Ben and the team."

"I don't think so," Bellakov said without turning.

"What? Are you mad?" Dan's brow was deeply creased. "Safety in numbers, man. Did you not see what just happened back there?"

Bellakov kept his eyes on the green walls all around them. He'd seen the smaller creatures sprint away, startled by the enormous fucking thing that had burst from the jungle. Those theropods, as the zoo girl called them, were mean suckers. They were like seven-foot-tall tigers with daggers on their feet. Going back might mean finding Ben Cartwright and his people, or it might mean walking straight into a pack of those pissed-off monsters.

Bellakov had seen how fast they moved, like a wolf pack but bigger, meaner, smarter, and a hundred times more deadly. And all he had was amateurs with a single shotgun, and the rest with handguns they probably didn't even know how to use.

He turned, fixing them with a stare. "Ain't happening."

"Hey, you're not listening." Dan reached out to grab his shoulder, but Bellakov spun, lifting his rifle to jam the butt into the tech millionaire's chest. Dan went down.

"It's *you* that's not listening." Bellakov righted the gun and held the muzzle pointed downwards but in Dan's direction. "They said they'd head towards the source of the river." He pointed. "That way. We can go back, and risk missing them, or perhaps coming face to face with those monsters."

Steve helped Dan to his feet, and Bellakov looked at each of their faces – fear, fatigue, and confusion – *good*, he thought. "Or we can head in the direction we *know* they'll go, and more than likely intersect trails."

"But they might need our help," Andrea implored.

Bellakov chuckled. "They've got Cartwright and Koenig – both seasoned warriors. You've just got me. They'll be fine." He turned to Barlow. "How you doin', boss?"

Barlow took off his hat and used one beefy arm to wipe his streaming brow before jamming it back on his head.

"Your logic is impeccable, Mr. Bellakov. Lead on."

"Nah ah." Bellakov pointed at Steve. "*You*; your turn to be out on point."

Steve just grunted. "Fine; ready when you are." He leaned towards Andrea. "You okay?"

She gave him a watery smile. "No."

He half smiled in return. "Me neither." He turned in the direction of where they believed the river was running from – inland.

*****

"We pick it up from where we know it exists – the plateau edge," Ben said.

"Works for me," Koenig agreed. "Then we can track it back – but finding it is the key."

"What then?" Jenny asked.

"In Benjamin's notes, he said there were caves at the inland lake. Maybe one is deep enough to take us back to the ground." He shrugged. "It's all I got for now."

Koenig checked his weapon. "We go silent, low, and as fast as we can. We do not want to be out here in the dark." He looked up and grinned at Ben. "It's your plan, big guy, so..."

Ben nodded and then led them out, followed by Emma and Jenny, with Koenig at the rear. Ben burrowed, squeezed, and eased his way through, trying to avoid having to hack his way forward using his long hunting knife. Their progress wasn't as fast as he wanted, but it was the quietest way they could manage.

Once, they all froze as they heard the sound of a massive body crashing through the undergrowth, followed by the screams of fear then pain, and gave their thanks it wasn't an agonized human voice.

They waited in silence as it devolved into the sounds of wet tearing before Ben waved them on again. They detoured in a wide arc around the kill zone, as the one thing they'd all learned was that the sounds and smells of death brought out more of the hunters.

Every foot they travelled stretched their nerves. In just a matter of hours, two of their party had been attacked and died gruesomely, and now they had been split up. So every shadow made someone jump, and every rustle in the underbrush caused a near panic.

146

Ben had fought in jungles before, but it had been against human adversaries, not something that wanted to eat you alive.

It took them another full draining hour in the humid mist-filled jungle before they came to the clearing at the edge of the plateau. Ben simply stopped and stared.

"Ho-*leeeey* shit," Emma said.

Walt Koenig chortled and cradled his gun. The jungle floor was well over a thousand feet below them, and the canopy cover was an unbroken field of green for as far as they could see.

Above them, the clouds hung heavily, and strangely, they were darker and thicker over the plateau above them. They even swirled slightly like they were in the eye of a cyclone.

But it wasn't the weather or the jungle that drew their attention, but instead the downed airplane.

"Old," Jenny said. "Looks like a Spitfire or something."

"I'm thinking World War II at least," Koenig added.

"Corsair Fighter," Ben said. "And yeah, you're right, World War II. They called them the bent-wing widow-makers – they were tough to land on carriers."

Ben began to walk towards it. "This poor sap probably got blown off course. They were doing a lot of work in the Pacific and I bet the carrier launched from Guadalcanal."

"A long way from home," Koenig said.

"Yep." Ben took a brief look over his shoulder to the jungle, and then put his rifle over his shoulder. The cockpit window was still sealed and covered over with vines. He laid a hand on the fuselage. "These bad boys had a Pratt & Whitney engine; that gave 'em 2,000 horsepower, and gassed up, had a range of 1,000 miles." He stepped up on the wing and rubbed at the cockpit canopy window, cupping his hands around his eyes to peer in.

He snorted softly, gripped the glass, and dragged it gradually back with a painful squeal of corrosion. The skeleton had its head leant forward and he immediately saw that the front of the skull was caved in.

Ben leaned his forearms on the edge of the cockpit. "Crash landing, died on impact. Probably for the best." He reached in to grab the dog tags still hanging around the bony neck.

"Lieutenant John Carter." He gripped them and tugged them free. "Rest in peace, buddy." He tucked the tags into his pocket.

Emma climbed up on the other wing and peered in. "Still in pretty good shape for a 70-year-old plane."

"Yeah, all we need is a tank of gas, a workshop, and a few hundred hours of a mechanic's time, and we're outta here." He smiled. 'We probably should have been here when he came down."

Ben leaned in again, looking at the skeleton. "If we were, maybe we could have…who knows." He patted the skeleton's shoulder. "Thank you for your service, airman." He was about to pull back but paused, looking from the cockpit, the wings, and then to the plateau edge – *pretty good shape for a 70-year-old plane*, she'd said.

An insane thought began to form, but then was quickly scrubbed away by logic. *Nah*, he straightened. *Not even I'm that mad*, he thought, and jumped down from the wing.

He took one last look back. *Yet.*

CHAPTER 25

Bellakov held up a hand and the group bunched up behind him. He held a finger to his lips, and then just let his senses reach out to the jungle.

The seconds stretched, each one seeming longer than the last. The group peered from him to the jungle and back again, and their eyes were large and round, like those of frightened sheep.

They're scared, and they need to be, he thought. The fact was, they were being tracked. On both sides of them, some *things* were keeping pace with them. Their footfalls were light, but he knew they were there.

Bellakov recognized the hunter's tread, as he was also a hunter. Plenty of times people had tried to kill him, and he knew what it was like to be shadowed by something or someone who wanted to kill, and he knew it now. Barlow eased in closer to him, the fat fool quivering like pink pudding.

"What is it?" he stammered.

"Predators," Bellakov whispered, and then pointed to Dan and Steve, then his eyes, and then back out into the jungle. He needed their eyes and ears, as well as their firepower.

Though there was no breeze to be up or downwind of, Bellakov knew that with their body odor, perfumes, and deodorants, they'd be leaving a scent trail dozens of feet wide to be picked up by every scent-tracking predator that passed across it.

And that wasn't all – he gritted his teeth as he looked down at the girl's leg; the bandage was red and damp – there was nothing like the coppery sweet smell of fresh blood to ring the dinner bell to call in the hungry diners.

"Stand and fight?" Steve asked.

Bellakov had considered it. He liked the kid's guts, but the fact was they had no idea how many of them there were. Added to that, he saw what happened when you made too much noise – it starts with the little fast ones, and ends with King fucking Kong lizard crashing the party.

He lifted his gun. "Not sure if we could bring one of those big mothers down. Might just piss it off. We're gonna have to make a run for it."

His head snapped around – more sound, moving now to get in front of them and cut them off. Time was up. "Lock and load; *everyone.*"

Steve had the shotgun, but everyone else just handguns. Andrea lifted hers from her holster, the weapon looking big and awkward in her hand. And worse, it shook from nerves.

"Ready?" He looked at each of them; they were wide-eyed and on the verge of panic. Couldn't be helped.

"Then *go!*" He charged out in front, rifle held up in two hands, using it as a battering ram and also ready to fire.

The sudden motion excited the creatures to attack, and they came out of the jungle, fast and low; this time, the things were no more than waist height, and a muddy, mottled brown. They ran on two legs and hissed, showing rows of teeth like a serrated knife. Little arms ended in clawed hands that were now splayed wide.

Dan fired first, missing. Steve fired off a round and blew the head completely off one of them. *Good lad*, Bellakov thought.

Behind them all was Barlow, gasping like a stranded fish. Bellakov turned, sighted, and took down one of the things that made a run at him. He waited, and Dan and Steve shot past him, Andrea came next and as she went to sprint past, he put a foot out, tripping her.

"*Hey!*" she screamed.

"Go, go, go," he yelled after the group.

Barlow finally caught up. "I can't...you have to..."

Bellakov grabbed him by the shirt and pulled him close. "Listen, you fat fuck, you run, or you stay; I ain't carrying you, got it?"

The man's wet eyes went wide and he nodded rapidly.

"Then here's a gift." Bellakov looked down at the struggling Andrea as she began to get to her feet. He lifted one large boot and stomped down on her ankle. There was a crunch of bone, and she cried out. He bent to rip the gun from her hands.

"Ow, ow, ow." The young woman held her leg, tears running. She looked up at him, more confused than anything else.

"Let's go." He dragged Barlow with him as Andrea wailed, holding up an arm to them.

The rustling in the bushes continued, but then the shriek of pain from behind them told him that the creatures had found their staked goat – just like all predator packs, they'd always go for the weakest, the stragglers, or the injured.

Bellakov stopped and turned. He hung onto Barlow and jerked the man around.

"Watch."

It reminded him of a dog attack – the animals seemed frenzied as they jostled for position, poking heads in to get at the shrieking woman. In only a few seconds, the heads that pulled back were gulping meat, with snouts now slick-red with blood.

The screams became sobs, and then silence. Beside him, he heard Barlow gag, and he dragged him closer

"Don't you fucking vomit; they'll smell it."

Bellakov turned back to the feeding frenzy. *Sorry babe*, he thought, *but you drew the short straw*. He still held Barlow by the arm and dragged him close for a second time.

"You owe me big time."

Barlow's head nodded like it was on springs.

They ran on but there were no sounds of pursuit, and after another 15 minutes, Bellakov felt it was safe enough to slow down. In another few minutes more, he stopped them. All were out of breath, but still alert.

Steve frowned, looking past him. "Where's Andrea?"

Bellakov ignored him. "Everyone okay?"

"*Where the fuck is Andrea?*" he asked more forcefully and stepped closer.

Bellakov sighed and reached out to place a large hand on the young man's shoulder. "I'm sorry…she's gone."

Steve knocked his arm away. "What? What do you mean *gone*? Gone where? We need to get her." He went to step past Bellakov with Dan set to follow him.

Bellakov put out one burly arm. "She's gone, *gone*. You understand what I'm saying?" He pulled the younger man in front of him, real close, and stared into his eyes. "*They* got her."

"But…" Steve's mouth opened and closed for a few seconds. "They got her? How? Where were you? Why didn't you try and help her? Why didn't you call us, *me*, I would have fucking well gone back for her."

Bellakov had the urge to punch the kid, hard, but held it in check, as he needed them all on his side. He pulled his face into a facsimile of sorrow, and just shook his head.

"Steve, there were too many. They would have overrun us all." He sighed. "Please, this is hard for me too, but we must go on and survive, try and find our friends." Bellakov reached out and gripped the young man's upper arms. "This is what matters now."

The two men locked eyes, and he could see that Steve's narrowed with distrust. After a moment, the fire in Steve's eyes went out and he seemed to deflate. He looked down at the ground and nodded.

"Good lad." Bellakov walked past the man. "This way." He and Barlow headed off into the jungle, and Steve and Dan followed.

*****

Bellakov heard the water before he saw it, and in another few

151

minutes, they came to the riverbank of a shallow stream no more than six feet wide. He waved them down and crouched on his haunches, gun across his thighs, and just watched for a while.

The waterway only looked a few inches deep, with maybe a little more in some areas. It was clear and not moving too fast. Feeder roots from huge trees thicker than his waist burrowed in at the bank and the tree trunks were moss-covered, ancient, and towering above them, creating a green roof over their heads. Bordering the bank, heavy fern fronds reached over the water and though the stream cut a corridor between them, there was a sand and gravel bank on each side.

It looked peaceful, and safe, but he waited and watched. He knew from his jungle hunting days that fresh water was a lifesaver, but it was also a dangerous place to be. When animals came to drink and dipped their heads to lap at the cool water, they were vulnerable – all carnivores knew that, and that went for carnivores both on land and in the water.

"What are we looking for?" Dan whispered.

"Anything." Bellakov watched as a few dragonflies the size of small birds hovered over the stream and then alighted on some rushes. He tried to listen, but there was the constant *zumm* of life from hidden insects buzzing, humming, and chirruping all around them. If there was something lurking down there, he needed to flush it out. He turned.

"*You*; Dan, was it?"

"Huh, yeah, me Dan. What?" Dan replied, frowning.

"Go down there and check for tracks on the bank." Bellakov kept his eyes on the water.

"Are you shitting me? I'm not going out there...*by myself.*" Dan's mouth dropped open in derision.

"Don't worry, you'll be safe." He tapped his gun. "I'll cover you and I'm the best shot of all of us." He shrugged. "Take your buddy if you want someone to hold your hand."

"This is not a good idea." Dan looked at Steve.

"We'll all be moving along the stream in a few minutes. But I want you to check for animal tracks now while I can cover you, rather than when we're all down there, okay?" He pushed Dan. "Hurry up, son; daylight's burning."

"Come on, buddy." Steve got up from his haunches and walked carefully down the bank. Dan followed in a crouch, mumbling about being a crash test dummy.

Bellakov watched the pair only for a moment before he turned his attention to the surrounding wall of jungle. Nothing edged closer or took a run at the pair, as they tentatively went to the bank, their heads turning one way then the other. Bellakov was also relieved to see nothing launched itself from the water, but didn't really expect it as it looked too shallow. However, there were deeper sections, and bottom line was, he had no idea what freaking things could even exist here, so they'd need to be careful.

He felt the gentle tug on his sleeve and turned to the moonfaced Barlow.

"Janus." He smiled creepily.

Bellakov was immediately on guard – Barlow never called him by his first name.

Barlow licked his lips. "I'm probably the slowest of you all. And I'm sure the temptation may come to leave me behind, like, well, you know who." He simpered again.

Bellakov continued to give him an impassive stare. The guy was a schemer and wasn't to be trusted. Besides that, the mercenary had already thought about dumping his fat ass if he slowed them down.

Barlow continued. "Janus, when that temptation comes, you will resist it, because you will remember the words I now speak to you." His fingers alighted on Bellakov's arm and began to gently tug at the fabric. "*Five million dollars*, no strings attached, and all you have to do for it is finish your job – and that is to get me home. Understand?"

Bellakov stared, letting the seconds stretch. "Ten million."

Barlow's eyes widened, but he nodded. "Ten million it is."

Money talks, Bellakov thought, and he let his face break open in a wide smile. He reached out a hand. "Deal."

Barlow shook it eagerly. "Good man, yes, *deal*."

Bellakov went back to watching the men in the stream. After five full minutes, the pair of men straightened and hiked their shoulders. Bellakov half turned.

"Looks okay."

Bellakov rose and then sauntered down, still wary, and when on the bank, he held up a hand for silence. He stood there, letting his senses take in the surroundings – there was no animal smells, no sound other than the small gurgle of water over rounded stones, and there seemed to be nothing he could see camouflaged behind the green fringe.

He walked out into the center of the stream that only came to his ankles.

"Move out; and walk in the water. It'll stop predators picking up our scent trail."

They began to head upstream, Bellakov in the lead, Barlow panting behind, then Dan and Steve at the rear. It was already 3pm, mid-afternoon. They needed shelter, or they needed a tree perch in the next few hours.

Bellakov knew more of them would be dead before morning. And it damn well wasn't going to be him…or his ten-million-buck meal ticket.

CHAPTER 26

Ben checked his watch – 4pm. Time was moving way too fast on them. He had the same coiled feeling in his gut like he had on some of the missions he undertook in Afghanistan, where he was always on edge, always ready, always strung piano-wire tight.

I left all that for a quieter life. Then I choose to do this – what kind of idiot am I? he wondered.

The streambed they moved along was shallow and clear. From time to time, small fish darted past his feet, but nothing hid in amongst the rounded rocks, and at the riverbanks, the rushes were too sparse for concealment.

A while back, he had spotted the impressions of boot marks. The tiny scrape of moss, the toe mark in sand, and the occasional squashed aquatic critter – the others had come this way, and they weren't that far in front.

Emma walked beside him, her handgun dangling at her side. "I know what you're thinking," she whispered.

He glanced at her and let one eyebrow rise. "Oh yeah. Lay it on me."

"You're wondering how the hell you got here?" She gave him a lopsided grin.

He bobbed his head. "How'd you guess?"

Her smile was fragile. "Because I'm thinking the same thing. We were like all the bored, spoilt, overfed, and pampered people of the modern world. We were just looking for a little adventure. Guess we found it."

He frowned down at her. "That's not true. For a start, we're not overfed."

She brightened a little at his attempt at humor.

"You know what the real problem was?" he asked.

She shook her head.

"Did any of us really think this place existed? I mean *really* think it existed? We underestimated, *everything*."

She nodded. "I sort of expected something, but, no, not like this. I thought maybe we'd spend a few days in the Amazon, take a few pictures, rack up a few mosquito bites, and then all head home with suntans and some cool stories to tell over beers."

"Me too." Ben stopped. "Uh oh."

"What?" Emma went with him. Behind them, Jenny and Koenig bunched up, but the hunter, Koenig, remained standing and keeping watch.

"Blood." He pointed at the tip of a rock just sticking from the water with a red streak. He looked upstream. "No way to tell if it's human or not."

Koenig spoke without turning. "There's no disruption on either bank; they never left the water."

"Good." Ben stood. He looked upwards and could just make out the cloud cover through the jungle canopy. The clouds were still low, angry, and unnatural, and seemed to be swirling almost like they were in the eye of a cyclone. He ignored it; he had enough to worry about.

"Let's pick up the pace."

They continued heading along the watercourse, trading a little silence now for speed, hoping to catch up with their friends.

CHAPTER 27

2 Hours Past Full Apparition

Comet P/2018-YG874, designate name Primordia, had passed over its perihelion, and though still bright in even the daylight sky, it had already achieved its closest point to Earth.

If Ben Cartwright could have seen through the cloud cover, he might have made out that the tiny streak in the sky was now moving into the left hemisphere, as Primordia's once a decade visit was coming to an end.

Soon it would vanish once again as it headed away from Earth, back out on its never-ending elliptical voyage through the solar system.

CHAPTER 28

The light was fading, and the ever-present cloud cover combined with the dropping sun to give them an early twilight. The light was weird, near purple, colored by the strange low clouds. And the heat and humidity never let up for a second.

They'd found the carcass a few miles back. They heard the sound of squabbling carnivores coming from a bend in the stream, and Ben left everyone behind a stand of thick pulpy-looking fronds as he crept forward.

The dozens of creatures reminded him of large turkeys, ripping at something he couldn't quite make out. He prayed it wasn't a person and edged even closer. It was only when one of the creatures had ripped the head of the victim free, that he saw it was some sort of armor-plated thing no bigger than a kitchen table.

The smaller animals should not have troubled the armored beast. Ben guessed that it had probably been killed by something else, and these things were undoubtedly scavenging on the remains.

Ben eased back and waved Jenny forward. The zoologist came and crouched beside him, and together they leaned out.

"Amazing," she breathed out.

"Yeah, but are they a threat?" Ben said over his shoulder.

The smaller biped creatures were frantic in their movements, jerking and squawking like a flock of birds, and their heads and necks were now streaked red with blood.

"*Dromaeosaurus, Saurornithoides*, or could be a dozen other types of smaller carnivore species," Jenny said. "They're scavengers, but in larger numbers, they may just decide to attack."

Jenny craned forward just as one pulled back with a chunk of meat in its mouth and gulped it down. "Their teeth are sharp and close together, creating a serrated scissor effect – they'd do damage to us soft human beings."

"Then we go around them." Ben pulled her back to the group.

"Roadblock," Ben said. "We'll need to detour."

The group needed to spend a considerable amount of time looping around the feeding frenzy, and then finding their way back to the stream. Detouring into the jungle meant it was slower going, and once they needed to hunker down as something large blundered past them back the way they'd come – Ben felt vindicated in his choice as he expected the smell of blood would draw larger more formidable beasts.

It was almost sundown when they finally reached the source of the stream. The group emerged from the green cave they had been travelling along and stopped to gape in awe.

"So big," Emma said. "It's not possible."

With the fading light, the huge body of water was already inky black. But even though there was no wind the surface wasn't still – ripples, bubbles, and V-shaped patterns were made by things moving beneath the surface.

Ben waved everyone down. "Why don't we just watch for a while; see who's home?"

Leathery-winged creatures with 12-foot wingspans glided on warm thermals to skim the lake's surface, now and then dipping three-foot-long toothed beaks down to snatch up wriggling fish before sharply pulling up and away.

As they watched, one spent a little too much time near the surface, and a huge massive black torpedo shape launched itself from below, grabbing the screaming animal and dragging it down in a thrash of bloody foam.

"Jesus; everything about this damn place is hell," Koenig said.

"No, this place is simply a snapshot of what our world was like about 100 million years ago," Jenny said. "Maybe to us soft little mammals, it's a nightmare, but to them, it's just, life." She looked up at the hunter. "Maybe to them, our world would be a nightmare."

"Yeah right, lady," Koenig scoffed.

"Over there." Ben pointed. "That cliff face; down on the waterline?"

Emma, Jenny, and Koenig followed his direction – at the far side of the lake on the waterline was a row of dark holes in the cliff, and all looked big enough to accommodate them.

"Looks like our digs for the night," Emma said.

"Let's just hope someone hasn't already made a reservation," Jenny said.

Ben eased to his feet and then looked skyward for a moment. "I estimate we've got about an hour of light left, and then it'll be darker than hell without a moon or stars. We need to be in there by then."

Koenig peered one way then the other. "Options: skirt the lake, left or right, or we go as the crow flies."

Jenny turned slowly towards him, her brow furrowed. "You did just see that pterosaur get taken a few minutes back, huh?"

"That big dumb bird wasn't carrying an assault rifle." Koenig grinned.

"We're not crossing the water in the dark, and we're not going to be acting as fish bait." Ben looked along the lake edge on both sides. "I think we'll skirt around to the left; seems to be the thickest growth – gonna make traveling a little harder, but will also give us the best cover."

"Pretty dense cover and some of those trees are huge." Koenig squinted. "No branches though, but plenty of predators could hide in there. Still think the other side is best, there's some good open space, we could make a run for it rather than slogging through more jungle."

Jenny scoffed. "Two things; those tall trees you spotted aren't trees."

Everyone turned back to the huge trunks and as they watched, one of the *trees* seemed to bend down and vanish, before reappearing.

"Is that what I think it is?" Emma asked.

"I think so; some sort of huge sauropod herbivore – spend their entire day just eating and could easily weigh a hundred tons. Looks like a herd of them." She turned to Koenig. "They're too big to be troubled by most predators, so if these guys are hanging around and don't seem agitated, it usually means there's no carnivores threatening them. And that's good for us."

"A hundred tons?" Koenig rubbed his neck. "This all makes no sense."

"What doesn't?" Ben asked.

"Look at them." He pointed his chin. "This plateau is huge, but not *that* huge. I've been in plenty of jungles, and tracked herds of prey animals and also big predators. And I can tell you right now those big guys should not be able to survive in this cliff-top greenhouse; it's just not damn big enough."

The group swung back to look at the sauropod's necks that must have been ten feet around. Ben could imagine just how big the bodies of the creatures were.

"I've thought the same thing." Jenny placed her hands on her hips. "This *entire* place doesn't make sense. And something else; these massive creatures were warm-blooded, so if anyone was doing thermal mapping overhead from either a LINDAR or satellite, they'd show up like Christmas lights, cloud or no cloud. They couldn't hide."

"Do you think people *do* know and are covering it up?" Emma asked.

"Unlikely," Ben said. "Governments leak like sieves. They'd never be able to keep this secret." He sighed. "I guess we just don't know enough about them or this place."

Jenny nodded, but her forehead was creased. "Yeah maybe." She continued to look along the lake edge.

"So which route?" Koenig asked.

Jenny turned to the far bank of the lake. "Walt, there's something else that makes me real nervous about the *easier* side you suggested." She pointed. "See those flat rocks near the water's edge? They've been smoothed and stained, and remind me of beaching stones at a seal colony rocks. I think something has been dragging itself up on those rocks from time to time…something big."

"Yeah, I see it." Koenig's eyes narrowed. "The thick jungle it is then. So what are we waiting for?"

Ben waved him on. "Then take us out, Mr. Koenig."

*****

Out in the oil-black water, and towards the far side of the lake, a mound eased to the surface. It glided towards the group as they stood on the bank where the trees came all the way to the water.

It stayed motionless for many minutes, before once again gliding closer, this time a little faster.

When the group moved back in amongst trees, it stopped and stayed on the surface for several more minutes. After a time, it slowly sank below the surface without making a ripple.

CHAPTER 29

Janus Bellakov sliced a huge vine that barred his way. He paused for a few seconds, just listening to the sounds of the jungle – they were all still there, the squawks, chirrups, hums and shrill cries – *good*. It was when those background sounds vanished that the shit usually came down.

They'd been attacked several more times, smaller creatures moving fast, but not big enough to really trouble them. Some of them only needed a good kick to send them screaming back into the jungle.

Finding the lake a while back had meant they could be linking up with the others real soon, and looking across the dark water, he'd seen the caves – he bet his last buck that both Koenig and Cartwright would head straight for them. And if that's where they were going, then that's what he'd do too.

Bellakov had chosen the route to the right that looked easiest to traverse, and soon he hoped to make it to a large flat area at the water's edge where he planned to make a dash for it. Once that was done, he expected to be in the caves well before it got real dark.

Bellakov's priorities were to be somewhere defensible, and with a goddamn fire, *pronto*. He half turned. Behind him, Barlow looked a wreck – nervous, exhausted, and his fear making him totally docile. The man was pathetic.

The other two were competent enough, and together they should be able to make it. Or at least the pair would put up enough of a fight, and distraction, so *he* could make it. Bellakov's one objective was to get off the plateau. First prize, he'd do it with Barlow and end up a rich man. But the bottom line was saving his own skin; anything and anyone else was expendable when it came to achieving that end.

They came to the edge of the flat rocks and Bellakov stopped.

"*Phew*, Jesus Christ, what's that smell?" Dan put a hand over his face.

"Like shit," Steve added. "Fishy shit."

"Keep it down," Bellakov growled.

The four men crouched, the fading light making them all indistinct shadows.

"I don't like it," Dan whispered.

Bellakov snorted. "And which part *have* you liked so far? The giant snake, your guide being eaten alive, or maybe…"

"Yeah, yeah." Dan shook his head. "You know what I mean."

Bellakov shrugged. "Maybe it's a dumping ground for these monsters. Good thing is, it'll mask our odor, right?"

Steve got to his feet. "Quicker we're at the cave the better."

"Good man." Bellakov grinned. "You take point. Head out about 20 feet and scout the terrain."

Steve's head snapped around. "*Seriously*? I had point at the stream."

"Yeah, *seriously*, you're good at it; now hurry the fuck up," Bellakov shot back.

Steve pointed at Barlow. "When's that asshole gonna do some work?"

"When I say. Now hurry up." Bellakov waved him on.

Steve grumbled, but gripped his shotgun and headed out.

*****

The creature gently lifted its head from the water for a moment, and then let it slide back down a few inches so it was below the surface. The freshwater mosasaur was forty feet long but squat and powerful. It had four paddle-like flippers that were the last vestiges of limbs, plus a scythe-like tail akin to that of a dolphin. It was a powerful water hunter, and an apex ambush predator.

It had spotted the creatures making their way along the shoreline a while back and had been tracking them ever since. It kept pace with them, but they had always been too far from shore for it to mount a successful attack. It *could* lever itself out of the water when it needed to on its paddle-like limbs, but only for short periods of time. Its real hunting ground was the water – unless something on land came close enough for it to catch.

It glided closer when it saw one of them walk out onto the rocks it sometimes used to dry its skin to remove some of the parasites that grew on its hide. It drifted closer, and closer, just a few feet from the shoreline now, and began to bunch powerful muscles.

Its huge tail was ready to propel itself from the water. It continued to watch, waiting. Like most carnivorous dinosaurs, rapid movement both excited and triggered it.

*****

Bellakov watched Steve walk carefully out onto the flat shelf of stone. While he did, the mercenary scanned the jungle at the water's edge, trying to pick out any movement or things lurking there.

He snorted; how the hell did he expect to see anything anyway, as the shadows were now absolute, and the jungle was turning to just outlines. A few bubbles popped to the surface on the lake, and Bellakov turned to them and continued to stare for a moment.

He eased around to Dan. "Hey, cover your buddy."

Bellakov looked over the water to the caves; they weren't that far now, a quarter mile, max. It'd be full dark by the time they got there, and he damn well hoped nobody was home, other than Koenig, Cartwright, and the others.

Barlow mopped his face with a damp handkerchief, and then tied it around his neck. Bellakov looked over his shoulder to the jungle again. He'd been in all manner of green hellholes, but this place, *this* even made the Congo look like a fun park – every goddamn nook and cranny had something waiting to pounce, bite, sting, peck, or generally rip 'em to shreds.

More bubbles came to the surface, pulling Bellakov's attention to the water again as this time they were a little closer. The mercenary eased to his feet, staring hard.

Fifty feet away, Steve stopped and turned and then waved them on.

"What are we waiting for?" Dan asked.

"Nothin'," Bellakov shot back at him. "Just give it a few more seconds, will ya?"

Barlow leaned closer to him. "What is it? Why are we waiting?"

Bellakov held up a hand, but also moved to stop Barlow rubbing up against him; the man reeked of a sour perspiration, undoubtedly fear oozing from every pore. Barlow was now a walking scent trail and would be attracting things from all over the freaking plateau. He had a mind to push him in the water.

If they made it to the cave, he'd make sure the guy washed himself off; otherwise, next morning when they tried to bug out, they'd be dragging every predator for miles with them.

"I'm thinking we're looking good." After another few seconds without any sign of attack, he decided to move them out. "We go fast. Me first, then Mr. Barlow, then you're up last, Dan." He turned to give Barlow a hard stare. "Keep up, or you're on your own."

Barlow huffed, but just clamped his lips tight and nodded once.

"Let's go." Bellakov gripped his gun and started out. As soon as they broke from the jungle, he felt exposed, and his neck prickled. At his heel was Barlow, and a few paces back, Dan, who stopped and turned to stare back the way they'd just come from. Across the other side of the ramp of flat stones, Steve waited just inside a stand of fern fronds.

Bellakov tried to see everywhere at once – the water, the jungle ahead, the walls of green beside them, and he also looked over his shoulder. Every one of his senses screamed a warning, but there was nothing for it now but to continue on. Behind him, Edward Barlow wheezed so loudly it sounded like he had swallowed some sort of tiny musical instrument.

"Shut it," he hissed back at the man.

The wheezing immediately stopped but was replaced by a squeak from one of his nostrils.

Dan started to jog to catch up to the group. Ahead, Steve grinned and stood cradling his gun as he waited for them. Bellakov felt relieved to be coming to the end of the flat slabs of stone, and he allowed his pressed lips to hitch into a small smile.

Then came the eruption of water.

Bellakov threw an arm up as beside him something that looked like a surfacing submarine launched itself from the lake. He and Barlow fell back as a V-shaped head split open to reveal a 3-foot mouth filled with needle-like, backward-curving teeth.

The head turned sideways, and Dan never stood a chance. The jaws clamped shut, catching his torso and one arm. The poor sap never even had time to cry out as the huge creature wallowed on the stones for just a second or two, before flipping sideways and then back into the dark water.

Then it, and Dan, was just gone, leaving only waves to lap up on the stones.

"Dan?" Steve's eyes were wide, and he braced his legs and lifted his shotgun.

The lake calmed. Silence returned.

"Go." Bellakov grabbed Barlow by the collar and hustled him towards the cover of the jungle. In another few seconds, they were inside the green barrier beside Steve, and Bellakov turned back.

Steve still stood, gun up, and pointed at the water. His eyes were wet and his mouth hung open. But even though the lake was smooth, a few bubbles popped at the surface, and the darkness made it impossible to make out if the liquid on the stones was stained with blood.

"He's gone." Bellakov turned away. "Move it."

"But…" Steve held his position, gun still pointed at the water.

"But what?" Bellakov scowled. "He's gone. That's it."

"Every…" Steve turned about. "…every goddamn thing, every goddamn place…" He shook his head.

"Move." Bellakov shoved him backwards, and then reached out to grab a trance-like Barlow. "No noise." The smell of death was about now, and he knew what that would bring.

"Nearly there, nearly safe." The mercenary didn't believe it for a second.

CHAPTER 30

Ben and Koenig crouched at the cave entrance, with Jenny and Emma keeping watch on the jungle behind them.

Koenig kept his rifle at the ready as Ben flicked on his flashlight and scanned the floor of the cave. Even though it was close to the water, it looked dry inside.

"Death," Koenig said softly.

"Yep," Ben agreed. "Something's dead in there for sure. It either went in there to die, or it was dragged in as something's recent meal."

Koenig craned his neck. "A million places to hide." He looked back over his shoulder. "I'll tell you right now, if there was something in there, it'd attack us. Most creatures that use caves as their lair don't take too kindly to strangers comin' a visitin'…and they defend them to the death."

"Okay, we're going in anyway." Ben half turned to the women. "Ready?"

Emma and Jenny nodded, guns also ready but pointed down for now. Ben eased to his feet. "Count of 3, 2, 1, *go*."

He went in and to the side. Koenig went to the other side, his own flashlight beam coming on and scanning fast. Both men had their rifles up. Emma and Jenny went in behind Ben, and after a few more seconds, the four stood inside breathing heavily.

"*Phew*," Emma said. "That's rank."

"Rotting meat…over there." Jenny pointed the beam of her own flashlight.

"I see it now." Ben walked closer. Partially hidden by a small rocky outcrop was the skull of a medium-sized creature. The hide was more a shell of bony plates that sat over a ragged-looking skeleton, and the bones still looked fairly fresh, but the carcass was empty.

"They don't leave much do they?" Koenig crouched down. "Ate everything edible. Right down to the bones." He frowned. "Weird that they didn't break the larger bones to get at the marrow."

"Maybe a larger carnivore dragged it in here, and smaller animals then finished it off." Jenny brows also knitted as she came closer. "And you're right, the bones look…scoured, like they were rubbed over with a wire brush rather than gnawed." She reached in to run her fingertips over a rib.

"*Ouch.*" She pulled her hand out.

"You okay?" Emma asked.

Jenny turned her hand over. There was a cut or abrasion on the meat of the thumb. "Yeah, must have caught it on a bone shard. Better throw some iodine on this." She looked up. "And if anyone else has some cuts or scratches, be a good time to douse them. Not sure what sort of ancient germs are up here."

Jenny sniffed her fingers and her eyebrows rose. "Odd; smells like…almonds or something."

"I can smell it too," Emma said. "Is it from the decomposition?"

Jenny continued to stare at her hand, and then sniffed it again. "Might be. Like who really knows what a rotting dinosaur is supposed to smell like."

"Let's get organized," Ben said. "Koenig, scout this place out while I get some branches together so we can get a fire going. Don't want anything else deciding to drag another carcass in here, or coming back to finish this one."

"I heard that." Koenig affixed his flashlight to the end of his rifle and headed off into the darkness of the cave's interior.

"Emma, Jenny, push some stones together for a fire pit." Ben turned to the cave mouth. "Be back in a few minutes."

"Ben…"

He turned at the sound of Emma's voice. She looked up round-eyed at him.

"…just be careful." She shared a nervous smile.

"Count on it." He saluted her and slipped outside.

Ben waited for a few moments. Even though it was a near impenetrable blackness outside now, the jungle was still alive with all manner of insects singing, whirring, and flinging themselves about in the dark. He could also hear crawling creatures rustling in the undergrowth. They needed the fire, *and* its smoke – the fire should keep inquisitive creatures at bay, and the smoke will dissuade flying insects from entering the cave – important if they were going to get some rest and not end up being turned into pin cushions.

Get on with it, he urged himself.

Ben moved quickly, darting, but pausing now and then to stop and simply listen. There was nothing he could detect, and in a few minutes had an armful of dry logs and some hair-like bark to use as tinder.

He was about to turn back to the cave when he heard the sound of branches being pushed aside. He froze, waiting. There was no doubt that something, or some *things*, were coming straight at him, not rushing, but creeping.

Ben lowered his pile of logs to the jungle floor and eased back upright. He carefully pulled his rifle from his shoulder. He hoped whatever it was would pass him by, but if not, he'd take the first one down and hope the rest might prefer the fresh kill instead of him.

Seconds ticked down, and he tried to calm himself and slow his breathing. The senses of these things were far in advance of his own and could probably smell his exhalations, his perspiration, and may even be able to detect his body heat.

He waited, his nerves stretching as the thing approached. A branch snapped, close, and then he heard something stumble and someone swear softly in the darkness.

"Jesus Christ, are you guys riding elephants?" Ben relaxed.

"Who's there?" a voice shot back.

"Ben Cartwright; over here."

The three men came forward, with Steve coming quickly to embrace him in a bear hug.

"Ben, *Ben*, thank God you're okay." Steve hugged him again. "Who's with you?"

"Koenig, Emma, and Jenny. That's it I'm afraid." He looked over Steve's shoulder. "And you?"

Janus Bellakov came out of the shadows. "Good to see you, Cartwright. Been a hellova trek." He pointed with his chin. "You in the caves?"

Ben ignored him and grabbed Steve's upper arms. "What happened?"

Steve exhaled and looked down at the ground. "We lost both Andrea and Dan – fucking monsters – it's only myself, Janus, and Barlow I'm afraid." The man's face crumpled, and Ben hugged him again.

"It's all right, buddy. We'll get through this." He held him back a step. "Let's go and see the rest. They'll be happy to see you."

He turned to the other two men. "Help grab some branches so we can make a fire." He crouched to gather up his logs again. "Hurry now."

*****

"We're back..." Ben spoke softly. "...found a friend."

They entered the cave and Bellakov stood in the entrance, looking over their faces. He nodded to Walt Koenig, with the man suddenly looking sullen in return.

Emma and Jenny got to their feet, their faces initially beaming, but then caught sight of Steve's expression.

"Where's... Daniel?" Jenny's voice was small.

"And Andrea?" Emma took a couple of steps forward.

Steve continued to stare at the ground.

"No, no, no; not Dan and Andrea," Emma agonized.

"Gone." Steve wiped at his nose and still couldn't meet their eyes.

"How... what happened?" Emma's fists balled.

"We were attacked," Bellakov said. "Lucky any of us are here."

"But *you* are." Emma's chin jutted.

"Yep," Bellakov replied, and Ben noticed the disbelieving look Koenig was giving him.

"How do you know they're dead?" Emma persisted. "Did you...?"

"That's enough." Ben sighed. "This place killed them, not anyone here. Our job now is to make sure it doesn't kill anyone else. There's safety in numbers."

Steve went and embraced both women, and just hung on for a while. Edward Barlow, who looked totally worn out, relaxed back into his avuncular self of old.

The logs were piled inside the ring of stones and in a few minutes the tinder caught, and then flames started to lick at the smaller sticks. Steve flicked off his cigarette lighter.

"Better than rubbing two sticks." He sat back on his haunches, his face still haunted. "Does anyone even do that anymore?"

"Sure they do, and still do," Ben said. "It's not hard, but you've got to be prepared to lose a bit of skin off your palms. But if it's the difference between being warm and dry or wet and cold, you make the effort."

As the fire took hold, an orange glow filled the cave. An added bonus was that the smoke masked the odor of corruption from the animal carcass.

Edward Barlow pointed. "Is it a good idea to be in a cave that has the rancid odor of a dead animal?"

"No, it's not," Ben replied. "But it's too big to drag outside. We might have to dissuade something from trying to take a look throughout the night – so we'll be taking turns on guard duty."

He looked at each of the group. "If anyone has any food bars, now is the time to share them around." He noticed Barlow give Bellakov a furtive look and guessed there'd be no sharing of *his* goodies.

As the tongues of flame rose, the dark corners of the cave were pushed back. Emma first stared, and then got to her feet.

"What the...?"

She walked to one side of the cave where there was a flat wall and flicked on her flashlight, adding its luminance to the fire's light.

"What is it?" Ben asked.

She turned. "You might want to see this."

The group followed her to the side of the cave, and Ben had to ease past a jostling Koenig and Jenny.

She pointed. "Your ancestor reaches out to you."

On the wall, scratched into the stone was writing. Ben came in closer and held up his own light. He then rubbed at some of the mineral excretions and algae that were masking some of the words. He began to read them.

"This is a lost world, and we are lost within it."

Ben used his palm, faster now, to wipe more lichen from the letters.

"Time is running out. If we delay, we'll be trapped here forever."

The two sentences made his stomach flip, and he couldn't imagine the horror for the two solitary men trapped here. He read the last line.

"They come at night. We know they're watching. BBC. 1908."

"BBC – Benjamin Bartholomew Cartwright," Ben breathed.

"They come at night." Koenig nodded. "And, they're watching." Koenig's mouth twitched. "I'm thinking maybe we need two on guard duty."

"Yeah, I'm thinking the same." Ben turned away. "Baxter never made it off the plateau. But somehow Benjamin did."

"Well, Ben the 1st is not giving away any clues today," Steve observed.

"Maybe he hadn't worked out how to escape yet," Koenig mused.

"Good point." Steve nodded. "So, tomorrow's another day." He looked up. "Who's on first shift?"

"Emma, you okay?" He saw that the young woman was still distracted, and her eyes were rimmed.

"Yeah, yeah, I'm fine." She walked a little closer to the words on the wall and reached up to touch them.

She didn't look it, Ben thought. *They were all being ground down.*

"I can do the first shift of two hours. Then Jenny and Walt, followed by Steve and Janus." Ben looked to Barlow. "Edward, you can do the last shift with me again."

Emma spun, frowning. "That's not fair, you doing two shifts." She jerked a thumb at Bellakov. "Make him do two shifts."

"It's not a problem; I won't be able to sleep anyway." Ben shrugged. "Besides, if it wasn't for me and that stupid notebook, you all wouldn't even be here."

"That's not true," Emma protested.

"Sadly, my dear, it *is* true," Barlow added. "Mostly."

Ben turned, his lips curled. "Except for you. If your men had done a better job stealing it from us in England, then you'd be here, and we wouldn't. So you're getting everything you deserve." Ben grinned menacingly.

"Easy there, young man. It was just a poor attempt at humor." Barlow returned Ben's glare with a half-lidded disinterest.

The group cleared a space around the fire, threw some more logs on, and then settled down to try and get some sleep. Ben and Emma moved to sit beside the cave entrance.

Ben handed her his canteen. "Try not to look back at the fire, it'll reduce your night vision ability."

"Got it." She took the canteen and sipped, and then handed it back. "I don't trust Bellakov, or his gross little paymaster."

He took the canteen. "Neither do I. But we need them. And once we're all off this plateau, we never have to see their ugly mugs again."

She nodded and then smiled, but it crumbled quickly. "What do you really think happened to Dan and Andrea?"

He looked back out at the darkness. "Steve said Dan was taken by something from the lake. He didn't see what happened to Andrea. I trust Steve's version." He shrugged. "That's all we can do."

She was silent for many minutes, ruminating. "So, tomorrow..." she began, "... What's the plan?"

He snorted softly. Frankly, he had no idea, but was determined to stay positive, if only for her.

"Priority one, we stay alive." He held out his canteen again, but she declined. He sipped and then stared out into the darkness. "We've been up on this plateau for less than a day, and we've already lost four people. So tomorrow, we use what we've learned from those tragedies to be a little bit smarter." He turned to her. "But bottom line, we need to find a way down, and maybe take some risks. Staying here is not an option."

She nodded, but then glanced at him. "Your great, great grandfather said that time was running out, and that there was a risk they could be trapped up here forever. What did he mean by that?"

Ben sighed. He also remembered Benjamin saying this place could only be found or rather, *seen*, once every decade. Nothing made sense anymore. He shook his head.

"I don't know exactly, Emm. But I have no intention of any of us being trapped up here for even one more minute, let alone forever."

Behind them, Barlow began to snore softly. Ben scoffed. "Glad someone is comfortable. Don't know how he does it."

"I think I'm like you. I couldn't sleep even if I wanted to," Emma said. "I just want to go home." She leaned against him. "Get me home, Ben; just get me home."

*****

The hours burned down just like the fire. The bodies tossed and turned, none of the group really falling into a fitful sleep. The two watching at the mouth of the cave also lapsed into a sense of lassitude, as the warmth of the night's humidity coupled with the smell of wood smoke became comforting and entrancing.

Outside, there was the ever-present noise of a jungle – things moved, scurried, and far out from the cave, something died, probably brutally. But close to them, all seemed calm.

But from the depths of the cave, eyes watched – a few at first, then hundreds, and then thousands.

The surge finally came around 3:00 in the morning.

*****

"Ouch."

Ben opened his eyes at the sound of Barlow's voice. The man shifted his sleeping bulk and relaxed again.

The first thing he noticed was the fire had burned down to a soft red glow. The second thing he was aware of was the almond-like smell that Jenny had first detected when they entered the cave was now pervasive and strong enough for him to pick it out over the top of the carcass, *and* the smoke.

Ben sat up, all vestiges of sleep falling away, and he let his eyes travel over the cave's interior. He saw the outline of Steve and Janus at the cave mouth, on their shift, and both doing their job staying focused on outside. Around the shrunken fire, there were the sleeping bodies of the group.

But now he was sure there was something else. Ben sat straighter and closed his eyes for a moment and concentrated – there it was; a small sound like dry leaves rustling, or perhaps very faint click-clacking like tiny knitting needles.

Barlow slapped at one fat leg and rolled over again, trying to get comfortable. The big man was the furthest inside the cave's interior as Ben guessed he wanted everyone between him and the cave mouth for added protection. Bravery didn't exactly flow like fire through this guy's veins.

Barlow grunted and slapped at himself again, and then he sat up, or rather jerked upright, with his eyes as round as silver dollars. But it was his scream that made the hair on Ben's head feel like it was standing on end.

Everyone was suddenly up and in a panic, and only then did Ben flick on his light and train it on the struggling man.

He wished he hadn't.

Edward Barlow was in the middle of a glistening carpet of shells – *insects* – all about as long as a thumb.

"*Jesus Christ.*" Ben shot to his feet. The wave was coming from the depths of the cave, and the sea of bodies had first found Barlow. In just the time that Ben spent watching, they had swarmed over the man.

Barlow thrashed and rolled, his screams becoming choked as the bugs also poured into his open mouth.

Ben went to charge towards him, but Jenny ran at him, shouldering him away.

"*Don't. Back off.*" She grabbed up one of the sticks beside the fire and used it to scoop a lot of the embers towards Barlow. The spray of red created a barrier that kept the insects back, but it did nothing to discourage them swarming over the man.

Barlow was now impossible to make out under the blanket of bugs, and he looked like nothing more than a man-sized pile of furiously moving tiny bodies.

Jenny brought another stick down on one of the bugs, and then snatched it up. She stared hard at it for a few seconds before yelping and flinging it away.

"*Modificaputis,* I think. A primitive form of cockroach." She shook her hand.

Steve held his shotgun pointed at the swarm. He looked panicked. "*They're fucking cockroaches?* They're huge, and they're goddamn eating him alive!"

"Don't fire that shotgun in here," Ben yelled.

"Backup," Jenny said. "The prehistoric version were carnivorous hunters – see the long legs?"

As they watched the mound rose up, and a low moan emanated from the centre of the pile that was once Barlow.

"Oh God." Emma put her hands to the sides of her head. "Make it stop."

A single gunshot rang out, and the mound collapsed. Ben spun to see Janus Bellakov pointing his rifle. The two men locked eyes momentarily, and eventually Ben nodded – it was a merciful release.

The group backed away. The fire had shrunk to a point of it being too small to be effective anymore, and as they watched, a glistening bone extended from one side of the pile, to break loose and drop onto the swarming carpet of insect bodies. It was an arm, now picked clean. Even the natural fibers in the man's clothing were being consumed.

"Who let the fire go out?" Ben asked.

"Doesn't matter; it's out," Janus said. "Now we know what your fucking ancestor meant by *they come at night*."

"They're watching," Jenny reminded them.

"Might have helped if he spelled it out just a little more, doncha think?" Bellakov sneered. "Well, we can't stay here."

"He's right," Jenny said. "These things won't stop until all the meat is gone." She gritted her teeth. "That's what the smell was – the insects giving off their pheromones, signaling to each other."

"Now we know why there wasn't anything living in here," Steve observed. "You come in here, you end up like that dead dinosaur...or Barlow. Poor sap."

"Gather your things," Ben said and turned to Jenny. "Will they follow us?"

Jenny looked back at the swarm. "I don't know. They would certainly be jungle foragers. Might be like army ants." She shrugged. "We just don't know enough about them."

"Maybe we should stay in the water for a while," Emma said. "They can't follow us there."

"Stay out of the water," Janus said.

"Huh?" Emma said, frowning.

Steve nodded. "Yeah, trust me, we don't want to get too close to the lake."

They edged to the cave mouth, and Ben turned to look at the Barlow mound of insects that was rapidly diminishing in size. From the side of the heap, something round and white rolled free – it was the man's skull, minus the jawbone or any meat inside or out.

"Not how he envisaged things were going to turn out," Walt Koenig said softly.

"Yeah, well, thanks for nothing, Barlow, you fat fuck." Bellakov bared his teeth.

Steve scoffed. "Remind me to have you come and say something nice at my funeral."

Ben checked his watch. "We've still at least an hour until daybreak." He had no idea if being out in the darkness was better or worse now. But they had no choice now. He turned away.

"Let's go – silent as we can." Ben headed out first.

*****

"New plan?" Emma whispered.

Ben turned to her. "I was going to ask you the same thing." He gave her a lopsided smile but doubted she could see him.

They moved quietly and quickly back the way they'd come. They were now out of food, shelter, and according to Benjamin's notebook, they were running out of time to escape, before something occurred to make leaving impossible. Ben had no idea what that could be, but his ancestor had been right about everything so far, so he didn't want to hang around to find out.

But the fact was, he had no idea what to do next, and no idea how to get off the plateau.

Except one.

Ben stopped, and Emma bumped into him. "We need to find that stream we came upon. I have an idea."

"What is it – all good ideas are solid gold right now?" Steve asked.

Ben waved them on and spoke over his shoulder. "I said I had an idea; I didn't say it was a good one."

*****

"Clouds are thinning." Bellakov craned his neck. "Thought I saw a glimpse of moon before."

Ben also looked up at the ever-present cloud cover. Hopefully, dawn was rushing upon them, but for now, it was still all in darkness…or mostly.

"I don't know," he said. "Looks weird. A bit like a cyclone the way it's moving about up there, and we're right in its eye." He continued to stare and saw through a small opening in the dark clouds a corner of the moon begin to appear.

"What the…?"

Ben frowned; it was wrong, bigger somehow…like it was closer.

"Clouds swirling, but there's no wind," Bellakov observed.

"Huh?" Ben turned briefly to the man, and then when he glanced back at the sky, the clouds had closed again. "Damn."

"I know what you're thinking; a bit of good ole sunlight would be great. There's just enough light and heat to turn this place into a freaking greenhouse. Just give me a few golden rays punching through."

Ben sighed. "Yeah, I heard that."

Bellakov walked up beside him, lowering his head and his voice. "You're going for the plane, aren't you?"

Ben looked at him, assessing, and then finally nodded. "Yep."

"Mad bastard." The mercenary snorted. "You know, even if you manage to get the engine out to lighten it for gliding, and the fuselage doesn't just fall apart, there's too many of us." He watched Ben closely as he spoke.

Ben shrugged. "The Corsair Fighter has a 41-foot wingspan, and empty can take the weight."

"The weight is one thing, but there's too many bodies. Simply won't all fit." Bellakov shrugged. "I like the plan though." He fell back a step. "I mean, what else we got?"

Emma sped up to walk beside him. "Are we going around in circles?"

"I don't think so." Ben turned to her. "We're retracing our steps; we haven't strayed too far off the trail we blazed."

"It's just that... *um*..." She grimaced and turned about. "We've been walking for hours. Added to that, the lake was huge, and the cave was in the side of a small mountain. I know Tepuis can be enormous, but this place is like an entire world up here."

Ben had already thought about that, but what did it mean? he wondered.

"She's right," Jenny added. "The population, size, and diversity of species up here is usually only represented by a large land mass. I don't get how these things can continue to survive, basically, on an island."

"An island," Ben repeated. "I don't have an answer for that. Nothing up here is normal, or makes sense."

Emma slipped and Ben caught her.

"Thanks," she said and wiped her greasy boot.

Ben looked down. There were crushed plants at their feet, still oozing slippery sap, and looking as though they'd been run over by tractor tires. He crouched, and Steve, Emma, and Jenny peered over his shoulder while Koenig kept his eyes on the jungle. Bellakov continued to stare up at the strange spinning cloud cover.

Ben saw that the tracks cut across their trail and kept going. He put his hands in the indentations. "What the hell makes a track like this?"

Koenig briefly looked down and over his shoulder. "Nothing I know. I would have said something lay down here, but I can see it was moving, and kept moving." He flicked on his flashlight and followed the depressions in the grasses and mud, until they vanished...just stopped and then *vanished*. "Never seen it before."

"I know." Jenny also crouched, and then looked up, her eyes round. "And you do too, Ben. Remember when we were down by the river and you found those tracks?"

Ben nodded and his head snapped back down. "You're shitting me?"

"I've been on trapping expeditions in the Amazon for the zoo. We hunted the giant green anaconda; they leave tracks like this, but on a much smaller scale." She rose to her feet.

But frowned. "But you said the tracks of the one we found by the river was big, and they didn't get much bigger." He pointed at the ground. "This thing is five times bigger."

"They *don't* get much bigger…in our time," Jenny said softly.

"I've also hunted anaconda," Koenig said. "They can be mean suckers – crush a full grown man down to mush. One that big?" He shrugged. "I don't want to meet it."

"We already did, once." Ben looked to Jenny.

"In the cave we climbed up in; one took Bourke. So big it filled the place." Her lips pressed together for a moment. "I hope it was the same one."

"And now dead." Ben looked up at her as silver light broke through the clouds.

"At last, we can…" Bellakov stopped talking and his brows snapped together as the setting moon was revealed.

Ben looked up. "That moon."

"Yeah, that's *some* moon." Steve gaped up at it.

"So big. I mean it looks like we could almost reach out and touch it." Bellakov shook his head. "Fuck I hate this place."

The moon vanished behind the clouds and threw them back into darkness. Jenny shone her light on the tracks again. "I think we need to get out of here."

"If it is another one, you think it might still be hanging around?" Koenig gripped his rifle a little tighter.

"Hanging around is right," Jenny said. "Look; the tracks on the ground disappear." She turned to the group. "Because I think it took to the trees."

"This gets better and better." Ben looked up, now feeling like they were being watched. "Let's keep moving…and everyone keep their eyes open."

*****

They continued to press on, weaving through the jungle as the light began to increase. Ben was sure this was the way they'd come, but still hadn't seen a single blaze mark he'd previously made. He was about to wave Koenig closer when he spotted the mouth of the stream.

"Thank God," he whispered.

"Self-doubt is a terrible thing." Koenig winked.

"Curse of the humble." Ben grinned and stepped out into the shallow water.

The stream cut a path through the dense jungle, and with the canopy roof, also created a dark cave. Ben paused, just letting his eyes run over *everything*. He then lifted his gaze to the canopy. The light was still weak, and the treetops knitted together in an unbroken ceiling of green. But thankfully, there was nothing that looked like a giant snake – not that he'd ever seen one before.

They'd been travelling now for a couple of hours, and the humidity was still energy-sapping. The clouds had dropped, so even as the light rose, the clouds had become a low-lying fog that twisted through the jungle like smoke.

He called the group in. "Let's take five."

He stepped out of the stream and felt a pang of hunger stab at his gut. He ignored it. They were out of food, and by rights, he should have been hunting. But hunting meant shooting, and he definitely didn't want that when silence probably meant their survival.

However, they needed to keep their energy levels up, so he might have to ask Koenig to use his hunting skills and see if he could either trap something or catch and kill it just with his knife. He looked down at the stream; he also remembered in some of the pools he had seen a few silver shapes dart back and forth, so fish wasn't off the menu either.

"Walt, let's scout ahead. The rest of you stay on guard."

"You got it," Koenig replied, shouldering his rifle.

Ben saw Bellakov stare hard at them.

"Back in five minutes." He saw that the mercenary continued to stare. "Scouts honor."

He and Walt Koenig then headed down along the edge of the streambed, walking for a few moments until he was sure he was out of earshot. Ben turned.

"That friend of yours, Bellakov; what's his number?" he asked.

Koenig's mouth turned down as he shook his head. "Don't really know him. Barlow brought us together. The guy was a mercenary and hunted everything from lions to people. He trusts no one, not even me." He shrugged. "Barlow kept him on a leash, but now he's gone, well..." he glanced at Ben. "I wouldn't turn my back on him."

"Didn't plan on it," Ben said. "And thanks."

They continued for another few minutes along the stream edge, and there were no more tracks or obvious dangers. A few small animals covered in fur or bristles that might have been primitive feathers, squealed and darted back into the jungle at their approach. It was a good sign – if there was game around, then there probably wasn't too many predators.

"We'll need to catch one of those soon," Ben said. "Without guns if possible."

Koenig nodded. "No problem. Just tell me when."

Ben crouched down at the edge of the stream. "This isn't good."

There were flattened areas all along the stream bank, three feet wide, and with odd markings that looked like something had been dragged.

Walt crouched, put his hand in them, and then lifted them to his nose. He looked up momentarily into the tree canopy. "One of those snake things." He turned to Ben. "You believe in coincidences?"

Ben snorted. "No." He turned. "So we both think it was following us before."

"Maybe, or maybe there's another one." Walt wiped his fingers on his pants. "Or maybe there's a lot of them."

"And that just makes me feel a hellova lot worse." Ben got to his feet.

Walt nodded. "Then you're gonna love this bit; it's almost impossible to hide from a big snake." He looked up. "They can *see* your body heat."

Ben exhaled and looked up at the dense overhead canopy. He could feel the damp fronds brushing his back and neck.

"Yep." Walt nodded. "The big guys like boas, pythons, anacondas and even vipers have these tiny holes on their faces called pit organs. They're used to detect infrared radiation." He smiled without mirth. "To them, we're just moving, hot sacks of food."

"Thank you, Walt; I feel much better now." Ben began to turn away. "Let's head ba…"

"*Hey…*" Walt quickly held up a hand. "*Don't. Move. A muscle.*"

Ben froze, staring over his shoulder at the man's face. He could see both alarm and fascination.

"What…*what*?" Ben said, trying to only move his lips.

"On your back." Walt shook his head, his brows up real high. "A fucking beauty."

"*What's on my back?*" Ben suddenly felt some extra weight there – like a large soft hand. "What the hell is it? I can feel it."

"A fucking spider bigger than your head." Walt angled his gaze. "*Wowee*; that's one big mother." He pulled back. "It's looking at me."

Ben turned a little more, getting pissed off. "Get it off."

"I ain't grabbin' that thing; looks dangerous." Walt's grin widened. "Besides; it might decide to run for it and head to higher ground, you know, up to your head and face."

"You bastard." Ben couldn't help grinning himself. "I'll get it myself." He began to look for a stick or something to reach back and wipe it away. But when he bent lower, he felt the thing move. Suddenly, he felt the first if its bristly legs against the skin of his neck. Instead of the soft finger-like touch he expected, he felt the pinprick sharpness of tiny hooks.

He slowly straightened. "Little help here."

"All right; will you hold still?" Walt retrieved the stick Ben had been reaching for. "Now don't move a muscle, a-*aaand*..."

Ben gritted his teeth, waiting.

"*Fore!*"

Walt swung, connected, and suddenly the weight on his neck and back was gone. There was the sound of an impact out in the jungle, but then a mad scrambling.

"That'll be ten bucks, buddy." Walt's grin was wider than ever. "Anything else I can help you with?"

Ben shook his head. "Put it on my tab. And while you're at –"

The crack of a rifle made him flinch, and then spin to the noise.

CHAPTER 31

Emma took a cloth, dipped it into the stream, and then used it to wipe her greasy brow and neck. The humidity made it feel like they were in a warm bath, and she felt dog-tired.

Steve loitered near a tree, shotgun cradled in his arms. Jenny crouched by a pool in the stream and stared into it, captivated by some fish, bug, or other aquatic animal. And the creepy Janus Bellakov glanced at each of them, his dark eyes like windows on a dead soul. The guy gave her the creeps.

"These fish; I think they're *Arowana*," Jenny said, frowning down into the water.

"Yeah, I was going to say that." Steve grinned.

Jenny looked up and chuckled for a moment before turning back and pointing. "But seriously, these guys have been around since the Jurassic."

"Uh-hu." Steve tilted his head. "More importantly, can we eat them? Raw is fine."

Jenny bobbed her head. "Probably; but they'd barely be a mouthful. Especially for a mouth as big as…" She looked up again and the smile froze on her face.

Emma swung to look at her and saw the woman's wide-eyed stare. Her eyes darted to where Jenny faced as she realised Jenny she wasn't actually looking *at* Steve but at something above him.

Emma's eyes moved upwards, following the scaly tree trunk, and further up into the paddle like fronds above him. Steve must have seen the expressions on their faces and began to look confused, and then fearful.

"What…*what*?"

Jenny began to make a tiny guttural noise in her throat, as no words would come. She lifted an arm to point.

In the canopy above Steve was the flicker of movement – a tongue, forked, and as thick as a man's arm. It had come from a diamond-shaped head, easily four feet across, with two glass-like eyes. The monstrous muscular body, twined within the branches of the tree, but also disappeared further back into the dark jungle. The thing was enormous and easily longer than a bus, or even *two* buses!

From the corner of Emma's eyes, she saw Bellakov, standing there, watching, but not making any move to help even though he had a rifle cradled in his arms.

Emma fumbled for her handgun as Steve finally looked upwards. The man reacted, first with alarm, and then by swinging the muzzle of the Mossberg shotgun up at the colossal snake hanging over him like an evil apparition.

Perhaps it was the movement, or the chemical signals of fear the man started to give off, but at that moment, the monster struck.

The V-shaped mouth sprung open, revealing hundreds of backward-curving teeth, each longer than Emma's hands, as the head shot forward, striking hard and driving Steve to the ground with a whoosh of his breath. The shotgun discharged, blasting into the trees as the coils of the snake piled down on top of him.

Steve was gripped from shoulder to groin in the mouth, his face more shock than pain as he was then lifted from the ground, and the coils began to wrap around him.

Emma pointed her handgun, but her hand shook like she was receiving an electric shock. She knew if she pulled the trigger she'd more than likely hit her friend instead of the snake.

"Shoot it," she screamed, but from the corner of her eye, she saw Bellakov ease back into the jungle a few steps, his gun up, but not aiming directly at the giant reptile.

Another shot rang out as Jenny stood, legs planted wide and two hands on her gun. She fired again, and this time must have hit the snake, as it jerked a bit and the massive knot of scaled muscle began to unravel. But instead of dropping its prize, it started to slide into the jungle, taking the now screaming man in its mouth with it.

"Hey!" Ben appeared with Koenig at his shoulder.

"Sn-*nn-naaake*." Emma turned, pointing. "*It*, the snake, *it's got Steve*."

Ben ran past her, sprinting into the jungle, with Walt right at his shoulder. Both men fired their guns, but even as they flew past, Emma saw that the massive creature had already vanished, gliding and shooting through holes in the jungle the men couldn't possibly follow. Horrifyingly, Steve's agonized voice could still be heard, but growing fainter by the second.

Emma sat down hard, her hands on her knees and gun pointed at the ground. She burst into tears, feeling helpless and empty, and scared shitless. She wiped her eyes, and then after another few moments, another emotion boiled to the surface.

With her teeth grit, she turned to where Bellakov loitered. "What the fuck?" She stood and marched up the opposite bank towards him.

"What's the matter with you? Why didn't you help?"

Bellakov's eyes were half-lidded and unflinching as he stared back. "I might have hit him. Same reason you didn't fire."

"Bullshit," she spat. "You're a hunter; you could have taken a shot." She bared her teeth at the man. "And that thing was over 50 feet long and as thick as a horse. You could have hit it anywhere. You're supposed to be a crack shot."

Bellakov inhaled, making his chest swell. His lips turned down as he looked over her head. "You misunderstand my position here, girlie. I'm not here as your fucking bodyguard. Best you remember that." He lowered his eyes to her, and all she saw in them was contempt.

"You fu..." Emma glared, but bit her lip. He was right. The guy was an asshole, and probably been in on the Ben beat down in the UK. She had nothing to gain by thinking he was actually part of their team. "*Fuck you.*" She turned away and waded back across the stream to where Jenny still sat in a daze.

The woman smiled tightly, but her eyes were brimmed with tears. "It was probably tracking us the whole time." She wiped at her nose. "I should have known when I encountered the first one – there's obviously a breeding population here." She looked up, real fear in her eyes. "We have no idea how many there are."

"*Shush.*" Emma put her arm around her. "Do you think...they might get Steve back?"

Jenny's mouth opened and she looked at her with incredulity. After a moment, she just shook her head.

Emma nodded. "I know, I was just...hoping." She motioned to Bellakov who was watching the jungle in the direction Ben and Koenig had gone. "That asshole did nothing."

Jenny let her eyes drift to the man. "I think... I think he probably knew it had been tracking us." Her eyes narrowed. "Maybe he let it take Steve in the hope that it would be sated and leave us alone."

"Oh Jesus." Emma felt a little sick at the thought. "Could that asshole basically be prepared to sacrifice one of us to save his own skin?"

Jenny exhaled shakily. "I don't think I want to know."

Emma ground her teeth. "I do."

*****

Ben and Walt pushed back out of the jungle, and Ben quickly found Jenny and Emma. He went to the zoologist and took her hand and then looked deep into her eyes.

"I'm sorry; he's gone."

She dropped her head. "I knew it."

Walt Koenig crossed to where Bellakov stood and the pair spoke quietly.

Ben released her hand and she walked away to sit down by herself. Emma put a hand up on his shoulder but her eyes went to Bellakov. "We tracked it for a while, but it could go places we couldn't. After a while, it just vanished; maybe into a hole or up into the trees." He shrugged. "I don't know."

"I think…" Emma continued to watch Bellakov and Koenig. "I think Bellakov let it happen." She looked up into Ben's face.

"What?" Ben frowned. "What do you mean?"

"He was just watching, standing back. He just let it happen, like he didn't care." She swallowed nervously. "He could have taken a shot, but he didn't." Emma folded her arms, tight, and went to sit with Jenny.

Ben remembered what Bellakov had said about the airplane: *there were too many people*, he'd said. He shook the thought away. *No way*, he thought. *But…*

He turned back to the jungle where the monster snake had taken Steve Chambers, his friend. The guy was always smiling, adventurous, and it only seemed like yesterday they were riding pushbikes together.

First Andrea, then Dan, and now Steve, gone. Only days ago, none of them had expected to be here, and now…

He jammed his handgun back in his holster, only from habit. The weapon was now empty. He took one last look at the dark jungle.

Goodbye, buddy, he whispered, and then turned away.

"Come on, people, we're out of here."

*****

In another hour, they found one of the trees that Ben had blazed, indicating their original path back to the clearing and the downed fighter plane. For some reason, the familiarity comforted them all the way to the clearing.

Ben held a hand up to his eyes and walked toward the plateau edge, feeling his hopes sink a little. The clouds had dropped, and where they stood was like a vast island amidst a sea of dirty cotton wool. The cliff wall still fell a few hundred feet to the cloud tops, but now everything else below it was hidden.

Strangely, the clouds slowly rotated, and the sky above was darkening even though sundown was many hours away. A slight breeze had sprung up, but seemed to come from below them, rising up over the cliff edge and into their faces.

Ben took in a deep breath and let it out slowly – whatever was happening, whatever Benjamin had feared would trap *him* in 1908, had begun, for *them*.

Bellakov eased up beside him, gun under his arm. "You know what they say about falling out of a plane?" He turned and grinned. "It's not the fall that kills you, but the sudden stop at the end."

Ben nodded. "Yep, if we can't see the ground, we can't find a clearing, and if we can't find a clearing, we'll probably glide into a stand of trees and end up like squashed bugs."

The others joined them. "I knew you were insane, but if I think you're planning to do what I think…" Walt slapped him on the shoulder "…then count me the hell in."

"Well? Would someone clue *me* in?" Emma asked.

"Both of us?" Jenny's brows were up.

Ben turned first to Bellakov. "Janus, give us some cover while I look this guy over. Don't want anything surprising us while we're between the jungle and a cliff edge."

"You got it, buddy." Bellakov turned to the jungle, walking a few dozen steps toward a boulder, and sitting down on it. He sat down in a place where he could keep one eye on the jungle, and one back on the group – *good enough*, Ben thought.

"Buddy now?" Emma glared at the man.

"Not even close." Ben headed to the Corsair Fighter plane carcass and first walked all the way around it. Then he went in close to run one hand over the metal skin, and then checked underneath it. The wheels had collapsed, but the pilot, Lieutenant John Carter, had done one hellova job in coming in clean, and making it over the lip of the cliff, *plus*, managing to stop just short of the tree line. *Carrier deck landing expertise*, Ben guessed.

Ben gritted his teeth, reached in and grabbed Carter's skeleton under the arms of the flight jacket. He eased him out, and then laid him carefully on the ground.

"Thanks for everything, Lieutenant. We'll take it from here."

He climbed back up to peer inside. The cockpit was intact and the rear empty. The plane's wings were primarily intact as well, but structurally, he wouldn't know until he was in the air whether they'd take the stress or simply snap off turning the plane into a torpedo. Ben chuckled mirthlessly – *only find out in the air* – talk about a death wish.

Ben reached in and moved the wheel, watching the effect on the wings. Amazingly, the flaps still worked, *just*. But when he tried the rear flap rudder, something pinged, and then it froze solid – not good, but also not a real tragedy as he doubted turning left or right would be a priority, and if he could manage a leveling out to keep the nose up, then that was first prize.

Ben rested his forearms on the cockpit edge and looked to the nose; the 13-foot, three-blade propeller was broken off, but the nose cone was still intact. Everything else was still there, and as he expected, it was the engine that'd be the problem – the Corsair used the largest engine available at the time: the 2,000 horsepower, 18-cylinder Pratt & Whitney Double Wasp radial – it was why it was so dominant in the skies.

But it was the source of all that muscle power that was the problem – the engine weighed in at 2,300 pounds of dead weight. Even if they were loaded in the back, they'd never weight-compensate, and they'd go nose-down immediately. Without an engine, they'd nosedive all the way to the jungle floor.

Ben straightened. The only way to achieve any semblance of a glide was to balance the weight, but first they needed to make the plane significantly lighter – at least *2,000 pounds lighter*.

Ben turned. "The engine has gotta go."

Walt Koenig blew air between pressed lips. "Got a winch and a tool shop?"

"No, but we got rocks as hammers, knives as screwdrivers, and muscles for leverage." Ben dusted off his hands. "Plus, we've got the most important ingredient of all." He turned and grinned. "Survival motivation."

Walt returned the smile and saluted. "Works for me."

Ben turned about for a moment and then looked back at the Corsair. He placed his hands on his hips, thinking through what they needed to do.

"Okay, people, we'll need all shoulders to the wheel. Walt and I will work on getting the engine removed. Once it's lighter, we can swing it around to face the cliff edge and then move it into place. We'll also need a path cleared – Jenny and Emma, going to need you to clear away as much debris as you can manage."

Ben's mouth curved into a smile. "And watch the edge; it's a hellova first step. Questions?" He waited; there were none. "Then let's do this."

Jenny and Emma set to shifting rocks, tufts of grass, and other debris, and he and Walt pulled off the panels of the engine housing at the nose of the fighter. Ben sighed and just shook his head. Walt leaned in on his elbows beside him.

"Never gonna get that all out." Ben exhaled slowly.

"Never thought we would," Walt replied. "So let's just get out what we can. Besides, to get the engine fully out, we'd need to deconstruct the plane, and maybe take the whole nose off. Don't want to do that as we'll distort the aerodynamics of the entire bird."

Ben reached in to tug on a few of the muscular-looking cylinders; several were already loose. "Okay, doable."

"Then what are we waiting for?" Walt pulled his hunting knife and started to work on some of the screw-heads.

The pair worked for several hours until Ben's knuckles were grazed, and his hands orange and black from ancient rust. The metal clanged down as they dropped piece after piece, and they quickly grew into a pile.

Ben looked up to see Janus Bellakov watching them. The man nodded, and Ben did the same in return. Ben pointed at his eyes then to the jungle. Janus nodded and turned away.

Jenny and Emma had basically cleared a runway, or rather *dragway*, to the cliff edge. If they managed to lighten the plane without destroying it, and then drag it to the lip, he still wondered whether he, or everyone, would be mad enough to actually sit in it and then let themselves tip over.

He laughed softly; of course they would. Because the alternative was dying up here, and by dying, that probably meant being eaten alive. *Or somehow being trapped here forever*. He frowned at the thought, still not understanding what his great, great grandfather had meant by that.

Ben looked at his watch – mid-afternoon – no wonder he was hungry. He paused, weighing up whether he should get Walt or Bellakov to try and catch some game. They'd given up on having Jenny scout for edible roots, nuts, or berries, as no one had ever seen any of the strange plants before, and as the creatures eating them had digestive systems far different from humans, then vomiting and diarrhea might be the least of their problems.

Ben looked at the pile of engine parts – not bad. The remaining engine block was refusing to give up any more odds and ends, and without a hoist, it wasn't going anywhere – it'd have to do.

"I think we're done here."

Walt held up his knife, the tip and edge warped and blunted. "We certainly are."

Emma and Jenny came and leant against one of the wings. "What now?"

Ben turned to look towards the cliff edge. It was a good two hundred feet and would take time to drag the plane to the lip without damaging it. Added to that, he didn't want to make the attempt when it was getting dark.

"I think we might have missed our window for tonight. But we can certainly drag this baby closer so we have a dawn launch."

"I vote we go now," Emma said. "I don't want to spend another minute up here."

Ben turned to her and then the cliff edge. He had to squint as dust and debris blew up over the rim, and the clouds continued to turn around them like they were in the center of a giant whirlpool. There was no sign of the ground at all.

Walt scratched his chin. "Yeah, I hear you. But by the time we get the plane to the edge, it'll be dark. Clouds are bad enough, but I reckon we can punch through those. But once we've done that, and if we do even make it that far, then we want to at least be able to try and glide to an open space. We need to see to do that." He half grinned. "Rumor has it that big trees might not bother to get out of our way."

Emma's eyes sparked. "Still think we should go for it; let's take a vote."

"Then I vote we wait," Jenny said, and sadness clouded her features. "Sorry, Emm, but if we can't see, we can't find a safe landing. And if we're gliding, there's no second chance."

Emma stared for a moment, but then exhaled and nodded once.

"It's settled," Ben said. "Let's turn this baby around." Ben waved to Janus Bellakov and called him back in.

"Ready to take off?" Bellakov asked.

Ben shook his head and wiped his hands. "Not until tomorrow. For now, we'll try and get it to the edge – take off first thing."

Bellakov's forehead creased and he put his hands on his hips. Ben ignored him and turned to Koenig.

"Maybe Walt here can show us some of that hunting prowess he's been talking up." Ben winked at the man, who was fast becoming an indispensable ally.

"Oh a challenge? Then you just place your order, big guy." Walt grinned back.

Ben finally jumped down from one of the wings and stepped back to survey all their work. Satisfied, he set to organizing the group.

"We turn it clockwise. Janus, you get the tail, and the rest of us on the wings." He held up a hand. "And *please*, take it slow; I don't want to see the bottom ripped out of her."

They each took their positions around the Corsair. "On a count of 3," Ben said, and then: "And 2, and 1, and…*heave*."

Janus lifted the lighter rear end of the plane, and the others swiveled the heavier nose. It slowly spun a little easier than Ben expected and immediately filled him with some hope. In another few minutes of starting, resting, and restarting, they had the nose pointed towards the cliff edge.

"Well, that was the easy part," Jenny observed.

Ben slapped his hands together, and then wiped them on his pants. "Looking good, and we've all got tickets booked on a morning flight. Now, let's get her to the edge."

Each wing had a man and woman, with Janus lifting the tail section once more. They pushed, once again in fits and starts, moving the plane forward a few feet, and then stopping to rest and check they weren't tearing the bottom out. In two hours, they'd managed to move it halfway, and without losing too much airplane or human skin in the process.

"Rest," Ben said, turning and leaning back against the plane's fuselage. Sweat streamed, and he sipped from the warm contents of his canteen. He felt a little lightheaded, probably from fluid loss, but also as he hadn't eaten since the previous evening, and he knew his energy levels were flagging.

He looked up. The clouds were dropping and still turning like they were being stirred, and overall the light was fading. A gust blew grit into his eyes and he wiped at it. He estimated another hour of light left, and maybe two more hours of pushing – no choice but to just suck it up and get it done.

So they did.

The darkness fell, but the energy-sapping heat and humidity remained. As they got closer to the plateau edge, the breeze blew harder into their faces, at least drying some of their sweat.

Ben was heartened by the updraft, as it'd aid in the planes gliding ability. A down draft would have sunk them like a stone.

In another 30 minutes, the group had the plane with the nose on the cliff edge, and Ben knew that if they were all as tired as he was, it was as far as the plane was going that evening.

"*Ah...*" Emma looked from the plateau edge, to the Corsair, and then to Ben. "If we're all sitting inside this death trap, how exactly are we going to launch it?"

Ben chuckled. "I like your confidence." He held up a finger. "Watch and learn – so, got any rope left?"

"Sure, but only about 80 feet," Emma said and folded her arms, looking quizzical. "But it's our last length."

"Hopefully we won't need it anymore," Ben said. "So, when you were a kid, did you ever own one of those glider slingshots?"

Emma half smiled but shook her head slowly. "Nope."

"Hmm, deprived childhood, huh?" Ben turned back to the plane, now that he had everyone watching him. He walked around it, and then to the rear, crouching and placing a hand on the tail for a moment, satisfying himself.

"Normal gliders have a hook underneath them, usually at the front, and you attach a lead cable to them so an engine-driven plane can lift them up into the thermals. A toy glider also has one at the front, to attach the elastic from the slingshot."

Ben then made a V-shape with the fingers of one hand and pretended to pull back on an imaginary elastic between them.

"Then when you let it go, the plane shot forward." He dusted off his hands. "So, we have our glider, we have our rope to act as catapult, and all we need is the slinging force, and..." He turned about. "There." He pointed to a small boulder. "We push that rock until it's right on the very edge. Tie the rope to it, and the other end we hook around the Corsair's tail, but loose enough so it releases by itself."

Ben walked forward, staring out over the plateau rim. "The rock goes over, pulls the rope, which tugs on the plane, launching it over the edge, and then we are *airborne*."

Walt clapped once and laughed out loud. "I love it – then the rope on release will tug on the tail, also bringing the nose up. This crazy idea could goddamn work."

"And if the rope doesn't release when it's supposed to?" Emma looked unconvinced.

"Then the gliding may be a little bit shitty." Ben grinned. "And a lot quicker to the ground." He pointed. "Step one, and last job for the night. Let's get that rock a little closer to the front of the plane.

It only took Ben, Walt, and Bellakov 15 minutes to muscle the small boulder to the cliff edge and front of the Corsair, and then carefully slide it forward. Ben got down on his belly and inched towards the rim. He peaked over, squinting into the flying grit. It was dark, and he flicked on his flashlight – he could now see that where they perched was basically a jutting lip of stone, and then below them the cliff dropped away until it was well beyond his light.

It could work...*it had to work*, he prayed.

Ben tied the rope around the small boulder, and then crawled back to reach under the tail and carefully loop it over its underside. He tried the release a few times until he was satisfied.

Ben then stood and wiped his hands on his shorts. "That's it for now."

"Good work," Walt said. "So let me see what I can run down for our dinner." He checked his rifle.

Ben looked at the hunter and then back at the forbidding dark jungle. "Can't let you go in by yourself. I'll go with you."

"What?" Emma straightened and quickly looked from Ben to the menacing Janus Bellakov.

Bellakov saw the exchange and chuckled. "No, Ben, you need to stay here with your friends. You're probably a good shot, but I'm a hunter like Koenig. Together, we'll have more success, and be back here in a flash."

"Good idea," Emma said quickly.

"Yep." Jenny also nodded vigorously.

Ben looked across to Walt, who was stony-faced, but nodded once.

"Done," Ben said.

Walt Koenig gave him a small salute, and then both men turned on their heel and crossed the lengthy clearing to then head out into the black jungle. Ben watched them for a moment before turning away.

"Can we risk a fire?"

"Probably not," Jenny said. "But then again, we shouldn't eat raw meat as we have no idea what sort of internal parasites these things could be carrying." She grimaced. "Plus, we're out in the open." She hiked her shoulders. "I don't know."

Ben thought about the pros and cons. They needed their strength, especially for the arduous day he expected for tomorrow, so one way or the other, they were going to eat. He certainly didn't want to attract anything with the light or smells, but he knew from experience, raw food could be dangerous.

Ben also knew if they became infected, then even if they made it to the ground, they might not survive the trek out of the jungle. He decided.

"We light one, and then let it die down so we can cook in the embers. Keeping the food buried will also reduce the cooking odors. Deal?" He raised his eyebrows.

Jenny bobbed her head. 'Sure, what's the worst that could happen?" She smiled, but it didn't extend to her eyes.

CHAPTER 32

"Think it'll work?" Walt Koenig whispered over his shoulder.

"Yeah, I do," Bellakov responded. "I think the plateau will give the Corsair some good updraft. Sure, we'll come in fast, but provided the landing site isn't a row of freaking tree trunks, then it should be survivable."

Walt nodded but had his doubts. They were now about a third of a mile into the thick jungle, and he began to tread more softly.

Walt Koenig crouched and waved Bellakov down. The jungle was near pitch dark, and he relied on peripheral vision. It was an evolutionary thing about the human eye – it had both rods and cones, but it was the rods that were more sensitive to light, and these were gathered in greater number at the corners of the eye. He also relied on sound, smell, and even air density changes. But the biggest advantage he had was his brain.

The pair of men crouched in near silence for a few moments. They heard the drip of water, smelled the chlorophyll and sweet fragrance of blooming night flowers, and heard the tiny scuttling of insects among the leaf detritus. But further out, there was the sound of tentative footfalls.

Walt knew the ideal would be one animal the size of a turkey, or two the size of fat chickens – either would be a good meal for the five of them.

"You're pretty friendly with Cartwright now, huh?" Bellakov asked, breaking the silence.

Walt half turned. "He's an okay kinda guy. I guess he knows what he's doing."

"Don't trust him," Bellakov responded. "Don't forget whose side you're on."

Walt snorted. "There are no sides anymore, dumbass. Barlow is dead. Staying alive is the priority now, and by my reckoning, working with Ben Cartwright will give us a better chance of doing that."

"Yeah, staying alive is the priority," Bellakov whispered. "Survival of the fittest."

Walt noticed Bellakov was now close in behind him and went to turn. The blade entered one side of his neck at the carotid artery level, appearing out the other side in a spray of blood.

Immediately, he felt cold, unable to move, and found himself on the ground. Bellakov ripped the knife free and swung it at the ground a few times, flicking off the thick coating of arterial blood.

"Guess you chose the wrong side, *dumbass*." Bellakov reached down to wipe his blade on Walt's shirt. He straightened, looked around, resheathed his knife, and then vanished into the jungle.

Need to warn Ben, Walt Koenig thought as the cold and the pain went away. He then began to get sleepy. *Think I'll just rest awhile first.* He closed his eyes.

*****

Janus Bellakov sprinted from the jungle, head up and waving madly. Ben swung around and then went to one knee lifting his rifle and pointing just past him, waiting for the expected rush of a pursuer.

He half turned, but kept his eyes dead ahead. "Emma, Jenny, get in behind the plane."

He waited as Bellakov crossed the few hundred yards of clear land towards them and the cliff edge. The man rounded the Corsair and skidded to a stop, slamming his back up against the fuselage.

"*Fucking monster.*" He sucked in and blew out more air before turning to Ben. "Just came out of the jungle. Took Walt." He sucked in a huge gulp of air. "Nothing I could do."

"Ah shit." Ben felt his heart sink. He both liked and needed the man. "Was it chasing you?"

"Yes, no, I don't know." Bellakov gulped more air, his eyes round with fear. "I just freaking got the hell out of there."

Ben checked his gun. "We go after him, he could still be alive."

"*No.*" Bellakov reached out and grabbed Ben's shirt in his fist. "He's dead." His mouth set in a grim line for a moment. "No one could have survived what I saw – bit nearly in half."

Ben lowered his head.

"He was my friend too." Bellakov squeezed Ben's arm. "But we have to stay here, stick to the plan. First light, we get out of here." Bellakov looked at each of them. "Right?"

Emma just stared back from under lowered brows.

"What was it?" Jenny asked.

"What was what?" Bellakov frowned.

"What sort of thing attacked you? Biped, quadruped, snake…something else entirely?" she asked.

"I, I don't know. It came out of the darkness so fast; didn't see it clearly." He put his hands to his face and rubbed hard.

"Well, was it following you? Was there only one?" Jenny's frown deepened.

"I don't *fucking* know!" he shot back at her. "So lay off."

Ben watched the man closely. He was agitated but seemed evasive. He didn't doubt something had happened, but he didn't think Bellakov was the sort of guy to panic and run.

"Okay everyone, this is how it is," Ben said softly. "We stay here, stay quiet, and stay on guard. It's going to be a long night, but first thing in the morning, we take off."

They all agreed; what else could they do? They continued to watch the jungle for another hour, but above the constant background noise of a million insects, the scuttling and rustling, and nightly eat or be eaten sounds, nothing burst from it to charge down at them.

Finally, Ben sat down with his back to the Corsair. The dry metal skin of its fuselage cool compared to the thick night air. The fire they'd started had now been put out, as there was now nothing to cook. So they sat in silence, each lost in their own thoughts, hungry and miserable. *But still alive*, Ben thought.

Emma was next to him, and she pulled out her canteen, shook it, and then sipped from it. She nudged him and held it out.

He looked from it to her. "Any backwash?"

She snorted. "Plenty."

He took it from her. "As long as it's yours." He put it to his lips, but only allowed it to wet them, as he knew she'd need her precious fluid a lot more than he would. There was plenty of water in the jungle, but no way was anyone going in to collect it now.

He felt Emma shift a little closer to him. "What do you think our chances are, you know, of making it home?"

One in a hundred, one in a thousand maybe, he thought. He smiled and turned to her and lied. "Good, very good, as long as our luck holds."

"Okay." She sighed. "You know, even at school you were always a crap liar."

He chuckled. "Oh, you wanted the truth; why didn't you say that?"

She nudged him in the ribs. "Lay it on me."

He lowered his voice and leaned closer to her. "No doubt, it's gonna be tough. If the plane even holds together after we tip over the edge, it has to glide. Which is a big ask for an antique that was never designed for that. Then we have to hope that the nose stays up and we're not coming in so fast that we fly into the ground, or a tree or rock – remember, we have little maneuverability. And, I'm worried about visibility."

Emma exhaled. "Yeah, I hope that cloud lifts; I've never seen the weather act like this."

"Neither have I; it's not natural." Ben frowned. "And it's getting worse; I keep thinking back to Benjamin's notebook, and also the carving in the cave – he said this place is can only be seen for a short period, and then…it can't be. I don't get it, but he seemed to think he needed to be gone before whatever happened, happened or he'd be stuck here."

"And then there's the comet. We seem to have a jigsaw in a million pieces," Emma agreed. "The interference ruining our communications and GPS, as well as the thick cloud cover. Does that mean it's invisible *now*, or it's harder to find later?" She snorted. "Does it move, sink, become invisible?"

She sighed and sat quietly for a few moments before nudging him again. "Tell me you'll get me off here."

He nudged her back. "We can do it."

Even in the dark, he saw her smile and nod. "That's the spirit," he said.

"I was always an optimist." She leaned on him. "I always knew you'd come back one day; how's that for optimism? That turned out to be true."

"Get some rest," he said.

"Oh yeah, right." She looked up at him. "I have one more question?"

"What is it?" He looked back down at her.

"How many parachutes do we have?" She laughed softly, and her crooked smile and boldness made his heart swell.

"One for the pilot." He leaned towards her, and she him. He kissed her, feeling soft lips that were flaky dry. Even after all this time, her hair still smelled of hints of apple shampoo.

"When we get home," he whispered, "I'm going to take you out for the biggest most expensive dinner you have ever seen in your life."

She leaned her head against his shoulder. "Yeah, sure, promise a girl anything when she's trapped on a hidden plateau and might be eaten by monsters."

Ben put his arm around her shoulders. "Don't worry." He tilted his head back and looked up into dark boiling clouds that now swirled like dirty froth. Lightning moved within them. "We'll make it."

*****

"Let's load 'em up." Ben turned and grinned. "Does everyone have their boarding pass?"

"Yep, first class." Emma grinned and slapped his shoulder.

Ben looked up again and saw that the bilious-looking clouds were now showing a hint of dawn light – it was nearly time. He leaned his head back, thinking through the plan he'd made, but then jerked forward.

"What the hell…?"

It was the vibrations that made him come instantly alert. He carefully extricated himself from Emma and inched up to peer over the Corsair's tail. It was still dark, but dawn wasn't far off now.

Bellakov crept up beside him, keeping low and just allowing his eyes to peek over the fuselage. In another few seconds, Jenny and Emma were also aware something was happening.

"I see them," Bellakov said.

"The size…unbelievable," Ben whispered.

The animals were around eight feet tall at the shoulder, on four legs that all ended in elephantine stumps with flattened claw-like nails. There were no scales, rather just a pebbled skin with brown and black blotches on their hide. The creature's heads were bony looking, about two and a half feet in length on long squat necks. All were low to the ground.

"Plant eaters – a herd of them," Jenny said, breathlessly. "Maybe *Unescoceratops* or even an *Aquilops* – see the flat beak-like mouths? Much bigger than I expected."

"Yeah, I guess everything looks bigger when it has meat on its bones," Bellakov jibed.

"Well, if they're happy, then it means there's nothing that's worrying them – no predators. So, feel free to stick around, tubby guys," Emma said

A few of the animals sauntered closer, picking at sparse patches of reed-like grasses as they neared the plateau's edge. The herd had initially reminded Ben of cattle, but now up close, that impression vanished. Where a cow's eyes had a mammalian liquid warmth, the small eyes in the large box-like heads of these creatures were like the soulless buttons of a reptile.

They continued to search out the grasses, and Ben noticed that where the team had shifted the Corsair, there was a small stand of the same plant species. And they'd dropped the plane right on top of it.

"If those things get much closer, they might nudge the plane," he whispered.

"Like hell." Bellakov lifted his rifle.

"*Don't do that*," Jenny insisted. "They're basically just giant cattle."

"Just a little discouragement then – just to the one in front." Bellakov began to aim.

Ben reached out to lower the man's muzzle. "Don't want to bring anything else in for a look-see now, do we?"

"Should we get in the plane?" Emma asked. "Then if it nudges us over, we'll be ready."

"Yeah, and what if it nudges the plane and not the rock; we're liable to be over the edge and hooked up. Dangling like worms on a freaking hook," Bellakov derided. He pointed with his thumb. "I vote for a single round into the flank. For something that size, it'll just feel a bee sting."

Ben turned to Jenny. "Cattle, huh?"

Jenny shrugged. "Sure – big, clumsy, and harmless."

Ben glanced above them and saw the thick clouds had lightened enough for them to go. "Well then, let's move these guys out, *frontier style*." He got to his feet and took the rifle off his shoulder and handed it to Emma. "When I move these big girls on, we go. Everyone get in the plane and be ready. This should only take me a few minutes."

"Be careful." Emma started to rise, but Jenny grabbed at her.

"He knows what he's doing," she said and pulled Emma back down.

Ben opened his arms wide and headed towards the nearest colossal beast. "*Heeyaa, heyaa!*" he waved his arms.

They ignored him and he moved even closer, crossing more of the open ground than he wanted to. More yells, and this time a few of the big heads came up and turned towards him.

The closest beast to him stopped chewing to stare for a few seconds, before going back to working at the tough grass. Obviously deciding he was insignificant, it then moved a few more ponderous steps towards him.

"No, no, not this way, Bertha." Ben tried again waving even more energetically, and yelled even louder. "*Heya-aaaaa!*"

He was so close now he could smell them, and they were a mix of methane flatulence, and an odd sweet coffee and wet hair odor. He still had his arms out and was just contemplating his next move, when the closest beast's head jerked up, and its chewing mouth hung open, grass still protruding. It froze like that. Weirdly, it stared straight ahead, but at nothing.

Ben's eyebrows drew together and he lowered his arms. The thing had become so motionless it looked like someone had simply flicked its off-switch.

Ben briefly looked over his shoulder to the Corsair; three people were crammed into the cockpit, waiting for him, and he felt their eyes focused on him. He turned back to the herd; strangely, all of them were standing silent and still.

Ben swallowed in a dry mouth and the hair on his neck began to rise – something wasn't right.

"What's the matter, girl?" Ben looked from the animal to the dark wall of jungle. He knew that the massive tree trunks, dripping ferns, and strangling vines hid a million eyes. But some were more dangerous than others.

"You can sense something, can't you?" He started to back up. "Something I can't."

One of the largest of the creatures snorted and its head swung to the jungle. Ben could hear the animal taking deep sniffs, and then like a spell had been broken, it squealed and started to run. The herd followed and Ben felt the ground shake beneath his feet.

But what came next made his blood run cold.

The monstrous snake poured out of the jungle like a river of green and brown scales. Ben's eyes widened as a jolt ran through his body from his toes to his scalp. He was suddenly like all small prey animals in the presence of a large predator – he froze.

*****

Emma tasted bile at the back of her throat as fear made her empty stomach threaten to dry heave on her.

It couldn't be real, her brain screamed. How could something that huge move so fast, and so silently? The giant snake poured forth, sinuously, all polished scale and muscle; its four-foot-wide diamond-shaped head pointed like an arrow at the panicking beasts.

Ben was frozen to the spot, but the herd's terror had turned to mad panic and that urged them on to greater speed. They began to split; their goal obviously was to be anywhere that was as far away from the snake as they could get – some stampeded for the jungle, some along the cliff top, and a few toward the plateau edge. Horrifyingly, these were the ones on which the snake turned its unblinking gaze.

Emma felt hypnotized and stared with mouth open as she watched the beasts pick up speed to what they thought might have been safety. They never stopped or even slowed as they neared the cliff. Unfortunately for Ben, that meant they were bearing down on him as well. And the snake followed.

"Ru-*uuun!*" she screamed, so loud she felt veins pop out on her temples.

Ben finally turned and then sprinted, angling out of the beast's path. Jenny added her voice, and Janus Bellakov finally hung the barrel of his gun out of the cockpit. He began to fire.

Emma continued to scream and wasn't sure if Bellakov hit any of the creatures, as it certainly wasn't making any difference.

The snake continued to pour forth, pausing for a moment as if to select its meal, before shooting forward. The bulky herbivores come to the cliff edge and Emma wasn't sure if they realised their mistake at the last moment, or just didn't care, perhaps thinking that going over the edge was preferable to being crushed and then devoured alive.

They didn't stop or even slow as their huge bulks went over the edge and sailed into space. The snake arrived just seconds too late, and its mouth opened in anticipation, as it must have thought about taking a grab at one of the falling beasts.

"Oh God." Jenny grabbed at her arm. "This is like what killed Bourke in the cave…a monster."

Fully out in the open now, Emma could see the colossal size of the reptile – it was about 70 feet in length and as wide around as a small car.

"*Ben!*" She waved him on.

He continued to sprint toward the plane.

"Stop running," Jenny whispered.

"*Huh?*" Emma looked from her to Ben. And then she understood. The diamond-shaped head swung towards him; the snake had lost one meal, and a fleeing creature out in the open immediately presented it with another.

Ben looked over his shoulder, saw it, and then put his head down and accelerated.

"Sto-*ooop!*"

And then what? she wondered. *Dumb idea.*

"Ru-*uuun!*" She knew he had no choice now.

Bellakov continued to fire, and she vaguely only noticed that he wasn't hitting anything, until she felt the plane lurch.

It hit her hard – *the bastard wasn't firing at the monster, but at the freaking rock.* Bellakov was trying to launch without Ben.

"You sonofabitch," Ben yelled, obviously seeing what the mercenary was trying to do.

Ben looked like he was trying to squeeze every last ounce of speed from his legs, but he began to slow as fatigue must have felt like he was dragging lead weights.

"*Stop it,*" she yelled at Bellakov and grabbed his collar. She saw that Ben still had too far to go and was never going to make it, and she leaned out to point to the nearest edge of the plateau.

Bellakov ignored her and continued to fire at the rock. Then, to Emma's horror, she felt the plane begin to slide over the edge.

"*Oh, no, no, no.*"

Just like Ben had hoped, the plane began to be tugged forward. Bellakov tried to drag forward the ancient canopy over the cockpit but it snagged on something.

Emma felt insane fear and anger and grabbed Bellakov's collar and shook it, as Jenny screamed in his ear. Emma then began to beat the man with her fists, but all he did was hunker down and grip the controls.

She raged and tore at his hair, pulling clumps out and then dug nails into his face. Emma pulled her handgun free just as Bellakov jerked an elbow back that struck her cheekbone, making her see stars for a moment. When her senses returned, the gun was gone.

She heard Ben's voice again and saw that he'd finally run out of plateau and was right on the absolute rim. He turned to look at her, once, and only for a moment, before vanishing over the edge.

"No-*ooo!*" Emma stood up in the cockpit.

"He jumped." Jenny's mouth hung open, before she turned, and her expression turned to wide-eyed terror. "*Ack.*"

Emma spun to look at the woman and then her head snapped around to where she stared.

"Oh God." The snake's attention had been dragged to the only thing left moving on the plateau edge – *them.*

"Come *on*, you fucker," she heard Bellakov grunt and start to jerk in his seat as though trying to force the Corsair to move faster.

"Get out." Emma felt terrible fear run through her as the monstrous snake bore down on them. "*Out,*" she hissed again, grabbed Jenny's arm and tugged. But Bellakov whipped out an arm across her chest, holding her in place.

"Sit *fucking* down!" he screamed.

Jenny looked up at her, her eyes wet. *Go,* she mouthed.

Time was up; the snake was only a hundred feet away and would cross the distance to them in seconds. The plane began to tilt.

Jenny fought with Bellakov, the plane was going over, and the snake was there. Emma looked to where Ben had jumped. She made up her mind and leapt from the tipping plane.

*****

Ben had seen the narrow ledge only five feet down – it may take his weight and it may not. He had no choice; he jumped down. It held.

After a few moments, he began to hear the screams of the two women. *Please, not them,* was all he thought, as he looked up over the edge.

The snake closed in on the sliding Corsair and he saw a figure leap free on the opposite side, roll on the ground and then scramble away on her belly – *it was Emma!*

Ben raised his hand to wave as the plane reached the plateau rim. Emma belly-crawled toward him, and he helped her over the ledge, as the snake's massive head shot out on its coiled neck and caught the rear of the plane.

"Jenny." Emma sunk down. "Oh God."

Jenny's scream was like a siren, and the sound of gunfire was continuous. Even though the snake was basically a 70-foot pipe of solid muscle, it still couldn't hang onto the entire weight of the Corsair, and its body began to slide. Self-preservation kicked in, and it opened its mouth, releasing its prey.

Ben couldn't tear his eyes away. The Corsair had been hanging straight down. The rock slingshot had detached, but the intervention of the snake had meant they didn't get any upward-forward lift.

The plane had no hope of getting into any sort of glide formation and would drop like a rock. As he watched, he saw a single figure clamber out from the cockpit canopy, and make a leap for the cliff wall. But the falling plane meant whoever it was never stood a chance. The Corsair and the body fell into oblivion.

"*Jenny!*" Emma screamed, and Ben put a hand over her mouth.

The monstrous snake watched the objects fall for a moment more, then an arm-thick forked tongue slid out to taste the air. It then began to coil back on itself, still tasting the air, as though searching for more interesting scents. Its huge head began to swing around. Ben eased both of them down.

He remembered what Walt had told him: *big snakes could see your body heat.* And even the top of a head peeking over a cliff edge might warrant an investigation from a hungry alpha predator.

Emma covered her face with her hands and began to sob. "You're alive," he whispered, and then put an arm around her and drew her in close. He then tried to force them both hard up against the cliff wall. With the other arm, he held his pitiful hunting knife pointed up at the cliff edge and stared towards the lip, watching, and waiting.

Minutes passed.

Then more minutes.

Ben wasn't sure exactly how long he waited, but curiosity was now gnawing at him. He tried to reach out with his senses, listening, smelling, or even feeling for vibrations in the stone. But he couldn't detect anything, and the wind around them was picking up, and with it came a continuous howl as it rushed up over the rim.

At last, he couldn't take it anymore, and he started to rise up. Emma grabbed at him and stared with wide eyes.

"Don't."

"Can't stay here forever." He lifted her hand free and squeezed it for a moment, before continuing to rise up.

When Ben got to the lip, he turned his head sideways, allowing just one eye to ease over the edge fractions of an inch at a time. At last, he was able to see.

He lifted a little more, letting his eyes dart left and right – there was no sign of the snake – *nothing*.

The bare rocky ground in front of the jungle was empty. Ben stared hard into that veil of green, trying to see in past the first lines of massive tree trunks, tree ferns, and huge tongue-like fronds. His neck prickled as his mind told him nothing was there, his eyes confirmed it, but his animal senses screamed a warning.

"Is it there?" Emma whispered.

"Can't see it." He reached down to grab her. "Come up and add your eyes. See if you can spot anything in the jungle I'm missing."

She exhaled and then rose up beside him, basically climbing his body. She peeked over the edge.

"Jenny," she squeaked.

"Didn't make it," Ben replied. He remembered seeing only one person get out, but then the body fall away into the misty void.

"It's just us now," she said softly.

"I know," he added.

"We're stuck here." Emma slumped back down and drew her legs up to her chest.

"If there's a way down, we'll find it." Ben turned down to her. "We can't stay here."

"Why not? I feel safe here." She looked up at him, her eyes wet. "Where will we go anyway?"

Ben sighed and stared out at the now swirling mist. The sun was rising, and hopefully it would lift the fog-like veils that were still hanging over them. He also expected that the ever-present cloud would rise and then the jungle floor over 1,000 feet below them would be laid out like a green carpet. He knew that Emma wouldn't find being on the cliff ledge so pleasant then when vertigo kicked in.

But she did pose the killer question – where exactly *would* they go? And if they couldn't get down, what then? Benjamin said they'd be trapped, so do they plan a life of living native up here? How long did he think they'd survive, weeks, days, hours?

But he remembered his military training; giving up was the mind killer. And that was something he'd never allow to happen. He crouched down beside her.

"We go back to where we came up. After all, we never fully explored the area; there might be another way into the tube we climbed up in, or another tube altogether." He put a hand on her shoulder. "We don't exactly have anything else to do."

His stomach grumbled, and he realised he hadn't eaten in so long, he'd forgotten what food tasted like. They could last days without food, but far less without water. But they needed both for energy and morale. Besides, if they did need to move quickly, the last thing they needed was to be fatigued.

"Come on; we forage as we go."

"Jenny said things could be poisonous," she muttered.

"We gotta take risks now, and be prepared to eat things…raw." He grinned, hoping to lift her spirits. "Live things."

She was having none of it. "We're in hell."

"At least we're in hell together." He half smiled.

She made a small sound in her throat. "Yeah, I guess." She looked up. "Hey, were you always an optimist?'

He looked at her, thinking about the question for a moment.

"You know what? I did two tours in Afghanistan, one in Western Syria and a few skirmishes in some Iraqi provinces. I've fought hand-to-hand, with a gun, knife, and fist and boot. And I've been in some damn dirty hellholes." He half smiled. "In every one of those times, I knew I *could* die, but I always expected I wouldn't. Call it will to live, expectations of a higher purpose, luck or optimism, I just never surrendered then, and I won't now…and I won't let *you* now either."

Ben held out his hand. "Sometimes you gotta fight to win."

She smiled as she took his hand. "Yeah, yeah, I can do that."

Together, they peeked back over the rim again. It was now 10 in the morning and dust devils spun on the cliff edge. But there was nothing else.

"Is it safe?" Emma asked. "I can't see anything moving."

"I'd prefer if there was," Ben said. "Just one little beastie eating grass, without a care in the world."

"Yeah, I know what you mean." She exhaled.

"Well." He pulled in a cheek. "Here's a dumb question; when I asked you to take care of my gun, did it go in the Corsair?"

She groaned. "Yes."

"Okay, thought so." He shrugged. "Doesn't matter; we still have a couple of pistols; they should at least dissuade any pursuers."

"Ah, about that." She grimaced.

He slowly turned to her, his eyebrows up.

"I dropped it. When the snake was coming for you, I pulled it out, but it all got crazy real quick, and it got knocked out of my hand." She gave him a gritted smile.

"In the plane as well, huh?" He grinned.

She nodded. "I'm sorry." Her voice was small.

"What? Don't be. You made it out, and to me that's all that matters." He lifted her hand, looking deep into her eyes. "I give you my word I will never rest until I've got you home, okay?"

"And I'll never rest until we're both back at Ricky's Ribs having a cold beer." Emma sucked in a huge shuddering breath and then nodded. "We got this."

"You bet we have." Ben looked back over the edge towards his right-hand side of the clearing in the direction where they first came in. "You see that pile of rocks over there?"

She followed his gaze. "Yeah."

"That's where we're headed – we go fast and low. Ready?" He looked into her eyes, seeing fear and fatigue, but also determination.

"When you are." She placed her hands on the cliff lip.

"Let's do it." Ben went up and over the lip. His gun was held loosely in his hand and his shoulders were down. He turned but Emma didn't need his help, leaping up with ease and jogging beside him.

Ben tried to keep himself between her and the jungle, as they ran fast to the rocky outcrop. He couldn't help but turn to the dense green wall as his imagination conjured huge diamond-shaped heads and jewel-like eyes in amongst the fern fronds, coiled around massive moss-covered tree trunks or hanging from the overhead canopy.

In another few seconds, they were at the rocks with their backs pressed hard to them. Ben breathed in hard, the humid air thick in their throats, and he had to spit grit that was being flung around by the now swirling wind.

Emma leaned back on the rocks and rubbed at her eyes. She squinted. "Shit, sorry, bit light-headed."

"Don't worry, me too. We've used up our energy stores; we need food and water – food soon, and water now." He looked over the boulders, and then along the plateau edge to the next place of cover. "We left a lot of stuff behind after the explosion – maybe damaged, but we'll take what we can get. Might even be some weapons."

She snorted. "Let's dream big; we're also going to find another way down, right?" She grinned. "So let's hurry."

He kissed her, grabbed her hand, sighted on his next coverage target, and ran. And then ran to the next, and the next after that. The trip took over an hour, and only a few times the jungle reached the edge of the plateau, or the rocks looked unstable and they were forced to detour inland.

On the way, they passed various creatures, mostly bovine-like herbivores, with serpentine necks and vacuous eyes, or a few smaller carnivores that stared with a fox's cunning and followed them for a while. Only once did Ben have to throw a few rocks at their pursuers.

Finally, they crouched behind a tree trunk that measured twenty feet around, and its towering branches disappeared up into the roiling clouds. Just past some fallen trees was the scattered debris from the grenade explosion.

"Did that only happen two days ago?" Emma whispered.

"Yeah, I know, seems a lifetime." Ben could see the place where he had stood, by himself, as the first person out of the cave. He'd remembered being in a state of awe and wonder at the massive jungle.

"We underestimated it, didn't we?" Emma looked up at him.

"Yeah, yeah we did." He let his eyes travel over the strewn debris. "In my military training, it's drilled into us to never underestimate an enemy. I did it big time."

"No." She grabbed his arm and tugged on it. "This place *isn't* our enemy; it's just that we don't belong here."

"You're so right," Ben said. "And if Benjamin somehow made it down in 1908, then that's the riddle that we need to solve. But first, we need supplies…any supplies – there." He motioned with his head and crept forward.

In amongst the strewn debris of rocks from the cave, they could see Bourke's backpack, burned up and torn open. The man's pack once held a few rations, but these were gone and not even the foil wraps of his protein bars remained.

The bloody remains of the man had also vanished, and it even looked as if the rags of flesh and the blood splatters had been licked clean from the rocks.

They wandered through the debris and Emma found an unopened water bottle, and together they shared a few sips.

"Looks like we weren't the only ones seeking out the supplies," Emma said, tucking the bottle into a thigh pocket.

"Yeah, damn." Ben sighed. "Nothing much salvageable." He dropped the remains of the backpack. "C'mon, let's look for another entrance."

Together, they walked along the front of the collapsed cave mouth. There were a few deeper holes, but they either ended after a few feet, or were far too narrow to allow even Emma's slim body to slide into.

Emma crouched staring in longingly. "Could we maybe widen it somehow?"

Ben crouched beside her. "We'd need equipment, or at least heavy tools…and a few weeks. The rock here is too dense and all we've got is a few hunting knives and our bare hands."

"So no." Emma found a rock and sat down, her hands on her knees.

"Getting late."

Thunder cracked and made her cringe. Ben's head swung around, but he couldn't see where the storm front was. In fact, it seemed like it had come from all around them. The wind was a constant now, and Emma had to hold the hair back from one side of her face.

"What the hell was that?" Her teeth were gritted.

"Dry storm maybe. Like you said, we're gonna need shelter soon." Ben reached up to wipe a sleeve across his damp brow. The constant perspiring was another way they were being drained, and meant they needed to take more water in than was going out.

"Just remember, Benjamin got down, *somehow*. And he didn't climb back into the temple."

"These tabletop mountains are riddled with caves," she replied. "From the top, bottom, and sides. He must have found another one that took him down." Emma rubbed both hands up through her hair, the sweat making it stay slicked back for a moment even in the wind.

Ben sat down beside her, and she turned to him.

"I don't get it. These things up here; all these monsters. Why aren't they down there, in the jungle? I mean, if Benjamin was able to climb up and down, and the ancient Pemon Indians, why don't these things get down? Why isn't the jungle overrun with them – not exactly too many predators to challenge them?"

"Maybe they have." Ben turned to her. "In Benjamin's notebook, he talks about coming across the body of a large animal at the foot of the plateau, dead, but there was something alive inside it that the natives killed. He thought it might have fallen...now, I think he was right." He picked up a small stick and then started to doodle in the sand at their feet.

"But when I was doing research before we came down here, I read about an ancient Amazon legend. Every country has them." He half smiled. "Remember, we've got Bigfoot, Scotland's got Nessie, and in the Congo, they even have their own local dinosaur legend called a *Mokele Mbembe*."

But in this place, there is something called a *Yacumama*; means *mother of the river*. It's supposed to be a monstrous snake that eats people whole."

"Don't remind me." Emma shuddered, and then looked up. "You think they're down there already?"

"Maybe. I don't know anymore." He sighed. "I wish Jenny was here; she'd know more. But if you remember, she told us about that fossil they found in a coal mine in Colombia, it was a giant snake called a *Titanoboa*. Colombia is real close, so this thing lived right here, so it makes sense."

She shook her head. "I just think that if these things are here 365 days a year, then there should be more evidence. Nature has a weird way of getting out, up, off and down, from any confine."

"Hmm." Ben had wondered about that himself. He looked down and saw that he had drawn a long coiling body in the sand. He quickly wiped it away. Jenny had told him that the monstrous snake was alive at the time of the dinosaurs, but outlived them by another 10 million years. How?

Jenny had thought the massive snakes were alpha-alpha predators and fed on dinosaurs. They were the ultimate survivor and with a body that was so heavily muscled, they gave off a lot of heat and so could live through periods of cooling – there was no *reason* for them to go extinct. Emma was right; why weren't there more of them down on the jungle floor?

Emma picked up a handful of small stones and began to flick them from her palm. "I can't see the jungle anymore." She scoffed. "Is it even still down there?"

Ben sat back. The cloud hadn't lifted as he expected, and the weird thick clouds swirled like they were in the centre of a bath and the water was draining down the plughole. Except it all seemed to be being drawn towards them, and then upwards into the sky. Ben looked up; there was nothing but a boiling ceiling of clouds there too.

"So, we need to find the canoes and travel along those rivers again. If they're still there." Emma laughed bitterly. "If we get down."

"*When* we get down." He smiled back at her, trying to radiate a confidence he didn't feel.

Emma stood and held out a hand. He took it and she groaned as she helped in hauling his 225-pound frame to his feet.

"Then we search along the plateau edge – further down." She turned to look back in at the dark foreboding jungle just in from them. Mist twined in and around the trunks and dripping fronds. "Besides, I don't exactly feel like going back in there yet."

Ben felt a little lightheaded and knew the search for food and water would eventually drive them in whether they liked it or not. "Let's just remember what Jenny told us; *things* live in caves."

She raised her eyebrows. "Oh, so you're saying we should be careful?"

He chuckled. "Yeah, right, I didn't need to say that, did I?"

*****

Emma watched Ben walking a little in front of her. His broad shoulders and large frame were carried lightly. The man knew what he was doing, and he chose to walk between her and the jungle as a shield. She knew that too.

She smiled. She always liked him, and him coming back had made her heart dance with excitement, anticipation, and the promise of something good. Her *Joie de vivre* had vanished and she just wished now that when they all sat around talking about searching for the missing notebook, she had stopped them at that. There had been multiple opportunities along the way, and she had ignored them all, allowing her curiosity to override her judgement.

Maybe it's her fault, she thought darkly. Maybe she had urged Ben to go along with the adventure as a way to keep him interested and not leave town. Great plan, and now there was just the two of them, and instead of them sitting home together or in some bar and grill having cold beers and ribs, they were stuck in some prehistoric hell.

Emma looked at the roll of his shoulders again; the raw power of the man made her feel safe. She imagined what it would be like if he was gone – she'd be soon dead, and she probably wouldn't even care. But while *he* was alive, more than anything she wanted to be alive too.

They came to a stream that had pooled at the plateau edge. It poured over the lip and an updraft brought a veil of water mist back up at them. At its center, the swimming pool-sized pond looked quite deep, and more interestingly, they saw darting fish there.

Ben looked to the plateau edge, and then back to the jungle. "We're going to have to re-enter the jungle here. Not sure I want to take my chance wading out into that water without knowing what else is living in there."

Emma nodded. "I don't think it's big enough for some big beast to live in. But I guess a lot of little things with too many teeth is just as bad."

Ben took one last glance at the jungle before staring into the water. "One thing's for sure, we are at least going to try and catch some of the fish." He looked along the pool edge and saw where there were some marshy edges closer to where the jungle started.

He took a last look at the pool's center and then sucked in a breath. "Okay, I'm going to wade into the shallows, and try and coax some of those babies into the reeds. And that's where you'll be waiting for an ambush."

"I'm so hungry, I'll grab 'em like a bear – *with my teeth.*" Emma grinned. She quickly found a six-foot-long stick, and drew her knife to knock the end into a spear shape. She held it up to examine.

"Ready, Tarzan?" Ben grinned.

"That's Jane to you." She nodded and then nodded towards the water. "Come on, let's see what you've got."

Ben waded in, pulling his knife, just in case something decided *he* was on the menu rather than vice versa.

The water wasn't that clear, and he felt a gravel-like bottom under his feet. Clumps of weed and water grasses were becoming sparser the deeper he went. Silver torpedo shapes shot past him, one, two, and then another. Several were now between him and the reeds – just where he wanted them.

He took one last look at the deeper area of the pool and then started to turn, holding his arms out, as if herding cattle.

"Come on, guys, in you go."

Ben could see out in front of him some of the shapes moving into the shallower water where the reeds poked up, and Emma waited with her sharp stick poised.

There came a splash from behind him, and he spun – at the center of the pond, something lumped and a V-shape started to head towards him.

"Ah, shit." He began to back up, his knife ready.

Ben half turned. "How you doin' there, Emma?" He continued to back away from the deeper water, his eyes fixed on the surface.

There was silence, and he wanted to turn, but knew that there was something in the water that might be a lot bigger than the fish...and it was making its way toward him.

"Emm?" Ben tightened his grip on his blade. "*Emma?*"

There was the sound of splash behind him, and then: "*Ha!*"

He continued to back up, as there came a sound of wet flapping. "Got one; a beauty."

"Then I'm outta here." He turned and started to run with high-legged strides out of the water. He saw that Emma was already moving up onto the dry bank with a fish flapping on the end of her stick.

When he got to the shallows he spun, just in time to see something the size and shape of a dolphin angle away, the water lumping as it turned,

"*Jesus.*" He blew air through his lips. "This place."

He crossed to Emma who had already placed the fish on a rock and was using a knife to push it off the stick. She then pinned it down, holding it ready for him to work on. "Careful; looks a bit like a catfish, and I think there's spines behind its head and gills." She looked up, brows raised. "Anyone for Cajun-style blackened catfish?"

"I'm thinking more, catfish, sashimi style." Ben reached forward. "Hold that sucker down." He began to slice the fillets from it, laying them out on the dry rock. The blood ran down, and he immediately became concerned that the odor might attract the hunters.

"We need to be quick." He stuffed a bit in his mouth. It was cold, muddy tasting, and he suddenly remembered why he liked sushi – because he used to drench it in salty soy sauce – not because he liked raw fish.

He chewed the meat from the tough skin and spat that out. "I've had better."

Emma lifted a slice and held it over her mouth, winked at him, and then popped it in. She closed her eyes as she chewed and after a while removed the tough skin from her mouth.

She then smacked her lips. "Right now, just about anything would taste good."

Ben turned. "It's a good place to fish. As long as we don't go out too far." He nodded towards the pond. "Something out there got a little too curious. We should get this down quickly, fill up our canteens, and then head off before something else catches the scent of blood."

"Yeah." She nodded and popped another piece of fish into her mouth.

In another few seconds, the fish was gone, and Ben lifted the head with a string of bones attached and tossed it out into the center of the pool. Almost immediately there was a surge from a few different places as whatever was in there converged on the still-bleeding remains.

Ben then tossed sand and gravel up onto the bloody rock, but his hands were still sticky and smelled of fish.

"Let's wash our hands and get moving."

There was no way they could wade through the pool, and it extended right to the plateau edge so the only way forward was to follow the stream up into the jungle until they found a place shallow enough to cross. They had no choice but to enter the jungle depths.

Ben crept forward, and his feet squelched in a particularly muddy area. The tree roots were now growing mangrove-like up on stilt-like roots to try and stop their trunks drowning in the soaked landscape.

Unfortunately, the further they went, the more the river deepened and when he peered up along the water course, he saw it wasn't getting any better further in. In fact, the jungle seemed more tangled, darker, and primordial, turning into a marshy bog-land.

Swarms of tiny black flies nipped at them and created a constant background whine in their ears.

"I don't like it," he whispered.

"I stopped liking it days back," Emma responded softly. She nudged him. "Look."

He followed her gaze. Underneath the stilt-like roots of a massive tree was a mound of rounded objects that looked like off-white river stones. Ben craned his neck, frowning at first as his mind tried to sort them into something recognizable.

They were each about two feet long, not round or oval, more oval-but-stretched like giant vitamin capsules.

"They look like leather," Emma murmured.

"Yeah, like big, rubber footballs." His memory nagged at him. "They remind me of something. I feel like I've..." Then his mind jumped back to a Congolese jungle mission from ten years back where his squad came across a python clutch – the massive snake had laid its eggs in a nest, and they looked the same – except less than about one-quarter of the size.

Mother of the river, he remembered as they stood on the edge of the water. He suddenly felt like he received an electric shock.

"Oh shit." He grabbed Emma and started to drag her back the way they'd come.

"What?" She frowned as she backed up.

"Snake eggs," he choked out and dragged her faster.

Emma gasped and her eyes widened. She turned and started to burrow through the mad, green tangle of vines, but Ben held on.

"Slowly...silently," he whispered.

Ben tried to see everywhere at once, and he felt his neck tingle. There were just too many places that they could be ambushed from.

He held onto Emma, slowing her, but his mind kept screaming at him to run, and his legs wanted to obey.

He had to let Emma go so he could burrow a path for them through the thick tangle of vines, creepers, and fleshy fronds. His neck continued to prickle, but he needed to force himself to slow down – he'd seen the way the snake had been attracted by movement, so a couple of soft and warm bipeds, moving fast, would have drawn attention from any snake for hundreds of feet.

There was a crash behind him, and Ben swung back, gun up. But it was only Emma who had slipped and fallen to the ground. She grimaced and shook a hand she had just grazed against a rock.

"I'm okay." She rubbed it against her chest.

They arrived back at the stream, still deep, and Ben stared, weighing up the risks. "Damn it, we go for it; it's as shallow and narrow here as anywhere else." He steeled himself. "Follow me."

He gritted his teeth, gripped the knife, and headed in. The jungle was dark here, and it meant the water was like ink.

"Ah, Jesus." He immediately sank to his waist and his boots were sucked into the ooze on the bottom. His testicles shriveled from fear.

Emma was right behind him, *right* behind him, and she hung onto his shirt so close he felt her body continually bumping into his. He edged forward, keeping his arms and shoulders high, trying to see everywhere at once.

Ben felt his nerves tightening, and he kept waiting for the monstrous diamond-shaped head to rise up from below – *Mother of the Water, Mother of the Water* – he wished his mind would shut the hell up.

He placed his boot on something that wriggled out from under his foot, and a jolt of fear and revulsion shot through him. Thankfully, it squirmed away and didn't come back to take a piece out of his leg.

In another few moments, he put his foot on a rock, and then another, and then the stream was shallowing out as they reached the other side.

"Jesus." He felt a surge of relief but didn't slow. He reached back to grab Emma and kept tugging her with him as he entered the jungle. But it was only for a short distance, as he knew they needed to follow the stream back to find the plateau edge again.

Ben held Emma's hand now, and she gripped his hard. He wanted to live and wanted *her* to live more than anything he had ever wanted in his life.

We can make it, he told himself. *They had to.*

*****

The massive snake, a female *Titanoboa*, was 70 feet long and four foot wide at its girth. It wasn't a dinosaur, but one of the largest true land reptiles that ever lived on the planet, and ever would.

It slid along the jungle floor, pouring around tree trunks and over the top of ferns. Its hunt had been unsuccessful, and its hunger now gnawed away at it.

It would return to its clutch to check on the eggs, but then take another scout of its territory. There was always game, and if need be, it could hunt the creatures in the rivers and pools as well.

The reptile returned to the riverbank, and its tongue continued to flick in and out tasting the air. It froze – there was something different – something that it had never sensed before.

Its muscles coiled, expecting a challenge or threat. Even the biggest hunters knew to avoid something of its size, but they may have come looking for its eggs.

It tasted the air again, only just picking up the faint odors of the creature's exhalations, and there was something else.

It poured forward, coming to a rock at the stream edge and lowering its head. There were traces of blood. Its tongue shot out faster and faster, and actually dipped into the scraping. Its mind gathered the information and formed an image, and then a direction.

The things had dared to invade its territory. But the scent also excited its digestion and once again its hunger flared.

The huge diamond-shaped head swung around. And then like a molten river of scales and muscle, it forged forward, flowing across the river in seconds.

CHAPTER 33

12 Hours Past Apparition

Comet P/2018-YG874, designate name Primordia, was now arcing away from the third planet to the sun to continue on its eternal elliptical voyage around our solar system.

Its magnetic presence that had dragged at the planet's surface and even distorted the very air was lessening in intensity by the seconds and in just a few more hours would vanish completely.

The clock was ticking down, and soon there would be another 10 years of calm over the jungle mountaintops of the Venezuelan Amazon jungle.

CHAPTER 34

Thirty minutes later, Ben and Emma emerged back out onto the plateau's edge, this time on the opposite side of the pond and stream. They wasted no time making their way along its edge, heading east.

The wind seemed to come from everywhere at once, oddly drawing from the plateau edge and up into the sky. Ben looked out over the rim and saw that the jungle below was beginning to become visible, but was indistinct – not just from the usual cloud haze, but this time it seemed a little oily and distorted, as if he was looking at it through a dirty or warped window. He ignored it for now, putting it down to fatigue. *Besides*, he thought, *they had enough to worry about.*

He looked over his shoulder. "How you doin'?"

Emma nodded. "Good." She smiled back, squinting from the grit in the maelstrom. Ben saw she had dirt smudged on her forehead and cheek, her eyes were rimmed and watered, her shirt was torn, and there was dried blood on one of her hands. In the other, she held her hunting knife, backwards, dagger style. She looked tiny, tired, but still full of bravado. Ben knew he loved her then. And would fight and die to keep her alive.

They came to a broad patch of vacant ground where the jungle seemed to have been pulled back but was matted with some type of creeper that had thick rope-like tendrils running across it.

In amongst them, Ben noticed bulbous fruit-like things and used his blade to cut one free. Emma wandered a little closer to the cliff edge.

Ben lifted the fruit to his ear and shook it – something rattled inside like dry seeds. He lifted his knife and sliced the fruit in half, trying to be careful not to get too much sap or juice on his hands. He knew that it might be toxic, but his mouth watered, and at this point, he was prepared to take a risk.

His blade struggled to cut the fibrous bulb to begin with, but then it cracked through and the thing broke in half.

"*Gak!*" He flung it away and stood shaking his hands – the thing hadn't been fruit at all, but some sort of insect egg. Hundreds of spindly, multi-legged monstrosities burst free running in all directions, and the ones that escaped now sought hiding places, under the vines, under the bulbs, and up on his legs. He started to dance and back away.

"How's dinner looking?" Emma chuckled wearily.

Ben shook his hands and stomped his feet to shake off the bugs. "Well…" He shook his arms again. "Fruit's off the menu."

"Hey, look." Emma crouched, cleared away some soil and gravel, and lifted an old revolver. She shook it and then blew dust from it. "Looks old; heavy." She held it up, sighting along it, and then crossed to him.

Ben could see that the long-barreled gun was brown with age with rotating cartridge cylinders and wooden inserts on the grip. She held it out and he took it from her.

"Wow." He immediately saw the imprint. "It's a Colt; gotta be over a hundred years old if it's a day." He looked into the cartridge chambers and saw they were empty. He tried to break it open, but it was fused closed.

Ben knew immediately it was the sort of weapon someone would have possessed back in 1908. He slowly looked up at her.

She met his eyes. "Benjamin?"

He nodded and turned to the cliff edge. "He was here." He flinched as a wave of grit was hurled into his face. He spat some out. "And the gun being empty tells me that he wasn't at the start of his expedition."

"This might be where he ended up." Emma turned back to the plateau edge. "And if this is where he ended up; then this is where he was…before he got down."

Emma held a hand up to her eyes, squinting. The wind was getting stronger, whipping the hair madly across her face. She had to plant her legs wide to keep her balance. Thunder exploded around them, but it remained dry.

"What the hell is going on? Is this a storm brewing?" She looked up.

Ben followed her gaze; the clouds above them looked ominous, but were now swirling and somehow pulling up at the center.

"That's all we goddamn need." He tucked the old gun into his belt.

"What do we do?" Emma stood with her legs braced. "Find shelter?"

"No, I think we're outta time." Ben gritted his teeth. "Benjamin was here, *right here*, over a hundred years ago, and something important happened. Let's look around; there might be some clue as to what he did next, or where he went."

Ben squinted as the wind became like a living thing, picking up debris and hurling it at the pair. There was a howling all around them, which masked the noise they made, but also hid the sound of the jungle behind them.

Emma headed to the plateau edge, and Ben walked closer to the jungle. He was looking for anything that might indicate a cave opening, a passage, some carved notes, or any sign or signal from his ancestor.

A big arrow carved into a rock would be good, Benjamin old boy. He snorted at the thought, but kept sweeping the ground with his gaze. There were many rocky outcrops here, and the vine-covered ground hid multiple lumps, bumps, and depressions in the tepui's skin, but so far, nothing that dropped below a few feet.

Emma got to the plateau's edge, and stood with her legs braced staring down for a moment. He watched her as she crouched down and started to pull on something on the cliff edge. Then she got right down on her belly and edged forward, looking over the precipice.

"What're you doing?" he yelled over the top of the wind. She didn't hear, so he cupped his mouth. "Hey, what're you doing?"

She half rolled. "I thin...cave dow...there."

Many of her words were lost to the wind but he got the gist. He grinned and gave her a thumbs up. "How far down?"

She smiled back. "I'm a climber...for me...not far...all...but y..." She shrugged and turned back over.

The wind screamed around them, and the temperature began to drop. He had to throw an arm up as a vicious spray of sand and gravel whipped his face. When Ben lowered it, for some reason the hair on his neck began to prickle.

He slowly turned.

*****

The massive *Titanoboa* snake flowed towards the plateau edge. Small animals screamed away from its path, recognizing one of the alpha predators of the land, probably hoping that they weren't in its sights as a meal that day.

The reptile slowed as it came to the jungle edge, just before the open ground. Its tongue flickered as it spotted the two small creatures it had been pursuing. Their body heat made them flare red and it tasted the air, catching their scent.

It edged forward some more, this time right up to a line of heavy fern fronds that created a border between the dense jungle and open ground. It rose up, its massive diamond-shaped head now over a dozen feet from the jungle floor. The snake was a muddy brown with a slight green tiger stripe and when it remained motionless, its camouflage rendered it almost invisible.

Two glass-like lidless eyes focused on the pair, and an arm-thick forked tongue flickered out – the taste of blood came from the one closer to the edge – it chose that one first.

The *Titanoboa's* massively muscled body coiled, readying itself for the ambush attack.

*****

The swirling air, the flying grit and debris, and the roar of the wind, all of them seemed to fall into a void as Ben straightened.

He'd had the sensation before in the deserts of Syria; he'd led a mission in to get in behind enemy lines and find and destroy an ammunition store. On that night, there was no moon, and they had their quad night-vision goggles in place, the eerie four lenses and their armor making the Special Forces operatives look robotic and inhuman.

The advantage of night vision technology was it used any available light by amplifying it but turning everything a ghoulish green. That night, the desert had been flat and still, and Ben had that same feeling then as he did now.

Back then, he'd waved everyone down, and switched to thermal – and then he saw them – the spider holes, all around them, and in the slit of each of the trapdoors the tiny flare of body heat.

And they had walked right in amongst them.

Of the eight mission team members he walked in with, only four of them walked out. Instincts and overwhelming firepower had saved their lives that night.

But now Ben had the same gut feeling as that fateful night. And this time, all he had was a knife and a 100-year old Colt revolver.

Ben turned slowly, carefully scanning the jungle edge. Even though the wind howled around him, he felt like he was in a vacuum as he stared hard into the jungle. He was trained to pick out even the most inconspicuous discrepancies, furtive movements, and even myriad forms of camouflage. But they were all built around the human form.

It was the tiny flickering of the tongue he saw first – not coming from something near the ground, but over a dozen feet in the air. He traced the movement back to its source, and only when he concentrated could he pick out the enormous snake. Its camouflage was so perfect that even if it were only a few feet from them he still would have missed it.

Horrifyingly, he saw that it wasn't watching him, but its unblinking gaze was riveted, arrow-like, on Emma who was forty feet from him and still crouching at the plateau's edge.

"Emma." Ben gripped the blade so hard his knuckles popped. He gritted his teeth, wanting to keep his movements to a minimum and also keep watch on the snake, but he knew she'd never hear him.

Fuck it, he thought, and yelled: "*Emma!*"

"*What...?*" She half turned, holding a thick vine in her hand. "Hey...think... found...something." Her words were still being blown away as she rose to her feet, dragging some of the vine with her. "... goes all the way...edge...like rope." She straightened hanging on to it. "... I bet...used it to climb down...cave..."

Like liquid, the monster snake glided forward a few feet. Ben could see that it had singled Emma out and its focus was intense. This close, its size scared the shit out of him – it seemed made of solid muscle, inevitable and unstoppable. The thing was more a force of nature than an adversary.

How fast could it move? he wondered. Snakes were fast, but not as fast as a running person. But that was a normal-sized snake; this thing could potentially outpace them in seconds.

Ben looked from one side to the other, seeking options. From the corner of his eye, he saw Emma finally turn to him, and her expression fell away as she must have seen his intense stare and then followed his gaze. She dropped the vine and froze.

"Oh Jesus, no." Her shoulders hiked and her hands came up in front of her as if pushing it away. "*B... B... Ben?*"

He quickly looked towards her. She had the cliff edge behind her, and the snake in front of her. He bet if she ran left or right, the monster would run her down in a blink.

Emma started to back up.

You sonofabitch, he thought. *I'm bigger; why aren't you focusing on me?*

"*Hey!*" he yelled at it. "*Hey-hey!*" He waved his arms.

The snake's head swung towards him.

"Stop that!" Emma screamed.

Her yell brought the thing's head back to her. This time, it began to shoot towards her, far too fast for something of its size. Even from where Ben stood, he saw Emma's eyes go wide.

"Ru-*uuun!*" she screamed to him as she turned to the cliff edge, got down on her belly, and started to back herself over the lip. The monstrous snake flowed towards her.

Ben could feel the grind of gravel beneath his feet as the thousands of pounds of reptile bore down on Emma.

"*Hey, you sonofabitch.*" Ben ran at it, scooping up a fist-sized rock and launching it at the draft-horse thick body. It struck the metallic looking scales, hard, and simply bounced away.

Ben felt his stomach flip as he watched Emma struggle on the cliff edge. The thought of what she was trying to do made him feel giddy. She was a good climber, but the wind now brutally sucked up over the cliff edge, and her hair whipped around her face, making her eyes useless.

The snake was only a few dozen feet from her when Ben got to its tail, raised a boot, and stomped down hard – *nothing*. He chased it for a moment, and then grabbed on – it was like trying to stop a runaway Mack truck and his feet slid on the ground with the snake not even noticing his efforts.

Emma looked up. There was just her head, shoulders, and fingertips above the lip. For a brief moment, her eyes met Bens, and then she grabbed one of the vines and dropped from sight.

The snake's head lunged forward, slamming down hard on the cliff edge, and continuing on, beginning to follow her over the edge. Its massively heavy, 70-foot-long body slid across the cliff edge, grinding and severing the vines.

"No-*ooo*!" Ben picked up a huge rock with both hands, strained every muscle in his body to raise it above his head, and then he slammed it down on the tail, hoping to stop the snake picking Emma off the cliff wall, or wherever she was perched.

The rock crunched down on the tail tip, denting the armored scales. He finally got its attention – the snake's head jerked around to him.

Good, he thought.

And then: *Oh, fuck no.*

He started to run.

CHAPTER 35

Emma had seen the cave mouth about fifty feet down when she had leaned out over the plateau edge. The vines hanging down were thick, strong, and fibrous enough to provide good handholds – as a climber, she could do it easily. She bet Ben wouldn't have any trouble either.

She bet her last dollar that if Ben's ancestor went anywhere, it was into that damn cave.

She had to shut her eyes as a tornado of debris was now spinning around them. With her eyes pressed to slits, she looked down towards the jungle floor – it was blurred as though there was a veil of gauze hanging in front of it.

Emma went back to examining the cliff face – not just sheer, but leaning outwards, without even a handhold – even as an experienced climber, she knew that she'd only be able to scale down with the vine.

Over the screaming howl of the wind, she could just make out Ben yelling to her. She rolled over and got to her feet. Ben looked funny, weird, and his body was all hiked in agitation. She followed his gaze and felt the shock run from her toes to her scalp.

The snake was only fifty feet from her, and its head was pointed at her with that horrifying unblinking glare with an intensity that was almost hypnotizing.

"Ben?"

She gulped. Out in the open, there was nothing to hide the full horror of the beast – it towered over them, and its brown and green body emanated raw power. To the creature, they were like mice to a normal-sized snake. Emma remembered what had happened to Steve – the monstrous snake had grabbed him in its mouth and took off with the struggling man like he was nothing but a rag doll.

She heard Ben yell again, and from the corner of her eye saw him jumping up and down waving his arms. She knew exactly what he was trying to do.

"*Stop that,*" she screamed.

What was it Ben had told her only hours before? That it was attracted by movement – *okay then, you big asshole, see if you can follow me.*

"Ru-*uuun!*" She spun to the cliff edge and started to slide over. The effect was instantaneous – the snake came for her.

Seconds mattered, and instincts took over she dropped down on the vine hand-over-hand. She ended up about five feet out from the cliff and cave mouth, and she started to swing her legs back and forth, creating a pendulum effect. She realised she needed a few more swings to be able to launch herself into the cave just as a huge shadow loomed over her.

Time was up; one last swing and then she let go. She landed just on the very lip of the cave mouth – her arms pin-wheeled for a second or two, and she went into a crouch, rolling forward, just as the snake slammed against the cave entrance.

She turned, ripped out her pathetic-looking blade, and held it up. Emma backed further into the depths of the cave. If the snake decided to follow her, she was as good as dead.

The shadow passed over, but then the vines from out front all fell away as if they'd been cut.

"No."

She ran to the cave mouth but skidded to a stop. She couldn't bring herself to peer out in case the huge head was right there, waiting to snap her up. Her eyes began to fill up as she realised she was trapped inside, and Ben out.

Emma knelt and said a silent prayer, hoping he was safe. Outside the cave the wind became like a living thing, and it forced her backwards. She waited for many minutes, and then an hour, but the cave mouth now looked like a thick curtain had been thrown over it. Mist began to fill the cave, and everything outside became oily looking and distorted.

She was torn; with the vines gone, not even she could make it back up now. Should she wait and see if Ben returned? Or should she try and climb down, make it back to try and get help?

Emma struggled towards the mouth of the cave but had to hang onto the wall and claw her way to the edge. The maelstrom battered at her and threatened to pull her from her place of safety and fling her into the void. She held an arm up to her face and looked upwards – there seemed nothing there. Everything was now cloaked in a thick mist and it was like the entire world had gone away.

The sky, air, and ground boiled and spun and even the fillings in her teeth hurt. *What the hell is going on?* she wondered.

A battering gust blew her off her feet and ten feet back into the cave. It was then she knew she'd never be able to climb up, or Ben down to her. She could only pray that he could hold on until she returned with help. If anyone could survive, it was her Ben Cartwright.

She turned to the dark cave. It was full of fog, and at the back, a dark hole in its floor dropped into its belly. She stood at its edge and peered down; she had no light, no rope, and no choice. But she did have one driving thought: *I'll save you, Ben*, she demanded of herself.

Emma eased herself over the edge.

CHAPTER 36

End of Apparition

Primordia was gone from the 3rd planet. It was now on its way to the middle star where it would be grabbed by its gravitational forces and then flung back to begin its decade-long elliptical voyage around our solar system all over again.

The magnetic distortion on the eastern jungles of Venezuela had ceased, doorways closed and pathways erased. On the surface of the tabletop mountain, silence and stillness settled over the sparse grasses and fissured landscape.

The monsoon-like rains dried, and the clouds parted, then cleared. The wettest season was at an end, and once again, there would be 10 years of calm over a single jungle mountaintop in the depths of the Venezuelan Amazon jungle.

CHAPTER 37

Venezuelan National Institute of Meteorological Services

Mateo snorted. "Well, seems you were right."

"*Hmm*, of course, I usually am." Santiago looked up from his screen. "About what?"

Mateo pointed. "The cloud has dissipated over the eastern jungle and the satellite can see the ground again. It was only temporary, just like you said."

Santiago reached up to pull the battered notebook from his shelf once again. He leaned back and tossed it onto the young meteorologist's desk.

"Make a note, sign it, and then in ten years' time, it might be you telling a younger version of yourself that the effects are limited, temporary, and nothing to be concerned about."

Mateo smiled and grabbed the book, flipping open its pages. "Weird though."

"Yes it is, *was*. We haven't solved all of our world's mysteries just yet." Santiago smiled. "It's what makes the place so interesting."

CHAPTER 38

It was three weeks later that Emmaline Jane Wilson was carried out of the Amazon jungle – alone, near death, and fevered. It made worldwide headlines; the mystery of the missing Cartwright party had been solved, they had said.

Emma's initial version of events was dismissed as nothing but hallucinations brought on by jungle fever, dehydration, and perhaps an impact to her head – she had certainly been in a terrible physical state when she was found.

All other members of the team were presumed dead. Ben's mother, Cynthia, flew down to meet her, and had listened intently to every word. Instead of dismissing her story, Cynthia had used her considerable wealth to hire a team of soldiers and a helicopter, and formulated a plan to head back in to find her lost son.

Cynthia had remarked that the jungle had consumed one Cartwright over a hundred years ago, and she wouldn't let it take another.

Emma was still weak, but wouldn't let the older woman go without her. She had the location and an idea of where they needed to go. It took a full day of flying before they even found the original river, and then more navigating at a low altitude, literally on the treetops, so they could follow the glimmer of the hidden river to where it sunk into the ground.

Then they slowed as she pointed out their long climb up to the massive tabletop mountain. Oddly, there was no cloud, and the sun shone bright, warm, and clear – it all seemed so different.

"*There.*" She pointed, leaning from the helicopter door so far one of the soldiers had to grab her arm and hang on. The chopper started to lift towards the plateau top, higher and higher.

Emma felt her heart galloping like a horse in her chest and her hands curled into fists. *Please be there, please be there*, she silently repeated, just her lips moving.

The helicopter came abreast of the plateau top and she put a hand to cup her ear, and then moved the small microphone bead at her mouth. "Not too close; there are giant…"

Things, up here, she was going to say, but the words wouldn't come.

The chopper hung in the sky like a giant dragonfly, and she snatched up the binoculars and put them to her eyes. Her forehead creased, deeply.

The plateau top had a few scrubby trees, grasses, and was pocked with caves and fissures. There was a large body of water at its center, but it looked more like a shallow pond than the inland sea she remembered.

Where was the massive jungle? Where were the tree trunks that towered into a cloud-filled sky, and the tangled vines, fleshy fern fronds, and the goddamn primordial jungle? And where were the boiling clouds and thick fog that intertwined over and through everything? She looked up; the sky was blue and clear.

Emma felt a coil begin to tighten in her stomach and she could feel the weight of Cynthia's stare. She grasped the small bead-like mic at her mouth to speak to the local pilot.

"This plateau…it was covered in clouds, and…" She looked at her wristwatch; it *still* worked. "…and the entire area was magnetic or something."

He looked confused for a moment and began to shake his head, when he seemed to suddenly recollect something. He put his hand to the mic.

"I think, yes, but is only sometime." He shrugged. "Very rare."

"What; *rare*? What does that mean?" Emma turned to Cynthia who looked perplexed and extremely anxious.

"Where is he?" Cynthia looked back at the empty plateau top. "There's nothing."

Emma grimaced and turned back to the pilot. "What does that mean?"

The pilot looked to his copilot and they spoke rapidly in Spanish for a few seconds before they came to an agreement.

"Every ten years." He bobbed his head. "About, I think."

Emma felt lightheaded and a little nauseous. "I don't understand, I don't understand."

The pilot went on. "Very strange and unique to this area. Big electrical storm, I think, just here, make electronics not work. Very rare, but we need to avoid when happening. Visibility very bad, dangerous, everyone stays away for a few days, a week." He bobbed his head. "Then all goes away."

Emma stared with glassy eyes. Her mind felt like it was short-circuiting and refused to process the information. The pilot half turned again.

"Been happening forever. Pemon call it *karutu salu* – time of lizard."

His copilot shook his head and the pair argued for a moment. The pilot shrugged.

"Andreas says *lizard* is not right – more like *time of snake*."

"And then it goes away…for ten years." Emma frowned. "No, no, no, not true." *Every ten years – every ten years – every ten years.*

But she knew it was true. It was just like it said in the notebook. She put her hands to each side of her head. "Not true." She barely heard Cynthia yelling her name.

Ben, she thought. *My poor Ben, trapped there for ten years. My Ben.*

She slumped, feeling giddy, but then her jaws clenched tight. *I'll be back, I promise, Ben*, she thought, *in ten years*.

Emma fell to the floor of the helicopter and everything went dark.

EPILOGUE

Benjamin Cartwright ran like never before in his life. Damp green fronds slapped at him and elastic vines tried to lasso every part of his body. But he barged, burrowed, and sprinted as if the devil was after him.

Because it was.

The thing that followed him was like a river of muscled flesh that pushed trees from its path, and its carnivore's breath was like a steam train huffing and hissing as it bore down on him. He whimpered, pivoting at a boulder and changing direction. The hissing-roar came then, making leathery-winged avian creatures take flight from the canopy overhead, and making him shiver in his ragged, sweat-soaked clothing.

Cartwright accelerated, and immediately there was a breeze on his face as the jungle opened out. He skidded to a stop at the cliff edge. His shoulders slumped.

Where he had expected to see the plateau edge falling away to a thick jungle canopy over a thousand feet below, there was now an unrecognizable vista stretching to the horizon – it was a jungle valley, primordial, and large long-necked beasts ambled amongst the towering trunks. In the air, leathery-winged Pteranodons glided on warm thermals.

The haze, the clouds, the hurricane-like winds, the oily distortion that had been in the air were all gone.

Emma was gone, *everything* was gone – no, that wasn't right; it just hadn't happened yet.

His eyes began to water as a creeping realization sunk in. Where they'd been wasn't a hidden plateau at all, but instead they had all stepped through a hidden doorway, reaching back millions of years. They'd stepped through, and unfortunately for him, the door had closed before he could escape.

He remembered Benjamin's warning about being trapped here forever; now he knew what he was referring to. But he knew too late.

Primordia came only once every ten years. He stepped closer to the cliff edge, and the updraft flapped at the rags of his clothing. In his hand, he held a single knife…all he had left.

Behind him, the trees began to be pushed aside as his pursuer finally caught up to him. He grimaced and turned. The foliage burst open and the hissing-roar made him cringe back a step. The monstrous snake rose up, towering over him, all coiled muscle, glistening scales, and teeth

230

as long as his forearm.

He *would* survive; he was trained to do it. In ten years, he'd damn well still be here.

The snake began its attack, flowing towards him like a reptilian train – time was up – Ben turned back to the cliff edge and jumped.

END

PRIMORDIA

AUTHORS NOTES & THE CUTTING ROOM FLOOR

Many readers ask me about the background of my novels – is the science real or fiction? Where do I get the situations, equipment, characters or their expertise from, and just how much of any element has a basis in fact?

In the case of the hidden plateau in the Amazon jungle, the novel, The Lost World, was my blueprint. However, myths and legends surrounding some of the creatures found there, and perhaps still living, persist to this day.

The Lost World by Sir Arthur Conan Doyle

The Lost World was a novel created by Sir Arthur Conan Doyle and released in 1912. It was about an expedition to a tabletop mountain plateau in the Amazon basin of South America where prehistoric animals still survived.

Doyle was already famous for his Sherlock Holmes novels, and this book, written just for fun, went on to become enormously popular. It's almost impossible to count the number of times it has been published, reprinted, and re-released, and there have been numerous radio and movie adaptations.

The setting for The Lost World is believed to have been inspired by reports of Doyle's good friend Percy Harrison Fawcett's 1906 expedition to a remote jungle plateau in Bolivia. Doyle was said to have been intrigued by the tale of the remote plateau with dangerous, impenetrable forests where Fawcett was said to have seen *"monstrous tracks of unknown origin."*

However, there may have been another inspiration: a 1996 Science Fiction Studies review of an annotated edition of the novel suggested that the author was also greatly interested in the Pacaraima Mountains plateaus; Mount Roraima in particular.

Mount Roraima is the highest of the Pakaraima chain of tepui plateaus in South America and was first described by the great English explorer Sir Walter Raleigh in 1595. Its enormous flat-topped summit is bordered on all sides by cliffs rising over 1,000 feet and was wrapped in many local myths and legends and said to be home to strange creatures, gods, and monsters.

Titanoboa and the Yacumama

There were tales of monster snakes existing in the Amazon jungles for centuries, and they would have forever remained myths if not for a chance discovery in a coal mine in Colombia in 2008. It turned out that a monster snake lived at the time of the dinosaurs and in fact outlived them by nearly 10 million years.

Fossils of an enormous snake were discovered and paleontologists estimated its length to be well over 50 feet. They had no idea whether the specimen found might even have been representative of the largest of its kind, so they could have grown to twice that.

The snake, called Titanoboa, wasn't just long but solid muscle that was as thick around as a draft horse and would have weighed in at over 3,000 pounds!

The monster snake lived during the Paleocene epoch, and also a 10-million-year period immediately following the Cretaceous-Paleogene extinction event. The Titanoboa would have fed on the last of the dinosaurs and to this day, many scientists agree there is no reason for it to have become extinct.

They also agree that over-sized snakes could still exist in the Amazon basin. And that brings us neatly to the legend of the *Yacumama*, the Mother of the River.

In the mythology of the indigenous people of South America, the Yacumama is a monster, fifty paces long, and believed to live in various areas of the Amazon River, estuaries, and lagoons. According to the legend, the Indians would need to blow into a conch horn before entering the water, as this would bring it to the surface, forcing the Yacumama to reveal itself.

Experts believe that if the creature exists, it is more than likely to be a species of giant anaconda.

During the year 1906, the explorer Percy H. Fawcett (mentioned above), a friend and inspiration to Arthur Conan Doyle, claimed to have found a giant anaconda while traveling through the Amazon River. He shot the creature and when he measured its body stated it to be nearly 60 feet in length. He went on to say that they found trails in the swamp mud that were six feet across that supported stories by local Indians and rubber pickers that the anaconda sometimes reached an incredible size, completely eclipsing the one he had shot.

To this day, monster hunters still mount expeditions to the Amazon in search of the *Mother of the River*. Only time will tell if they are successful and determine whether the creature is still there.

Tepuis and the Canaima National Park

A tepui is a tabletop mountain or mesa found in the Guayanan Highlands of South America, especially in Venezuela and western Guyana. In the native tongue of the Pemon, the indigenous people of the area, the word *tepui* means "house of the gods" and can also be an area that is taboo.

Canaima National Park is a 12,000 square mile park in southeastern Venezuela that is home to indigenous Pemon Indians that have an intimate relationship with the tepuis, and believe they are the home of the gods, demons, and "Mawari" spirits.

The park is home to lush jungles, exotic animals, and plateaus of rock called tepuis, which have vertical walls and almost flat tops and occupy about 65% of the park. These geological islands create a unique biological environment as species can become trapped at their summit for millions of years, or perhaps even longer, as they are very ancient sandstone that have a granite base that is up to 3 billion years old.

Their sheer cliffs and waterfalls (including Angel Falls, which is the highest waterfall in the world, at 3,287 feet), create spectacular landscapes. The most famous tepui in the park is also the tallest called Mount Roraima.

These ancient geological structures date back to a time when South America and Africa were part of the Pangaea super-continent.

The Strange Effects of a Comet

A comet is a solar system body that, when passing close to the sun, warms and begins to release gases producing a visible atmosphere or coma, and sometimes also a tail. They have a wide range of orbital periods, ranging from just a few years to potentially several millions of years. The appearance of a comet is called an apparition.

A significant comet impact on the Earth's surface would be devastating depending on its mass and composition. But, even if they don't make landfall, the full astral effects of a comet simply passing *close* to our planet is not yet known or fully understood. However, we have been able to observe other events within our solar system to make educated guesses.

On October 2014, Comet C/2013 A1, designate name: Siding Spring, plunged the magnetic field around Mars into chaos, said Jared Espley, NASA's Goddard Space Flight Center in Greenbelt, Maryland. "We think the encounter blew away part of Mars' upper atmosphere, much like a strong solar storm would."

Comet Siding Spring, like most comets, is surrounded by a strong magnetic field. When it passed close to Mars, the comet's coma washed over the planet, with the dense inner coma potentially reaching the surface. For a period of time, Mars was flooded with an invisible tide of charged particles from the coma, and the powerful magnetic field around the comet temporarily merged with, overwhelmed, and distorted, the planet's own magnetic field.

Those Damn Bugs!

While doing research for my latest novel, I came across a few species of creepy crawlies that were truly horrific – so naturally, I had to use them! Both lived about a 100 million years ago, and I think you'll agree we can all breathe a sigh of relief that both aren't around today!

The Hell Ant

A reader sent me information on something fantastic that lived during the Cretaceous period – the HELL ANT (no, seriously!).The newly discovered species of prehistoric Formicidae, or Hell Ant, as dubbed by its discoverer, had a physiology that lived up to its Underworldish name. They were huge and armor-plated with gruesome mouthparts and metal-infused spikes on their head used to impale their victims and then drink the running blood.

No other living ant species had such exoskeleton cranial anatomy. The larger of the species had a horn-like appendage that jutted out over their tusk-like mandibles. As well as being like an iron-armored rhino, these ants may also been vampires – when their mandibles moved upwards, they formed a perfect "gutter" that might have funneled *hemolymph*, insect blood, down to the mouthparts.

The Killer Cockroach

The specimen was beautifully preserved in amber – a prehistoric cockroach that lived 100 million years ago during the age of the dinosaurs. But the *Manipulator Modificaputis* was like no other cockroach, past or present.

Based on its physical appearance, scientists suggest it was a nocturnal hunter in the ancient coniferous forests. Unlike most cockroach varieties today who are scavengers, this hunting specimen had long legs covered in dense hairs, long forearms capable of clasping prey, a moveable head on a long neck, and an extra set of eyes covered with an umbrella-like shield. Added to that, it had mouthparts that were like a buzz saw.

The Killer Cockroach is more anatomically closely related to the praying mantodeans, and although praying mantises are predatory, they are mostly sit-and-wait predators. But the *Manipulator Modificaputis* was a hunter, and certainly would have had the body and the skill to chase down and eat its prey alive.

CHECK OUT OTHER GREAT DINOSAUR THRILLERS

JURASSIC ISLAND
by Viktor Zarkov

Guided by satellite photos and modern technology a ragtag group of survivalists and scientists travel to an uncharted island in the remote South Indian Ocean. Things go to hell in a hurry once the team reaches the island and the massive megalodon that attacked their boats is only the beginning of their desperate fight for survival.

Nothing could have prepared billionaire explorer Joseph Thornton and washed up archaeologist Christopher "Colt" McKinnon for the terrifying prehistoric creatures that wait for them on JURASSIC ISLAND!

K-REX
by L.Z. Hunter

Deep within the Congo jungle, Circuitz Mining employs mercenaries as security for its Coltan mining site. Armed with assault rifles and decades of experience, nothing should go wrong. However, the dangers within the jungle stretch beyond venomous snakes and poisonous spiders. There is more to fear than guerrillas and vicious animals. Undetected, something lurks under the expansive treetop canopy . . .

Something ancient.

Something dangerous.

Kasai Rex!

CHECK OUT OTHER GREAT DINOSAUR THRILLERS

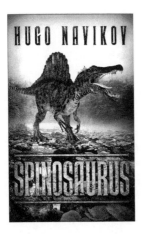

SPINOSAURUS
by Hugo Navikov

Brett Russell is a hunter of the rarest game. His targets are cryptids, animals denied by science. But they are well known by those living on the edges of civilization, where monsters attack and devour their animals and children and lay ruin to their shantytowns.

When a shadowy organization sends Brett to the Congo in search of the legendary dinosaur cryptid Kasai Rex, he will face much more than a terrifying monster from the past. Spinosaurus is a dinosaur thriller packed with intrigue, action and giant prehistoric predators.

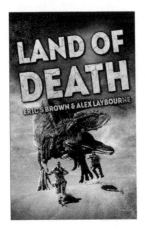

LAND OF DEATH
by Eric S Brown & Alex Laybourne

A group of American soldiers, fleeing an organized attack on their base camp in the Middle East, encounter a storm unlike anything they've seen before. When the storm subsides, they wake up to find themselves no longer in the desert and perhaps not even on Earth. The jungle they've been deposited in is a place ruled by prehistoric creatures long extinct. Each day is a struggle to survive as their ammo begins to run low and virtually everything they encounter, in this land they've been hurled into, is a deadly threat.

CHECK OUT OTHER GREAT DINOSAUR THRILLERS

WRITTEN IN STONE
by David Rhodes

Charles Dawson is trapped 100 million years in the past. Trying to survive from day to day in a world of dinosaurs he devises a plan to change his fate. As he begins to write messages in the soft mud of a nearby stream, he can only hope they will be found by someone who can stop his time travel. Professor Ron Fontana and Professor Ray Taggit, scientists with opposing views, each discover the fossilized messages. While attempting to save Charles, Professor Fontana, his daughter Lauren and their friend Danny are forced to join Taggit and his group of mercenaries. Taggit does not intend to rescue Charles Dawson, but to force Dawson to travel back in time to gather samples for Taggit's fame and fortune. As the two groups jump through time they find they must work together to make it back alive as this fast-paced thriller climaxes at the very moment the age of dinosaurs is ending.

HARD TIME
by Alex Laybourne

Rookie officer Peter Malone and his heavily armed team are sent on a deadly mission to extract a dangerous criminal from a classified prison world. A Kruger Correctional facility where only the hardest, most vicious criminals are sent to fend for themselves, never to return.

But when the team come face to face with ancient beasts from a lost world, their mission is changed. The new objective: Survive.

63227124R00146

Made in the USA
Middletown, DE
30 January 2018